THE SMURFS TALES

Peyo

Whoa!
Whew! That was a close smurf!
GLING GLING GLING GLING
BRRRRRRRRRRR
CLING BLIN
BING
CRAC
That was a smurfquake!
Everything okay? Anybody hurt?

PAPERCUTZ™
NEW YORK

THE SMURFS TALES #5

© Peyo - 2022- Licensed through Lafig Belgium - www.smurf.com

"The Smurfs and the Golden Tree"
BY PEYO
WITH THE COLLABORATION OF
ALAIN JOST AND THIERRY CULLIFORD FOR THE SCRIPT,
PASCAL GARRAY FOR THE ARTWORK,
AND NINE CULLIFORD FOR THE COLORS

"Lady Dolphine"
BASED ON AN IDEA BY PEYO
DELPORTE AND PEYO, SCRIPT
WALTHÉRY, ART

"A New Beginning"
BY LUC PARTHOENS AND THIERRY CULLIFORD, SCRIPT
LAURENT CAGNIAT, ART
PAULOMADDELENI, COLOR

"The Miniature Smurfs"
BY PEYO

Joe Johnson, *SMURFLATIONS*
Bryan Senka, Wilson Ramos Jr., *LETTERING SMURFS*
Léa Zimmerman, *SMURFIC PRODUCTION*
Matt. Murray, *SMURF CONSULTANT*
Stephanie Brooks, *ASSISTANT MANAGING SMURF*
Jim Salicrup, *SMURF-IN-CHIEF*

HC ISBN 978-1-5458-0887-0
PB ISBN 978-1-5458-0886-3

PRINTED IN CHINA
AUGUST 2022

Papercutz books may be purchased for business or
promotional use. For information on bulk purchases
please contact Macmillan Corporate and Premium
Sales Department at (800) 221-7945 x5442.

DISTRIBUTED BY MACMILLAN
FIRST PAPERCUTZ PRINTING

THE SMURFS AND THE GOLDEN TREE

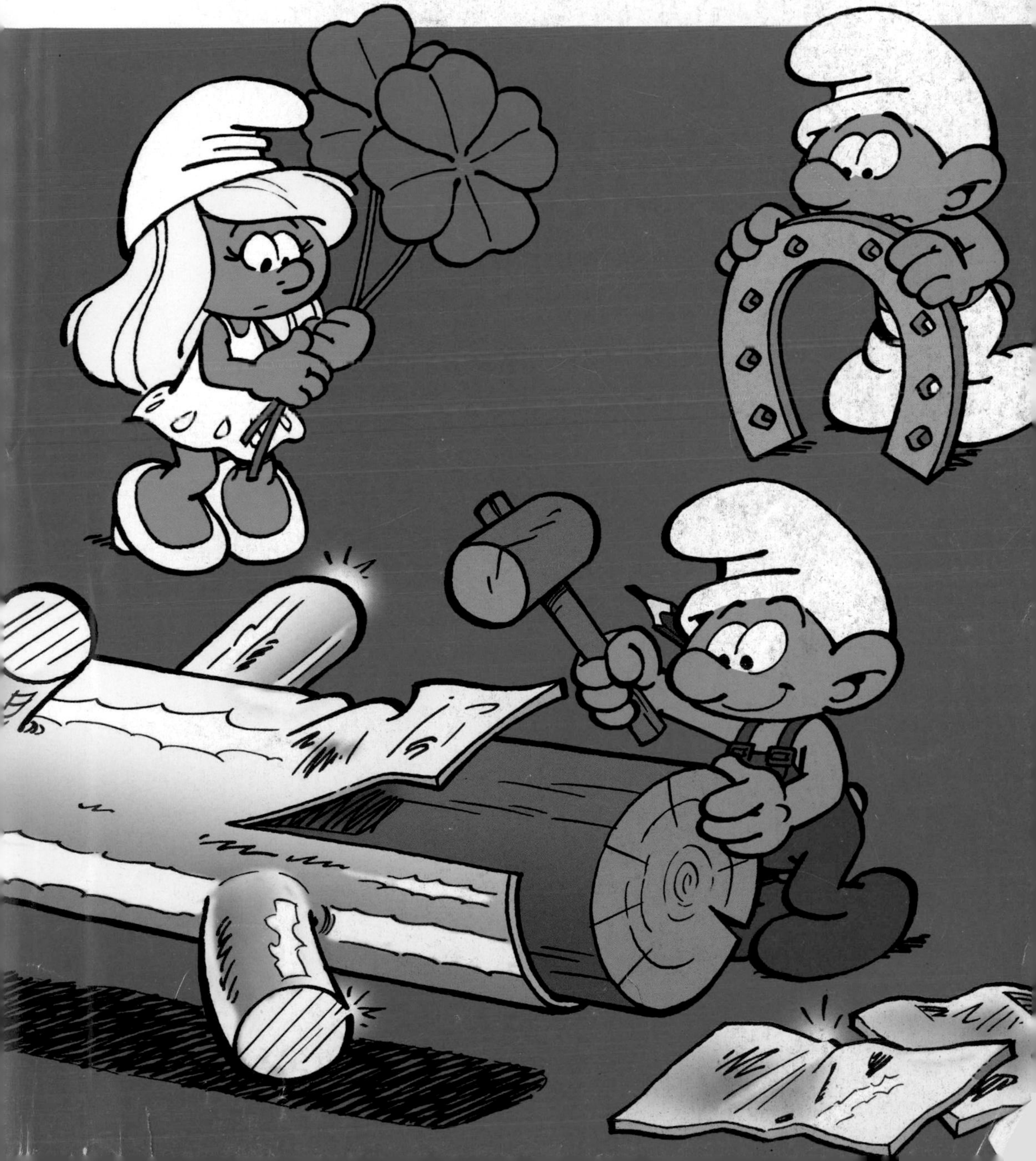

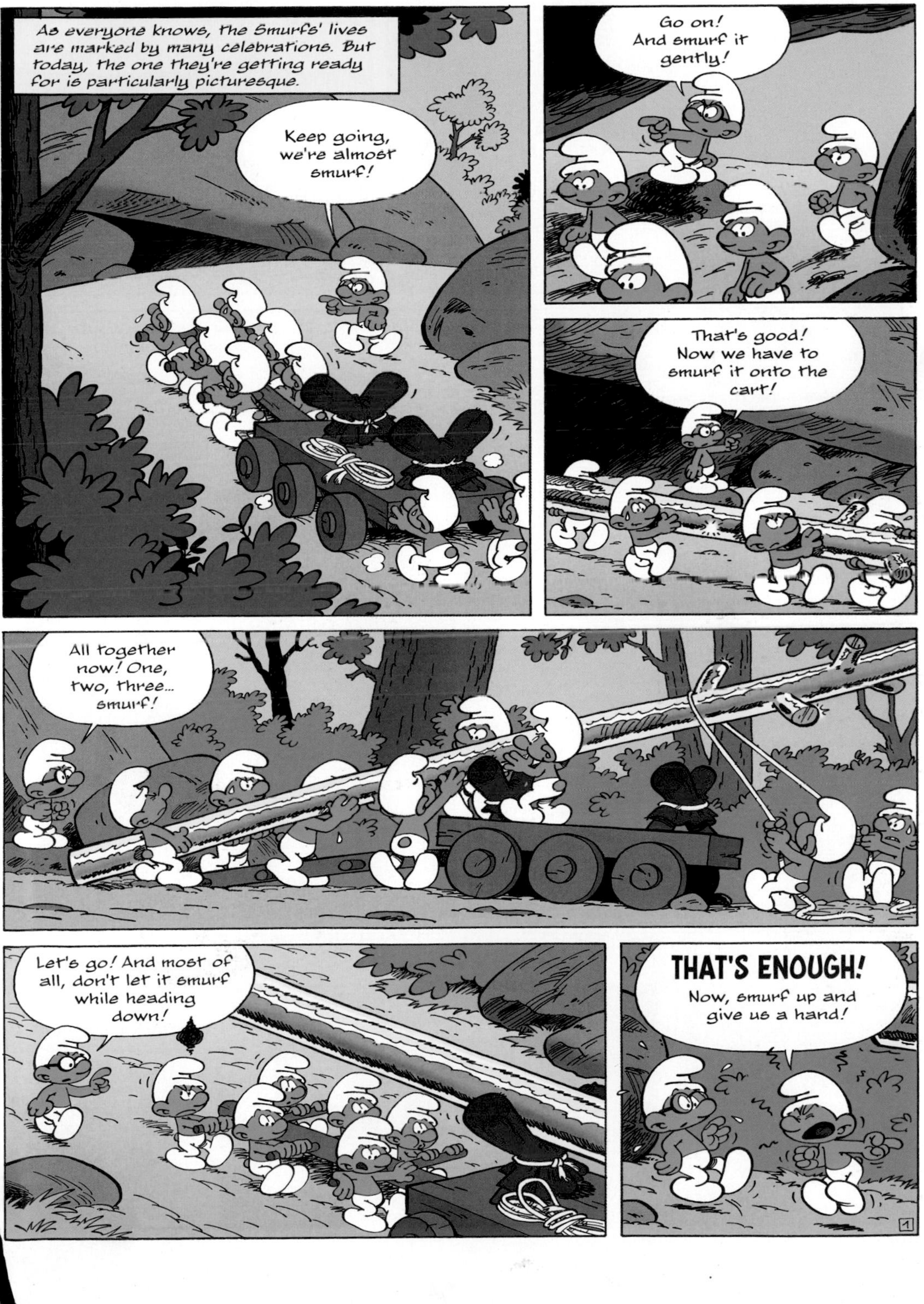

As everyone knows, the Smurfs' lives are marked by many celebrations. But today, the one they're getting ready for is particularly picturesque.
Keep going, we're almost smurf!
Go on! And smurf it gently!
That's good! Now we have to smurf it onto the cart!
All together now! One, two, three... smurf!
Let's go! And most of all, don't let it smurf while heading down!
THAT'S ENOUGH! Now, smurf up and give us a hand!
1

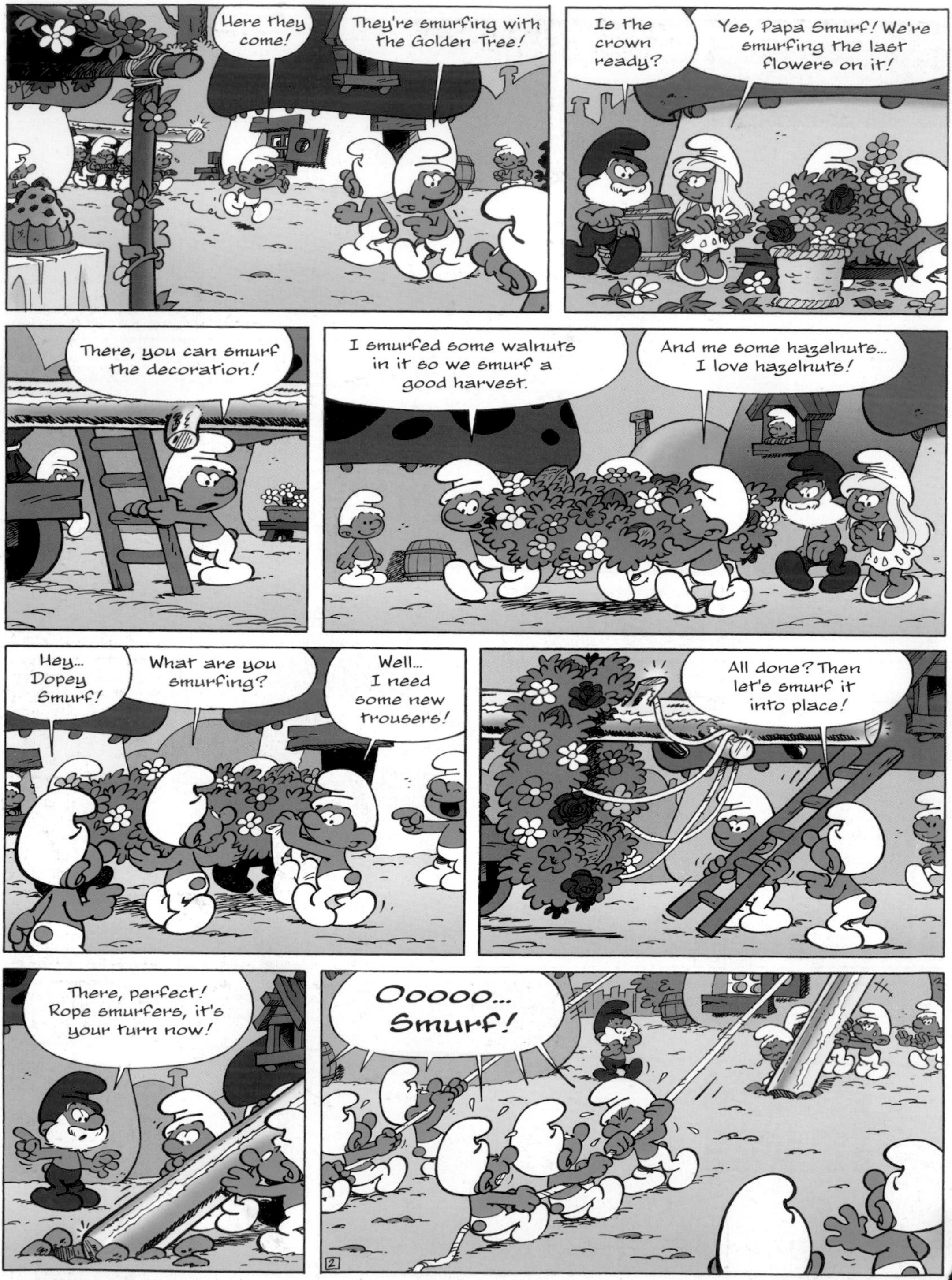
Here they come!
They're smurfing with the Golden Tree!
Is the crown ready?
Yes, Papa Smurf! We're smurfing the last flowers on it!
There, you can smurf the decoration!
I smurfed some walnuts in it so we smurf a good harvest.
And me some hazelnuts... I love hazelnuts!
Hey... Dopey Smurf!
What are you smurfing?
Well... I need some new trousers!
All done? Then let's smurf it into place!
There, perfect! Rope smurfers, it's your turn now!
Ooooo... Smurf!
2

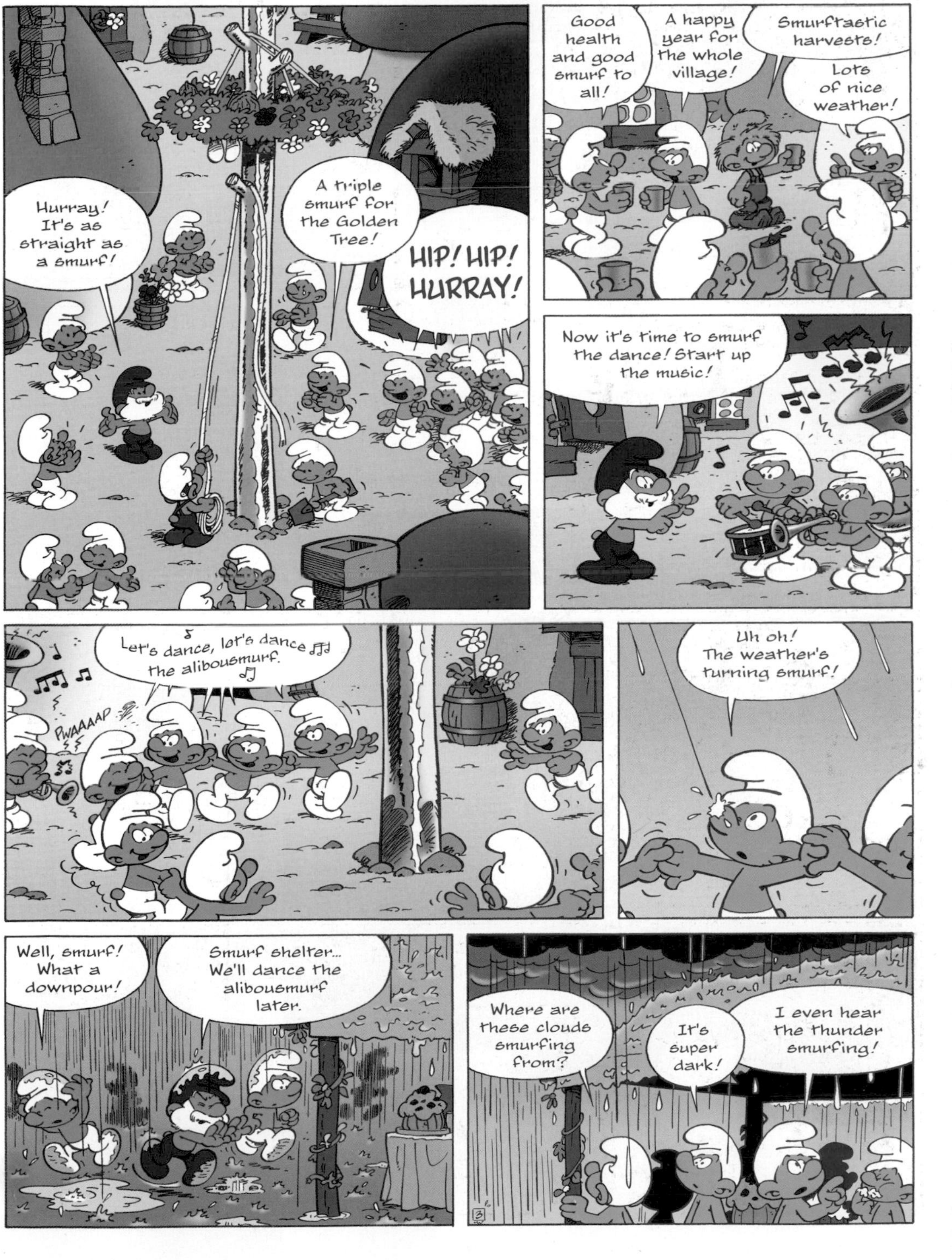
Hurray! It's as straight as a smurf!
A triple smurf for the Golden Tree!
HIP! HIP! HURRAY!
Good health and good smurf to all!
A happy year for the whole village!
Smurftastic harvests!
Lots of nice weather!
Now it's time to smurf the dance! Start up the music!
Let's dance, let's dance the alibousmurf.
PWAAAAP
Uh oh! The weather's turning smurf!
Well, smurf! What a downpour!
Smurf shelter... We'll dance the alibousmurf later.
Where are these clouds smurfing from?
It's super dark!
I even hear the thunder smurfing!

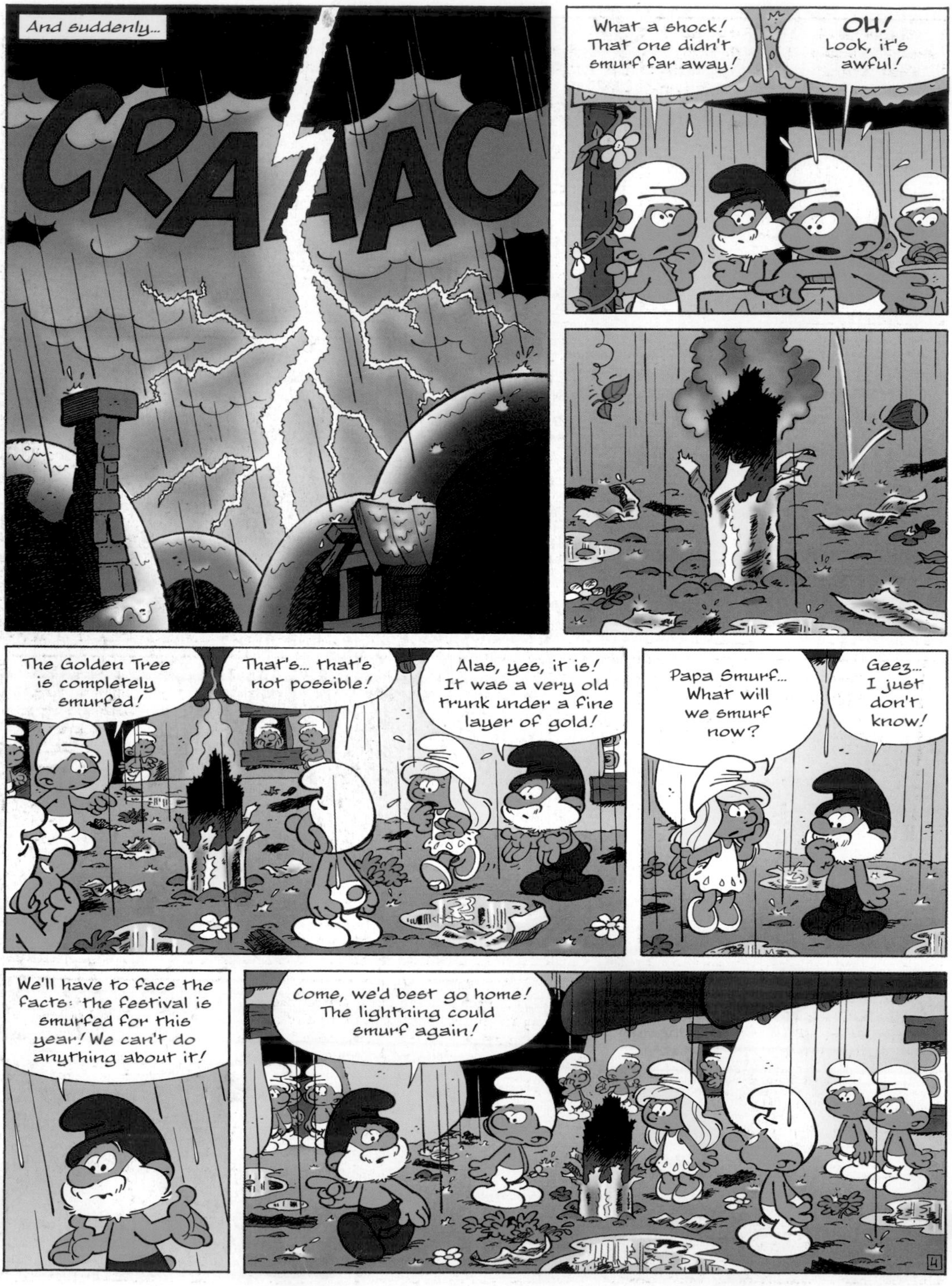

And suddenly...
CRAAAC
What a shock! That one didn't smurf far away!
OH! Look, it's awful!
The Golden Tree is completely smurfed!
That's... that's not possible!
Alas, yes, it is! It was a very old trunk under a fine layer of gold!
Papa Smurf... What will we smurf now?
Geez... I just don't know!
We'll have to face the facts: the festival is smurfed for this year! We can't do anything about it!
Come, we'd best go home! The lightning could smurf again!
4

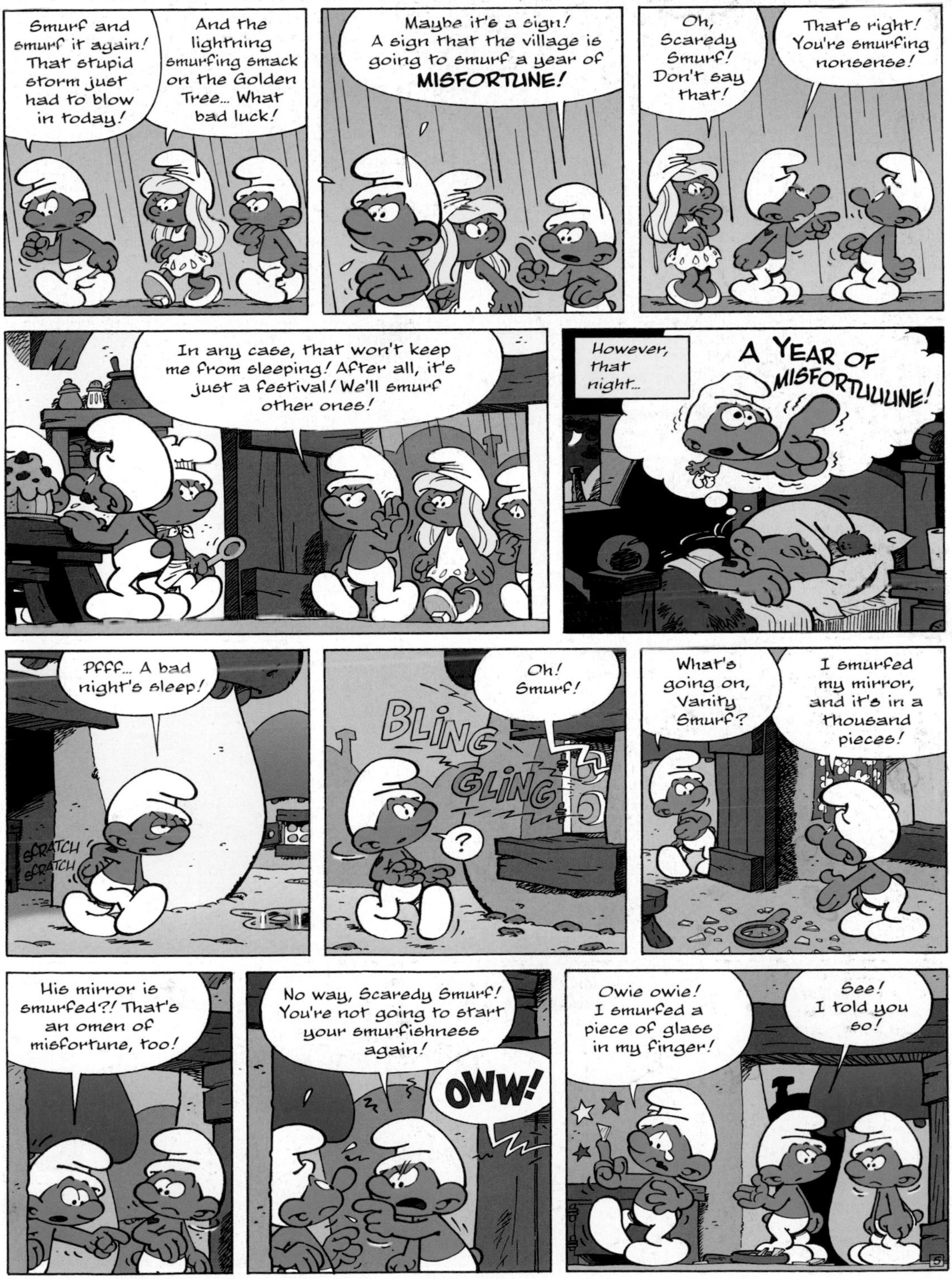
Smurf and smurf it again! That stupid storm just had to blow in today!
And the lightning smurfing smack on the Golden Tree... What bad luck!
Maybe it's a sign! A sign that the village is going to smurf a year of MISFORTUNE!
Oh, Scaredy Smurf! Don't say that!
That's right! You're smurfing nonsense!
In any case, that won't keep me from sleeping! After all, it's just a festival! We'll smurf other ones!
However, that night...
A YEAR OF MISFORTUUUNE!
Pfff... A bad night's sleep!
SCRATCH SCRATCH
BLING
GLING
Oh! Smurf!
?
What's going on, Vanity Smurf?
I smurfed my mirror, and it's in a thousand pieces!
His mirror is smurfed?! That's an omen of misfortune, too!
No way, Scaredy Smurf! You're not going to start your smurfishness again!
OWW!
Owie owie! I smurfed a piece of glass in my finger!
See! I told you so!
5

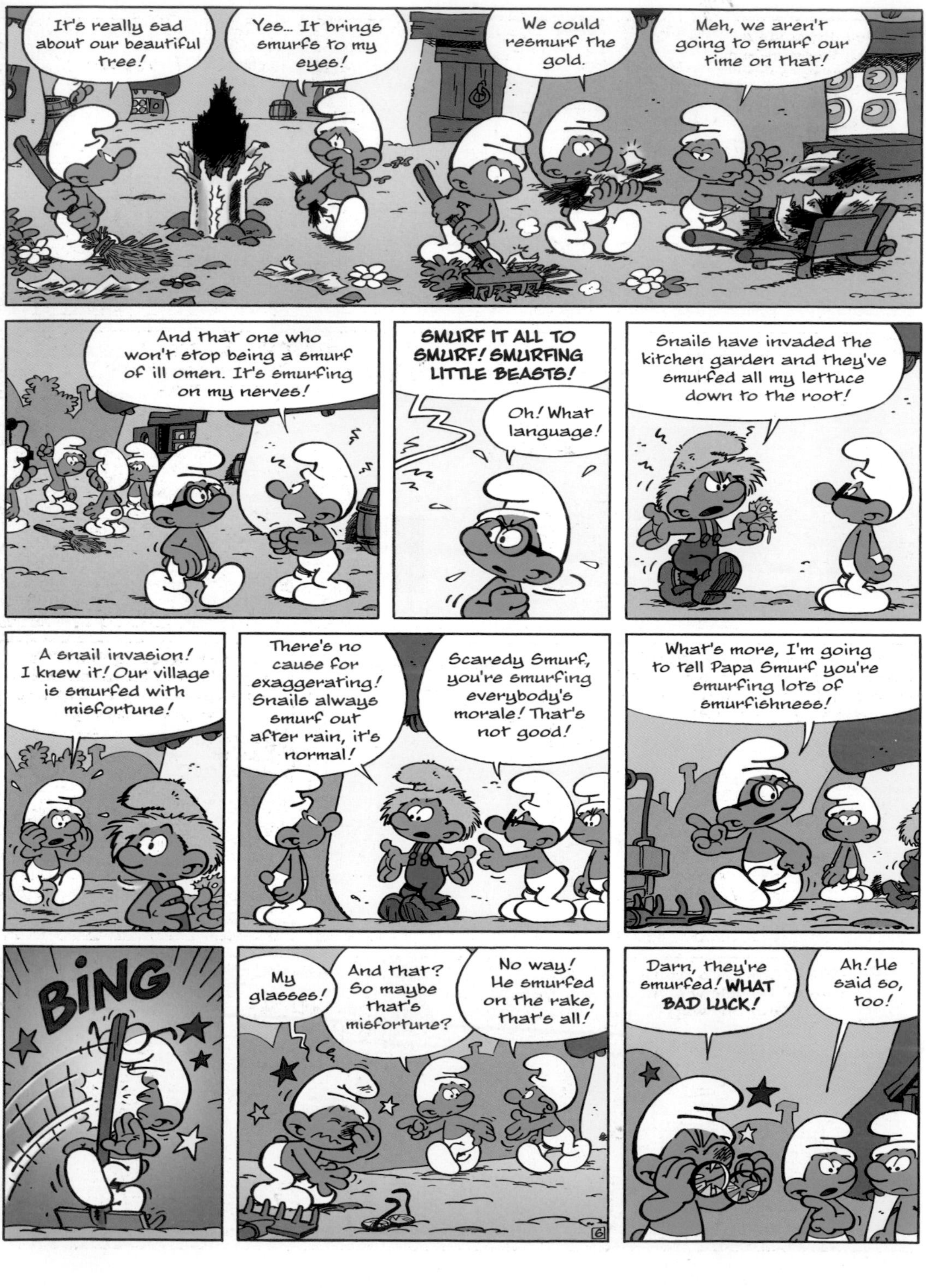
It's really sad about our beautiful tree!
Yes... It brings smurfs to my eyes!
We could resmurf the gold.
Meh, we aren't going to smurf our time on that!
And that one who won't stop being a smurf of ill omen. It's smurfing on my nerves!
SMURF IT ALL TO SMURF! SMURFING LITTLE BEASTS!
Oh! What language!
Snails have invaded the kitchen garden and they've smurfed all my lettuce down to the root!
A snail invasion! I knew it! Our village is smurfed with misfortune!
There's no cause for exaggerating! Snails always smurf out after rain, it's normal!
Scaredy Smurf, you're smurfing everybody's morale! That's not good!
What's more, I'm going to tell Papa Smurf you're smurfing lots of smurfishness!
BING
My glasses!
And that? So maybe that's misfortune?
No way! He smurfed on the rake, that's all!
6
Darn, they're smurfed! WHAT BAD LUCK!
Ah! He said so, too!

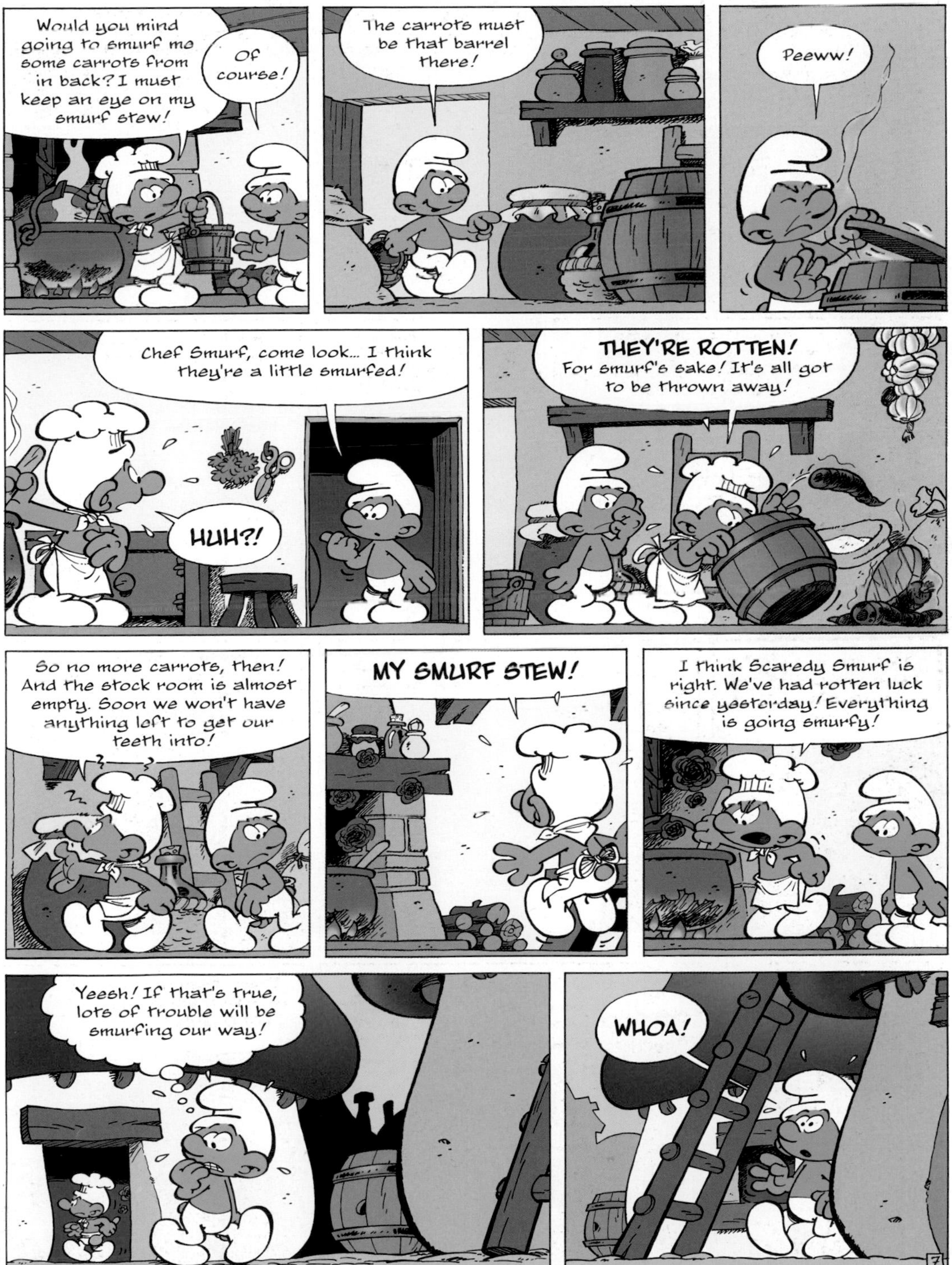
Would you mind going to smurf me some carrots from in back? I must keep an eye on my smurf stew!
Of course!
The carrots must be that barrel there!
Peeww!
Chef Smurf, come look... I think they're a little smurfed!
HUH?!
THEY'RE ROTTEN!
For smurf's sake! It's all got to be thrown away!
So no more carrots, then! And the stock room is almost empty. Soon we won't have anything left to get our teeth into!
MY SMURF STEW!
I think Scaredy Smurf is right. We've had rotten luck since yesterday! Everything is going smurfy!
Yeesh! If that's true, lots of trouble will be smurfing our way!
WHOA!
7

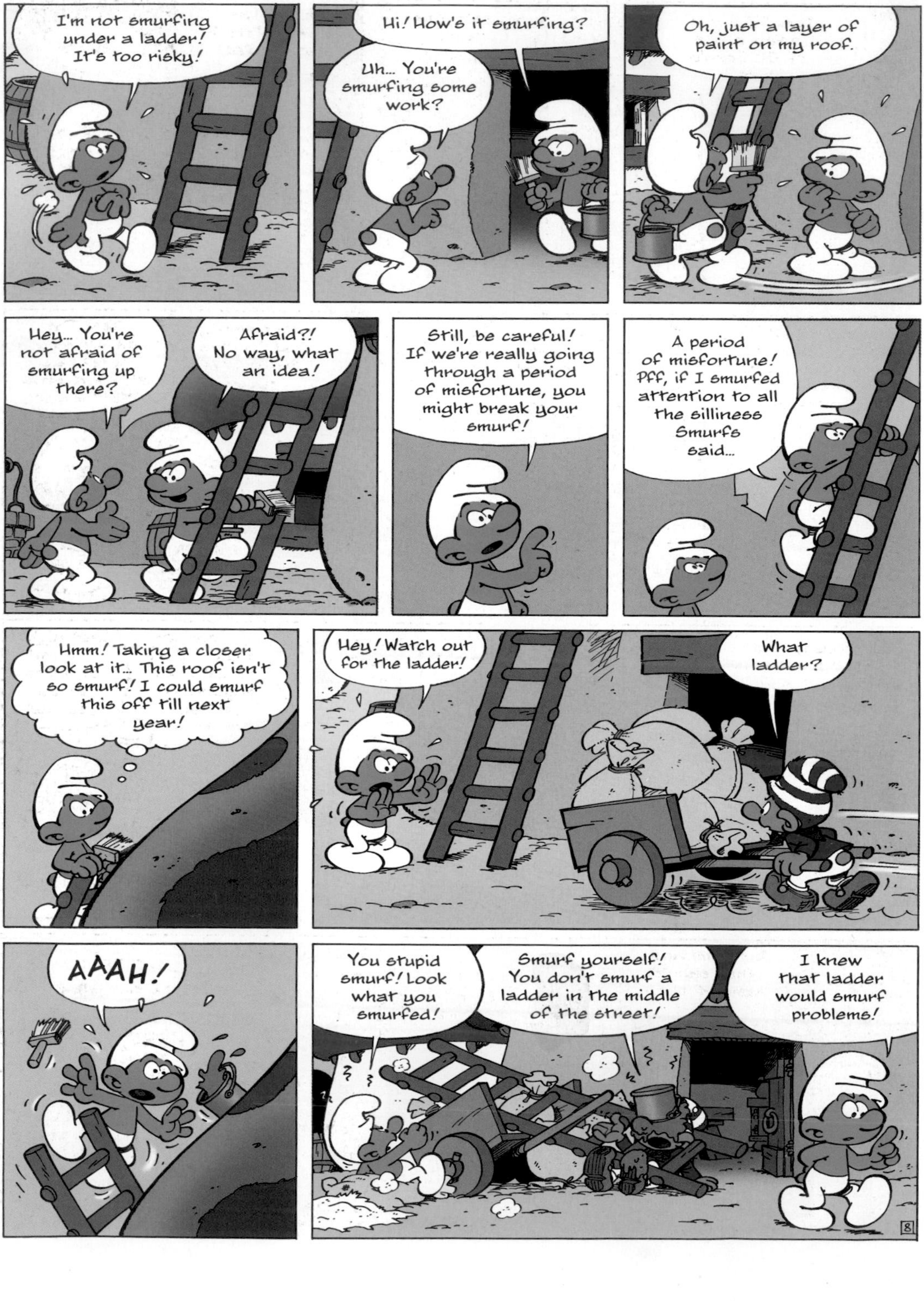
I'm not smurfing under a ladder! It's too risky!
Hi! How's it smurfing?
Uh... You're smurfing some work?
Oh, just a layer of paint on my roof.
Hey... You're not afraid of smurfing up there?
Afraid?! No way, what an idea!
Still, be careful! If we're really going through a period of misfortune, you might break your smurf!
A period of misfortune! Pff, if I smurfed attention to all the silliness Smurfs said...
Hmm! Taking a closer look at it... This roof isn't so smurf! I could smurf this off till next year!
Hey! Watch out for the ladder!
What ladder?
AAAH!
You stupid smurf! Look what you smurfed!
Smurf yourself! You don't smurf a ladder in the middle of the street!
I knew that ladder would smurf problems!
8

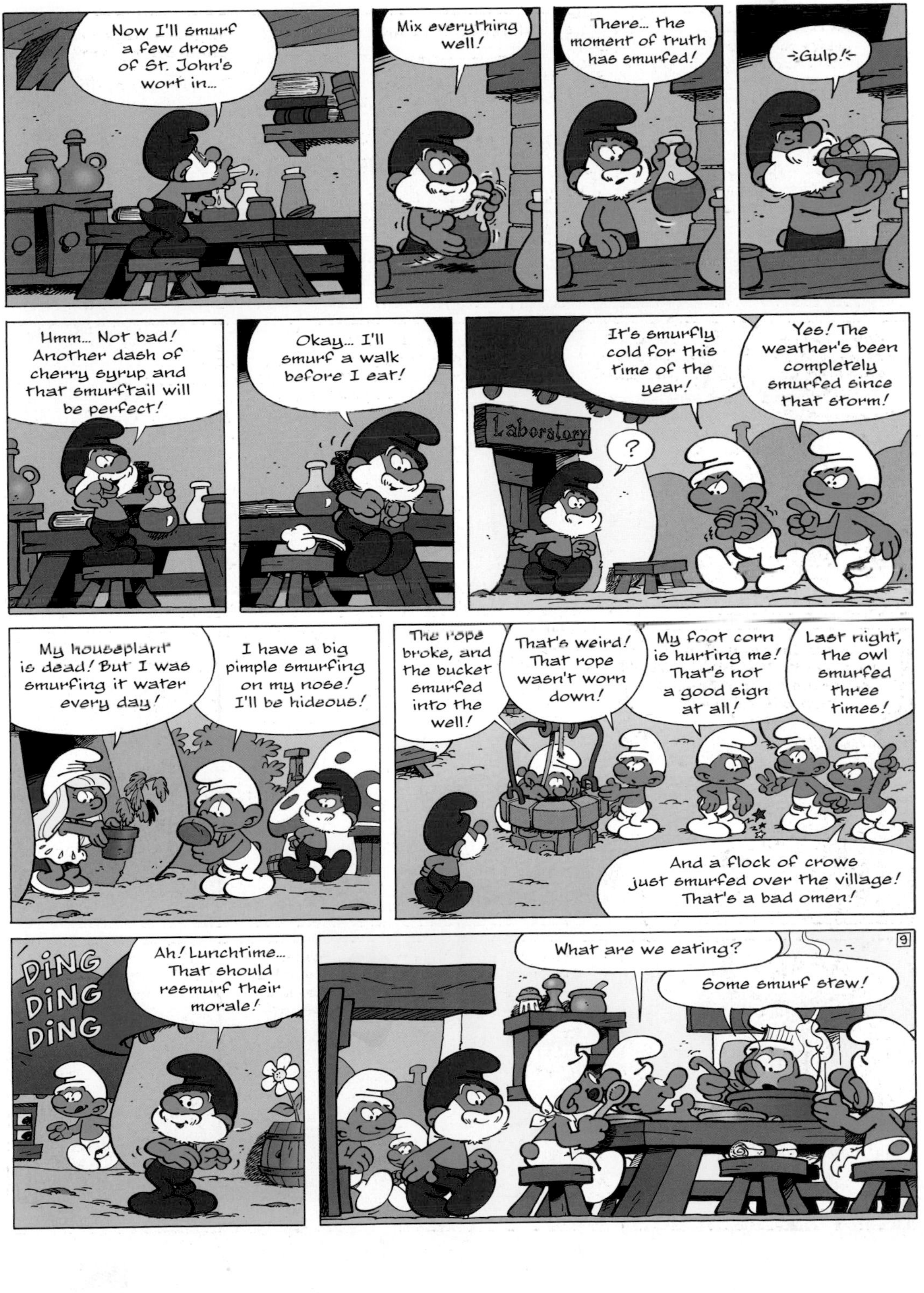

Now I'll smurf a few drops of St. John's wort in...
Mix everything well!
There... the moment of truth has smurfed!
Gulp!
Hmm... Not bad! Another dash of cherry syrup and that smurftail will be perfect!
Okay... I'll smurf a walk before I eat!
Laborstory
It's smurfly cold for this time of the year!
Yes! The weather's been completely smurfed since that storm!
?
My houseplant is dead! But I was smurfing it water every day!
I have a big pimple smurfing on my nose! I'll be hideous!
The rope broke, and the bucket smurfed into the well!
That's weird! That rope wasn't worn down!
My foot corn is hurting me! That's not a good sign at all!
Last night, the owl smurfed three times!
And a flock of crows just smurfed over the village! That's a bad omen!
DING DING DING
Ah! Lunchtime... That should resmurf their morale!
What are we eating?
Some smurf stew!
9

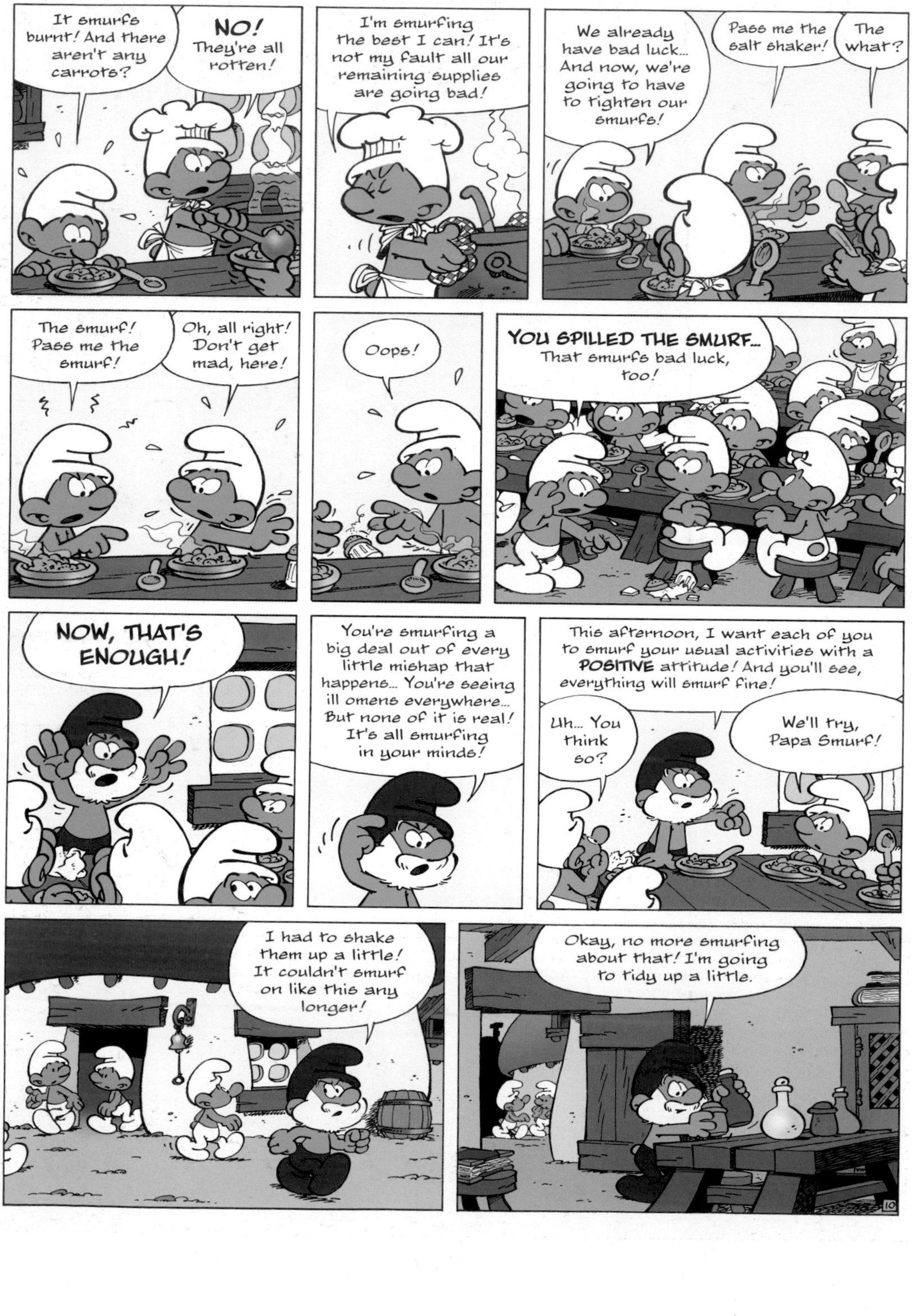
It smurfs burnt! And there aren't any carrots?
NO! They're all rotten!
I'm smurfing the best I can! It's not my fault all our remaining supplies are going bad!
We already have bad luck... And now, we're going to have to tighten our smurfs!
Pass me the salt shaker!
The what?
The smurf! Pass me the smurf!
Oh, all right! Don't get mad, here!
Oops!
YOU SPILLED THE SMURF... That smurfs bad luck, too!
NOW, THAT'S ENOUGH!
You're smurfing a big deal out of every little mishap that happens... You're seeing ill omens everywhere... But none of it is real! It's all smurfing in your minds!
This afternoon, I want each of you to smurf your usual activities with a POSITIVE attitude! And you'll see, everything will smurf fine!
Uh... You think so?
We'll try, Papa Smurf!
I had to shake them up a little! It couldn't smurf on like this any longer!
Okay, no more smurfing about that! I'm going to tidy up a little.
10

Whoa!

⌐Whew!⌐ That was a close smurf!

GLING GLING GLING GLING

BRRRRRRRRRR

CLING BLING
BING CKAC

That was a smurfquake!

Everything okay? Anybody hurt?

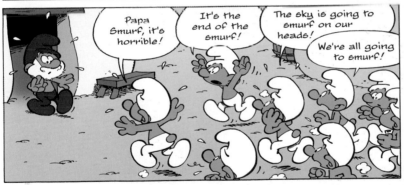

Papa Smurf, it's horrible!

It's the end of the smurf!

The sky is going to smurf on our heads!

We're all going to smurf!

QUIET DOWN!

Smurf your cool, for smurf's sake!

It was a smurf-quake, but it was only a little tremor! There's nothing to smurf about, I've seen dozens of them in my lifetime!

Considering your great age, that's quite likely.

But how many times was there a smurf-quake right after lightning destroyed the golden tree, huh? Huh?!?

Well... None, since lightning had never smurfed the golden tree before!

So you see! WEIRD stuff is going on!

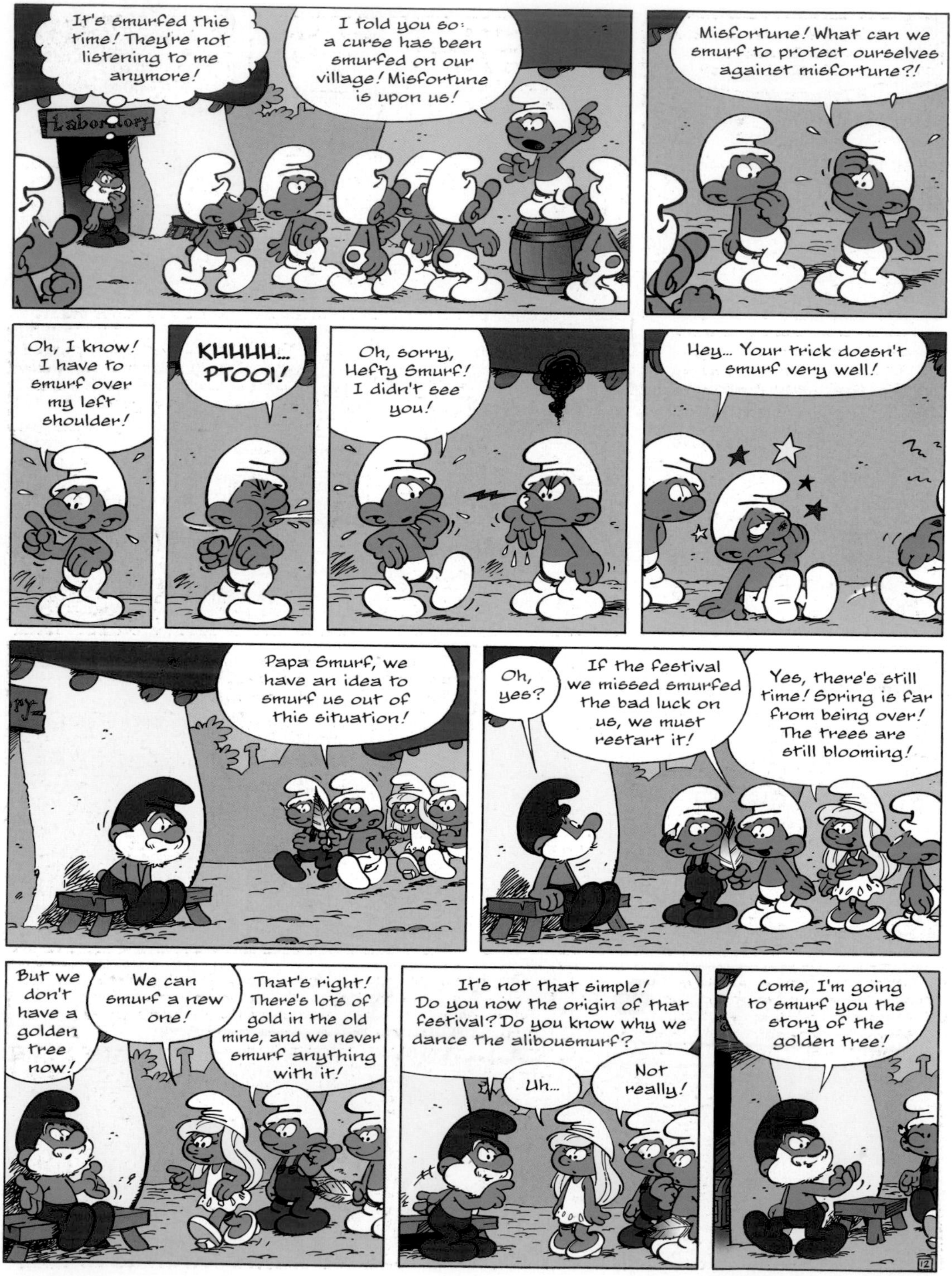
Laboratory
It's smurfed this time! They're not listening to me anymore!
I told you so: a curse has been smurfed on our village! Misfortune is upon us!
Misfortune! What can we smurf to protect ourselves against misfortune?!
Oh, I know! I have to smurf over my left shoulder!
KHHHH... PTOOI!
Oh, sorry, Hefty Smurf! I didn't see you!
Hey... Your trick doesn't smurf very well!
Papa Smurf, we have an idea to smurf us out of this situation!
Oh, yes?
If the festival we missed smurfed the bad luck on us, we must restart it!
Yes, there's still time! Spring is far from being over! The trees are still blooming!
But we don't have a golden tree now!
We can smurf a new one!
That's right! There's lots of gold in the old mine, and we never smurf anything with it!
It's not that simple! Do you now the origin of that festival? Do you know why we dance the alibousmurf?
Uh...
Not really!
Come, I'm going to smurf you the story of the golden tree!
12

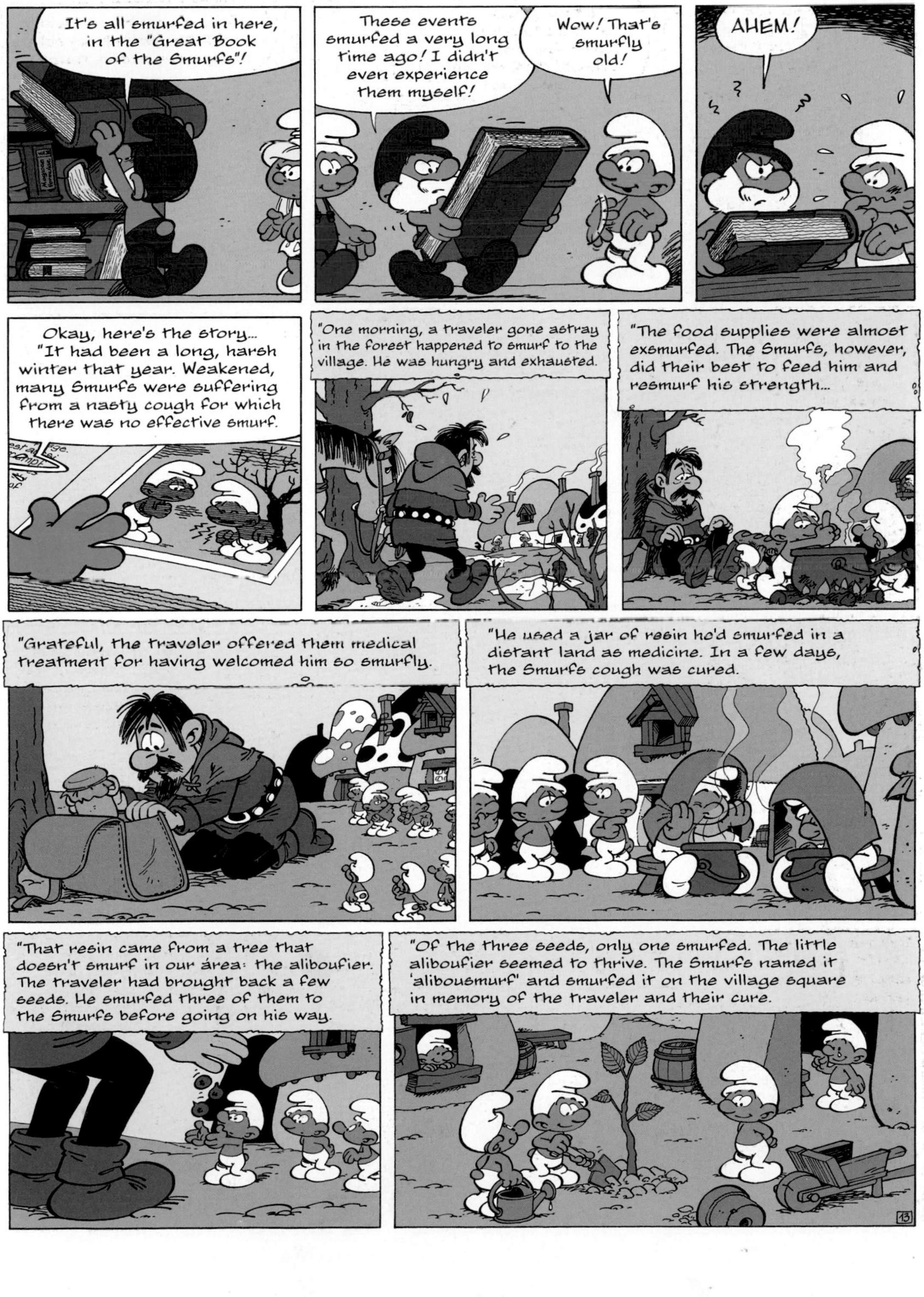

It's all smurfed in here, in the "Great Book of the Smurfs"!
These events smurfed a very long time ago! I didn't even experience them myself!
Wow! That's smurfly old!
AHEM!
Okay, here's the story... "It had been a long, harsh winter that year. Weakened, many Smurfs were suffering from a nasty cough for which there was no effective smurf.
"One morning, a traveler gone astray in the forest happened to smurf to the village. He was hungry and exhausted.
"The food supplies were almost exsmurfed. The Smurfs, however, did their best to feed him and resmurf his strength...
"Grateful, the travelor offered them medical treatment for having welcomed him so smurfly.
"He used a jar of resin ho'd smurfed in a distant land as medicine. In a few days, the Smurfs cough was cured.
"That resin came from a tree that doesn't smurf in our área: the aliboufier. The traveler had brought back a few seeds. He smurfed three of them to the Smurfs before going on his way.
"Of the three seeds, only one smurfed. The little aliboufier seemed to thrive. The Smurfs named it 'alibousmurf' and smurfed it on the village square in memory of the traveler and their cure.
13

"The following spring, the sapling smurfed pretty flowers. Overjoyed, the Smurfs started dancing to celebrate the return of good weather. They smurfed that new dance the name of the tree: the alibousmurf."

"Every year, when the alibousmurf bloomed, they celebrated the festival again while smurfing wishes for good health, good weather, and good harvests."

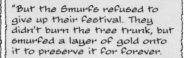

"Alas, another icy winter smurfed over the land. The young alibousmurf, a tree from the South, couldn't take it. In the spring, it didn't smurf out any leaves. It was dead.

"But the Smurfs refused to give up their festival. They didn't burn the tree trunk, but smurfed a layer of gold onto it to preserve it for forever.

"And that's how the alibousmurf became the golden tree that we smurf onto the town square every year when nature blooms again."

You see? The golden tree isn't just any old tree: it's an alibousmurf!

Well, we'll have to smurf a new one, that's all!

But remember, that tree doesn't smurf in our area!

That's right!

Then we're smurfed!

No! Let's not smurf hope! If an alibousmurf once grew here, there can be others nearby!

He's right, Papa Smurf!

We have to smurf a search!

It's our only chance! We've nothing to lose by smurfing!

Well! I see that I won't smurf that idea out of your heads...

SCRATCH SCRATCH

All right, then! I'm going to smurf a visit to the mage Homnibus! He's a great expert in plants and remedies!

Hurray!

We're smurfing on you, Papa Smurf!

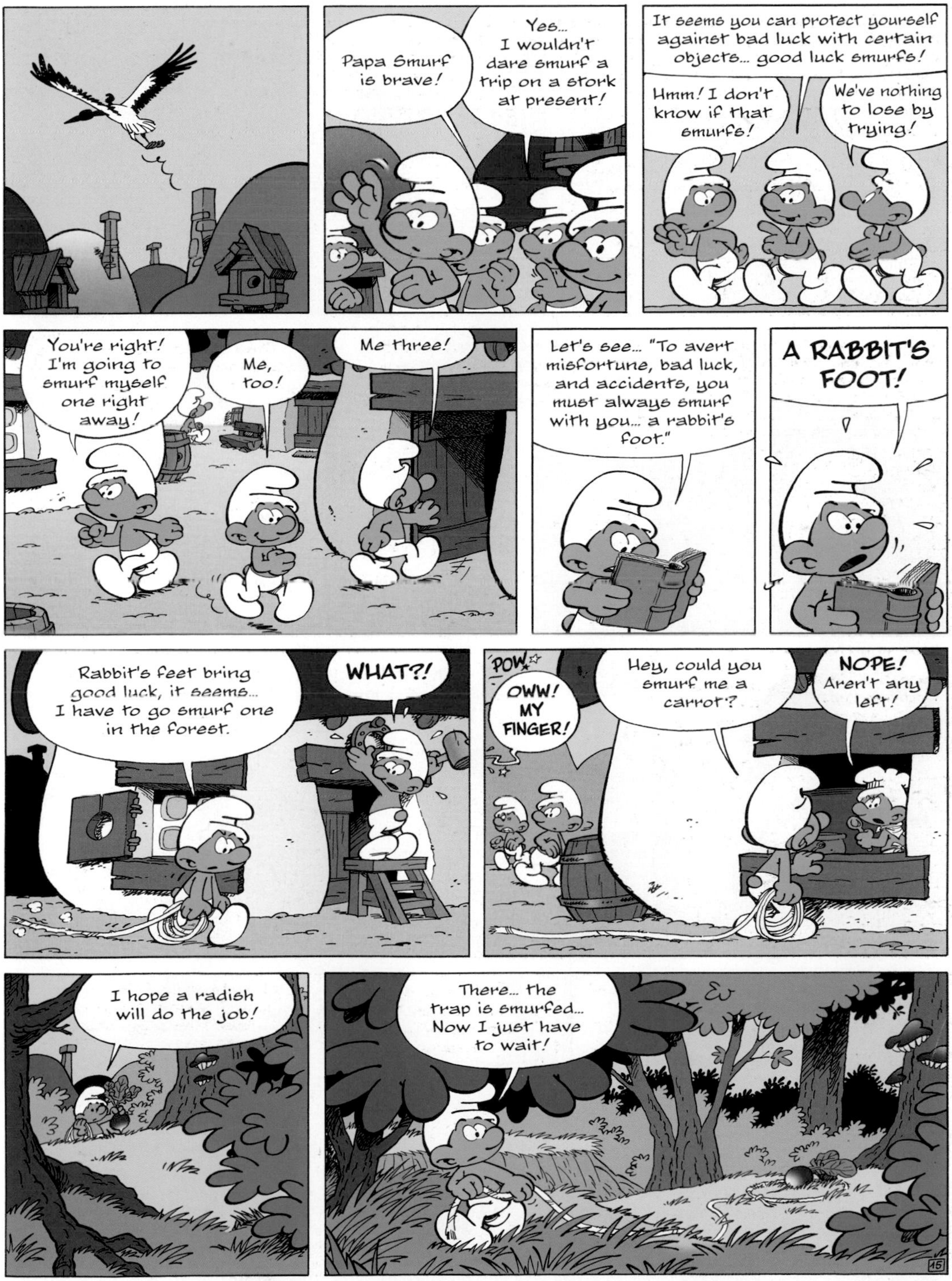

Papa Smurf is brave!
Yes... I wouldn't dare smurf a trip on a stork at present!
It seems you can protect yourself against bad luck with certain objects... good luck smurfs!
Hmm! I don't know if that smurfs!
We've nothing to lose by trying!
You're right! I'm going to smurf myself one right away!
Me, too!
Me three!
Let's see... "To avert misfortune, bad luck, and accidents, you must always smurf with you... a rabbit's foot."
A RABBIT'S FOOT!
Rabbit's feet bring good luck, it seems... I have to go smurf one in the forest.
WHAT?!
POW
OWW! MY FINGER!
Hey, could you smurf me a carrot?
NOPE! Aren't any left!
I hope a radish will do the job!
There... the trap is smurfed... Now I just have to wait!
15

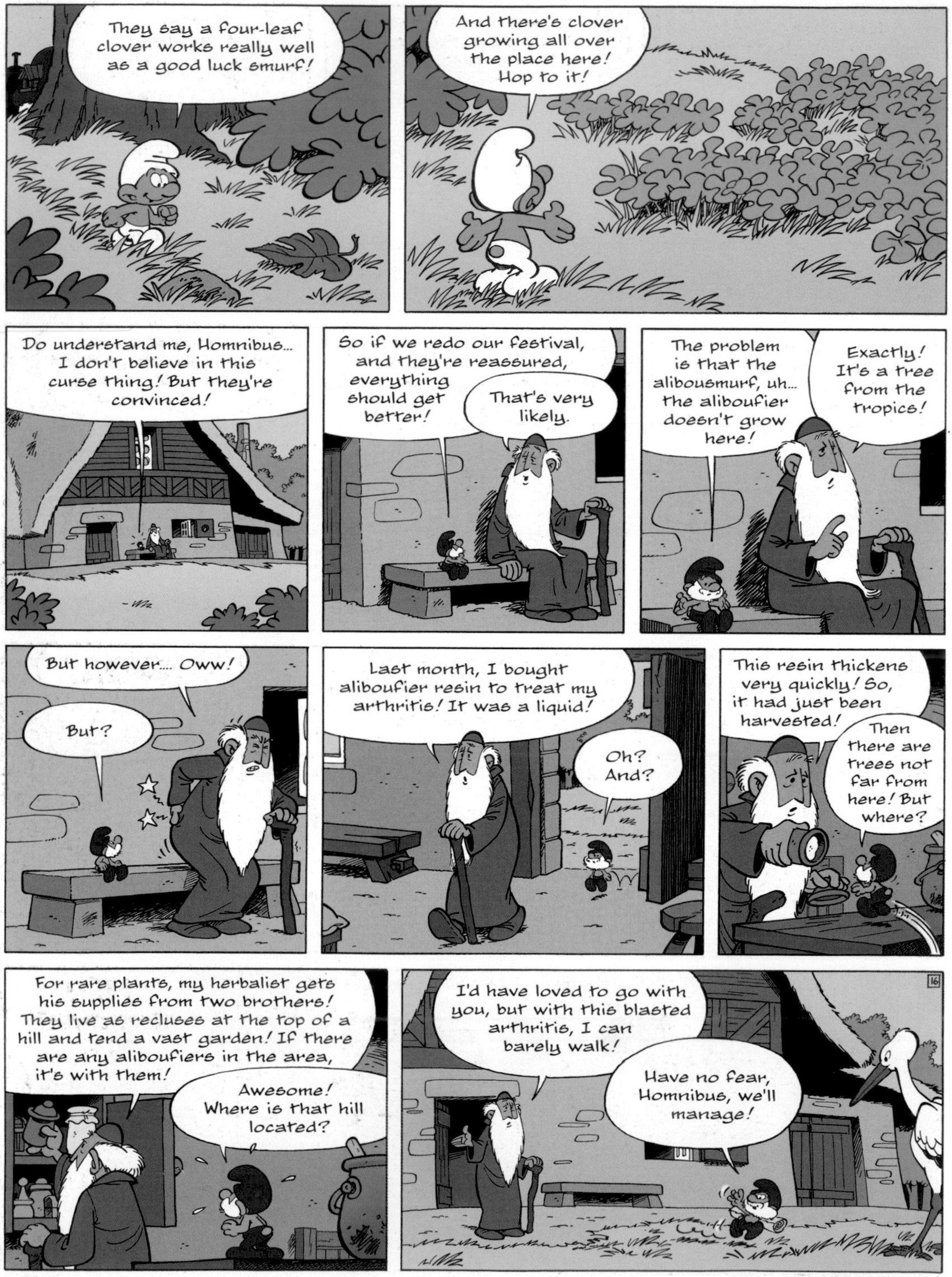

They say a four-leaf clover works really well as a good luck smurf!
And there's clover growing all over the place here! Hop to it!
Do understand me, Homnibus... I don't believe in this curse thing! But they're convinced!
So if we redo our festival, and they're reassured, everything should get better!
That's very likely.
The problem is that the alibousmurf, uh... the aliboufier doesn't grow here!
Exactly! It's a tree from the tropics!
But however.... Oww!
But?
Last month, I bought aliboufier resin to treat my arthritis! It was a liquid!
Oh? And?
This resin thickens very quickly! So, it had just been harvested!
Then there are trees not far from here! But where?
For rare plants, my herbalist gets his supplies from two brothers! They live as recluses at the top of a hill and tend a vast garden! If there are any aliboufiers in the area, it's with them!
Awesome! Where is that hill located?
16
I'd have loved to go with you, but with this blasted arthritis, I can barely walk!
Have no fear, Homnibus, we'll manage!

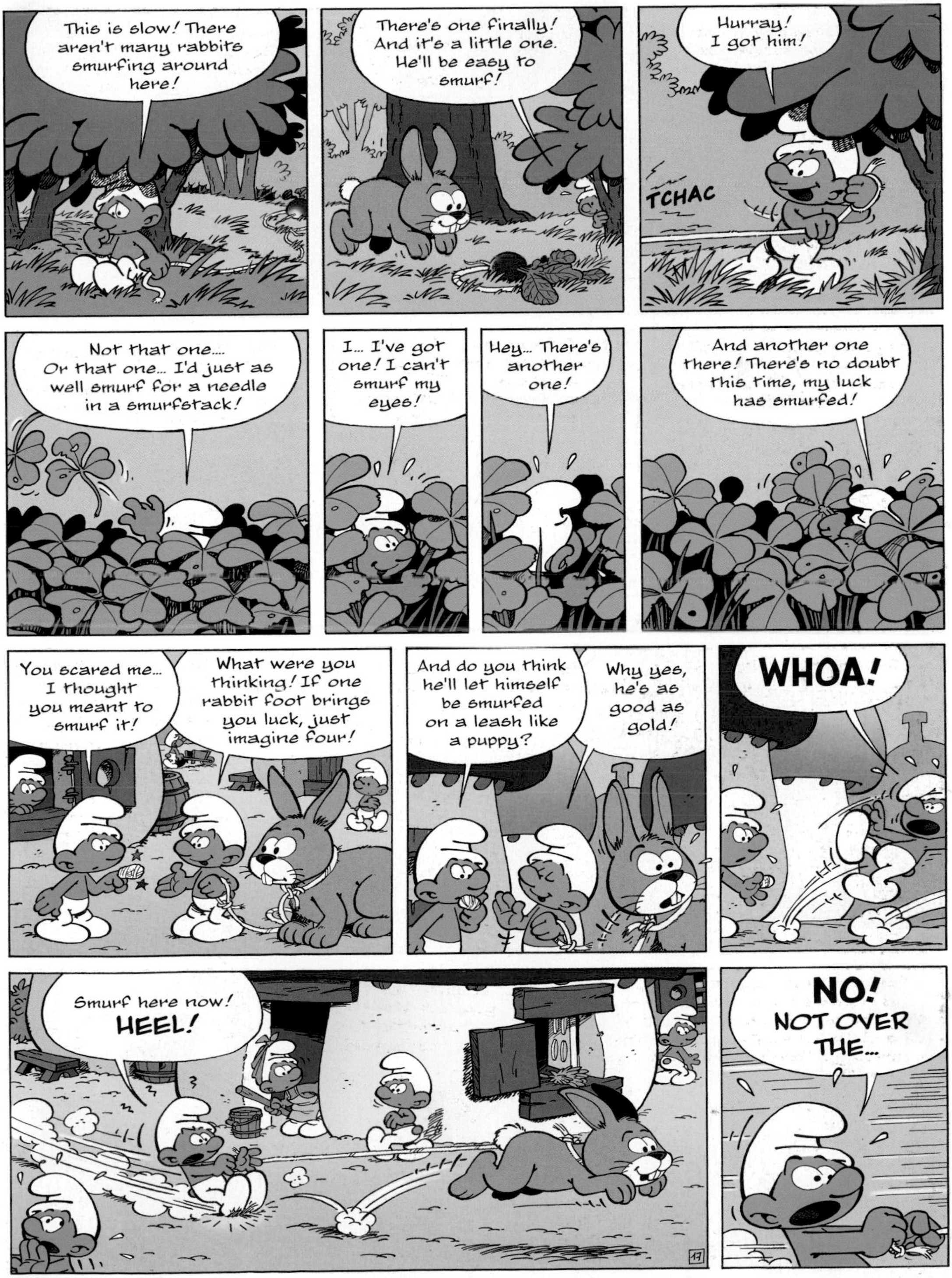

This is slow! There aren't many rabbits smurfing around here!
There's one finally! And it's a little one. He'll be easy to smurf!
Hurray! I got him!
TCHAC
Not that one.... Or that one... I'd just as well smurf for a needle in a smurfstack!
I... I've got one! I can't smurf my eyes!
Hey... There's another one!
And another one there! There's no doubt this time, my luck has smurfed!
You scared me... I thought you meant to smurf it!
What were you thinking! If one rabbit foot brings you luck, just imagine four!
And do you think he'll let himself be smurfed on a leash like a puppy?
Why yes, he's as good as gold!
WHOA!
Smurf here now! **HEEL!**
17
NO! NOT OVER THE...

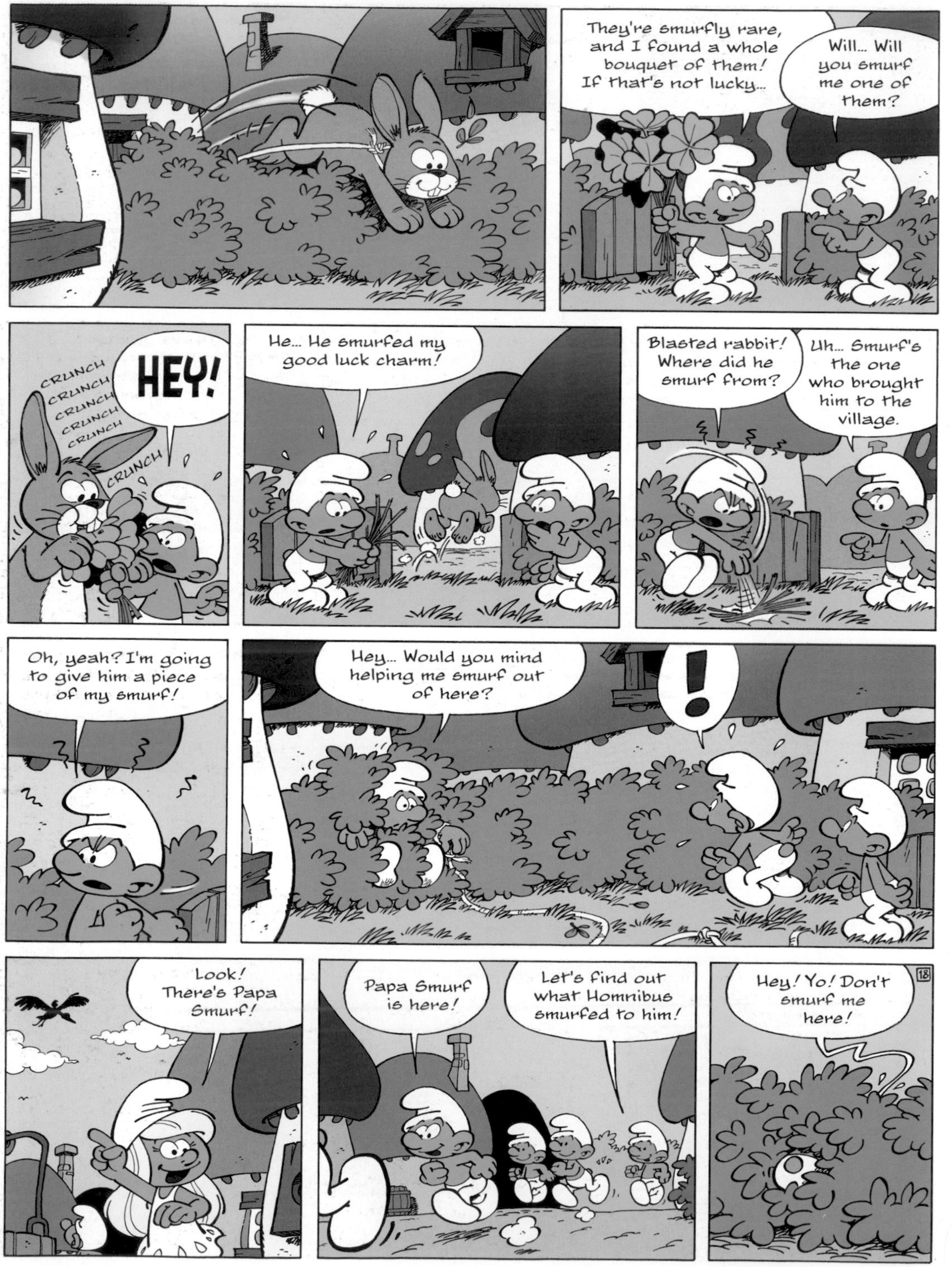
They're smurfly rare, and I found a whole bouquet of them! If that's not lucky...
Will... Will you smurf me one of them?
CRUNCH CRUNCH CRUNCH CRUNCH CRUNCH
HEY!
CRUNCH
He... He smurfed my good luck charm!
Blasted rabbit! Where did he smurf from?
Uh... Smurf's the one who brought him to the village.
Oh, yeah? I'm going to give him a piece of my smurf!
Hey... Would you mind helping me smurf out of here?
!
Look! There's Papa Smurf!
Papa Smurf is here!
Let's find out what Homnibus smurfed to him!
18
Hey! Yo! Don't smurf me here!

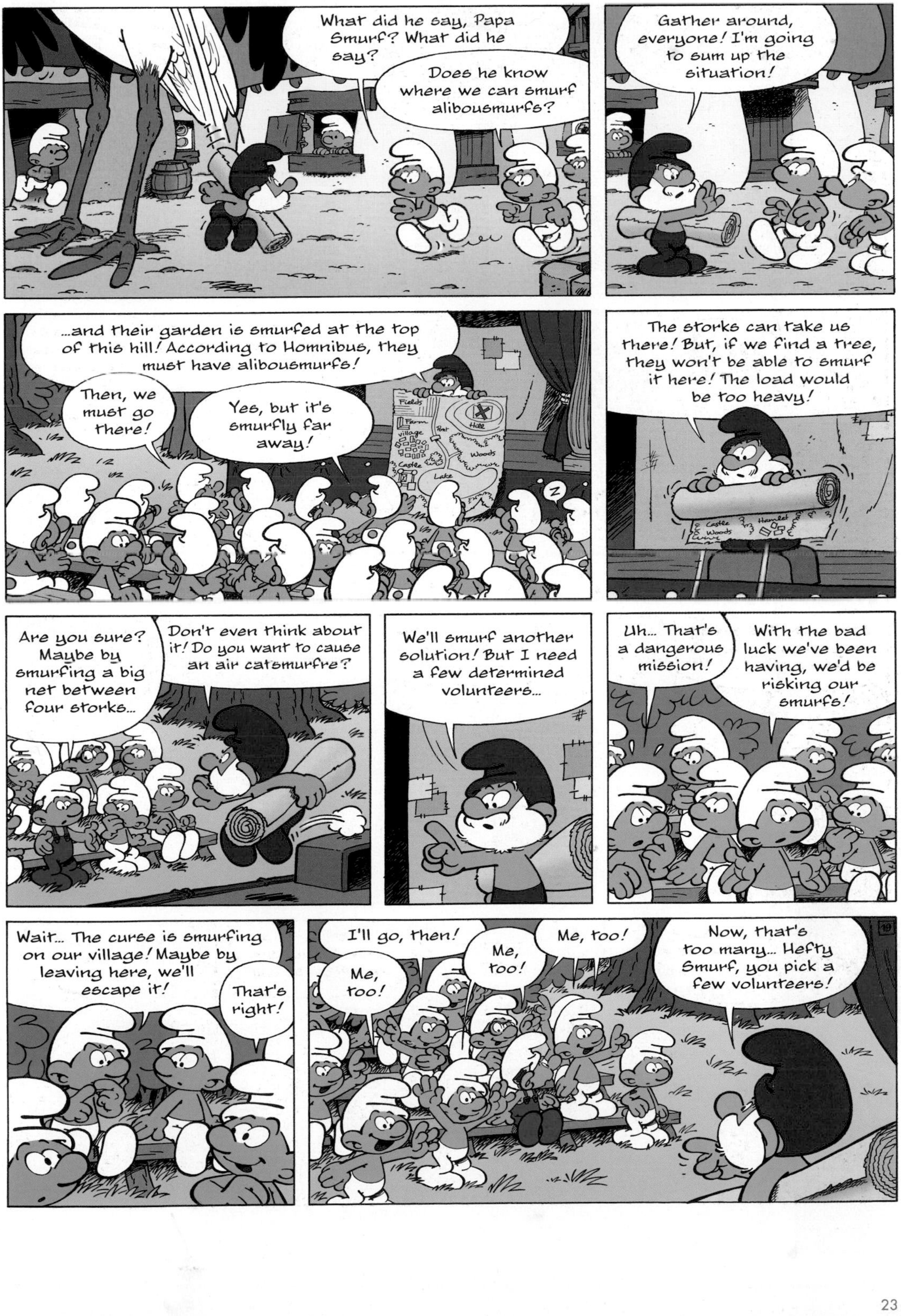

What did he say, Papa Smurf? What did he say?
Does he know where we can smurf alibousmurfs?
Gather around, everyone! I'm going to sum up the situation!
...and their garden is smurfed at the top of this hill! According to Homnibus, they must have alibousmurfs!
Then, we must go there!
Yes, but it's smurfly far away!
Fields
Farm
village
Castle
Hill
Woods
Lake
The storks can take us there! But, if we find a tree, they won't be able to smurf it here! The load would be too heavy!
Are you sure? Maybe by smurfing a big net between four storks...
Don't even think about it! Do you want to cause an air catsmurfre?
We'll smurf another solution! But I need a few determined volunteers...
Uh... That's a dangerous mission!
With the bad luck we've been having, we'd be risking our smurfs!
Wait... The curse is smurfing on our village! Maybe by leaving here, we'll escape it!
That's right!
I'll go, then!
Me, too!
Me, too!
Me, too!
Now, that's too many... Hefty Smurf, you pick a few volunteers!

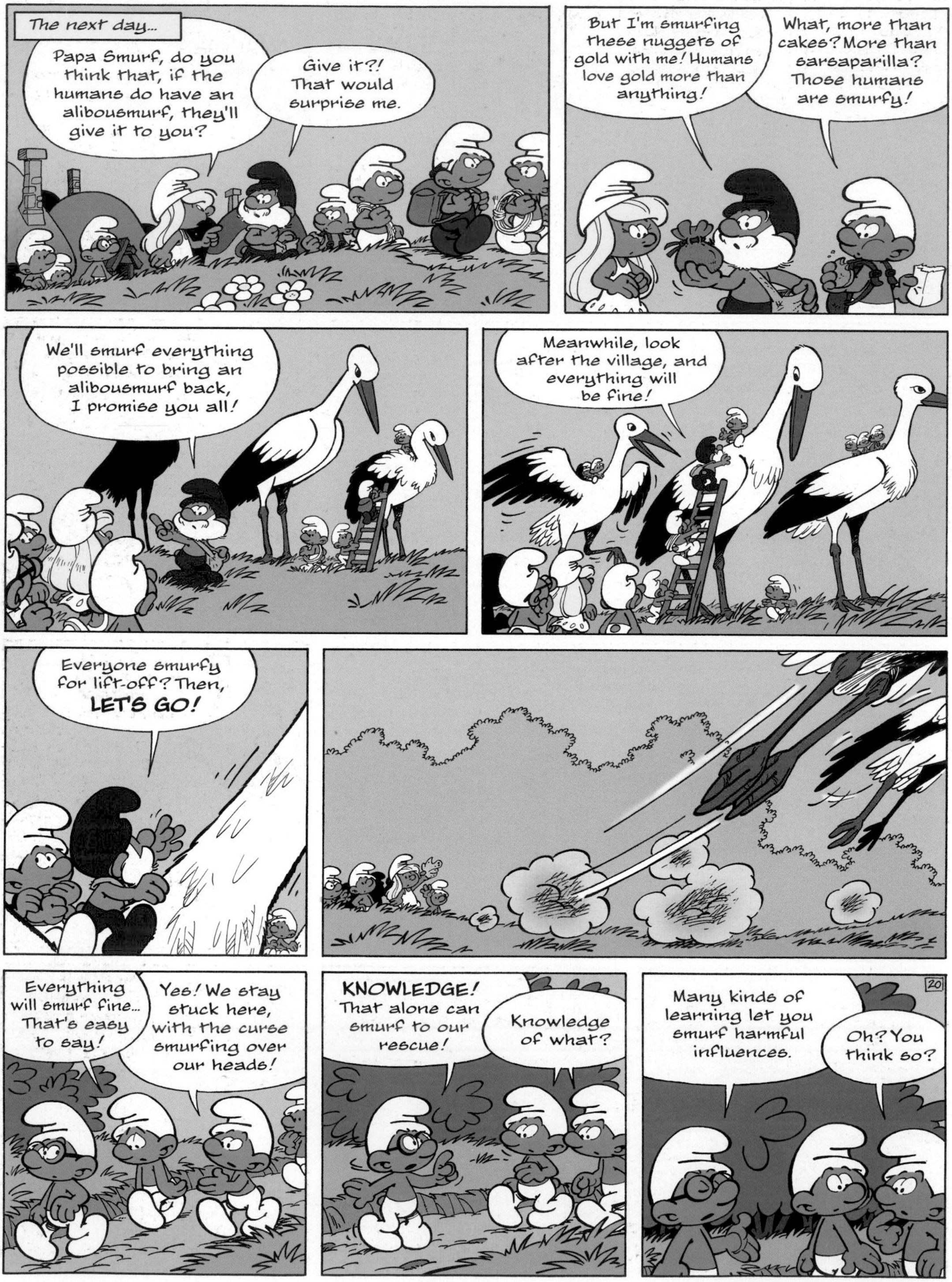

The next day...
Papa Smurf, do you think that, if the humans do have an alibousmurf, they'll give it to you?
Give it?! That would surprise me.
But I'm smurfing these nuggets of gold with me! Humans love gold more than anything!
What, more than cakes? More than sarsaparilla? Those humans are smurfy!
We'll smurf everything possible to bring an alibousmurf back, I promise you all!
Meanwhile, look after the village, and everything will be fine!
Everyone smurfy for lift-off? Then, LET'S GO!
Everything will smurf fine... That's easy to say!
Yes! We stay stuck here, with the curse smurfing over our heads!
KNOWLEDGE! That alone can smurf to our rescue!
Knowledge of what?
20
Many kinds of learning let you smurf harmful influences.
Oh? You think so?

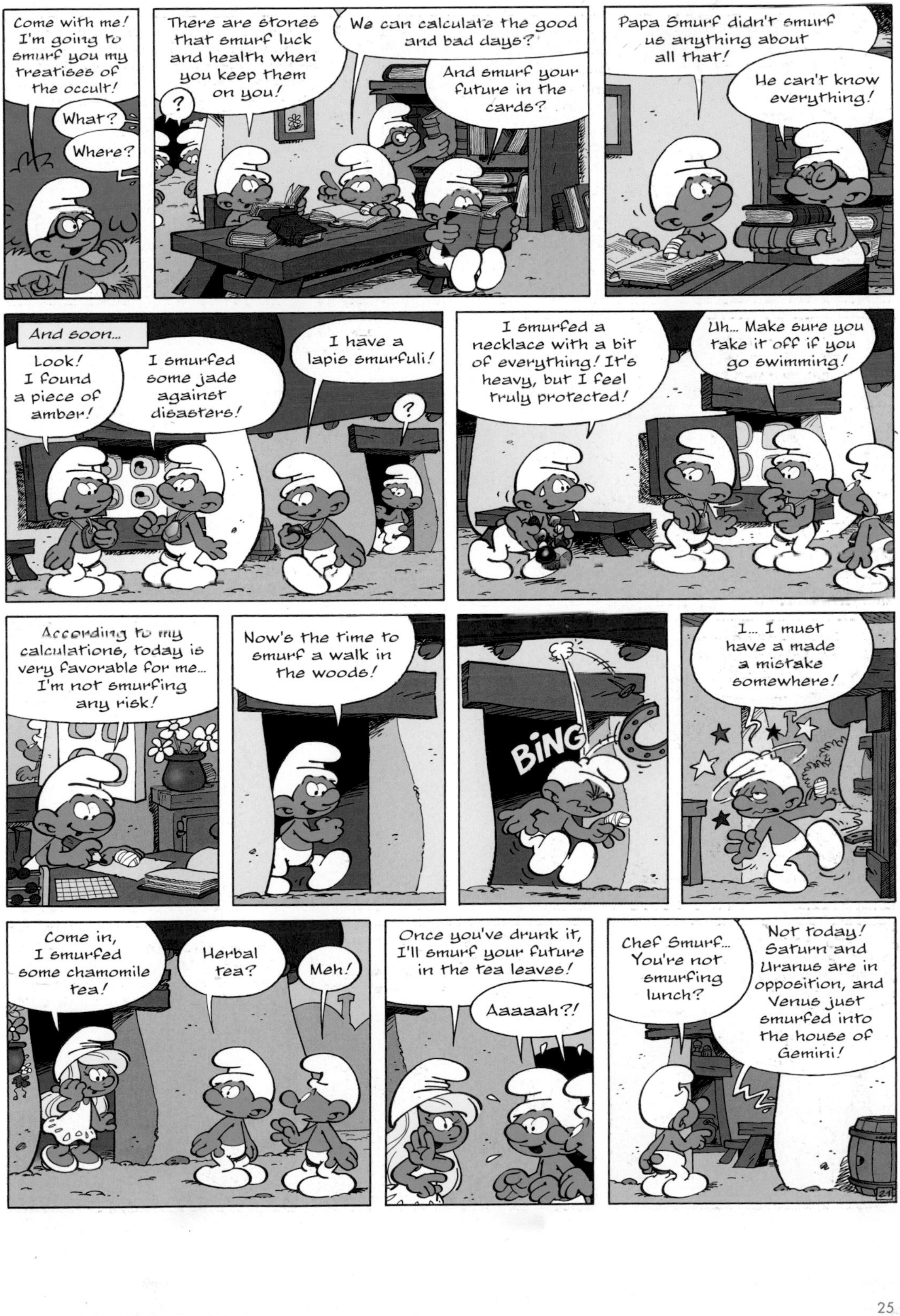
Come with me! I'm going to smurf you my treatises of the occult!
What?
Where?
?
There are stones that smurf luck and health when you keep them on you!
We can calculate the good and bad days?
And smurf your future in the cards?
Papa Smurf didn't smurf us anything about all that!
He can't know everything!
And soon...
Look! I found a piece of amber!
I smurfed some jade against disasters!
I have a lapis smurfuli!
?
I smurfed a necklace with a bit of everything! It's heavy, but I feel truly protected!
Uh... Make sure you take it off if you go swimming!
According to my calculations, today is very favorable for me... I'm not smurfing any risk!
Now's the time to smurf a walk in the woods!
BING
I... I must have a made a mistake somewhere!
Come in, I smurfed some chamomile tea!
Herbal tea?
Meh!
Once you've drunk it, I'll smurf your future in the tea leaves!
Aaaaah?!
Chef Smurf... You're not smurfing lunch?
Not today! Saturn and Uranus are in opposition, and Venus just smurfed into the house of Gemini!

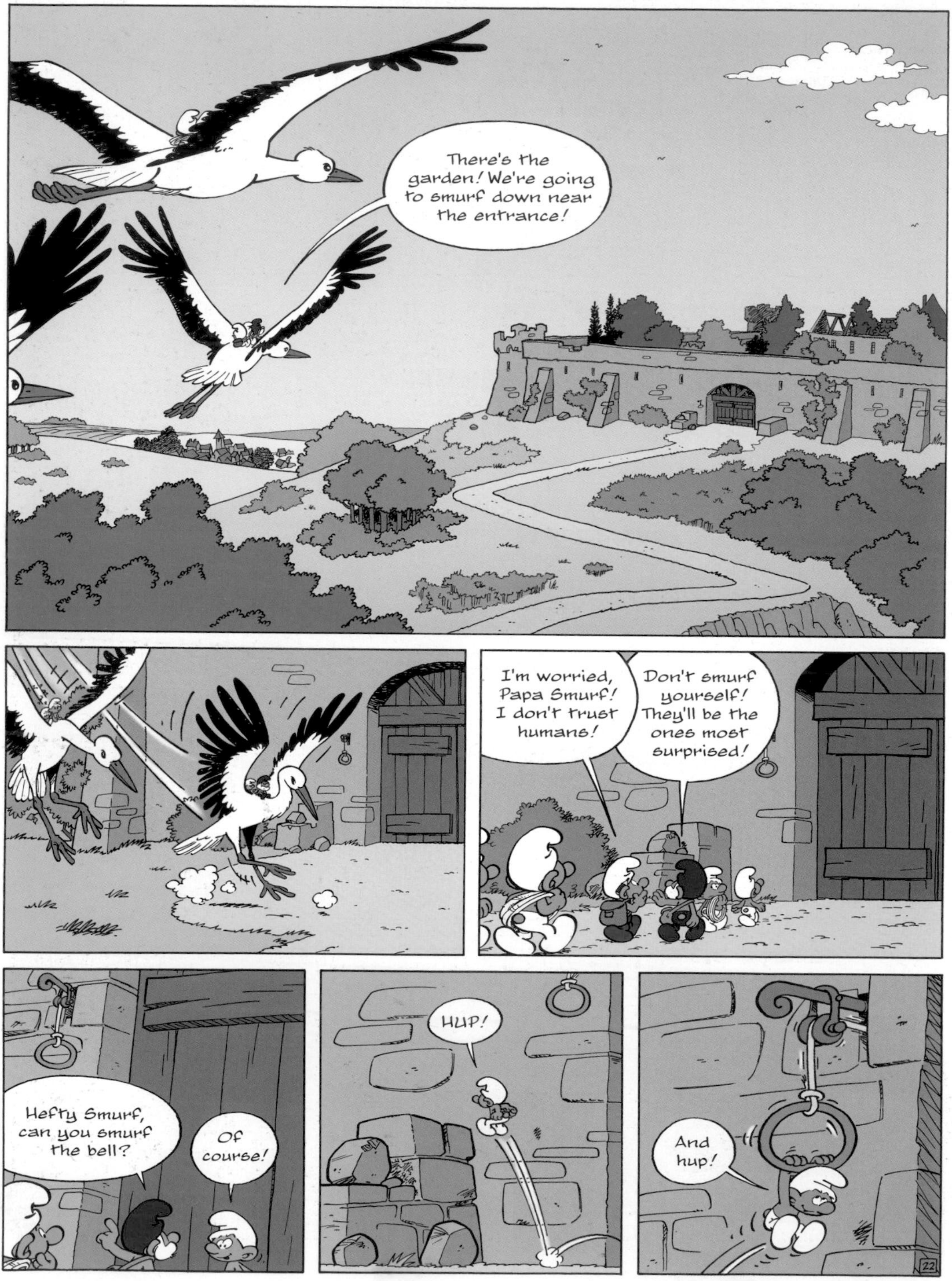

There's the garden! We're going to smurf down near the entrance!
I'm worried, Papa Smurf! I don't trust humans!
Don't smurf yourself! They'll be the ones most surprised!
Hefty Smurf, can you smurf the bell?
Of course!
HUP!
And hup!
22

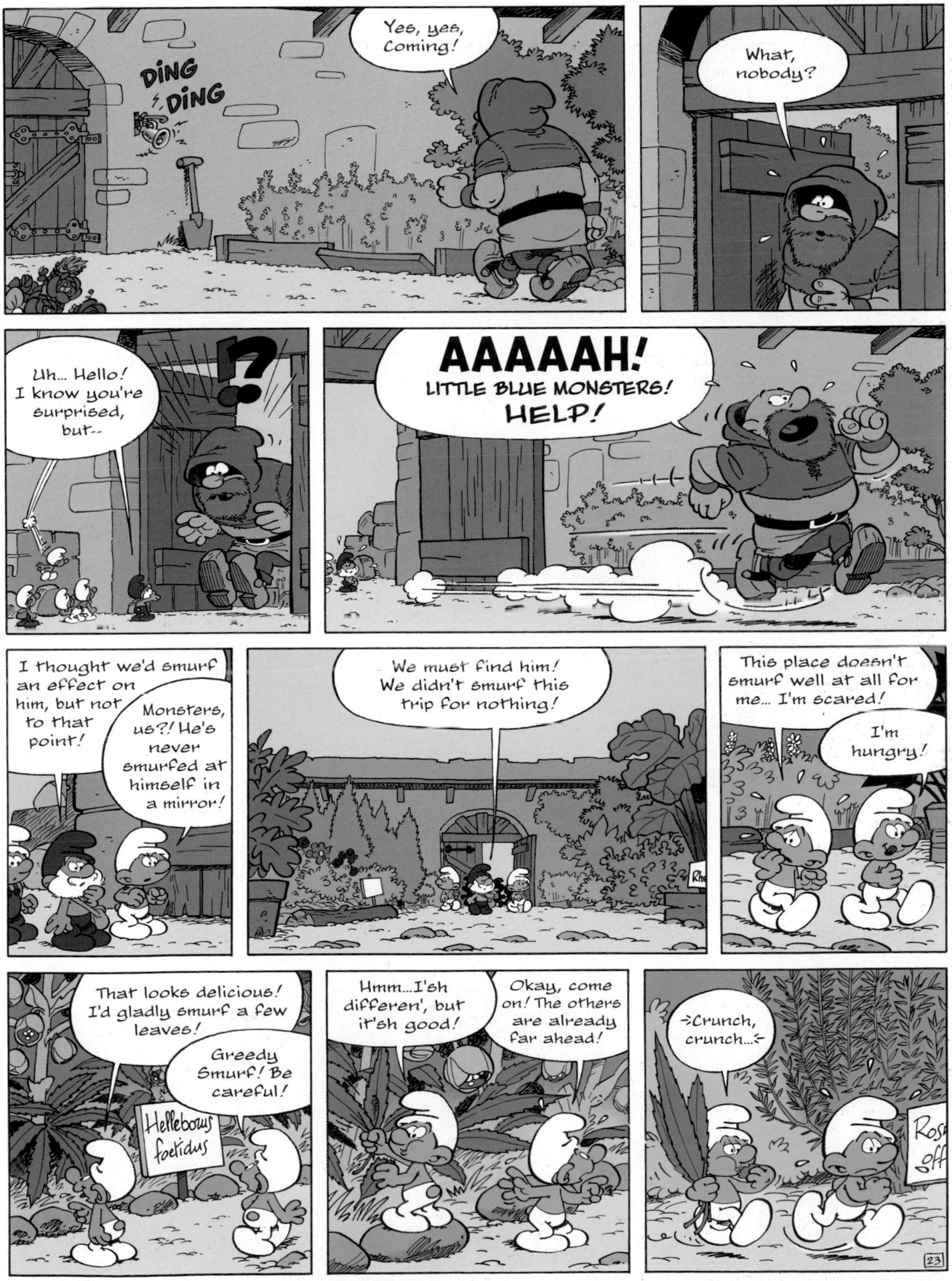
DING DING
Yes, yes, Coming!
What, nobody?
Uh... Hello! I know you're surprised, but--
AAAAAH! LITTLE BLUE MONSTERS! HELP!
I thought we'd smurf an effect on him, but not to that point!
Monsters, us?! He's never smurfed at himself in a mirror!
We must find him! We didn't smurf this trip for nothing!
This place doesn't smurf well at all for me... I'm scared!
I'm hungry!
That looks delicious! I'd gladly smurf a few leaves!
Greedy Smurf! Be careful!
Helleborus foetidus
Hmm...I'sh differen', but it'sh good!
Okay, come on! The others are already far ahead!
Crunch, crunch...
23

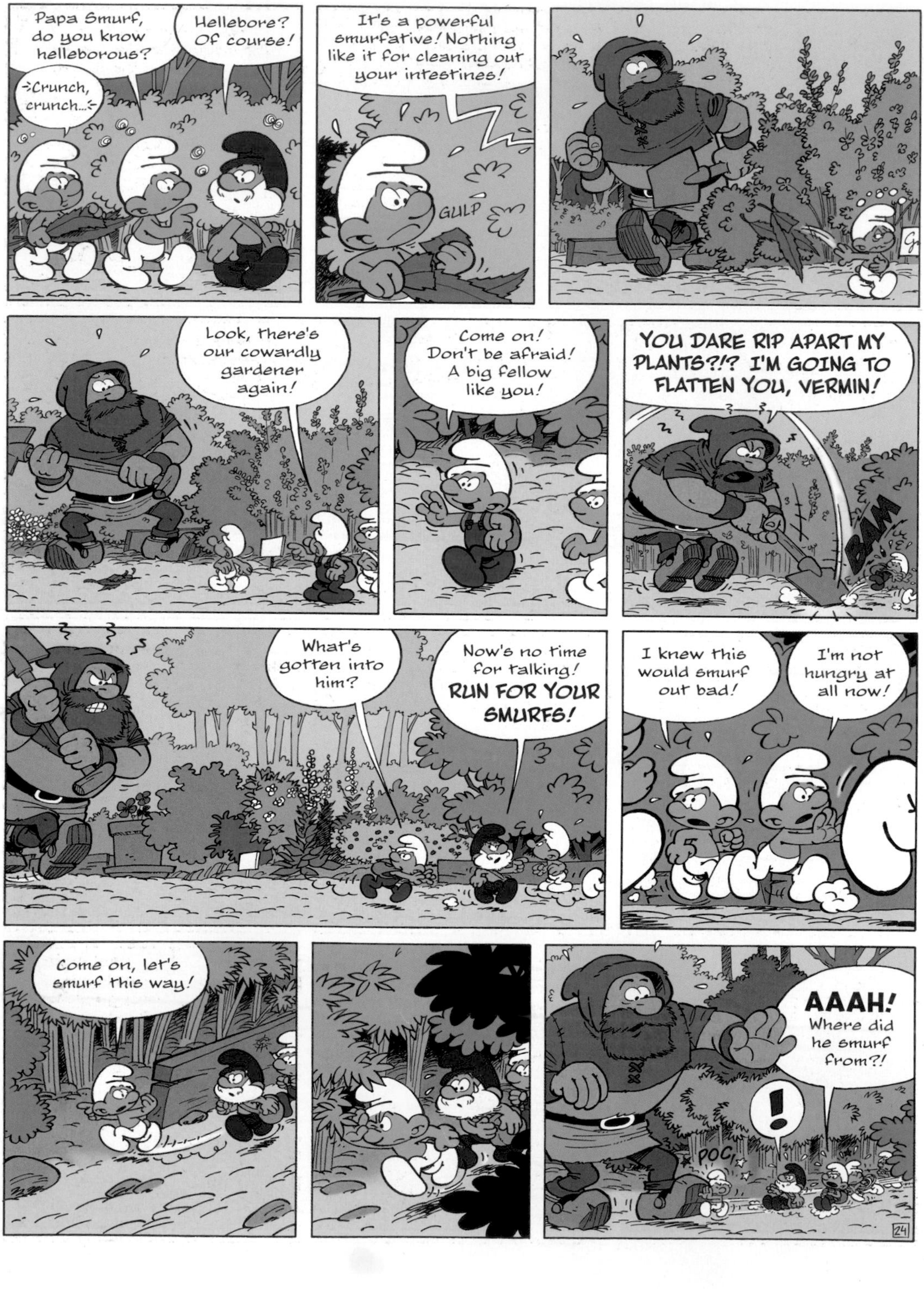

Papa Smurf, do you know helleborous?
Crunch, crunch...
Hellebore? Of course!
It's a powerful smurfative! Nothing like it for cleaning out your intestines!
GULP
Look, there's our cowardly gardener again!
Come on! Don't be afraid! A big fellow like you!
YOU DARE RIP APART MY PLANTS?!? I'M GOING TO FLATTEN YOU, VERMIN!
BAM
What's gotten into him?
Now's no time for talking! RUN FOR YOUR SMURFS!
I knew this would smurf out bad!
I'm not hungry at all now!
Come on, let's smurf this way!
AAAH! Where did he smurf from?!
!
POC
24

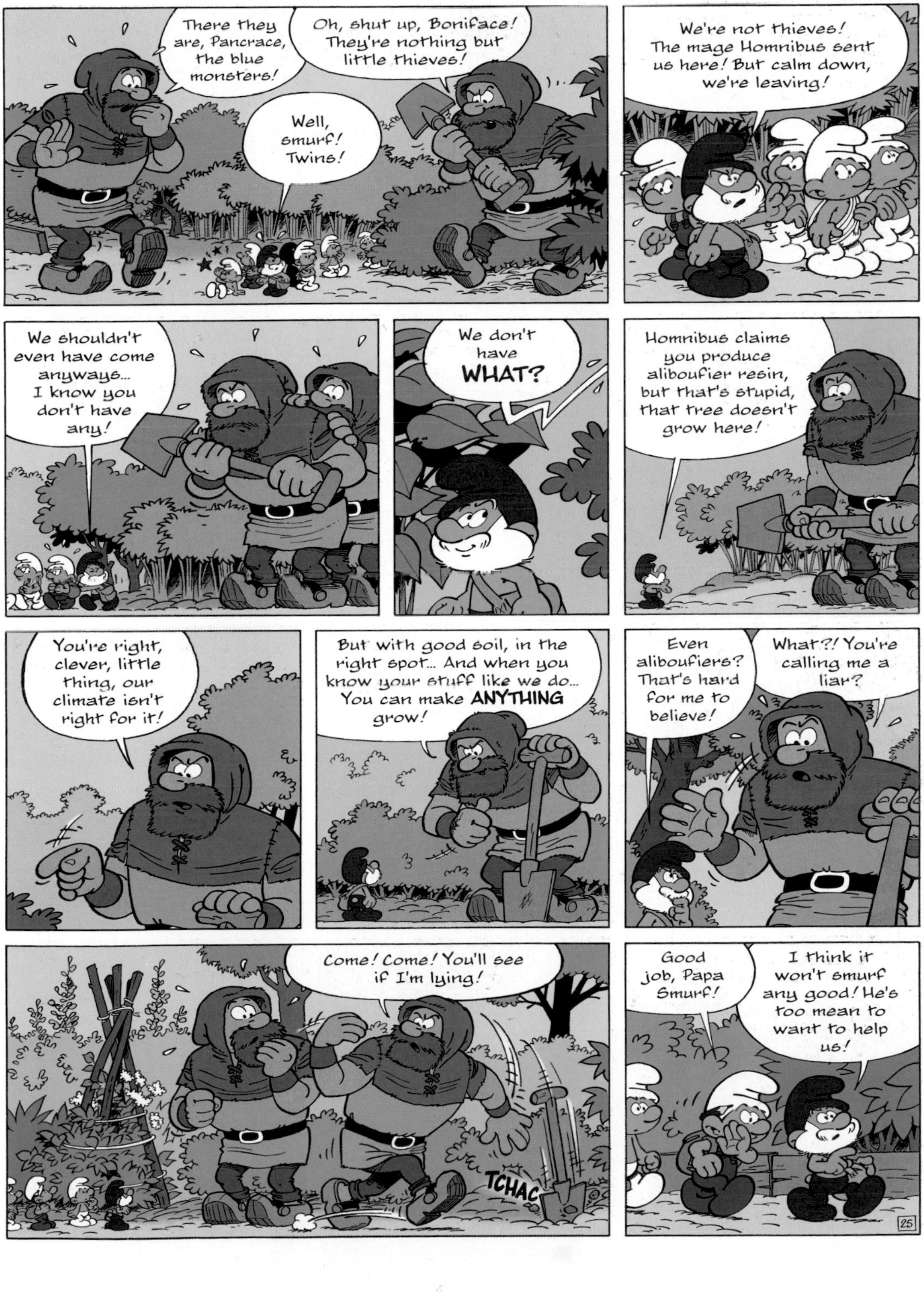
There they are, Pancrace, the blue monsters!
Oh, shut up, Boniface! They're nothing but little thieves!
Well, smurf! Twins!
We're not thieves! The mage Homnibus sent us here! But calm down, we're leaving!
We shouldn't even have come anyways... I know you don't have any!
We don't have WHAT?
Homnibus claims you produce aliboufier resin, but that's stupid, that tree doesn't grow here!
You're right, clever, little thing, our climate isn't right for it!
But with good soil, in the right spot... And when you know your stuff like we do... You can make ANYTHING grow!
Even aliboufiers? That's hard for me to believe!
What?! You're calling me a liar?
Come! Come! You'll see if I'm lying!
TCHAC
Good job, Papa Smurf!
I think it won't smurf any good! He's too mean to want to help us!
25

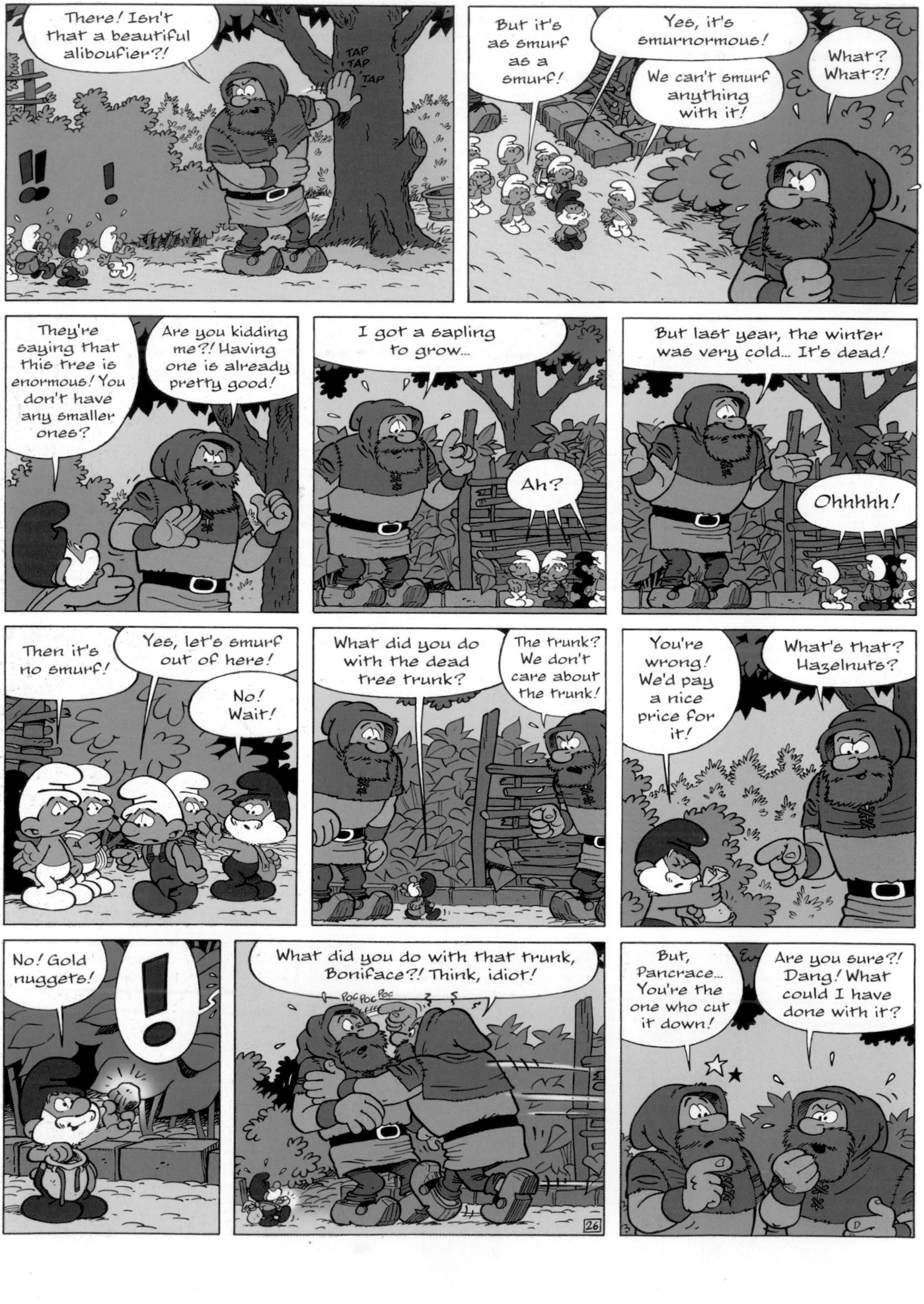
There! Isn't that a beautiful aliboufier?!
TAP TAP TAP
!!
!
But it's as smurf as a smurf!
Yes, it's smurnormous!
We can't smurf anything with it!
What? What?!
They're saying that this tree is enormous! You don't have any smaller ones?
Are you kidding me?! Having one is already pretty good!
I got a sapling to grow...
Ah?
But last year, the winter was very cold... It's dead!
Ohhhhh!
Then it's no smurf!
Yes, let's smurf out of here!
No! Wait!
What did you do with the dead tree trunk?
The trunk? We don't care about the trunk!
You're wrong! We'd pay a nice price for it!
What's that? Hazelnuts?
No! Gold nuggets!
!
What did you do with that trunk, Boniface?! Think, idiot!
POC POC POC POC
26
But, Pancrace... You're the one who cut it down!
Are you sure?! Dang! What could I have done with it?

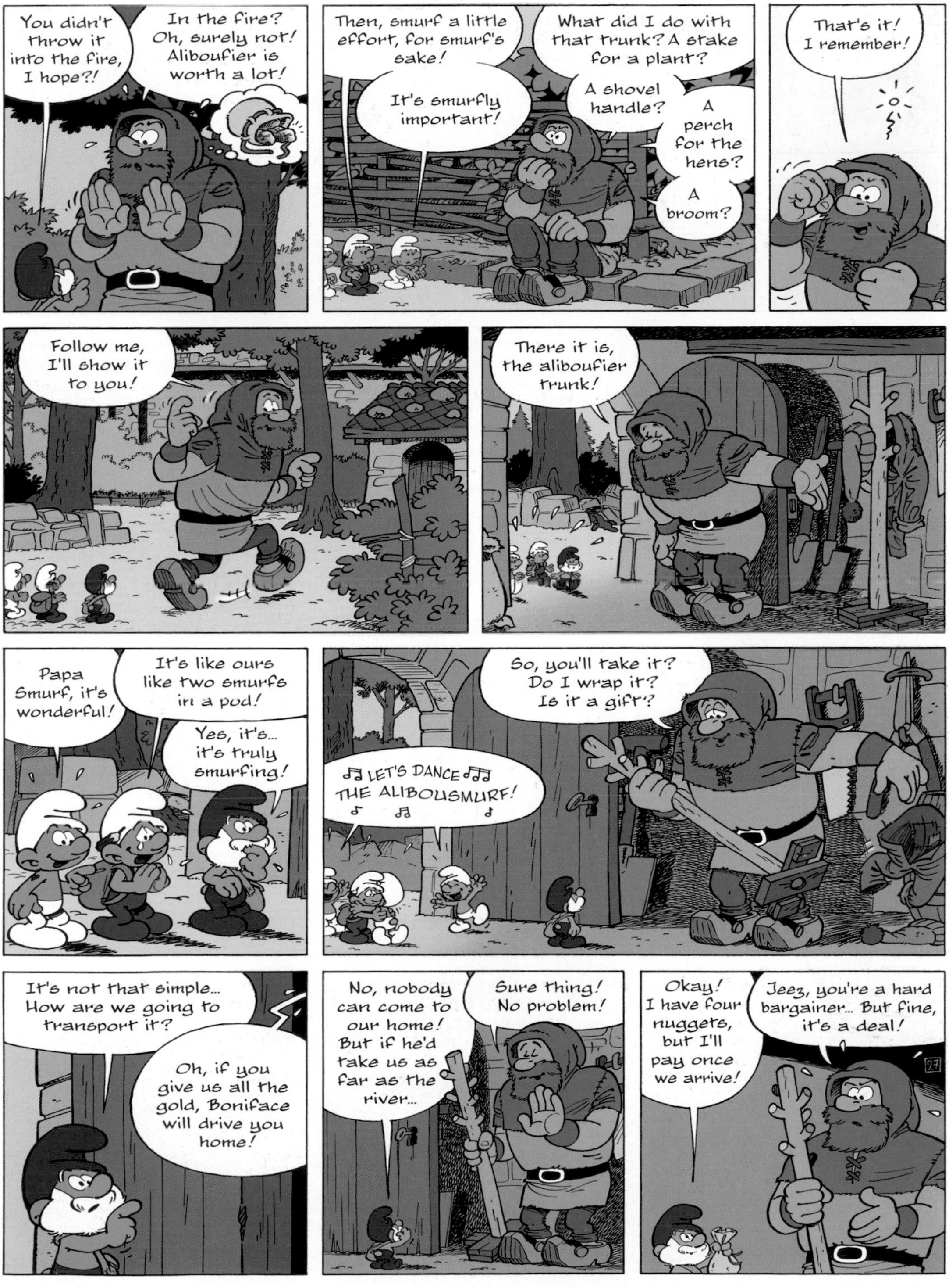
You didn't throw it into the fire, I hope?!
In the fire? Oh, surely not! Aliboufier is worth a lot!
Then, smurf a little effort, for smurf's sake!
It's smurfly important!
What did I do with that trunk? A stake for a plant?
A shovel handle?
A perch for the hens?
A broom?
That's it! I remember!
Follow me, I'll show it to you!
There it is, the aliboufier trunk!
Papa Smurf, it's wonderful!
It's like ours like two smurfs in a pod!
Yes, it's... it's truly smurfing!
So, you'll take it? Do I wrap it? Is it a gift?
LET'S DANCE THE ALIBOUSMURF!
It's not that simple... How are we going to transport it?
Oh, if you give us all the gold, Boniface will drive you home!
No, nobody can come to our home! But if he'd take us as far as the river...
Sure thing! No problem!
Okay! I have four nuggets, but I'll pay once we arrive!
Jeez, you're a hard bargainer... But fine, it's a deal!
27

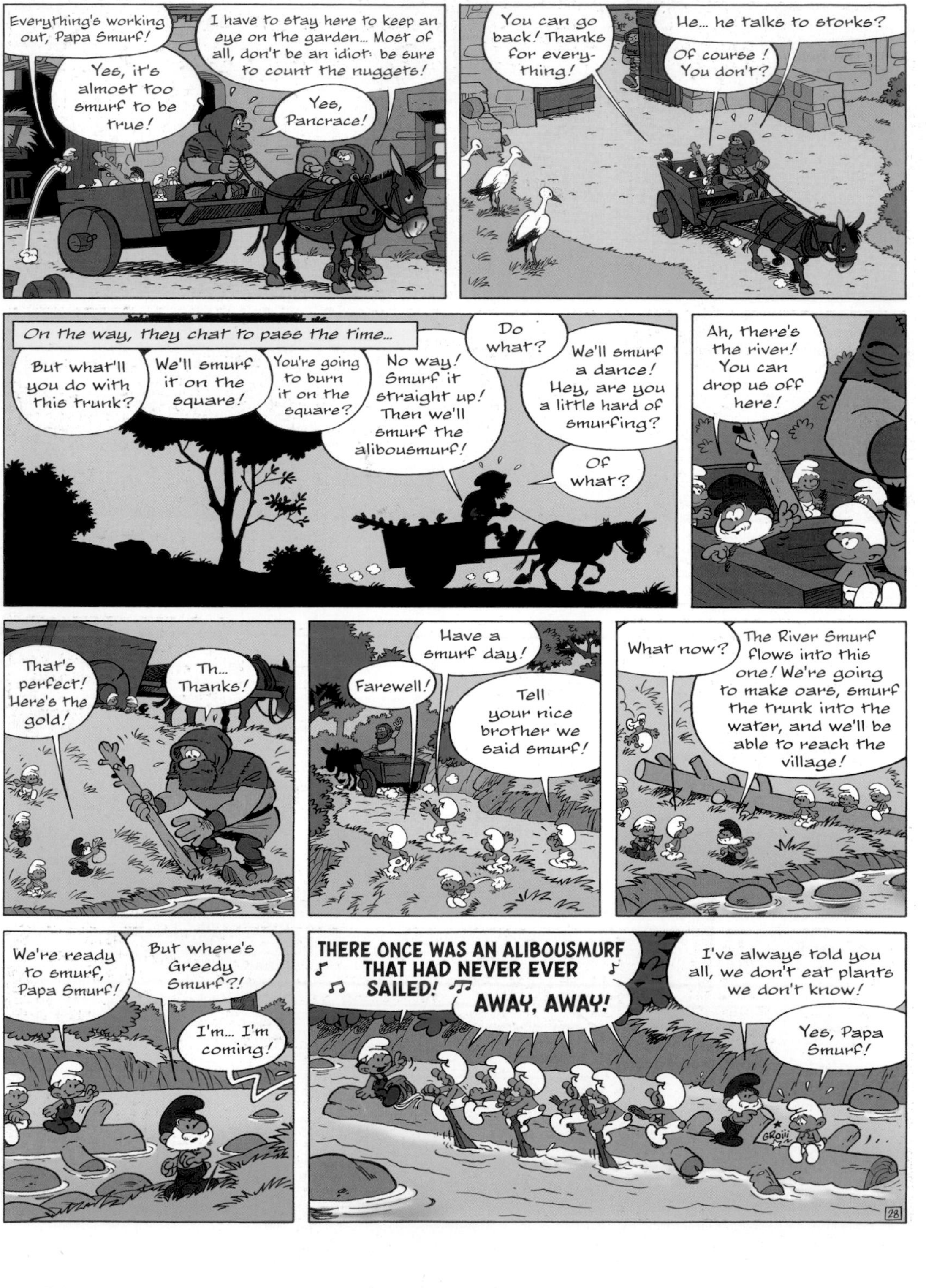
Everything's working out, Papa Smurf!
Yes, it's almost too smurf to be true!
I have to stay here to keep an eye on the garden... Most of all, don't be an idiot: be sure to count the nuggets!
Yes, Pancrace!
You can go back! Thanks for every-thing!
He... he talks to storks?
Of course! You don't?
On the way, they chat to pass the time...
But what'll you do with this trunk?
We'll smurf it on the square!
You're going to burn it on the square?
No way! Smurf it straight up! Then we'll smurf the alibousmurf!
Do what?
We'll smurf a dance! Hey, are you a little hard of smurfing?
Of what?
Ah, there's the river! You can drop us off here!
That's perfect! Here's the gold!
Th... Thanks!
Have a smurf day!
Farewell!
Tell your nice brother we said smurf!
What now?
The River Smurf flows into this one! We're going to make oars, smurf the trunk into the water, and we'll be able to reach the village!
We're ready to smurf, Papa Smurf!
But where's Greedy Smurf?!
I'm... I'm coming!
THERE ONCE WAS AN ALIBOUSMURF THAT HAD NEVER EVER SAILED!
AWAY, AWAY!
I've always told you all, we don't eat plants we don't know!
Yes, Papa Smurf!
GROiii
28

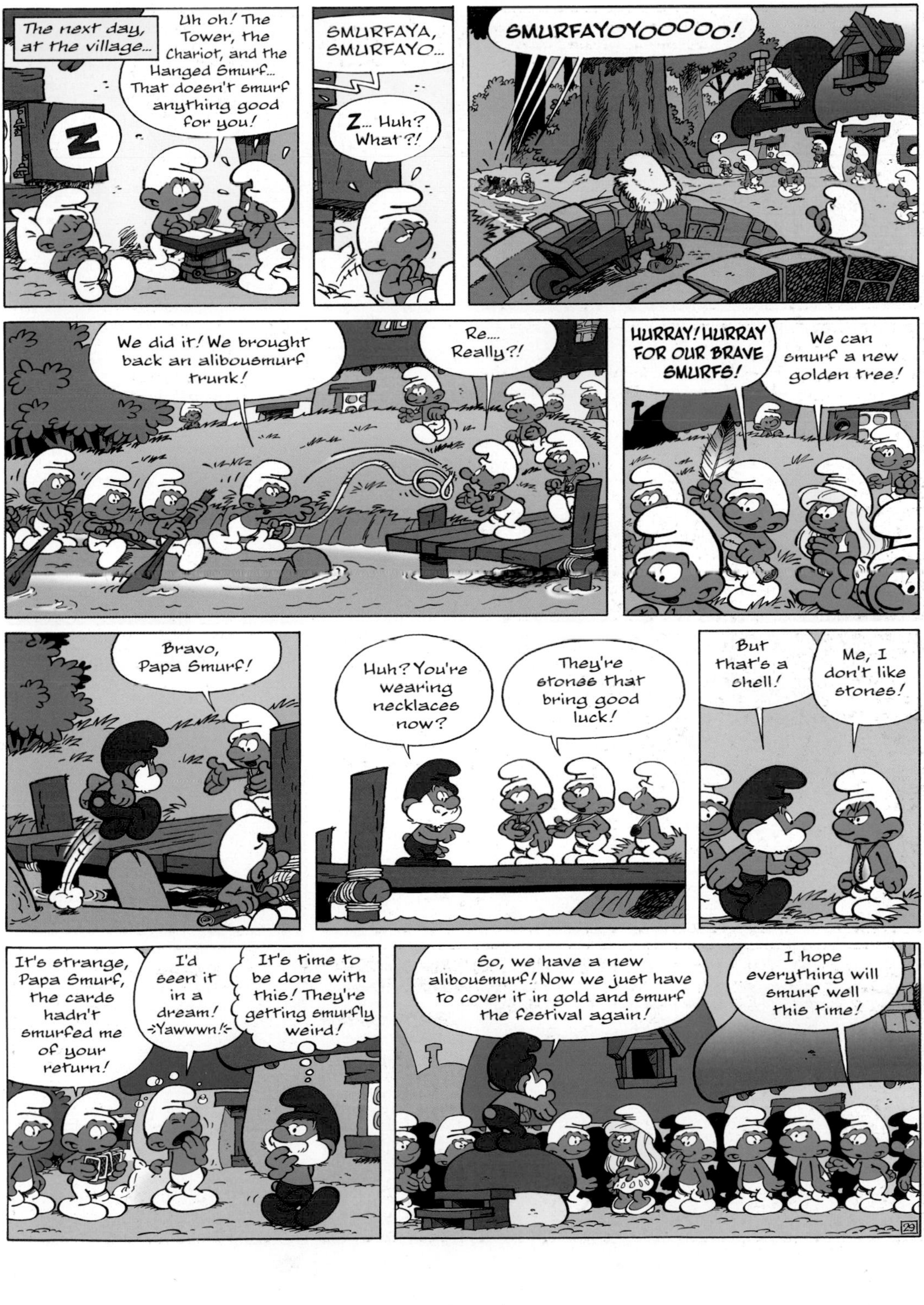
The next day, at the village...
Uh oh! The Tower, the Chariot, and the Hanged Smurf... That doesn't smurf anything good for you!
Z
SMURFAYA, SMURFAYO...
Z... Huh? What?!
SMURFAYOYOOOOO!
We did it! We brought back an alibousmurf trunk!
Re.... Really?!
HURRAY! HURRAY FOR OUR BRAVE SMURFS!
We can smurf a new golden tree!
Bravo, Papa Smurf!
Huh? You're wearing necklaces now?
They're stones that bring good luck!
But that's a shell!
Me, I don't like stones!
It's strange, Papa Smurf, the cards hadn't smurfed me of your return!
I'd seen it in a dream! -Yawwwn!-
It's time to be done with this! They're getting smurfly weird!
So, we have a new alibousmurf! Now we just have to cover it in gold and smurf the festival again!
I hope everything will smurf well this time!
29

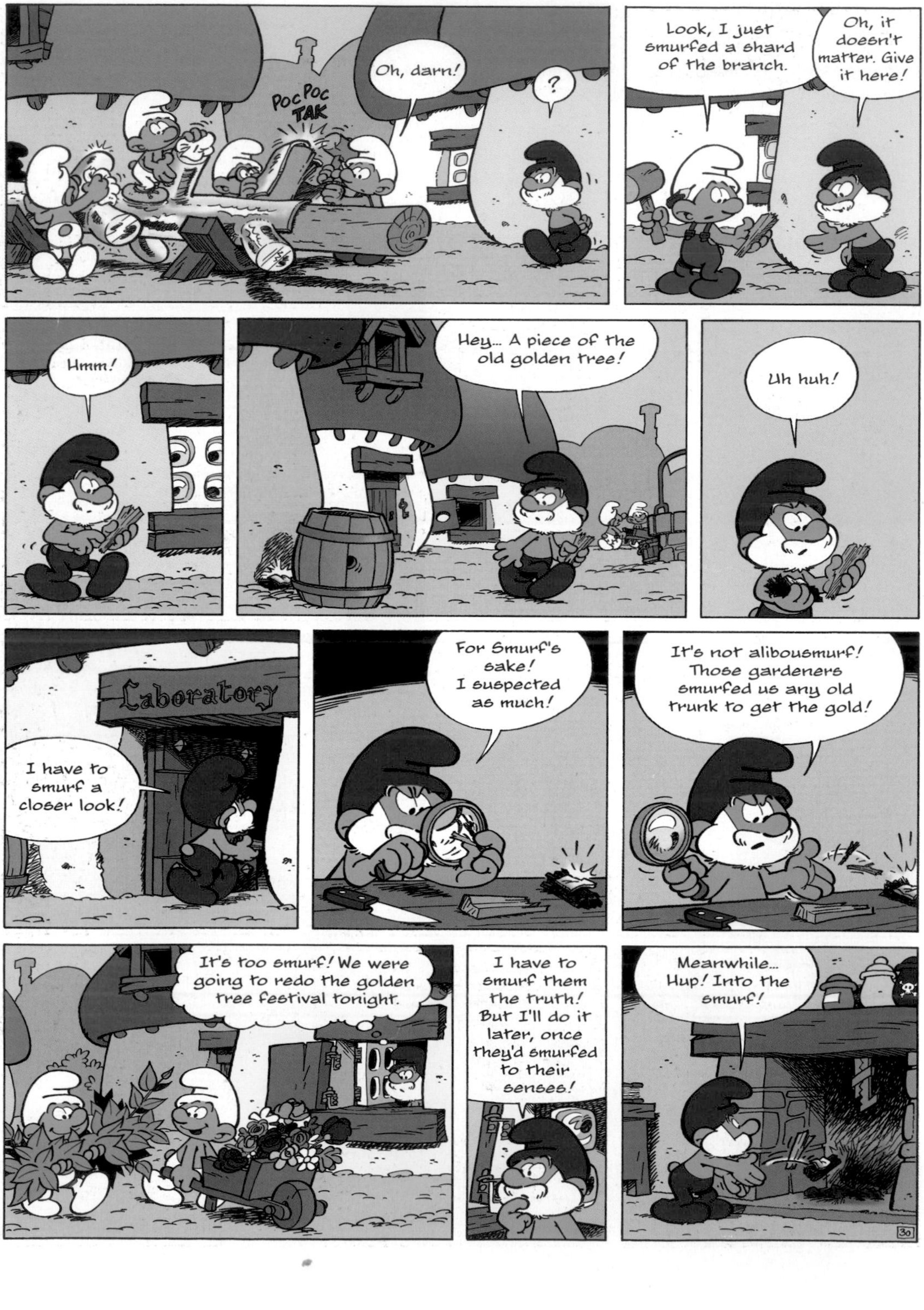
Oh, darn!
POC POC TAK
?
Look, I just smurfed a shard of the branch.
Oh, it doesn't matter. Give it here!
Hmm!
Hey... A piece of the old golden tree!
Uh huh!
Laboratory
I have to smurf a closer look!
For Smurf's sake! I suspected as much!
It's not alibousmurf! Those gardeners smurfed us any old trunk to get the gold!
It's too smurf! We were going to redo the golden tree festival tonight.
I have to smurf them the truth! But I'll do it later, once they'd smurfed to their senses!
Meanwhile... Hup! Into the smurf!
30

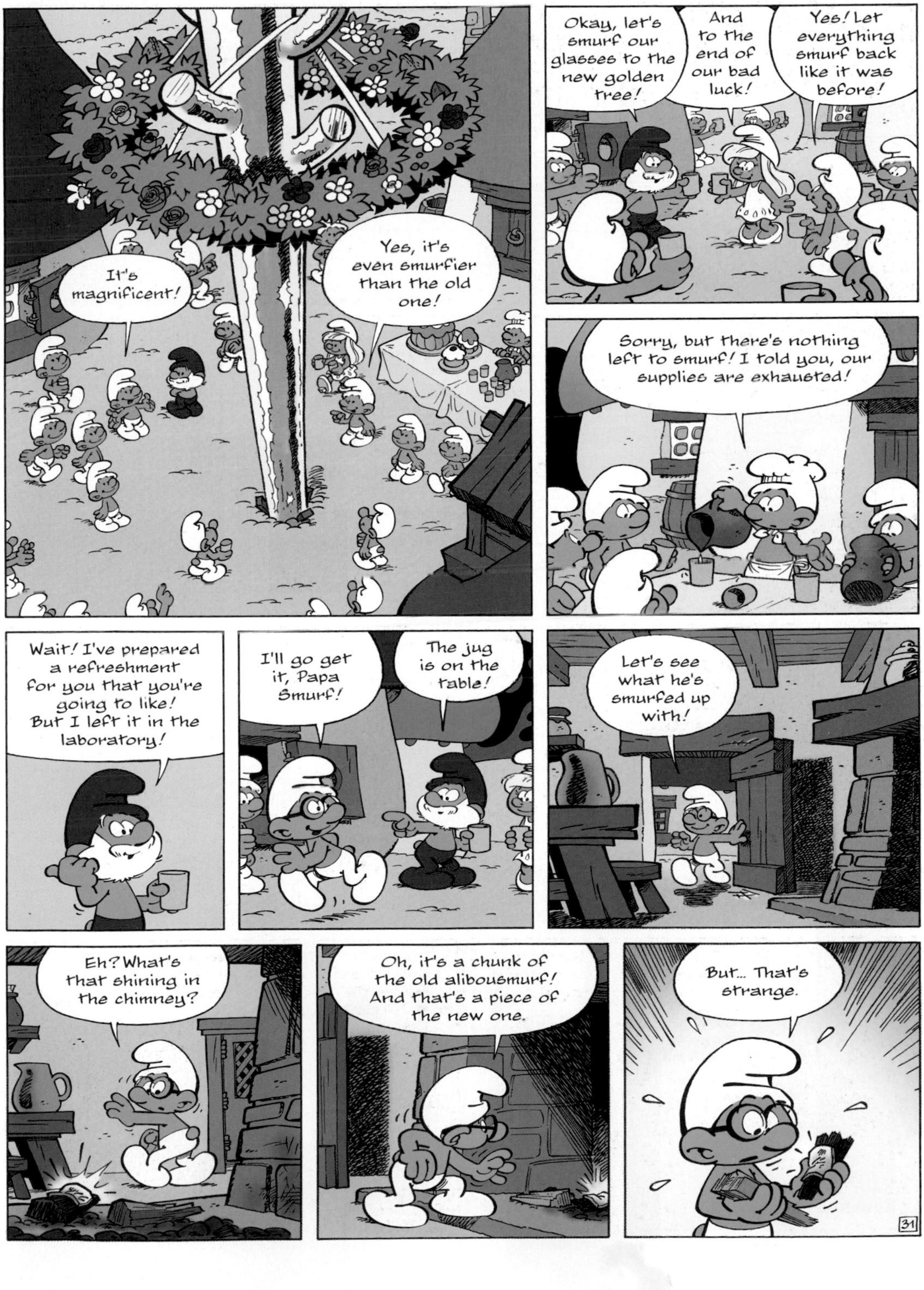
It's magnificent!
Yes, it's even smurfier than the old one!
Okay, let's smurf our glasses to the new golden tree!
And to the end of our bad luck!
Yes! Let everything smurf back like it was before!
Sorry, but there's nothing left to smurf! I told you, our supplies are exhausted!
Wait! I've prepared a refreshment for you that you're going to like! But I left it in the laboratory!
I'll go get it, Papa Smurf!
The jug is on the table!
Let's see what he's smurfed up with!
Eh? What's that shining in the chimney?
Oh, it's a chunk of the old alibousmurf! And that's a piece of the new one.
But... That's strange.
31

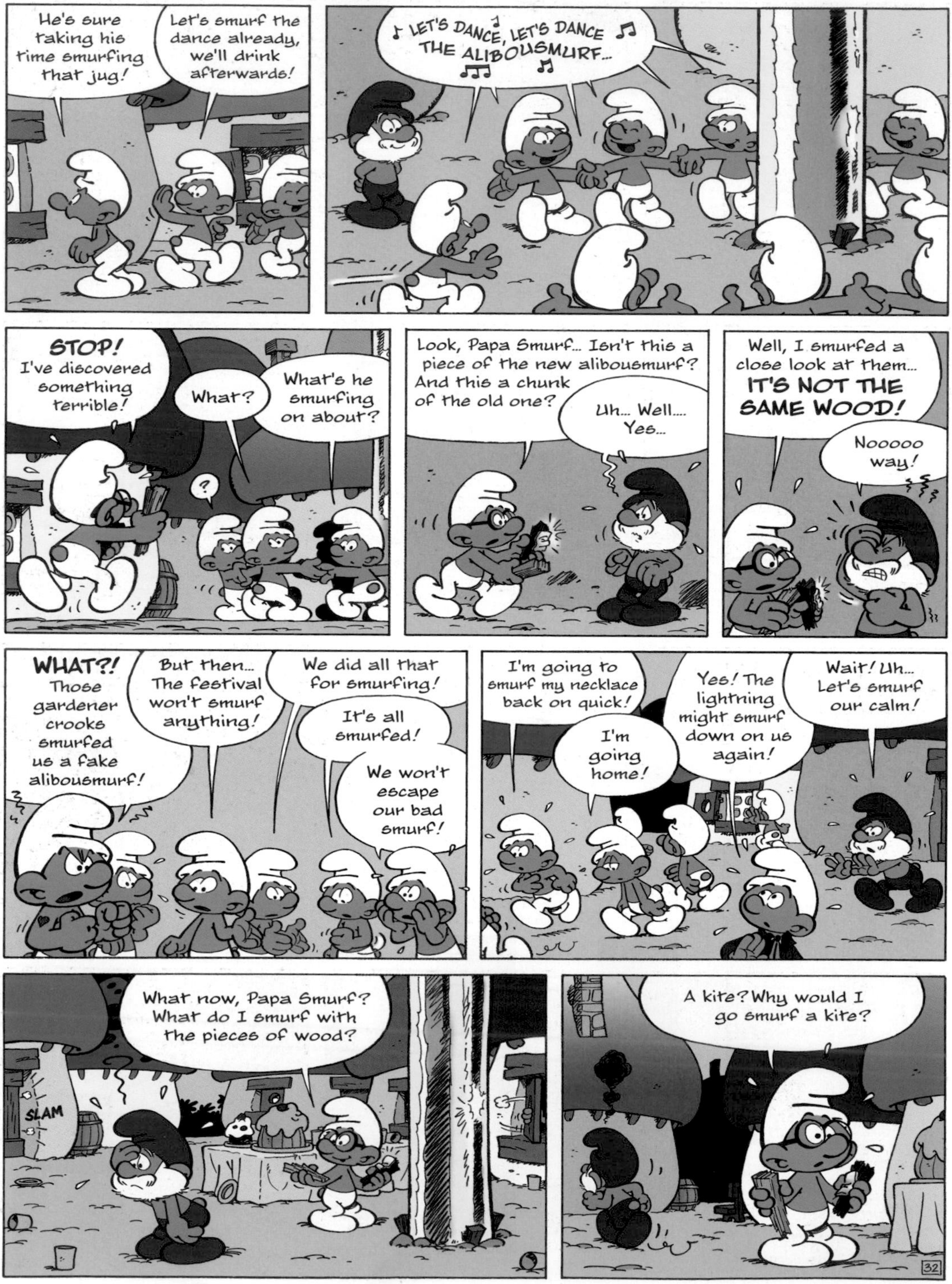
He's sure taking his time smurfing that jug!
Let's smurf the dance already, we'll drink afterwards!
♪ LET'S DANCE, LET'S DANCE THE ALIBOUSMURF... ♫
STOP! I've discovered something terrible!
What?
What's he smurfing on about?
?
Look, Papa Smurf... Isn't this a piece of the new alibousmurf? And this a chunk of the old one?
Uh... Well.... Yes...
Well, I smurfed a close look at them... IT'S NOT THE SAME WOOD!
Nooooo way!
WHAT?! Those gardener crooks smurfed us a fake alibousmurf!
But then... The festival won't smurf anything!
We did all that for smurfing!
It's all smurfed!
We won't escape our bad smurf!
I'm going to smurf my necklace back on quick!
I'm going home!
Yes! The lightning might smurf down on us again!
Wait! Uh... Let's smurf our calm!
SLAM
What now, Papa Smurf? What do I smurf with the pieces of wood?
A kite? Why would I go smurf a kite?
32

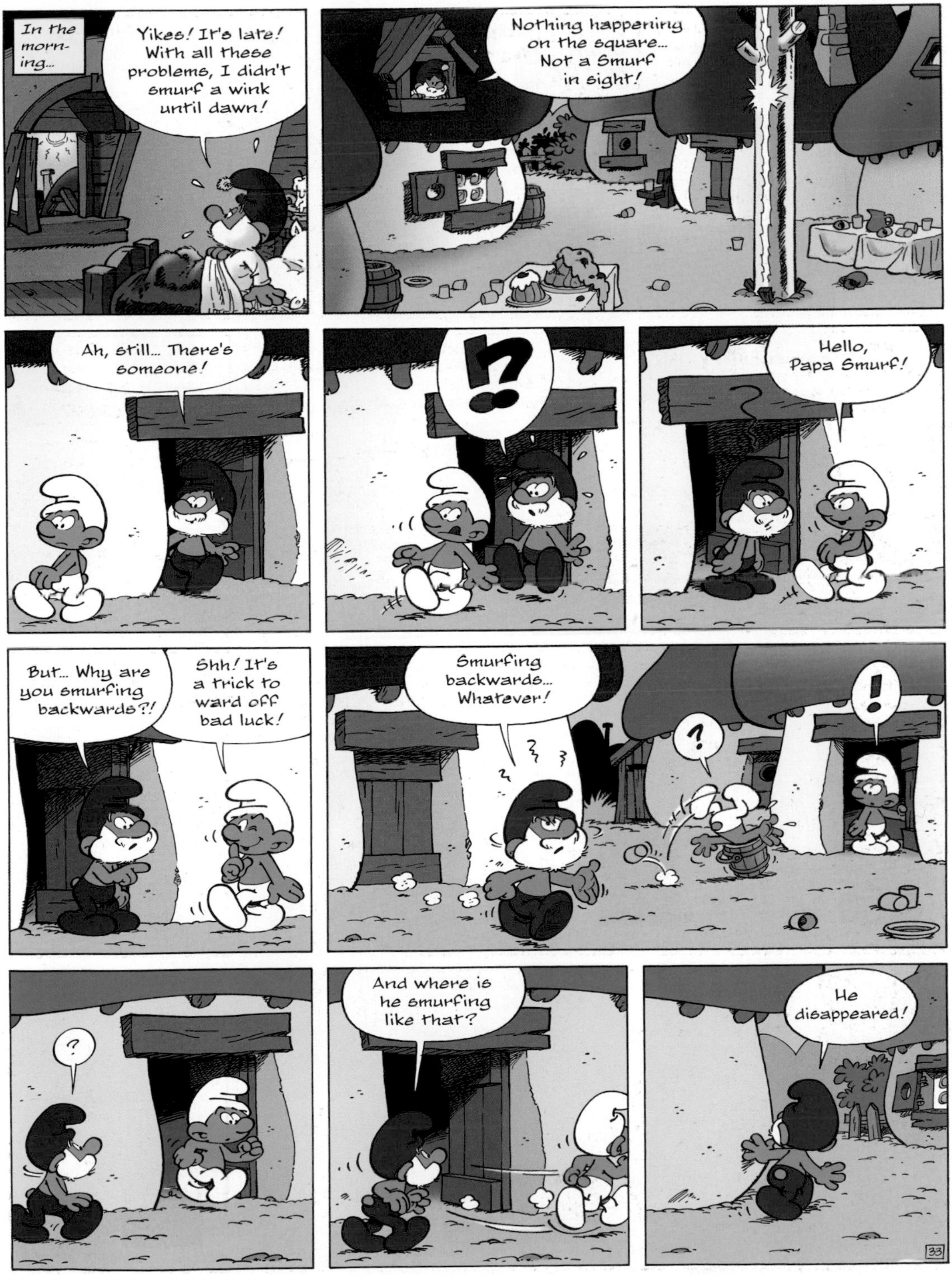
In the morning...
Yikes! It's late! With all these problems, I didn't smurf a wink until dawn!
Nothing happening on the square... Not a Smurf in sight!
Ah, still... There's someone!
!?
Hello, Papa Smurf!
But... Why are you smurfing backwards?!
Shh! It's a trick to ward off bad luck!
Smurfing backwards... Whatever!
?
!
?
And where is he smurfing like that?
He disappeared!
33

I wonder what's smurfed into him...

Sorry, Papa Smurf!

What's got you smurfing around like crazy?

I smurf around the house three times when I come out and when I go in! It brings good luck, it seems!

Come on, that's idiotic!

Excuse me, I still have two times around to smurf!

And... and what's that?

Painter Smurf's house is covered with smurffiti!

I'm the one who did it! These smurftistic signs are protecting my house against harmful influences! And I don't come out of my home anymore!

It's awful, they're going completely smurfy!

Lazy Smurf is the only one still normal!

PAPA SMURF! LOOK OUT!

>Whew!< You were going to smurf into my circle of protection!

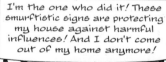

34

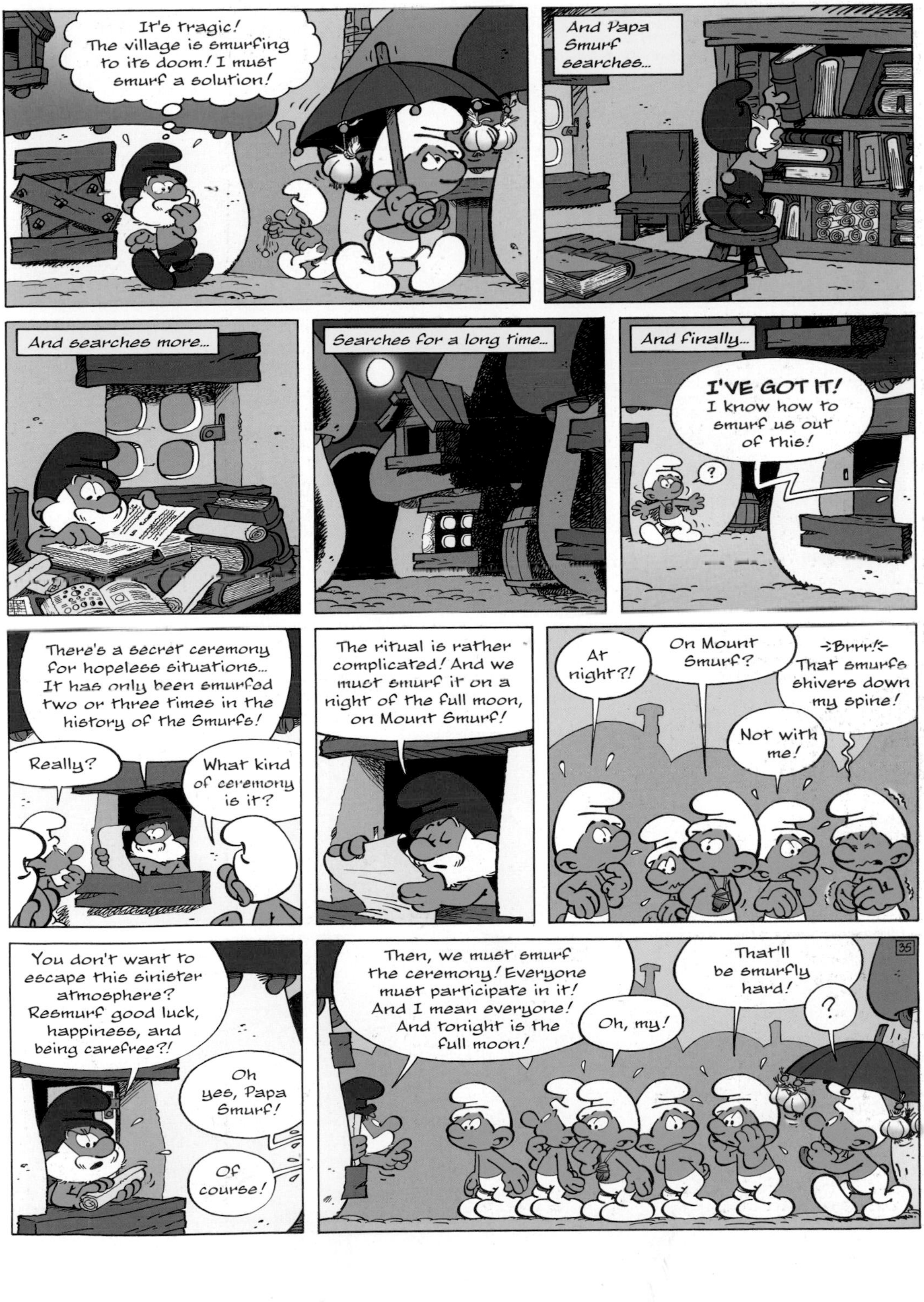

It's tragic! The village is smurfing to its doom! I must smurf a solution!
And Papa Smurf searches...
And searches more...
Searches for a long time...
And finally...
I'VE GOT IT! I know how to smurf us out of this!
?
There's a secret ceremony for hopeless situations... It has only been smurfed two or three times in the history of the Smurfs!
Really?
What kind of ceremony is it?
The ritual is rather complicated! And we must smurf it on a night of the full moon, on Mount Smurf!
At night?!
On Mount Smurf?
Brrr! That smurfs shivers down my spine!
Not with me!
You don't want to escape this sinister atmosphere? Resmurf good luck, happiness, and being carefree?!
Oh yes, Papa Smurf!
Of course!
35
Then, we must smurf the ceremony! Everyone must participate in it! And I mean everyone! And tonight is the full moon!
Oh, my!
That'll be smurfly hard!
?

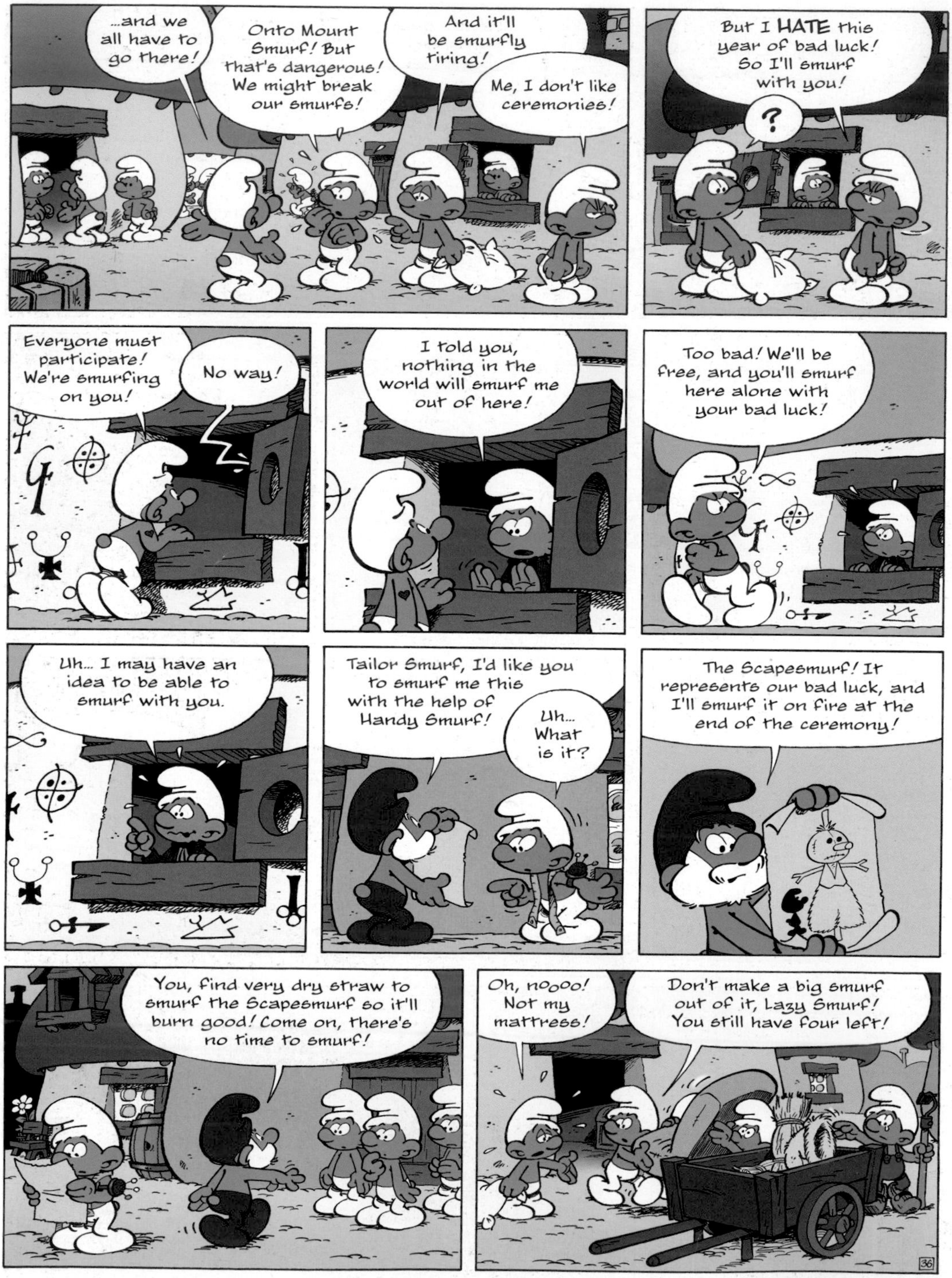

...and we all have to go there!
Onto Mount Smurf! But that's dangerous! We might break our smurfs!
And it'll be smurfly tiring!
Me, I don't like ceremonies!
But I HATE this year of bad luck! So I'll smurf with you!
?
Everyone must participate! We're smurfing on you!
No way!
I told you, nothing in the world will smurf me out of here!
Too bad! We'll be free, and you'll smurf here alone with your bad luck!
Uh... I may have an idea to be able to smurf with you.
Tailor Smurf, I'd like you to smurf me this with the help of Handy Smurf!
Uh... What is it?
The Scapesmurf! It represents our bad luck, and I'll smurf it on fire at the end of the ceremony!
You, find very dry straw to smurf the Scapesmurf so it'll burn good! Come on, there's no time to smurf!
Oh, noooo! Not my mattress!
Don't make a big smurf out of it, Lazy Smurf! You still have four left!
36

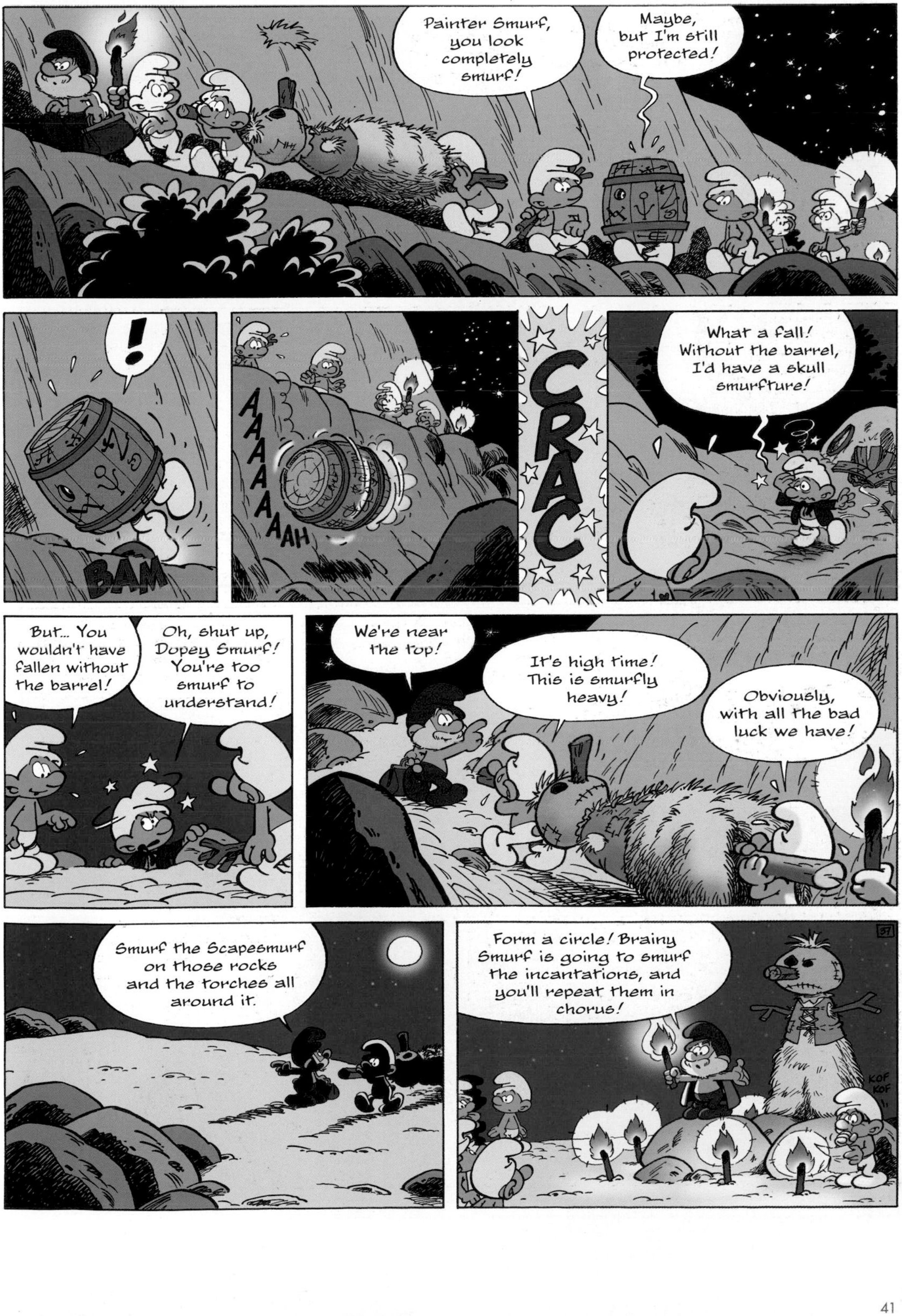
Painter Smurf, you look completely smurf!
Maybe, but I'm still protected!
!
BAM
AAAAAAAAH
CRAC
What a fall! Without the barrel, I'd have a skull smurfture!
But... You wouldn't have fallen without the barrel!
Oh, shut up, Dopey Smurf! You're too smurf to understand!
We're near the top!
It's high time! This is smurfly heavy!
Obviously, with all the bad luck we have!
Smurf the Scapesmurf on those rocks and the torches all around it.
Form a circle! Brainy Smurf is going to smurf the incantations, and you'll repeat them in chorus!
KOF KOF

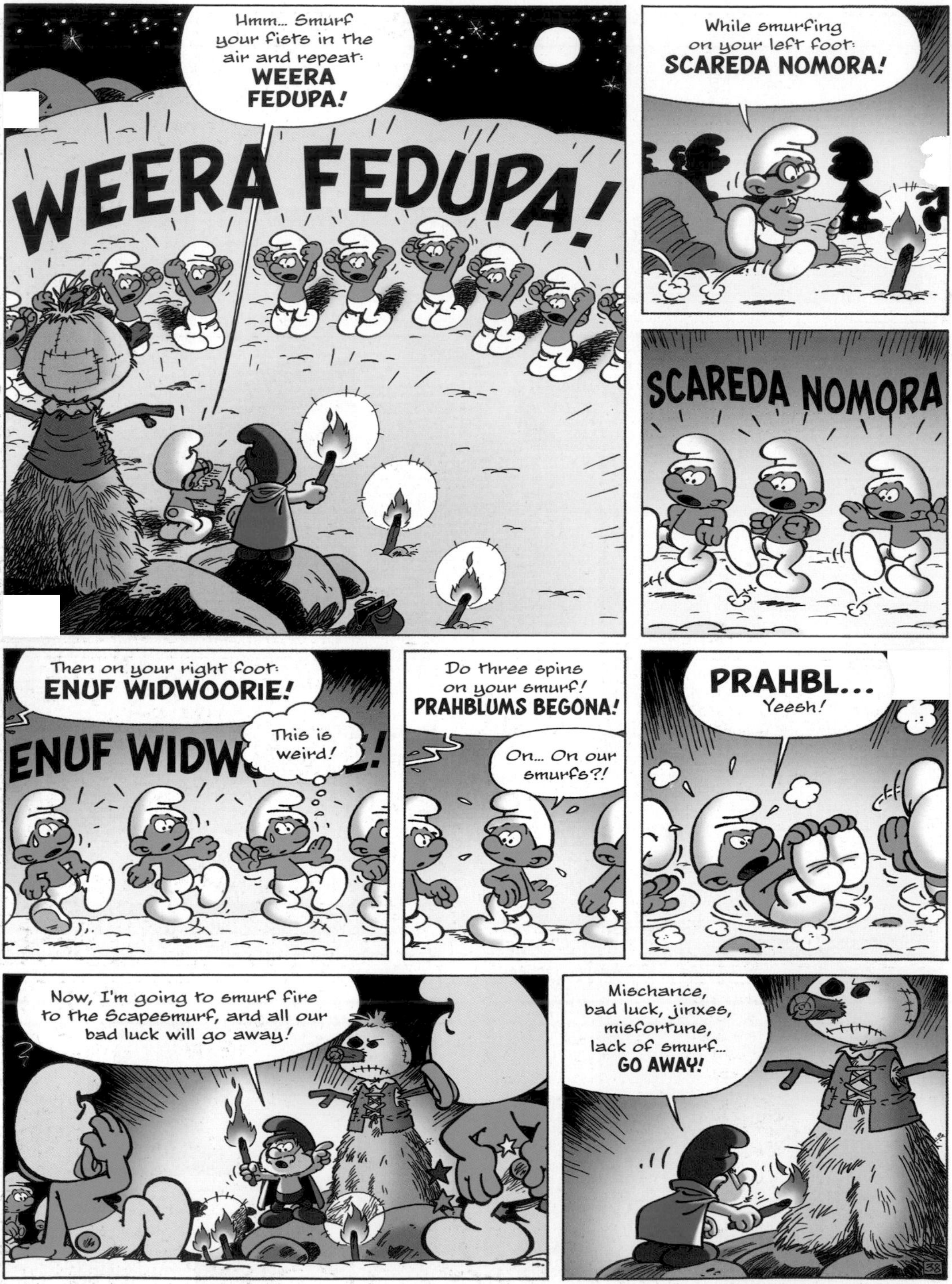
Hmm... Smurf your fists in the air and repeat: WEERA FEDUPA!
WEERA FEDUPA!
While smurfing on your left foot: SCAREDA NOMORA!
SCAREDA NOMORA
Then on your right foot: ENUF WIDWOORIE!
This is weird!
Do three spins on your smurf! PRAHBLUMS BEGONA!
On... On our smurfs?!
PRAHBL... Yeesh!
Now, I'm going to smurf fire to the Scapesmurf, and all our bad luck will go away!
Mischance, bad luck, jinxes, misfortune, lack of smurf... GO AWAY!
38

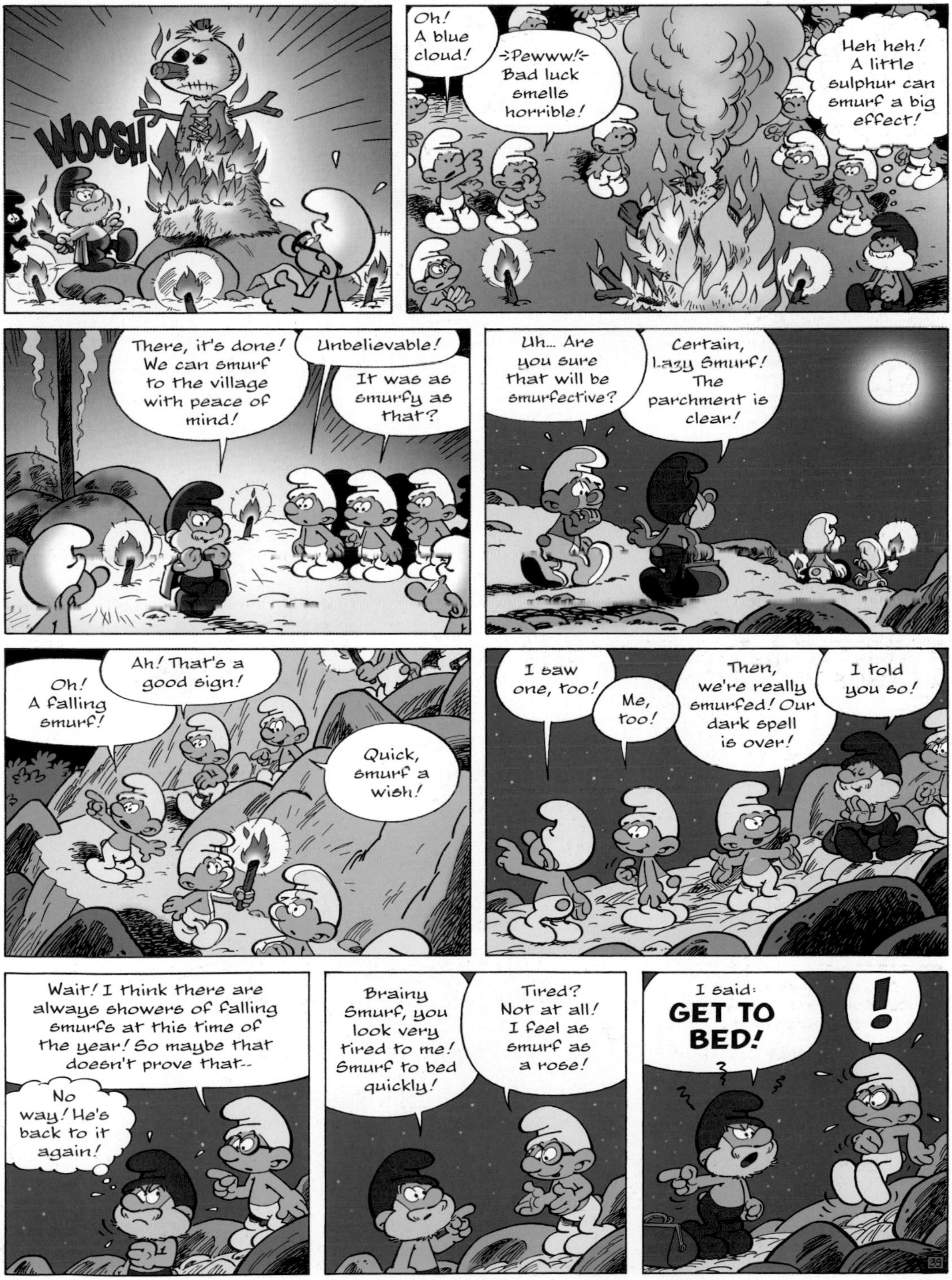

WOOSH
Oh! A blue cloud!
Pewww! Bad luck smells horrible!
Heh heh! A little sulphur can smurf a big effect!
There, it's done! We can smurf to the village with peace of mind!
Unbelievable!
It was as smurfy as that?
Uh... Are you sure that will be smurfective?
Certain, Lazy Smurf! The parchment is clear!
Oh! A falling smurf!
Ah! That's a good sign!
Quick, smurf a wish!
I saw one, too!
Me, too!
Then, we're really smurfed! Our dark spell is over!
I told you so!
Wait! I think there are always showers of falling smurfs at this time of the year! So maybe that doesn't prove that--
No way! He's back to it again!
Brainy Smurf, you look very tired to me! Smurf to bed quickly!
Tired? Not at all! I feel as smurf as a rose!
I said: GET TO BED!
!

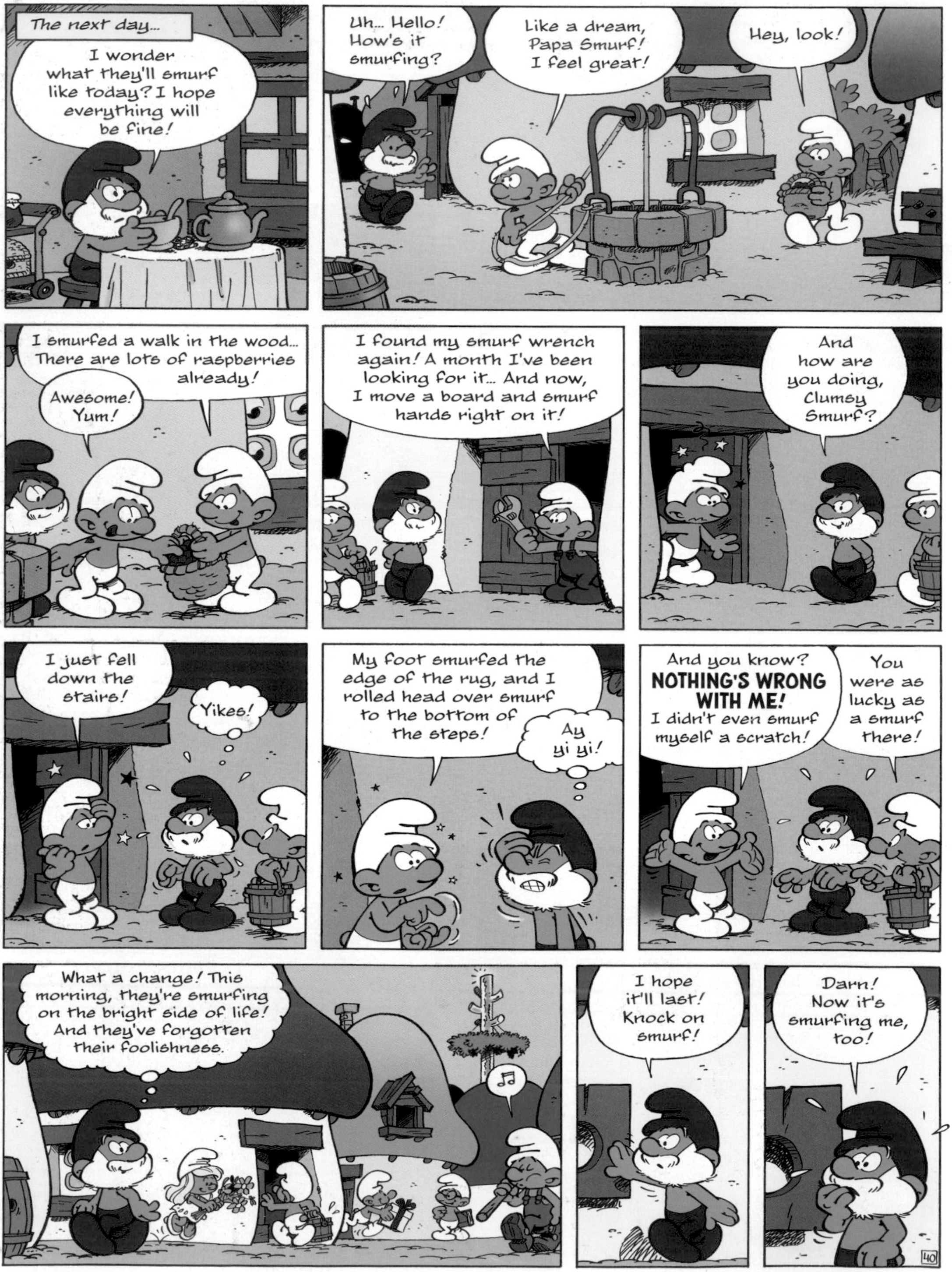
The next day...
I wonder what they'll smurf like today? I hope everything will be fine!
Uh... Hello! How's it smurfing?
Like a dream, Papa Smurf! I feel great!
Hey, look!
I smurfed a walk in the wood... There are lots of raspberries already!
Awesome! Yum!
I found my smurf wrench again! A month I've been looking for it... And now, I move a board and smurf hands right on it!
And how are you doing, Clumsy Smurf?
I just fell down the stairs!
Yikes!
My foot smurfed the edge of the rug, and I rolled head over smurf to the bottom of the steps!
Ay yi yi!
And you know? NOTHING'S WRONG WITH ME! I didn't even smurf myself a scratch!
You were as lucky as a smurf there!
What a change! This morning, they're smurfing on the bright side of life! And they've forgotten their foolishness.
I hope it'll last! Knock on smurf!
Darn! Now it's smurfing me, too!
40

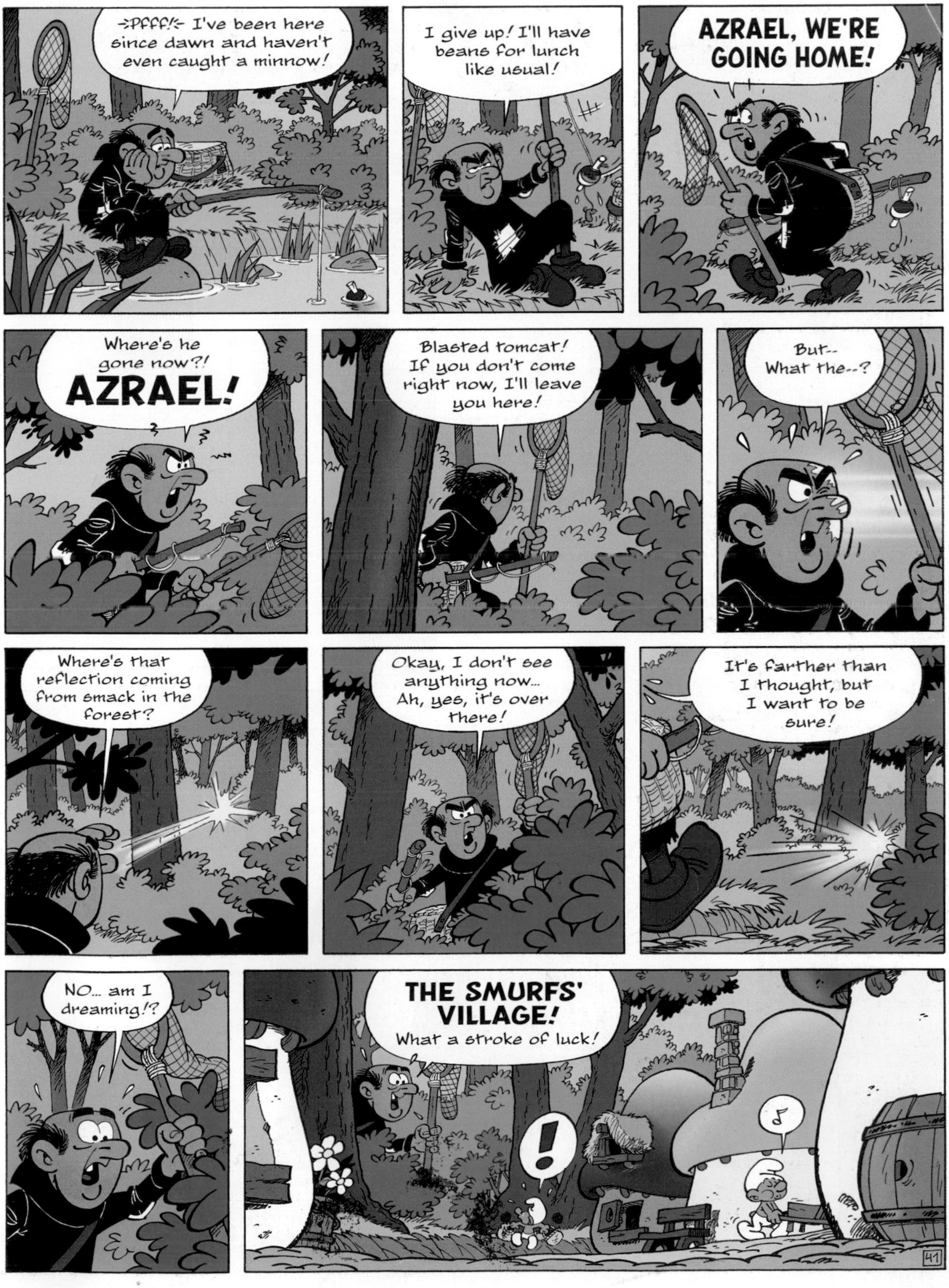

-PFFF!- I've been here since dawn and haven't even caught a minnow!
I give up! I'll have beans for lunch like usual!
AZRAEL, WE'RE GOING HOME!
Where's he gone now?! AZRAEL!
Blasted tomcat! If you don't come right now, I'll leave you here!
But-- What the--?
Where's that reflection coming from smack in the forest?
Okay, I don't see anything now... Ah, yes, it's over there!
It's farther than I thought, but I want to be sure!
NO... am I dreaming!?
THE SMURFS' VILLAGE! What a stroke of luck!
!
41

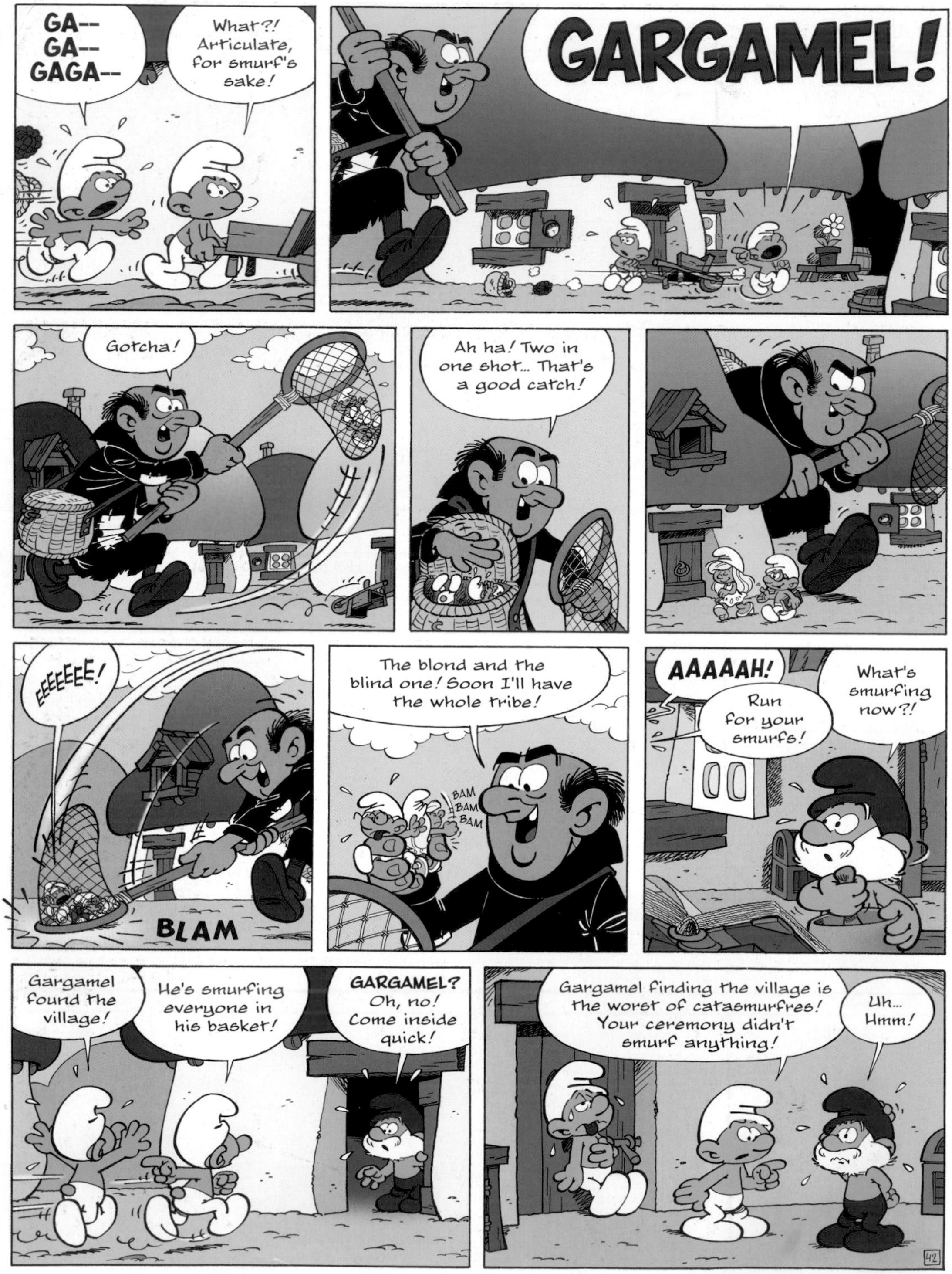

GA--
GA--
GAGA--
What?! Articulate, for smurf's sake!
GARGAMEL!
Gotcha!
Ah ha! Two in one shot... That's a good catch!
EEEEEEE!
BLAM
The blond and the blind one! Soon I'll have the whole tribe!
BAM BAM BAM
AAAAAH!
Run for your smurfs!
What's smurfing now?!
Gargamel found the village!
He's smurfing everyone in his basket!
GARGAMEL? Oh, no! Come inside quick!
Gargamel finding the village is the worst of catasmurfres! Your ceremony didn't smurf anything!
Uh... Hmm!
42

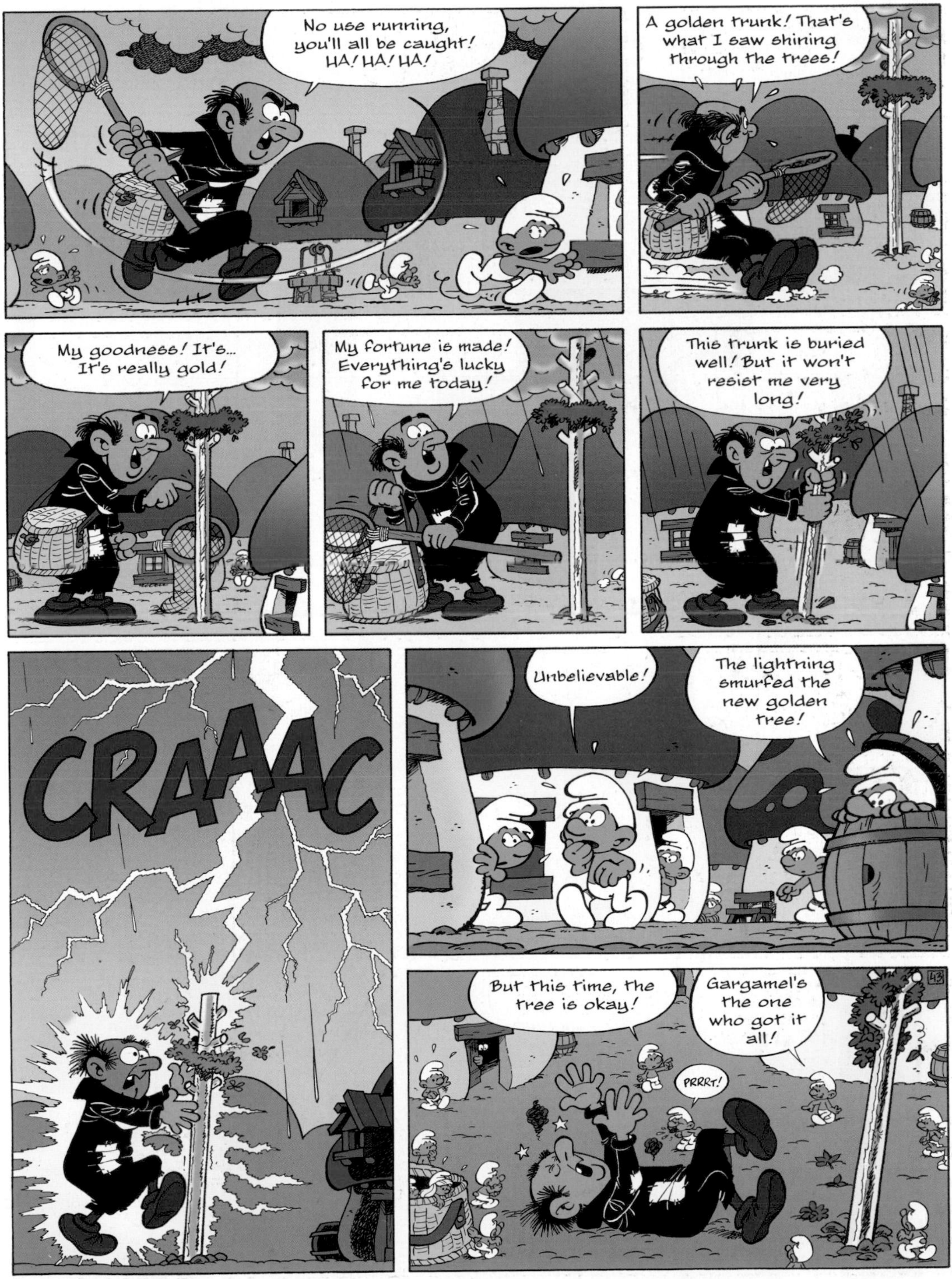
No use running, you'll all be caught! HA! HA! HA!
A golden trunk! That's what I saw shining through the trees!
My goodness! It's... It's really gold!
My fortune is made! Everything's lucky for me today!
This trunk is buried well! But it won't resist me very long!
CRAAAC
Unbelievable!
The lightning smurfed the new golden tree!
But this time, the tree is okay!
Gargamel's the one who got it all!
PRRRT!

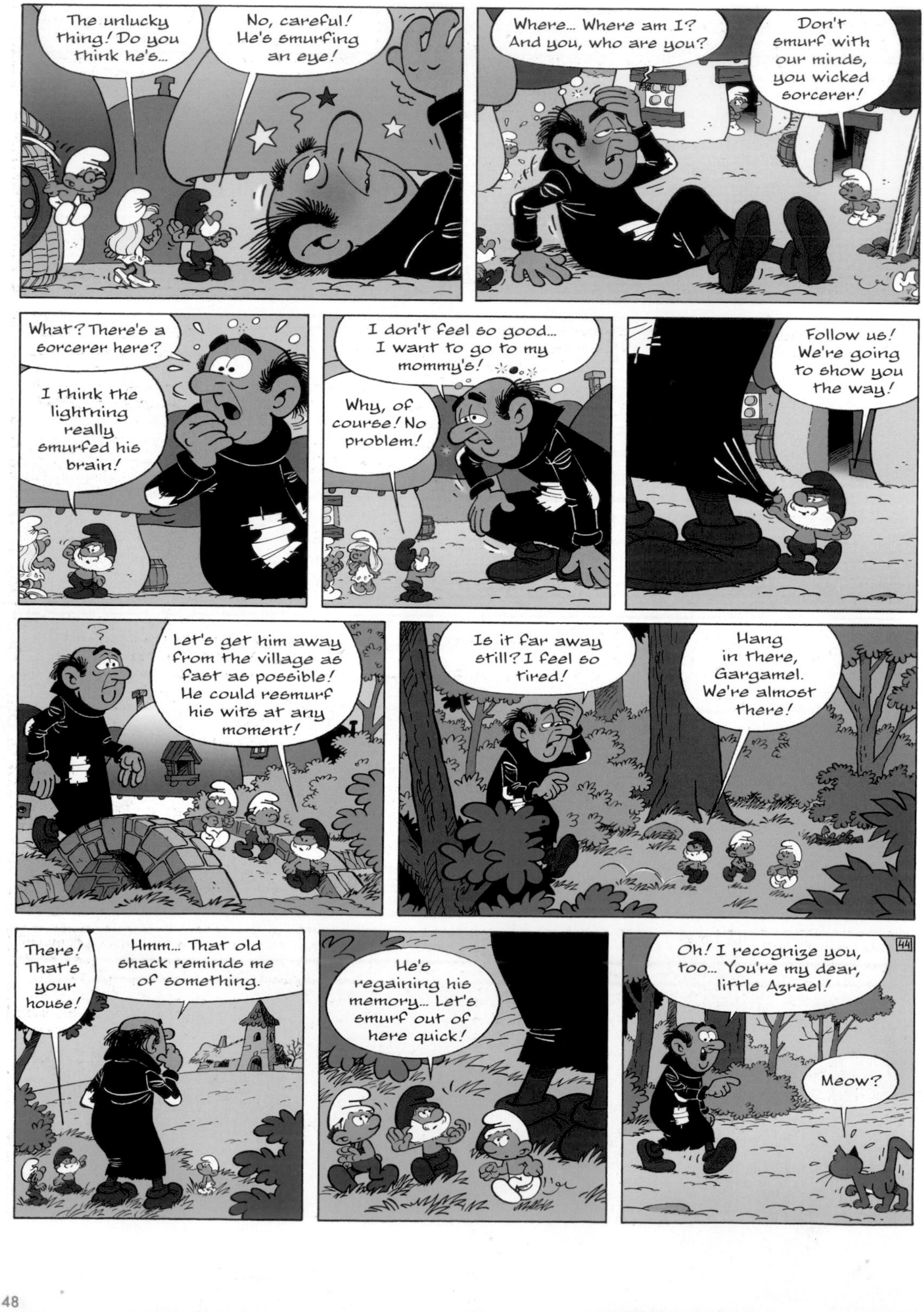
The unlucky thing! Do you think he's...
No, careful! He's smurfing an eye!
Where... Where am I? And you, who are you?
Don't smurf with our minds, you wicked sorcerer!
What? There's a sorcerer here?
I think the lightning really smurfed his brain!
I don't feel so good... I want to go to my mommy's!
Why, of course! No problem!
Follow us! We're going to show you the way!
Let's get him away from the village as fast as possible! He could resmurf his wits at any moment!
Is it far away still? I feel so tired!
Hang in there, Gargamel. We're almost there!
There! That's your house!
Hmm... That old shack reminds me of something.
He's regaining his memory... Let's smurf out of here quick!
44
Oh! I recognize you, too... You're my dear, little Azrael!
Meow?

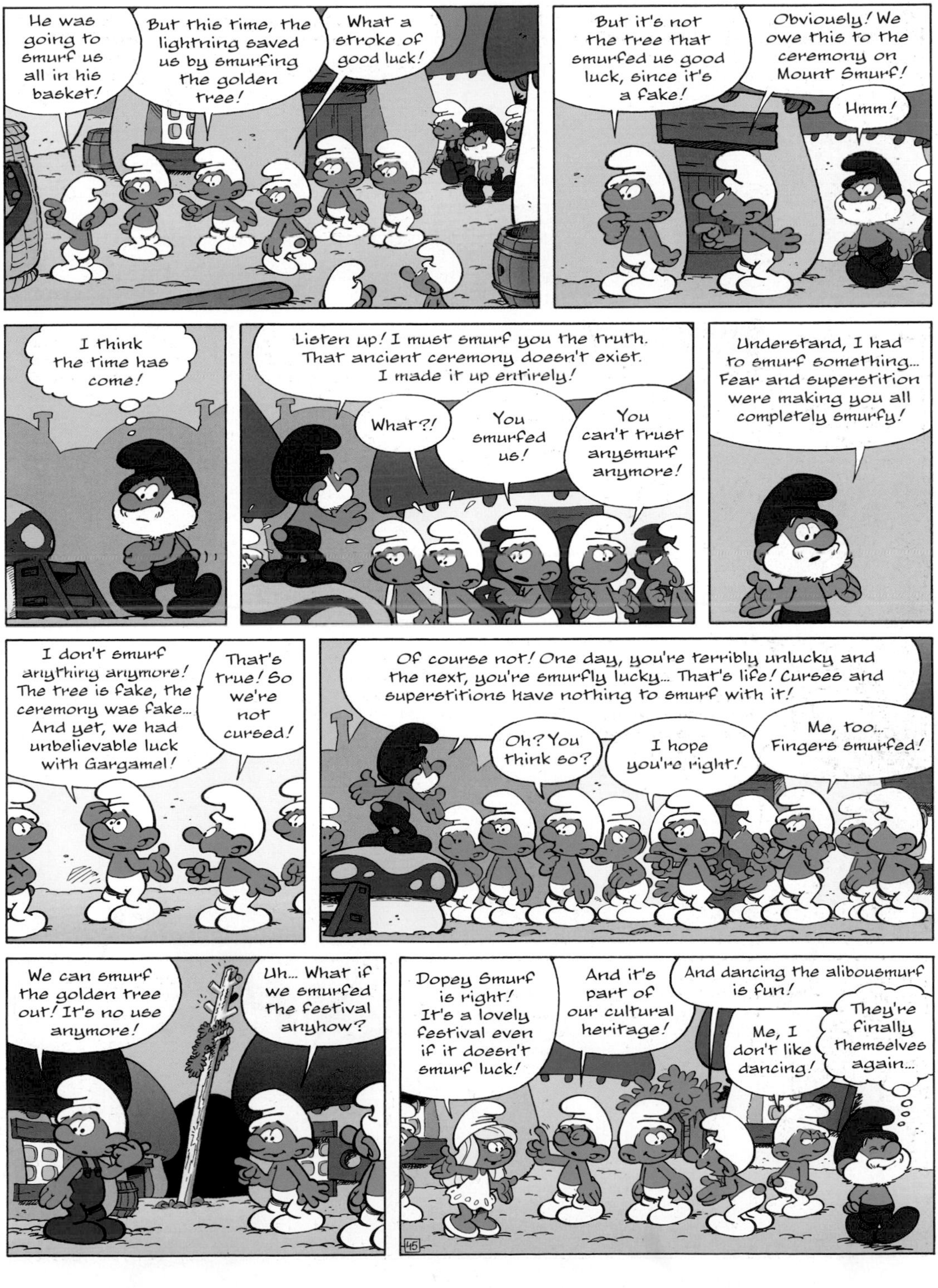
He was going to smurf us all in his basket!
But this time, the lightning saved us by smurfing the golden tree!
What a stroke of good luck!
But it's not the tree that smurfed us good luck, since it's a fake!
Obviously! We owe this to the ceremony on Mount Smurf!
Hmm!
I think the time has come!
Listen up! I must smurf you the truth. That ancient ceremony doesn't exist. I made it up entirely!
What?!
You smurfed us!
You can't trust anysmurf anymore!
Understand, I had to smurf something... Fear and superstition were making you all completely smurfy!
I don't smurf anything anymore! The tree is fake, the ceremony was fake... And yet, we had unbelievable luck with Gargamel!
That's true! So we're not cursed!
Of course not! One day, you're terribly unlucky and the next, you're smurfly lucky... That's life! Curses and superstitions have nothing to smurf with it!
Oh? You think so?
I hope you're right!
Me, too... Fingers smurfed!
We can smurf the golden tree out! It's no use anymore!
Uh... What if we smurfed the festival anyhow?
Dopey Smurf is right! It's a lovely festival even if it doesn't smurf luck!
And it's part of our cultural heritage!
And dancing the alibousmurf is fun!
Me, I don't like dancing!
They're finally themselves again...
45

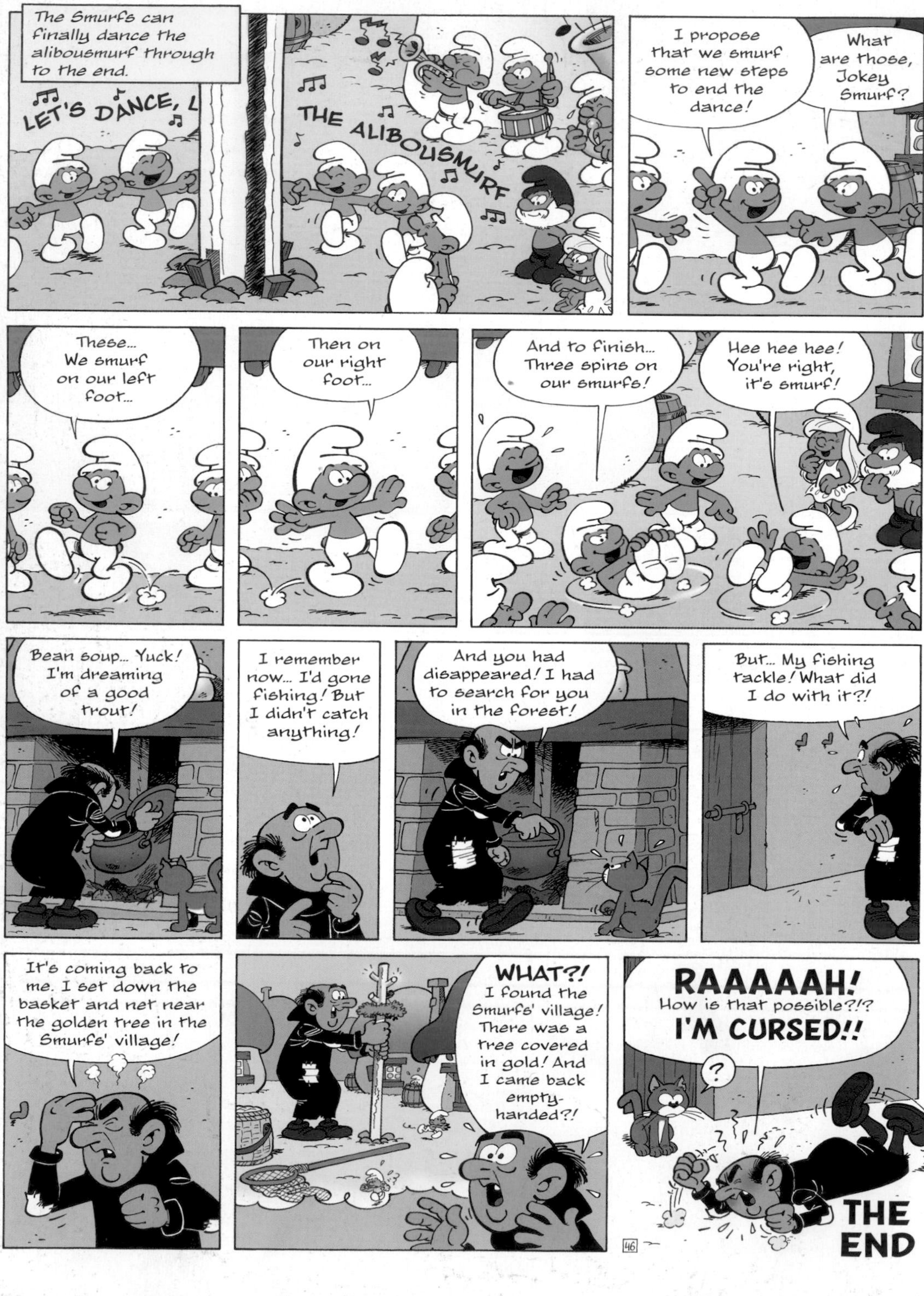
The Smurfs can finally dance the alibousmurf through to the end.
LET'S DANCE, L
THE ALIBOUSMURF
I propose that we smurf some new steps to end the dance!
What are those, Jokey Smurf?
These... We smurf on our left foot...
Then on our right foot...
And to finish... Three spins on our smurfs!
Hee hee hee! You're right, it's smurf!
Bean soup... Yuck! I'm dreaming of a good trout!
I remember now... I'd gone fishing! But I didn't catch anything!
And you had disappeared! I had to search for you in the forest!
But... My fishing tackle! What did I do with it?!
It's coming back to me. I set down the basket and net near the golden tree in the Smurfs' village!
WHAT?! I found the Smurfs' village! There was a tree covered in gold! And I came back empty-handed?!
RAAAAAH! How is that possible?!? I'M CURSED!!
?
46
THE END

THE ADVENTURES OF BENNY BREAKIRON

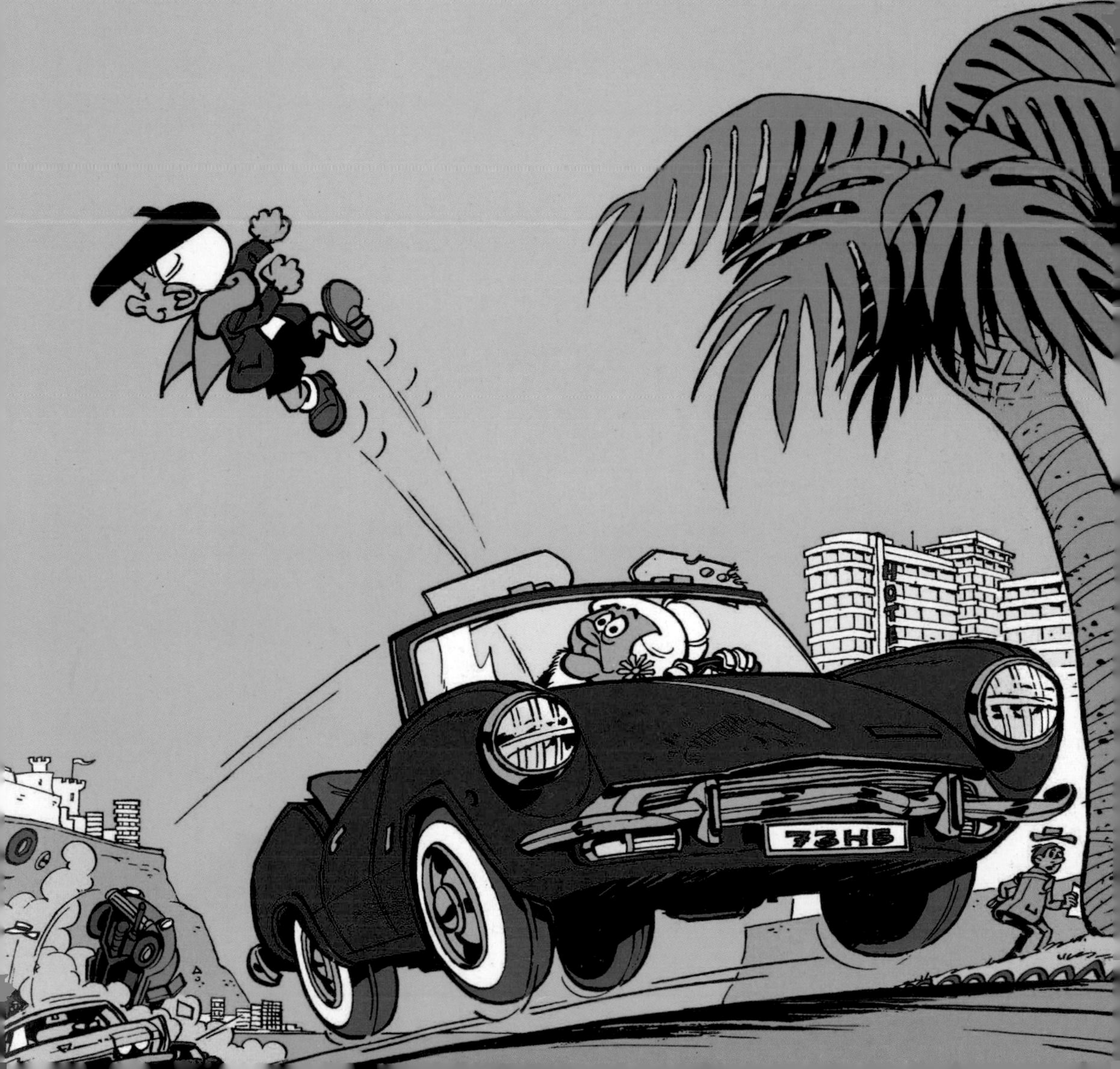

73HB

LADY DOLPHINE

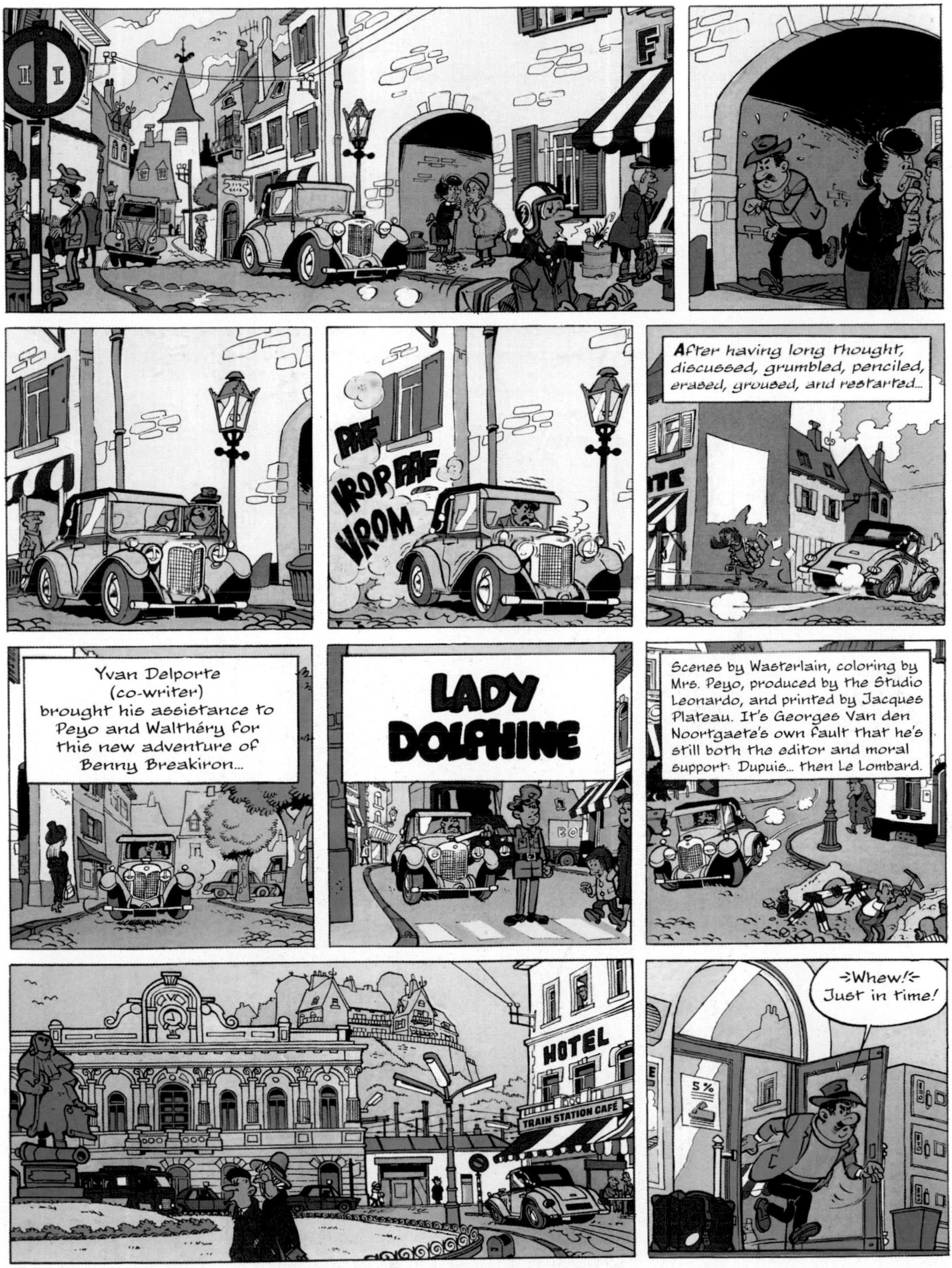

PAF
KROP PAF
VROM
After having long thought, discussed, grumbled, penciled, erased, groused, and restarted...
Yvan Delporte (co-writer) brought his assistance to Peyo and Walthéry for this new adventure of Benny Breakiron...
LADY DOLPHINE
Scenes by Wasterlain, coloring by Mrs. Peyo, produced by the Studio Leonardo, and printed by Jacques Plateau. It's Georges Van den Noortgaete's own fault that he's still both the editor and moral support: Dupuis... then Le Lombard.
HOTEL
TRAIN STATION CAFÉ
5%
Whew! Just in time!

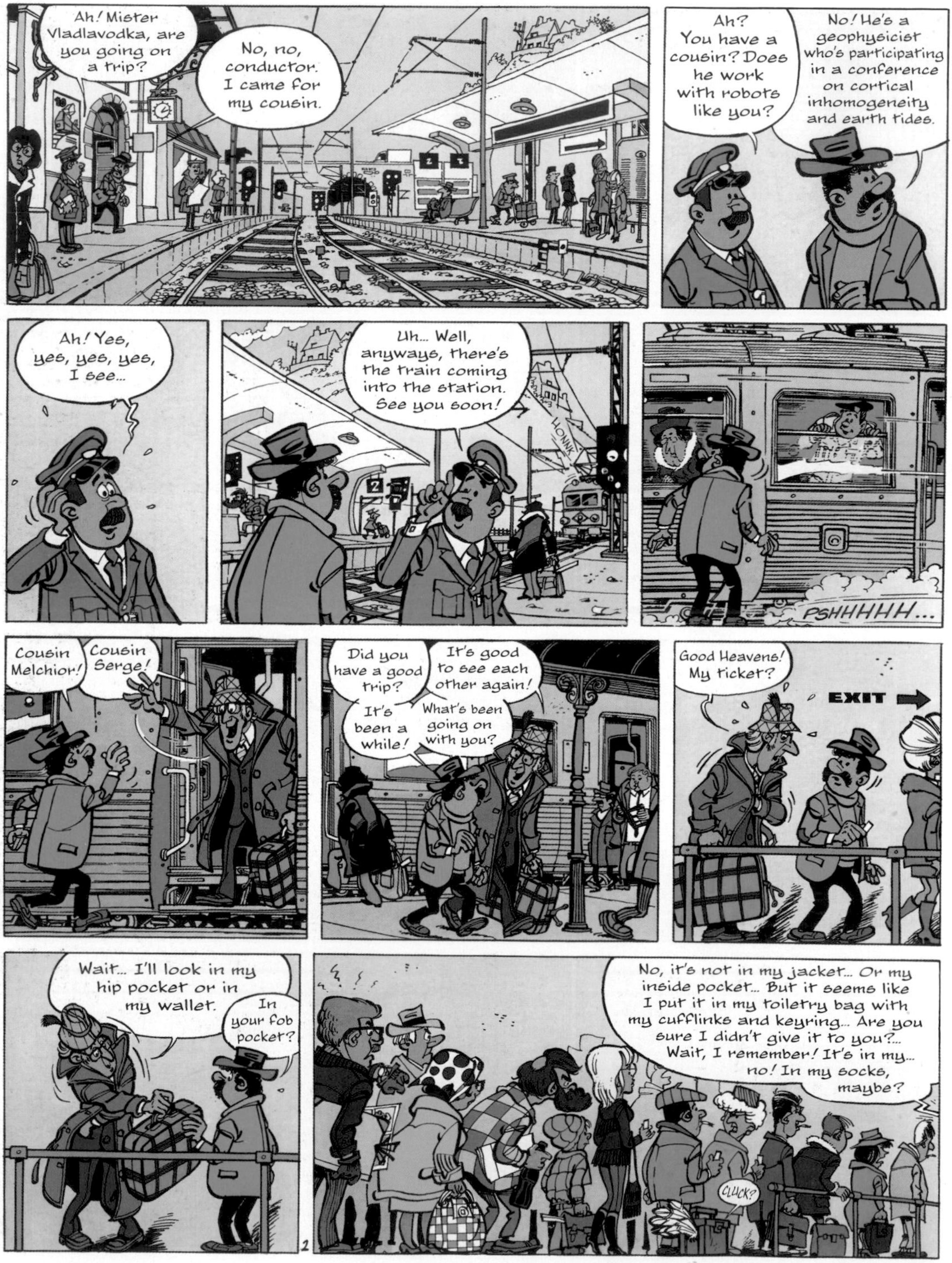

Ah! Mister Vladlavodka, are you going on a trip?
No, no, conductor. I came for my cousin.
Ah? You have a cousin? Does he work with robots like you?
No! He's a geophysicist who's participating in a conference on cortical inhomogeneity and earth tides.
Ah! Yes, yes, yes, yes, I see...
Uh... Well, anyways, there's the train coming into the station. See you soon!
HONNK
PSHHHHH...
Cousin Melchior!
Cousin Serge!
Did you have a good trip?
It's good to see each other again!
It's been a while!
What's been going on with you?
Good Heavens! My ticket?
EXIT
Wait... I'll look in my hip pocket or in my wallet.
In your fob pocket?
No, it's not in my jacket... Or my inside pocket... But it seems like I put it in my toiletry bag with my cufflinks and keyring... Are you sure I didn't give it to you?... Wait, I remember! It's in my... no! In my socks, maybe?
CLUCK?

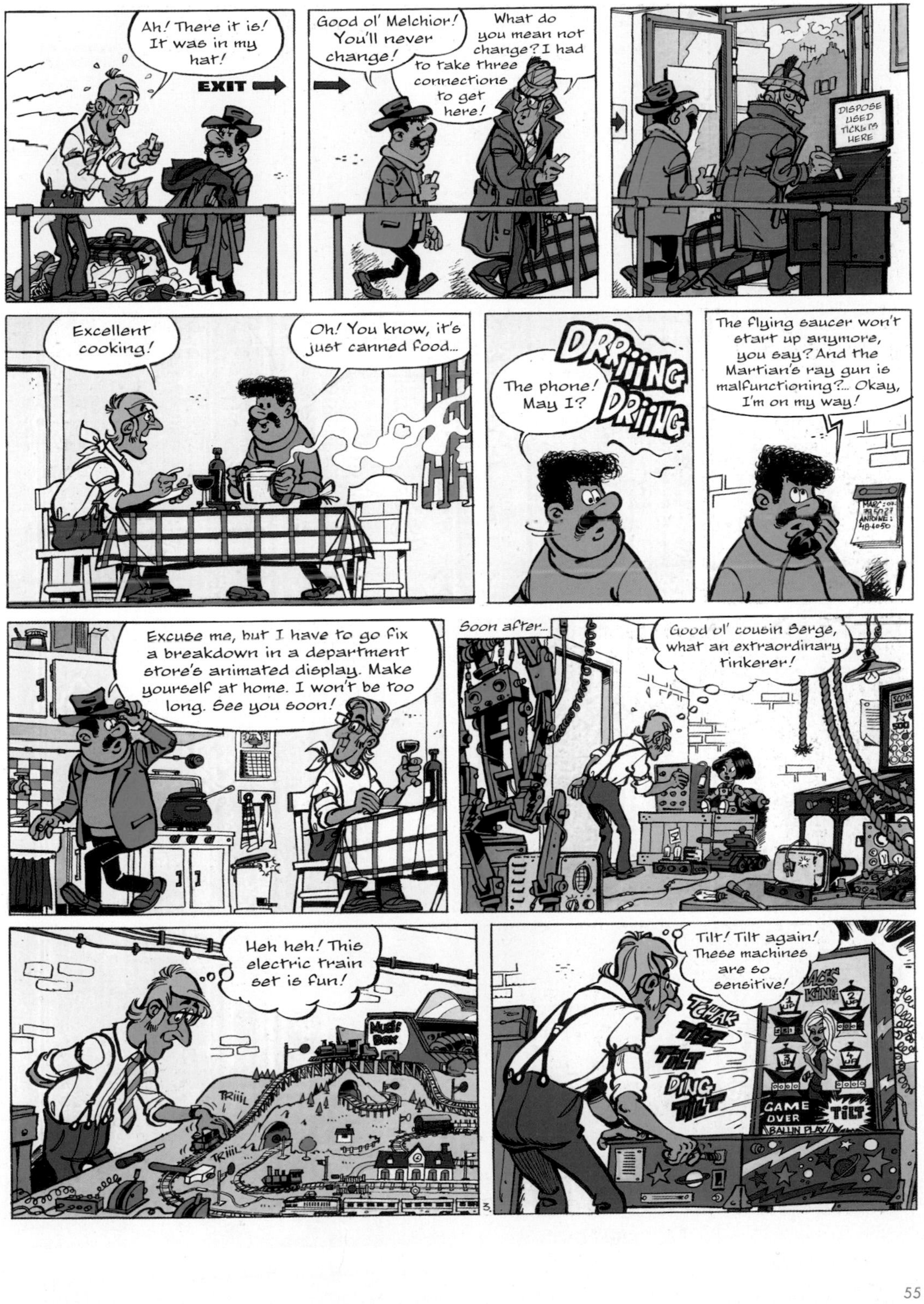
Ah! There it is! It was in my hat!
EXIT
Good ol' Melchior! You'll never change!
What do you mean not change? I had to take three connections to get here!
Excellent cooking!
Oh! You know, it's just canned food...
DRRIIING DRIIING
The phone! May I?
The flying saucer won't start up anymore, you say? And the Martian's ray gun is malfunctioning?... Okay, I'm on my way!
Excuse me, but I have to go fix a breakdown in a department store's animated display. Make yourself at home. I won't be too long. See you soon!
Soon after...
Good ol' cousin Serge, what an extraordinary tinkerer!
Heh heh! This electric train set is fun!
TRIIIL
TRIIIL
Tilt! Tilt again! These machines are so sensitive!
TCHAK TILT TILT DING TILT
GAME OVER
TILT

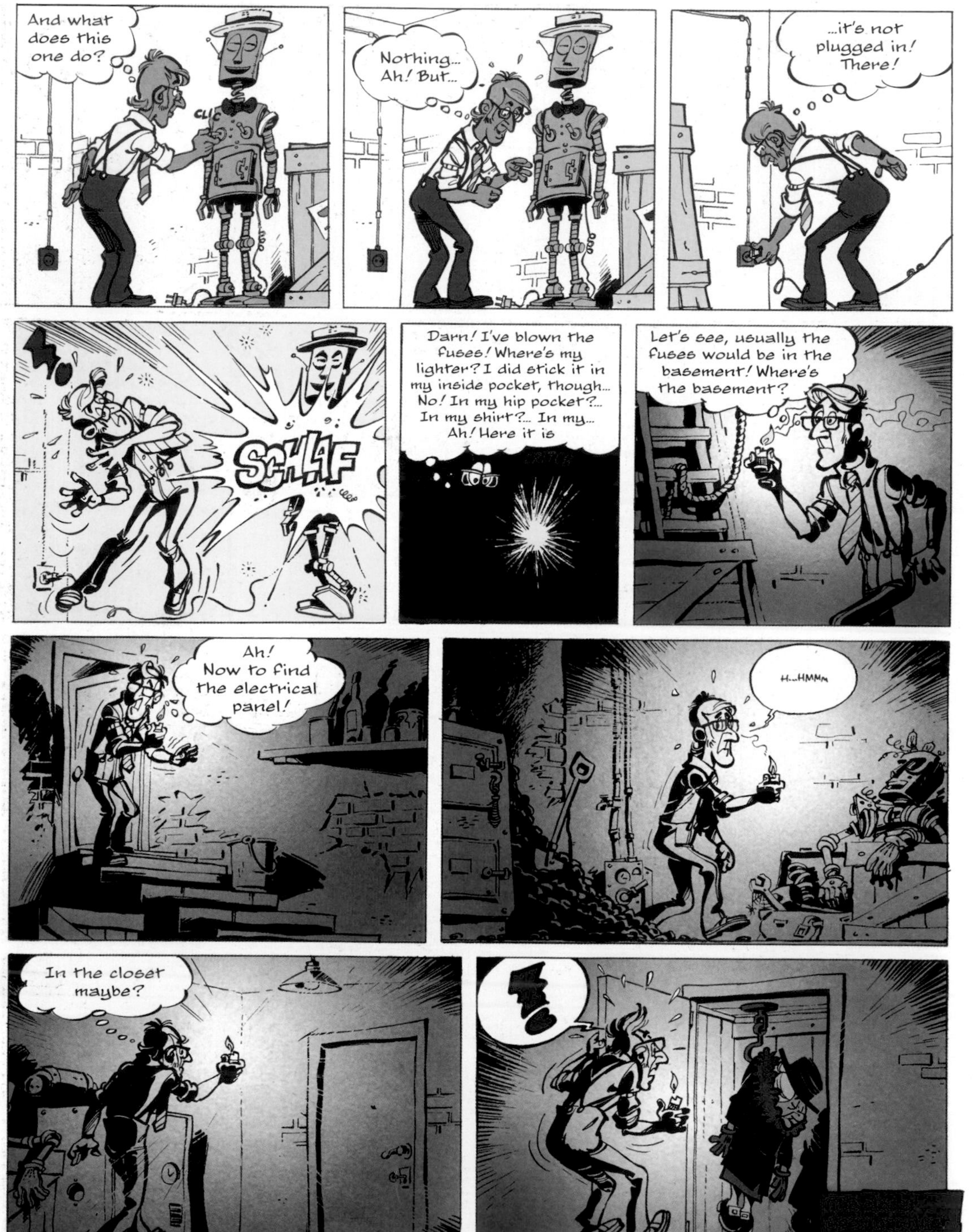

And what does this one do?
Nothing... Ah! But...
...it's not plugged in! There!
SCHLAF
Darn! I've blown the fuses! Where's my lighter? I did stick it in my inside pocket, though... No! In my hip pocket?... In my shirt?... In my... Ah! Here it is
Let's see, usually the fuses would be in the basement! Where's the basement?
Ah! Now to find the electrical panel!
In the closet maybe?

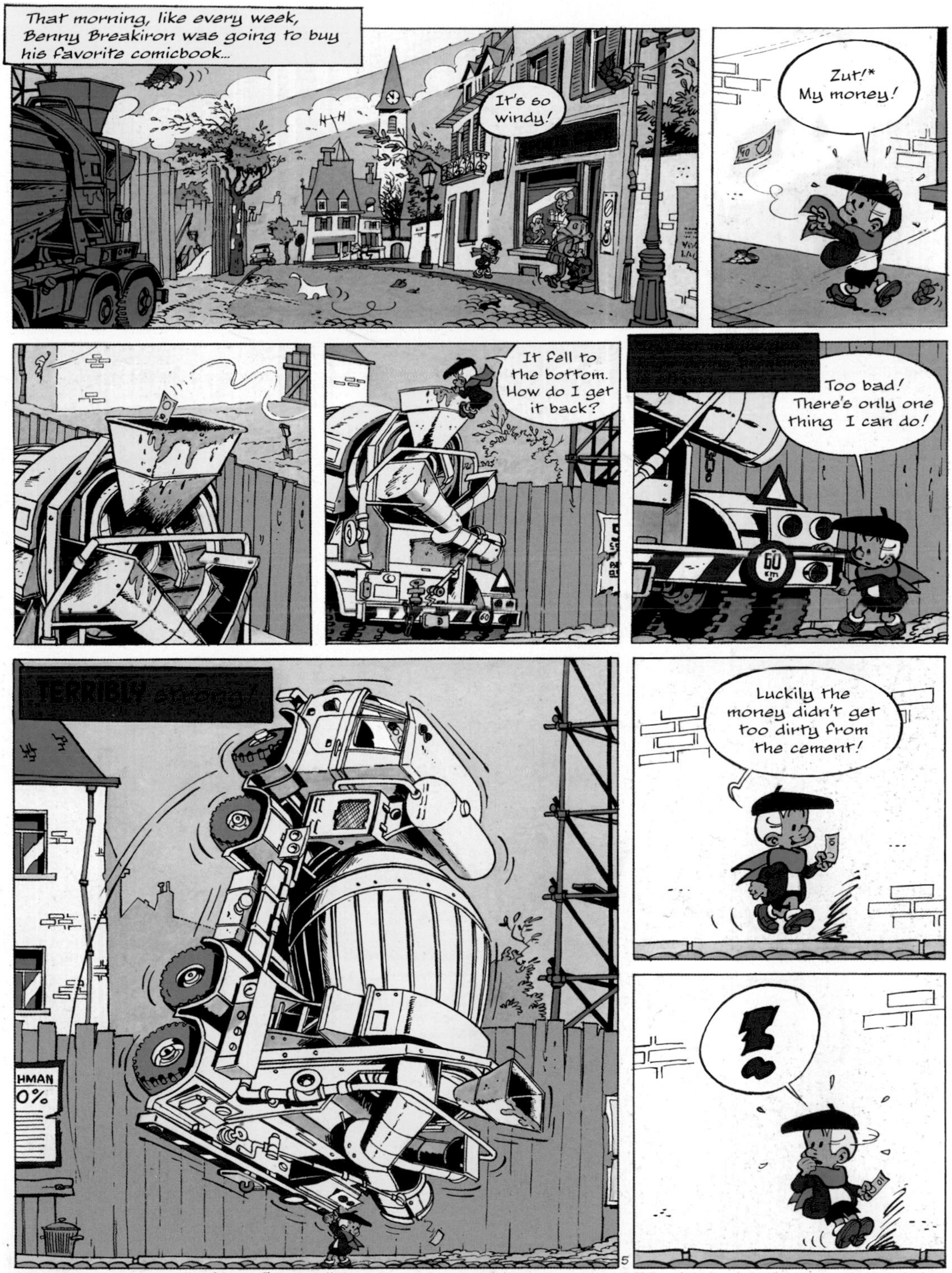
That morning, like every week, Benny Breakiron was going to buy his favorite comicbook...
It's so windy!
Zut!* My money!
It fell to the bottom. How do I get it back?
[redacted]
Too bad! There's only one thing I can do!
[redacted]
Luckily the money didn't get too dirty from the cement!

*French exclamation, like "Darn!" in English.

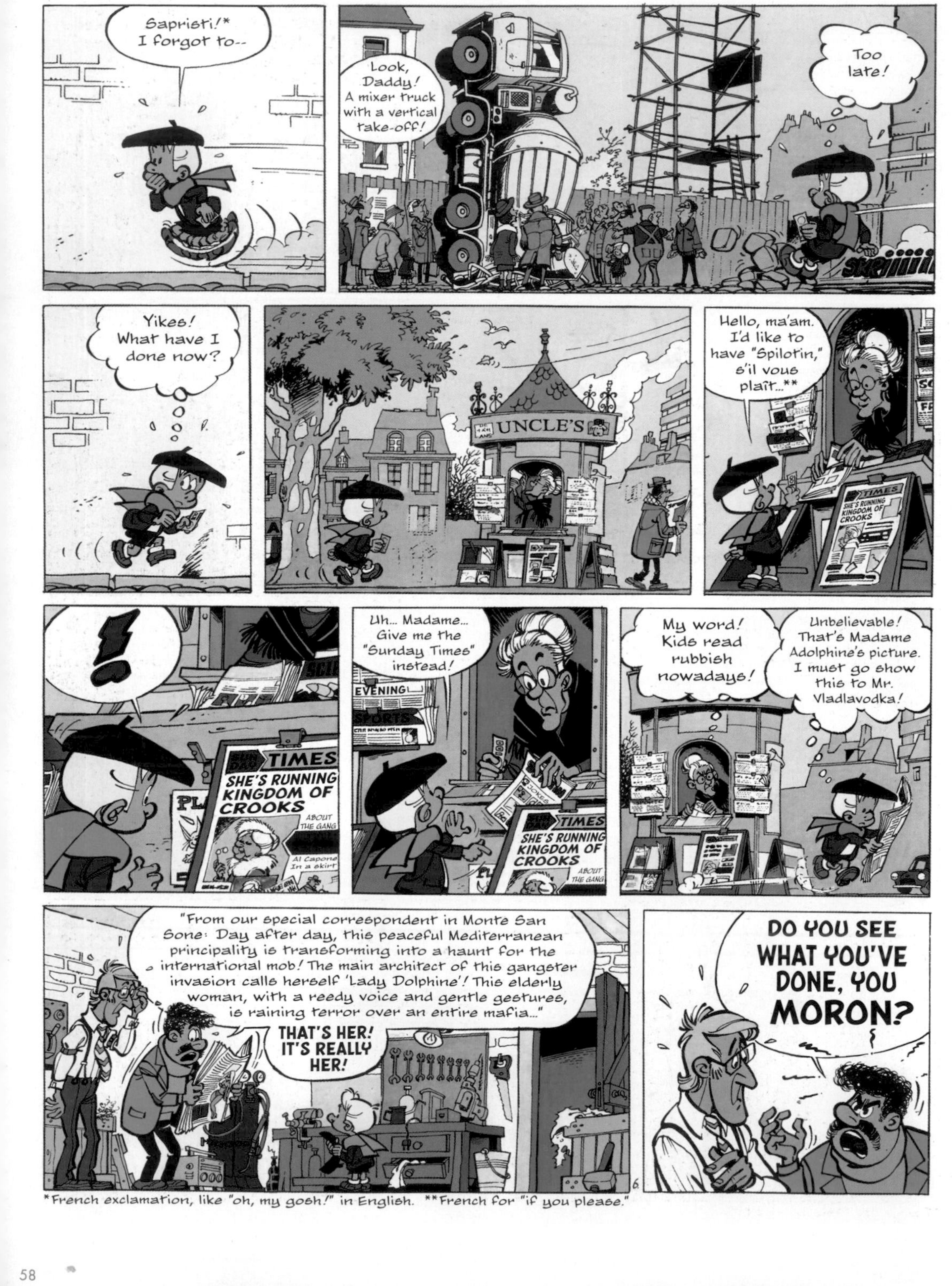

Sapristi!*
I forgot to--
Look, Daddy! A mixer truck with a vertical take-off!
Too late!
Yikes! What have I done now?
UNCLE'S
Hello, ma'am. I'd like to have "Spilotin," s'il vous plaît...**
TIMES
SHE'S RUNNING KINGDOM OF CROOKS
!
TIMES
SHE'S RUNNING KINGDOM OF CROOKS
ABOUT THE GANG
Al Capone In a skirt
Uh... Madame... Give me the "Sunday Times" instead!
EVENING
SPORTS
TIMES
SHE'S RUNNING KINGDOM OF CROOKS
ABOUT THE GANG
My word! Kids read rubbish nowadays!
Unbelievable! That's Madame Adolphine's picture. I must go show this to Mr. Vladlavodka!
"From our special correspondent in Monte San Sone: Day after day, this peaceful Mediterranean principality is transforming into a haunt for the international mob! The main architect of this gangster invasion calls herself 'Lady Dolphine'! This elderly woman, with a reedy voice and gentle gestures, is raining terror over an entire mafia..."
THAT'S HER! IT'S REALLY HER!
DO YOU SEE WHAT YOU'VE DONE, YOU MORON?

*French exclamation, like "oh, my gosh!" in English. **French for "if you please."

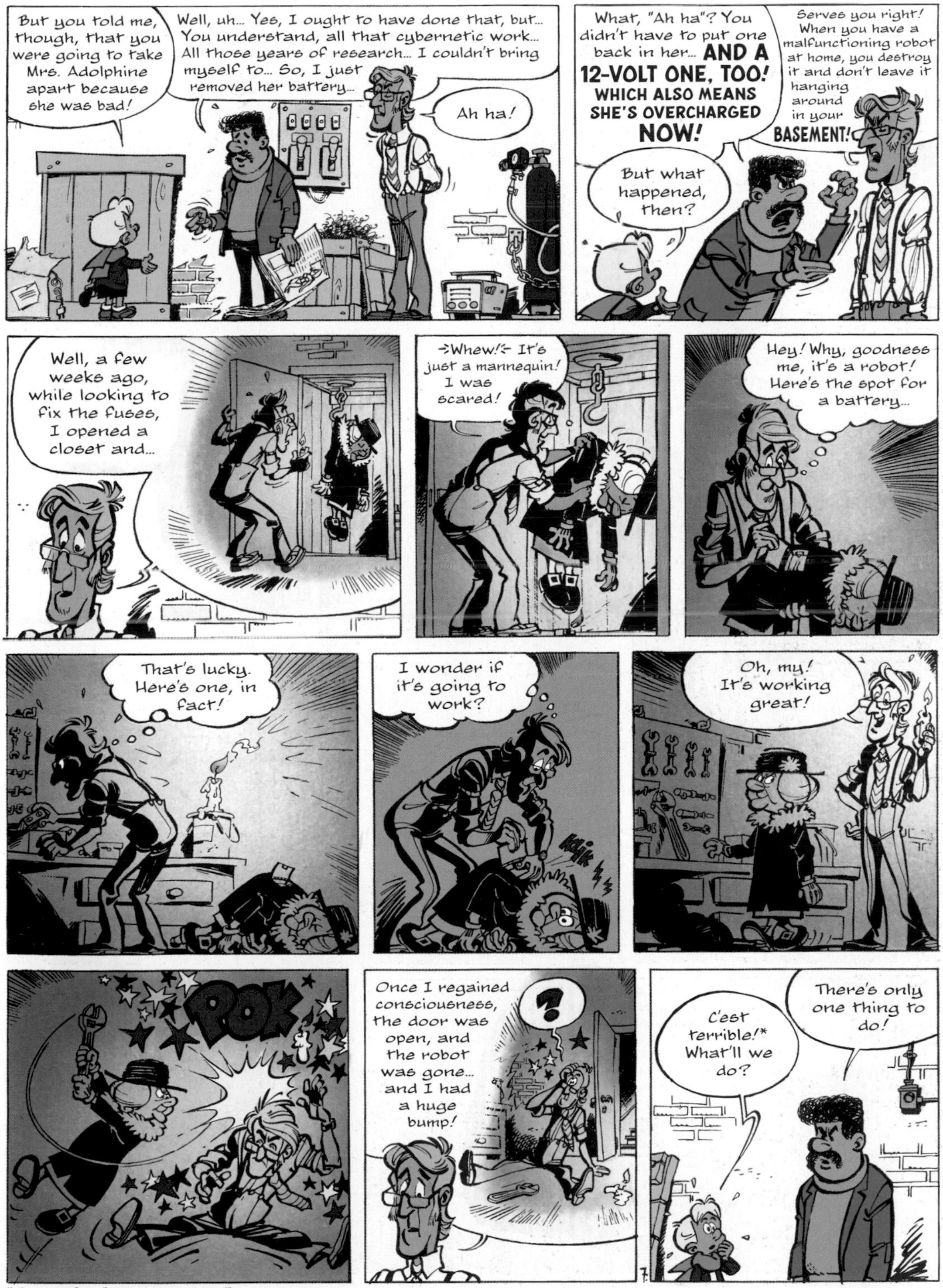
But you told me, though, that you were going to take Mrs. Adolphine apart because she was bad!
Well, uh... Yes, I ought to have done that, but... You understand, all that cybernetic work... All those years of research... I couldn't bring myself to... So, I just removed her battery...
Ah ha!
What, "Ah ha"? You didn't have to put one back in her... AND A 12-VOLT ONE, TOO! WHICH ALSO MEANS SHE'S OVERCHARGED NOW!
Serves you right! When you have a malfunctioning robot at home, you destroy it and don't leave it hanging around in your BASEMENT!
But what happened, then?
Well, a few weeks ago, while looking to fix the fuses, I opened a closet and...
Whew! It's just a mannequin! I was scared!
Hey! Why, goodness me, it's a robot! Here's the spot for a battery...
That's lucky. Here's one, in fact!
I wonder if it's going to work?
Oh, my! It's working great!
POK
Once I regained consciousness, the door was open, and the robot was gone... and I had a huge bump!
?
C'est terrible!* What'll we do?
There's only one thing to do!

*French for "This is terrible!"

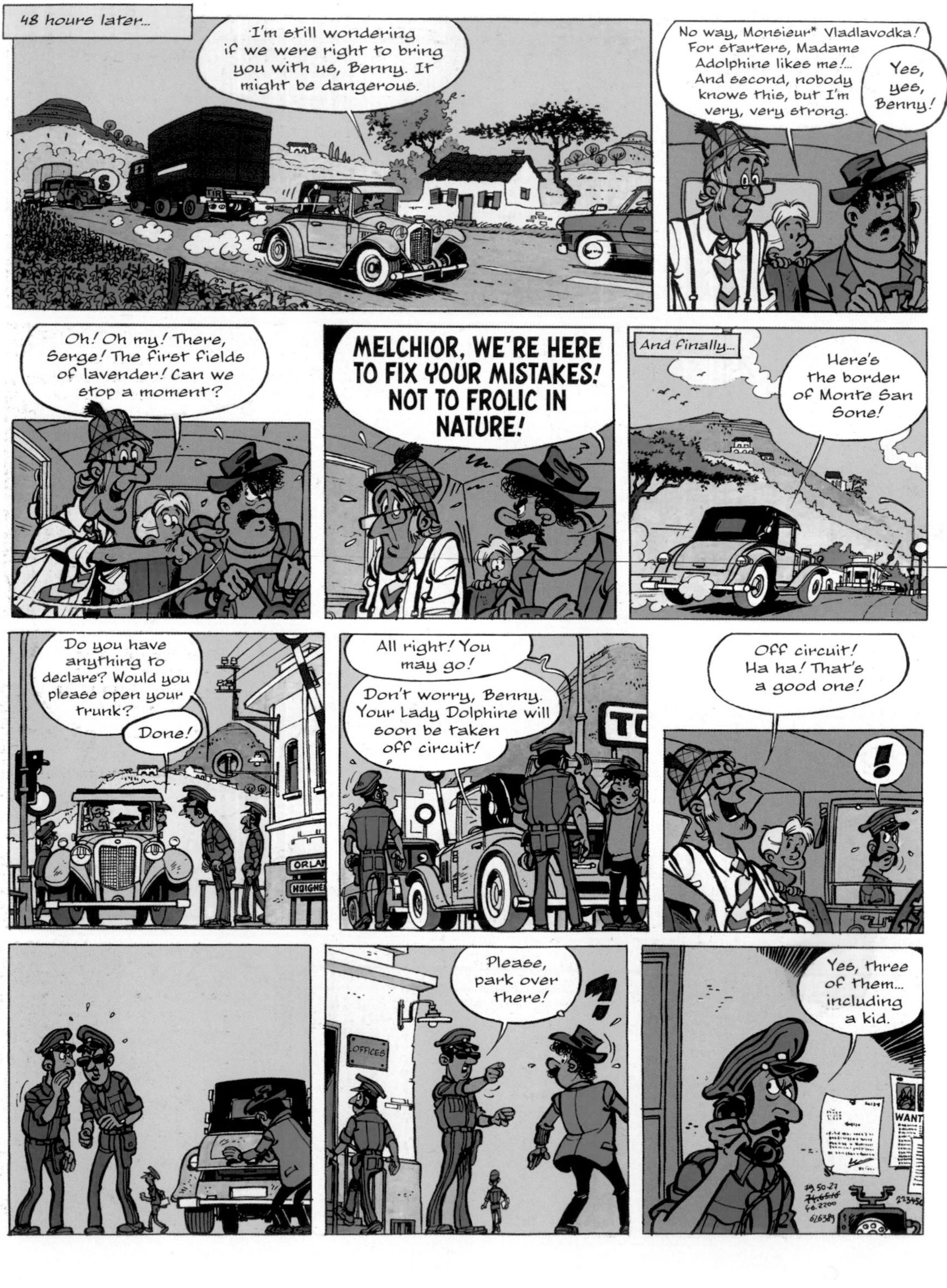

48 hours later...
I'm still wondering if we were right to bring you with us, Benny. It might be dangerous.
No way, Monsieur* Vladlavodka! For starters, Madame Adolphine likes me!... And second, nobody knows this, but I'm very, very strong.
Yes, yes, Benny!
Oh! Oh my! There, Serge! The first fields of lavender! Can we stop a moment?
MELCHIOR, WE'RE HERE TO FIX YOUR MISTAKES! NOT TO FROLIC IN NATURE!
And finally...
Here's the border of Monte San Sone!
Do you have anything to declare? Would you please open your trunk?
Done!
All right! You may go!
Don't worry, Benny. Your Lady Dolphine will soon be taken off circuit!
Off circuit! Ha ha! That's a good one!
!
Please, park over there!
Yes, three of them... including a kid.

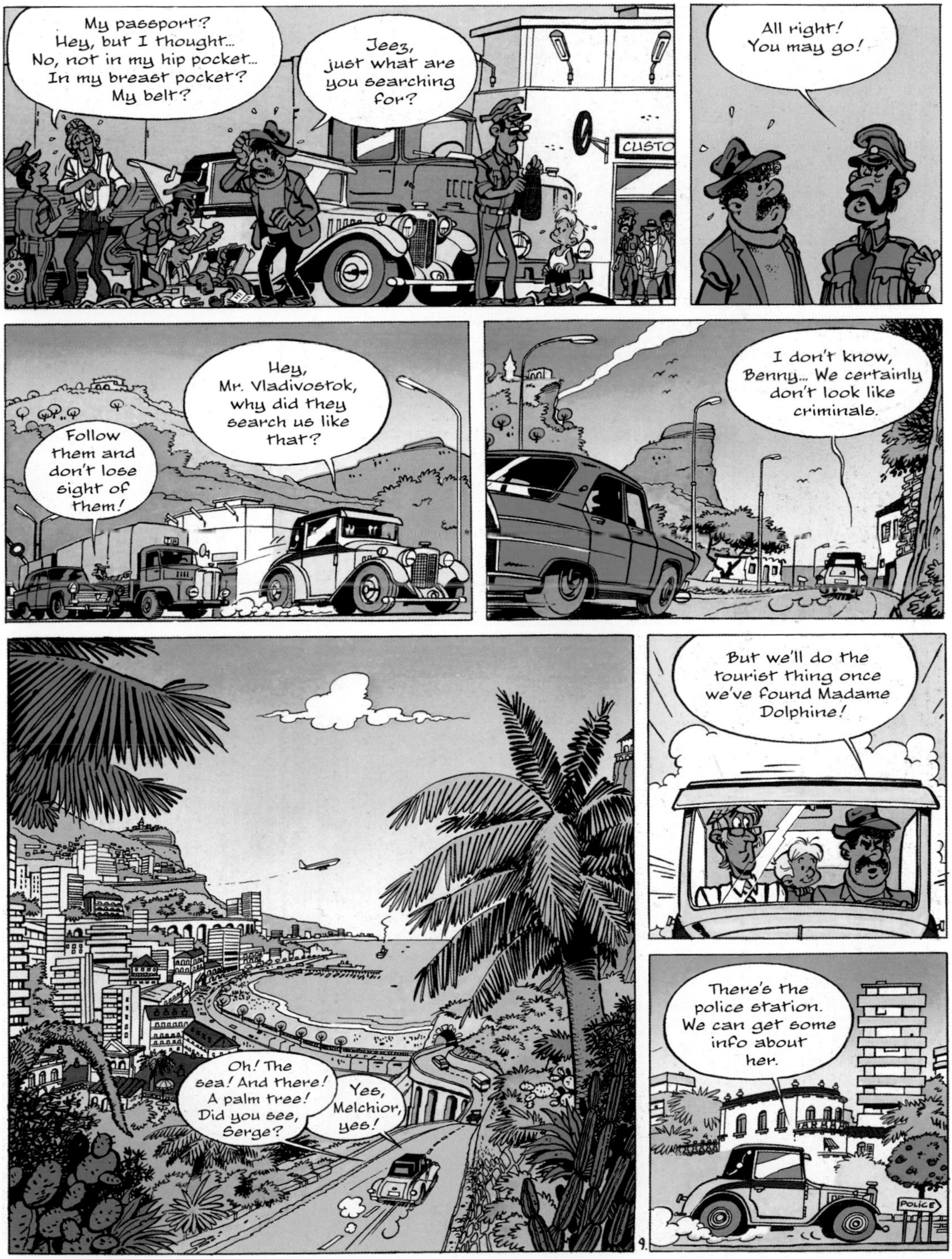
My passport? Hey, but I thought... No, not in my hip pocket... In my breast pocket? My belt?
Jeez, just what are you searching for?
CUSTO
All right! You may go!
Hey, Mr. Vladivostok, why did they search us like that?
Follow them and don't lose sight of them!
I don't know, Benny... We certainly don't look like criminals.
Oh! The sea! And there! A palm tree! Did you see, Serge?
Yes, Melchior, yes!
But we'll do the tourist thing once we've found Madame Dolphine!
There's the police station. We can get some info about her.
POLICE

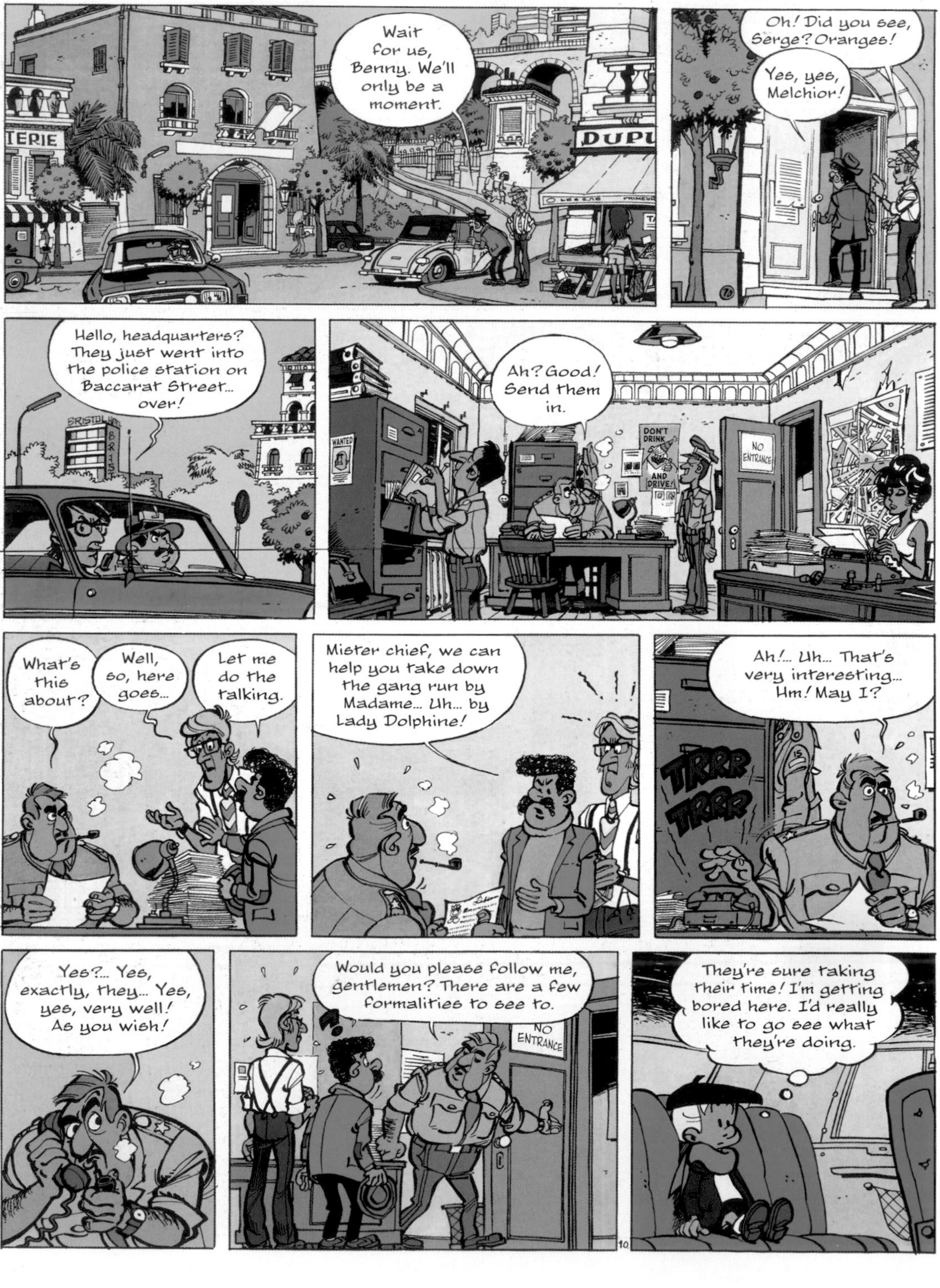
Wait for us, Benny. We'll only be a moment.
TERIE
DUPU
Oh! Did you see, Serge? Oranges!
Yes, yes, Melchior!
Hello, headquarters? They just went into the police station on Baccarat Street... over!
BRISTOL
Ah? Good! Send them in.
WANTED
DON'T DRINK AND DRIVE!
NO ENTRANCE
What's this about?
Well, so, here goes...
Let me do the talking.
Mister chief, we can help you take down the gang run by Madame... Uh... by Lady Dolphine!
Ah!... Uh... That's very interesting... Hm! May I?
TRRR TRRR
Yes?... Yes, exactly, they... Yes, yes, very well! As you wish!
Would you please follow me, gentlemen? There are a few formalities to see to.
NO ENTRANCE
They're sure taking their time! I'm getting bored here. I'd really like to go see what they're doing.

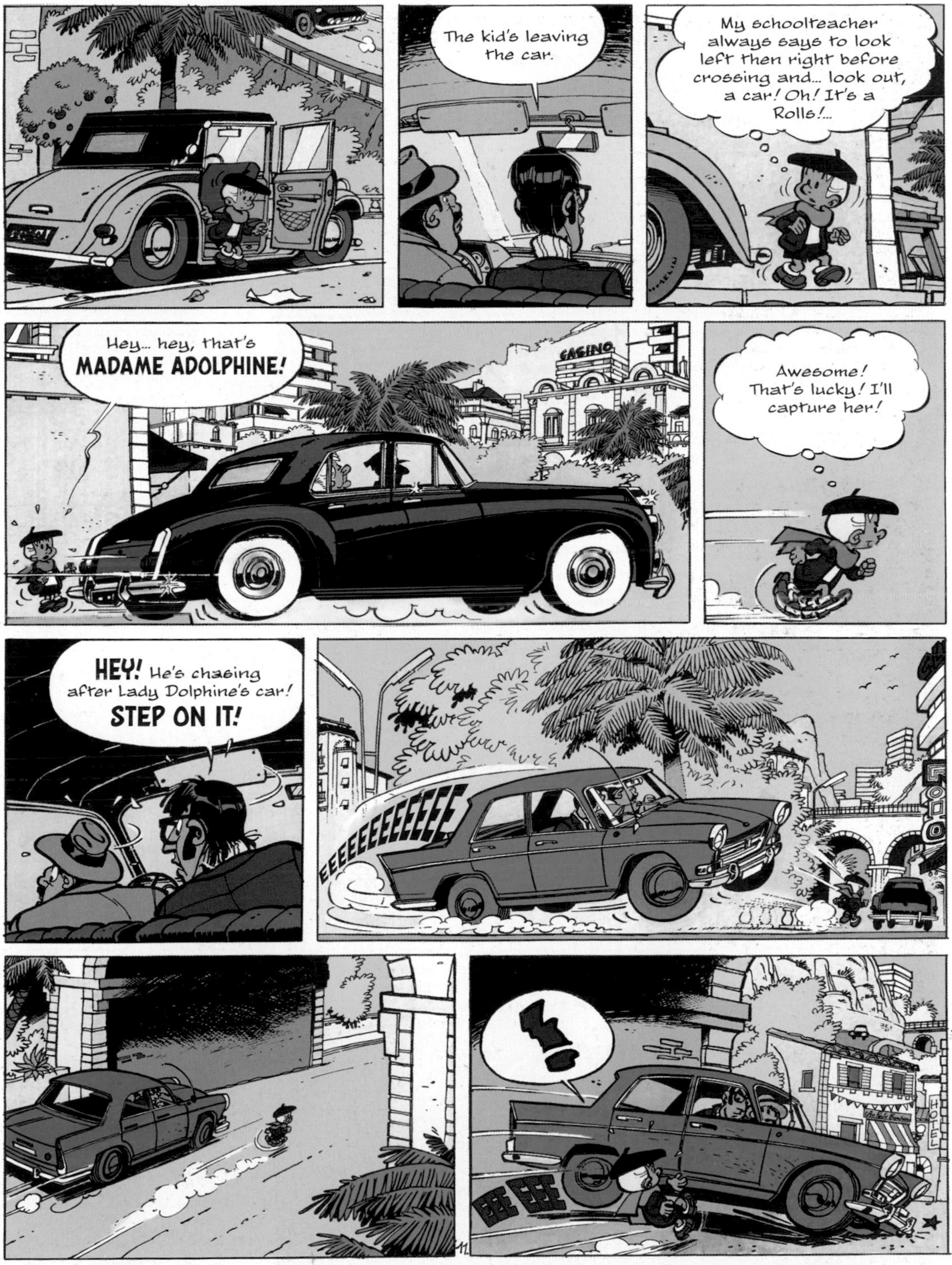
The kid's leaving the car.
My schoolteacher always says to look left then right before crossing and... look out, a car! Oh! It's a Rolls!...
Hey... hey, that's MADAME ADOLPHINE!
CASINO
Awesome! That's lucky! I'll capture her!
HEY! He's chasing after Lady Dolphine's car! STEP ON IT!
EEEEEEEEEEEE
HOTEL
EEE EEE

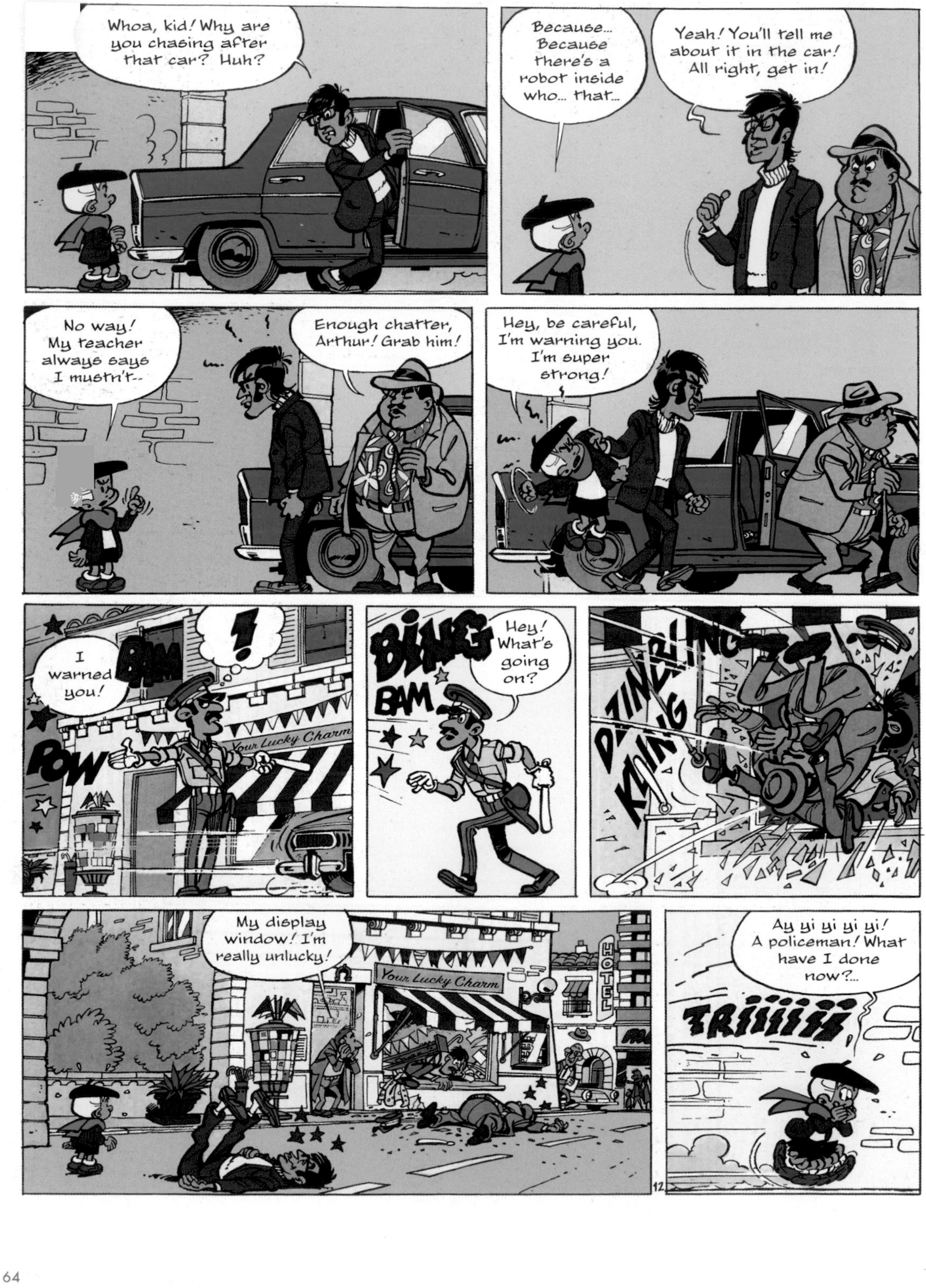
Whoa, kid! Why are you chasing after that car? Huh?
Because... Because there's a robot inside who... that...
Yeah! You'll tell me about it in the car! All right, get in!
No way! My teacher always says I mustn't...
Enough chatter, Arthur! Grab him!
Hey, be careful, I'm warning you. I'm super strong!
I warned you!
BAM
POW
Your Lucky Charm
BING
BAM
Hey! What's going on?
DZING
KLING
My display window! I'm really unlucky!
Your Lucky Charm
HOTEL
Ay yi yi yi yi! A policeman! What have I done now?...
TRIIIIII
12

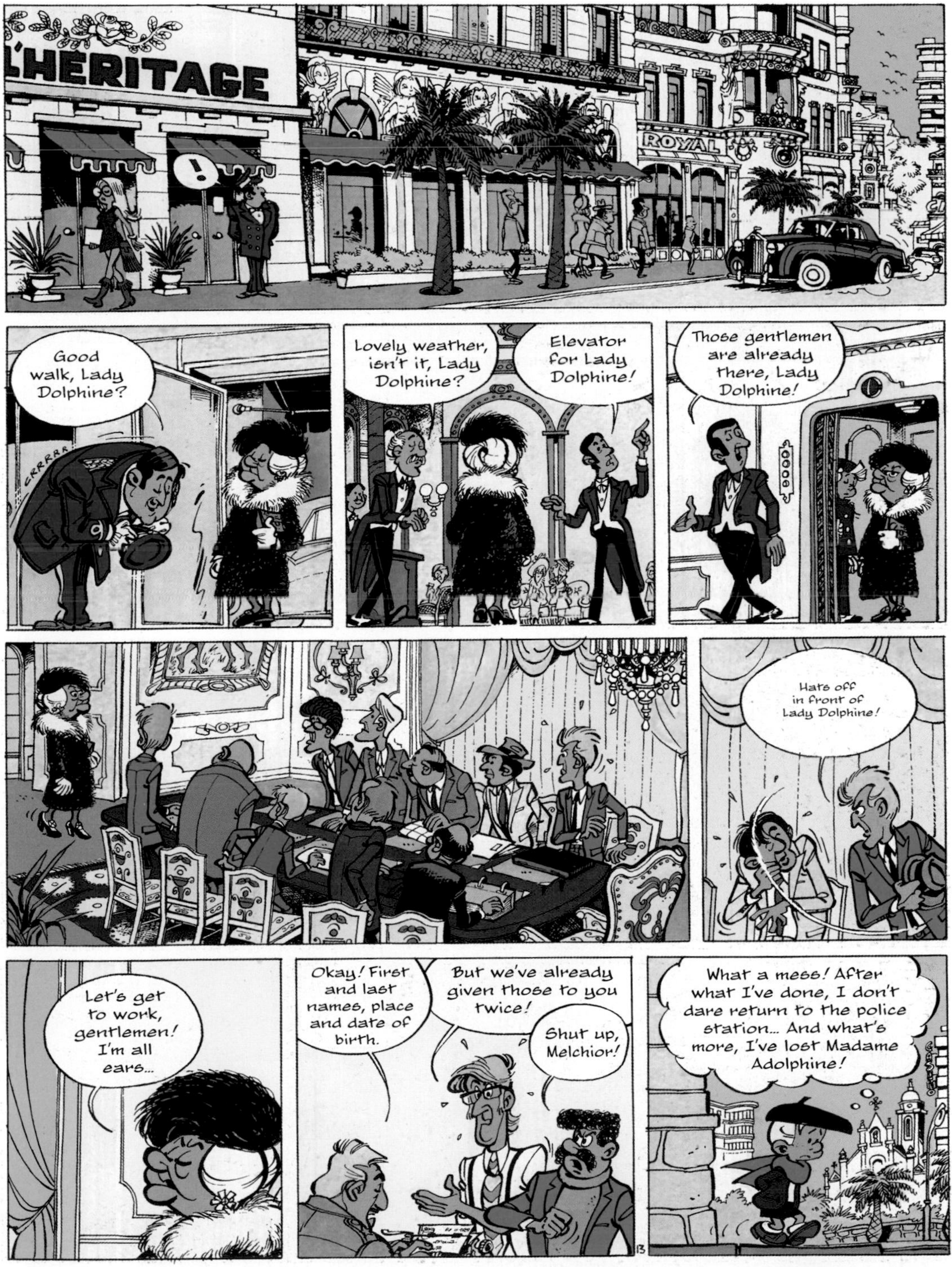
L'HERITAGE
ROYAL
Good walk, Lady Dolphine?
CRRRRR
Lovely weather, isn't it, Lady Dolphine?
Elevator for Lady Dolphine!
Those gentlemen are already there, Lady Dolphine!
Hats off in front of Lady Dolphine!
Let's get to work, gentlemen! I'm all ears...
Okay! First and last names, place and date of birth.
But we've already given those to you twice!
Shut up, Melchior!
What a mess! After what I've done, I don't dare return to the police station... And what's more, I've lost Madame Adolphine!

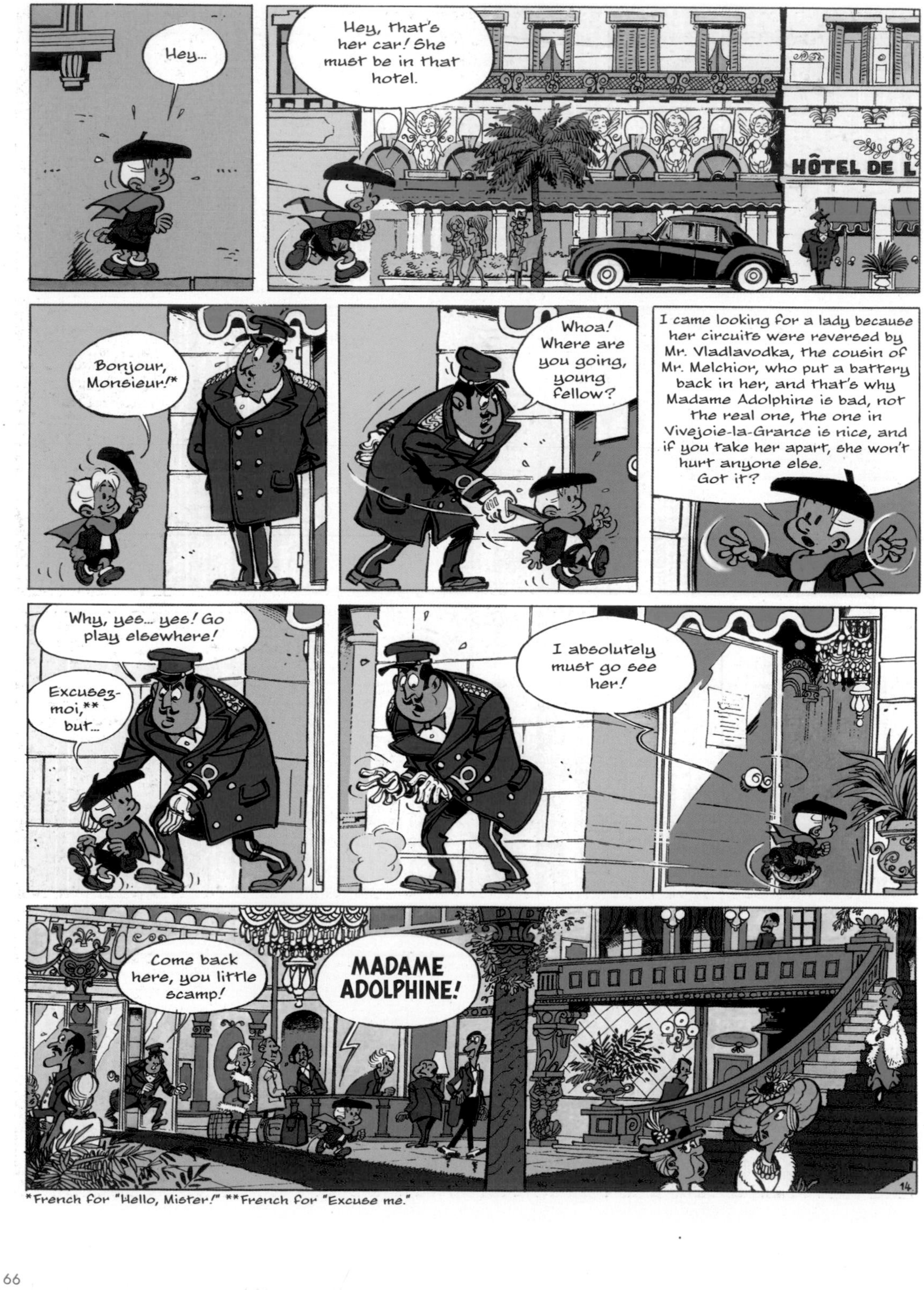

Hey...
Hey, that's her car! She must be in that hotel.
HÔTEL DE L
Bonjour, Monsieur!*
Whoa! Where are you going, young fellow?
I came looking for a lady because her circuits were reversed by Mr. Vladlavodka, the cousin of Mr. Melchior, who put a battery back in her, and that's why Madame Adolphine is bad, not the real one, the one in Vivejoie-la-Grance is nice, and if you take her apart, she won't hurt anyone else.
Got it?
Why, yes... yes! Go play elsewhere!
Excusez-moi,** but...
I absolutely must go see her!
Come back here, you little scamp!
MADAME ADOLPHINE!
14

*French for "Hello, Mister!" **French for "Excuse me."

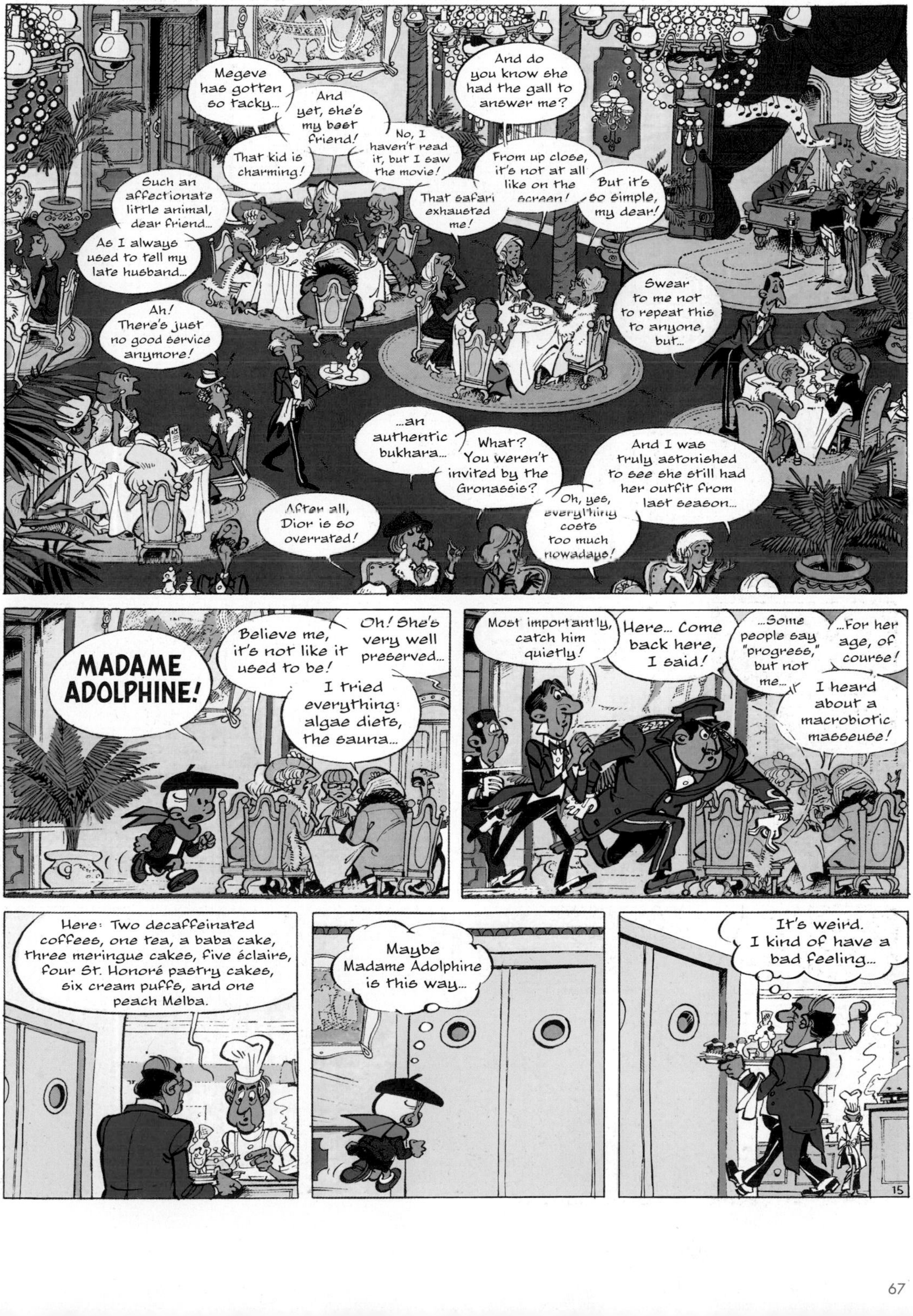

Megeve has gotten so tacky...
And yet, she's my best friend!
And do you know she had the gall to answer me?
That kid is charming!
No, I haven't read it, but I saw the movie!
From up close, it's not at all like on the screen!
Such an affectionate little animal, dear friend...
That safari exhausted me!
But it's so simple, my dear!
As I always used to tell my late husband...
Swear to me not to repeat this to anyone, but...
Ah! There's just no good service anymore!
...an authentic bukhara...
What? You weren't invited by the Gronassis?
And I was truly astonished to see she still had her outfit from last season...
After all, Dior is so overrated!
Oh, yes, everything costs too much nowadays!
MADAME ADOLPHINE!
Believe me, it's not like it used to be!
Oh! She's very well preserved...
I tried everything: algae diets, the sauna...
Most importantly, catch him quietly!
Here... Come back here, I said!
...Some people say "progress," but not me...
...For her age, of course!
I heard about a macrobiotic masseuse!
Here: Two decaffeinated coffees, one tea, a baba cake, three meringue cakes, five éclairs, four St. Honoré pastry cakes, six cream puffs, and one peach Melba.
Maybe Madame Adolphine is this way...
It's weird. I kind of have a bad feeling...
15

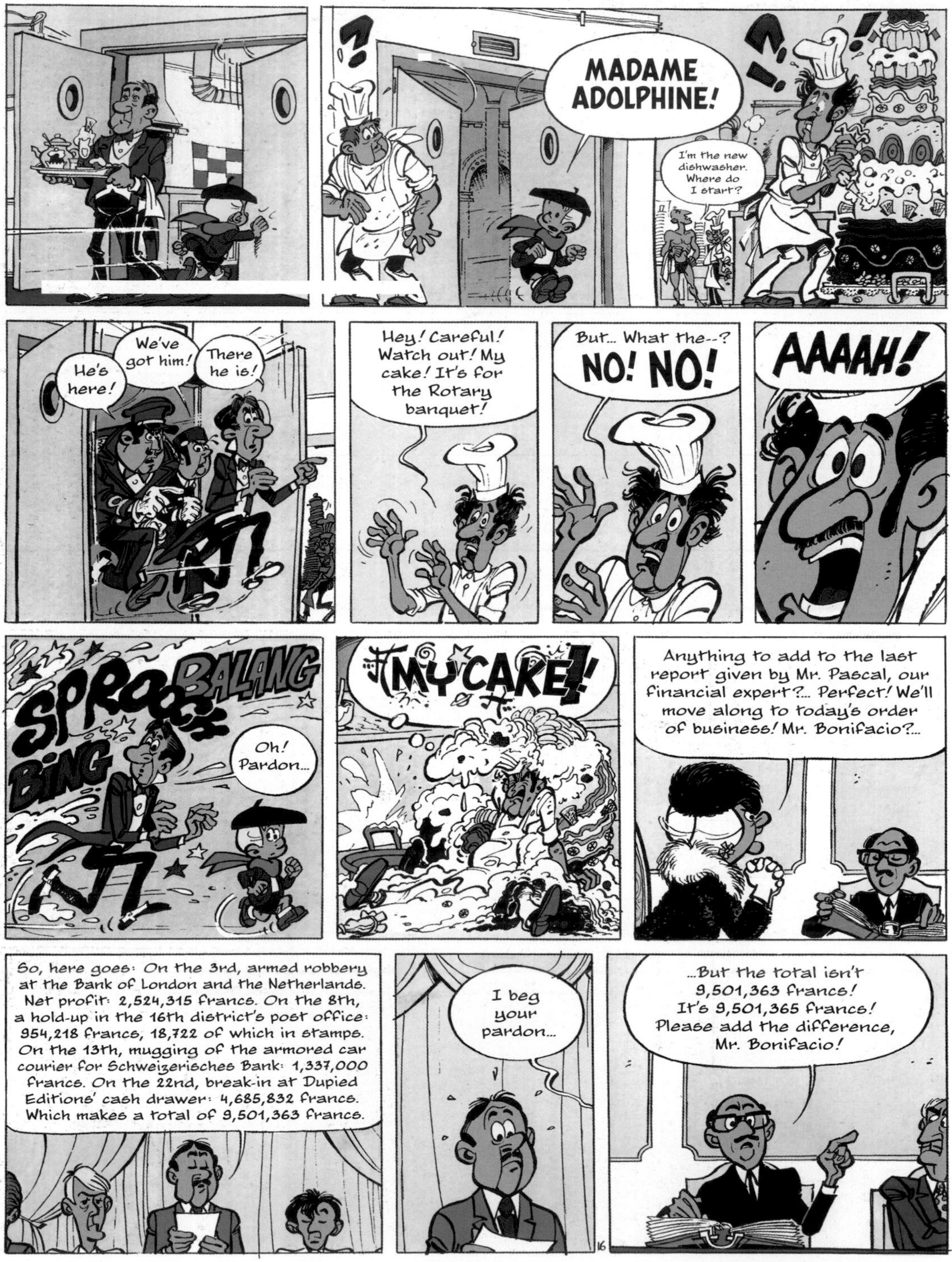
MADAME ADOLPHINE!
I'm the new dishwasher. Where do I start?
He's here!
We've got him!
There he is!
Hey! Careful! Watch out! My cake! It's for the Rotary banquet!
But... What the--?
NO! NO!
AAAAH!
SPROOOCH
BALANG
BING
Oh! Pardon...
MY CAKE!
Anything to add to the last report given by Mr. Pascal, our financial expert?... Perfect! We'll move along to today's order of business! Mr. Bonifacio?...
So, here goes: On the 3rd, armed robbery at the Bank of London and the Netherlands. Net profit: 2,524,315 francs. On the 8th, a hold-up in the 16th district's post office: 954,218 francs, 18,722 of which in stamps. On the 13th, mugging of the armored car courier for Schweizerisches Bank: 1,337,000 francs. On the 22nd, break-in at Dupied Editions' cash drawer: 4,685,832 francs. Which makes a total of 9,501,363 francs.
I beg your pardon...
...But the total isn't 9,501,363 francs! It's 9,501,365 francs! Please add the difference, Mr. Bonifacio!
16

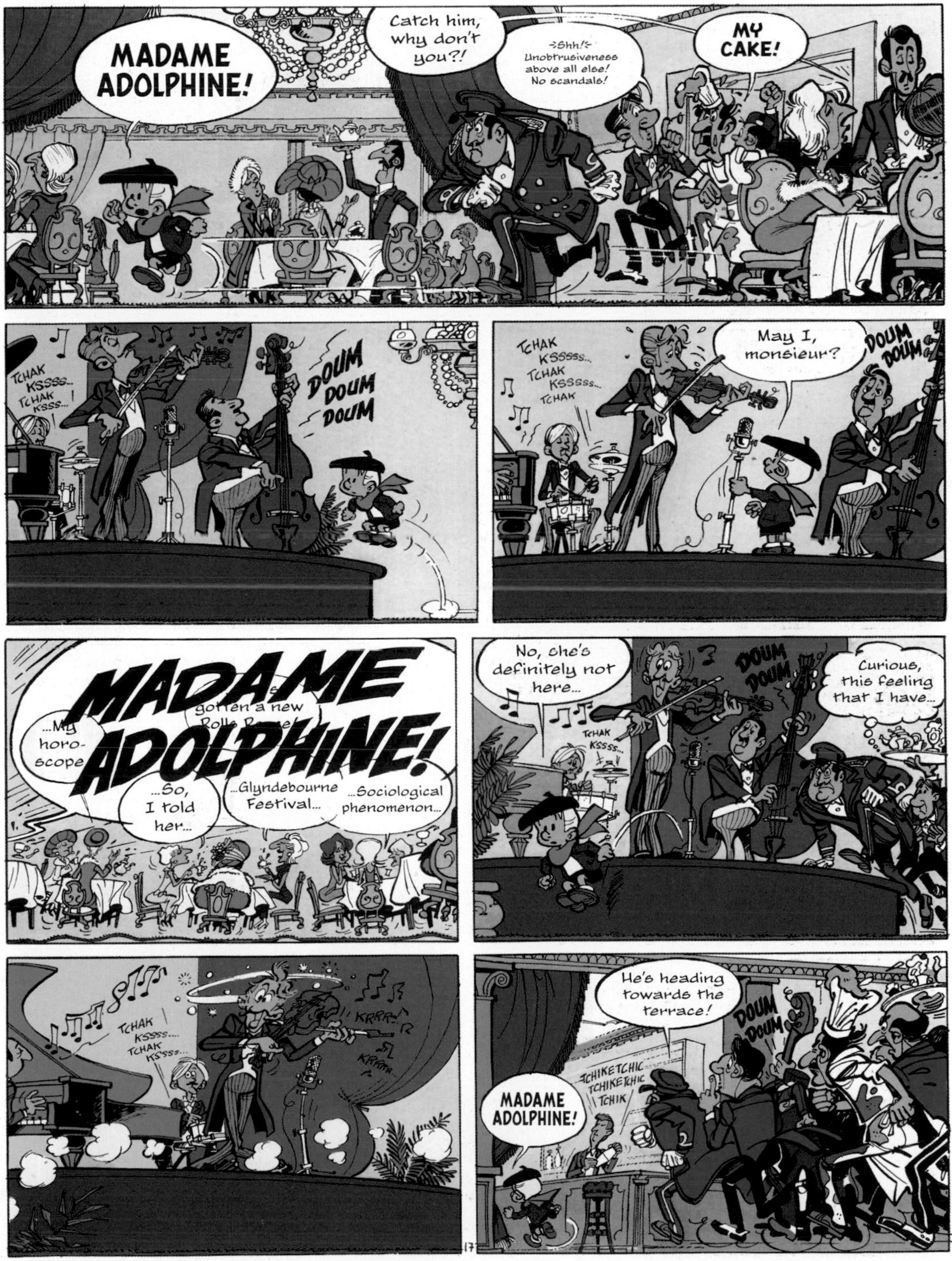
MADAME ADOLPHINE!
Catch him, why don't you?!
Shh! Unobtrusiveness above all else! No scandals!
MY CAKE!
TCHAK KSSSS.. TCHAK KSSS...
DOUM DOUM DOUM
TCHAK KSSSSS.. TCHAK KSSSSS... TCHAK
May I, monsieur?
DOUM DOUM
MADAME ADOLPHINE!
...My horoscope
gotten a new
...So, I told her...
...Glyndebourne Festival...
...Sociological phenomenon...
No, she's definitely not here...
TCHAK KSSSS...
DOUM DOUM
Curious, this feeling that I have...
TCHAK KSSSS... TCHAK KSSSS...
KRRRR!
He's heading towards the terrace!
DOUM DOUM
TCHIKETCHIC TCHIKETCHIC TCHIK
MADAME ADOLPHINE!

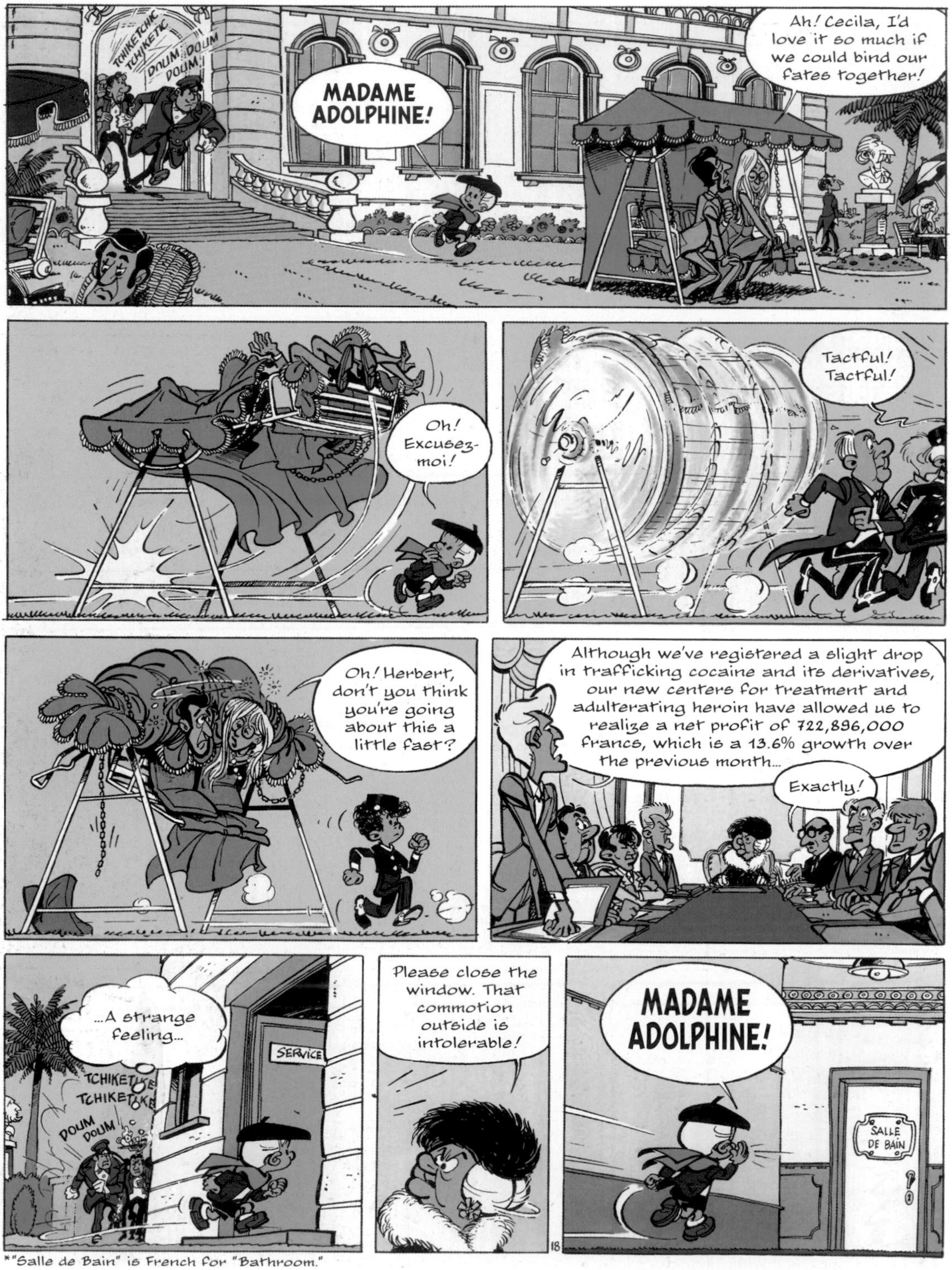
TCHIKETCHIC TCHIKETIC
DOUM DOUM DOUM DOUM
MADAME ADOLPHINE!
...Ah! Cecila, I'd love it so much if we could bind our fates together!
Oh! Excusez-moi!
Tactful! Tactful!
Oh! Herbert, don't you think you're going about this a little fast?
Although we've registered a slight drop in trafficking cocaine and its derivatives, our new centers for treatment and adulterating heroin have allowed us to realize a net profit of 722,896,000 francs, which is a 13.6% growth over the previous month...
Exactly!
...A strange feeling...
SERVICE
TCHIKETIKE TCHIKETAKE
DOUM DOUM
Please close the window. That commotion outside is intolerable!
MADAME ADOLPHINE!
SALLE DE BAIN
18

*"Salle de Bain" is French for "Bathroom."

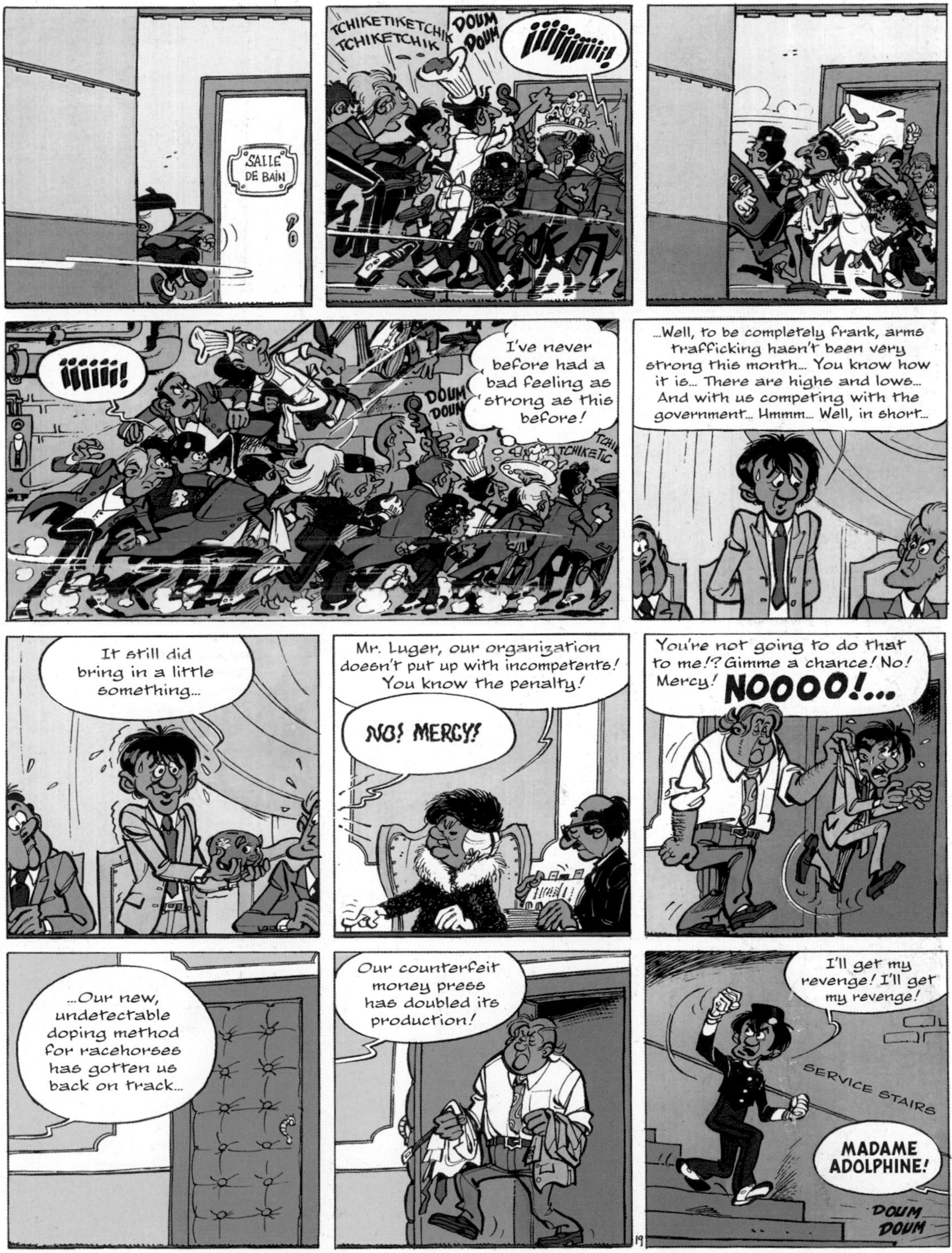

SALLE DE BAIN
TCHIKETIKETCHIK TCHIKETCHIK
DOUM DOUM
¡¡¡¡¡¡¡¡¡¡¡¡!
¡¡¡¡¡¡!
I've never before had a bad feeling as strong as this before!
DOUM DOUM
TCHIKETIC
...Well, to be completely frank, arms trafficking hasn't been very strong this month... You know how it is... There are highs and lows... And with us competing with the government... Hmmm... Well, in short...
It still did bring in a little something...
Mr. Luger, our organization doesn't put up with incompetents! You know the penalty!
NO! MERCY!
You're not going to do that to me!? Gimme a chance! No! Mercy! NOOOO!...
...Our new, undetectable doping method for racehorses has gotten us back on track...
Our counterfeit money press has doubled its production!
I'll get my revenge! I'll get my revenge!
SERVICE STAIRS
MADAME ADOLPHINE!
DOUM DOUM

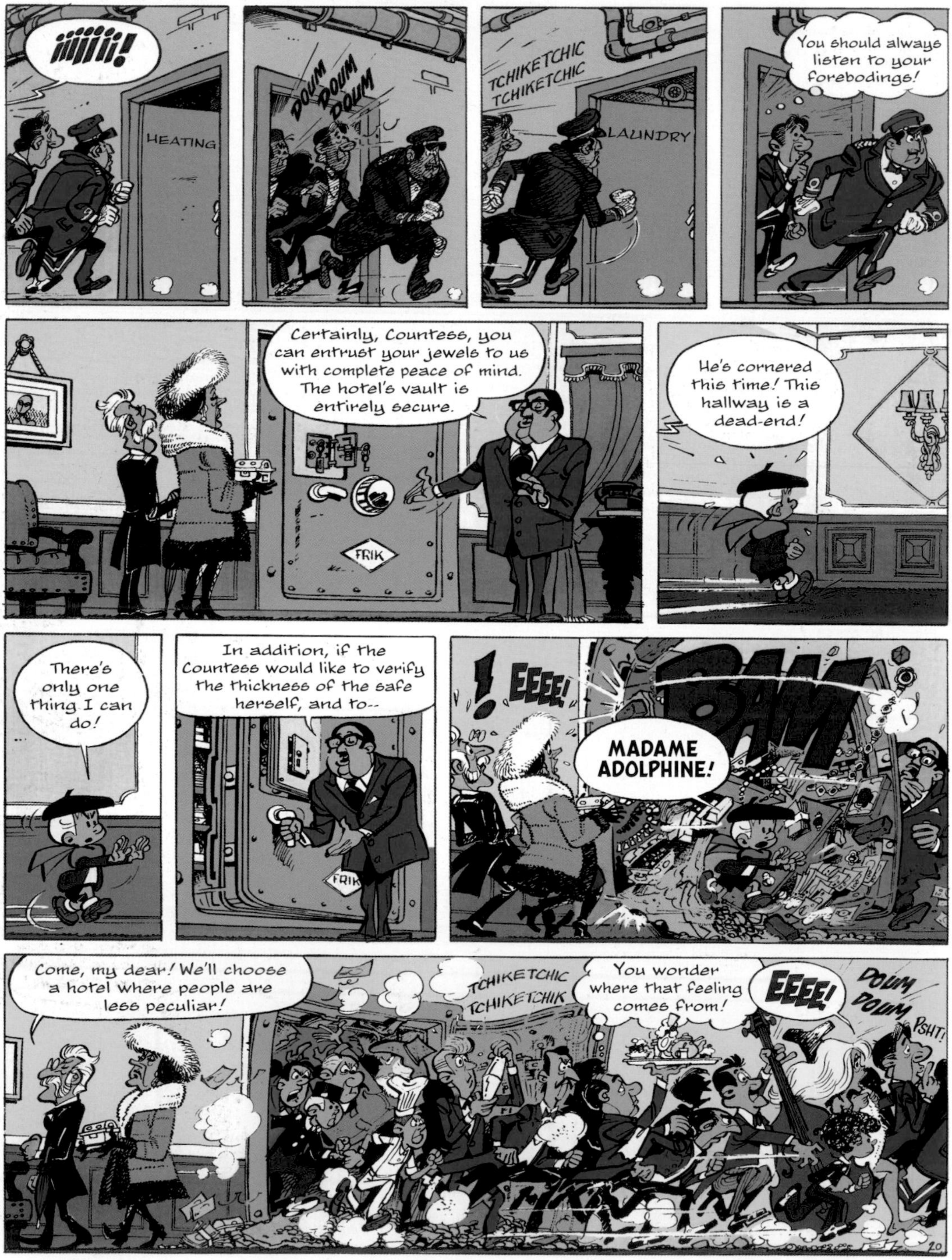
iiiiiii!
HEATING
DOUM DOUM DOUM
TCHIKETCHIC TCHIKETCHIC
LAUNDRY
You should always listen to your forebodings!
Certainly, Countess, you can entrust your jewels to us with complete peace of mind. The hotel's vault is entirely secure.
FRIK
He's cornered this time! This hallway is a dead-end!
There's only one thing I can do!
In addition, if the Countess would like to verify the thickness of the safe herself, and to--
FRIK
! EEEE!
BAM
MADAME ADOLPHINE!
Come, my dear! We'll choose a hotel where people are less peculiar!
TCHIKETCHIC TCHIKETCHIK
You wonder where that feeling comes from!
EEEE!
DOUM DOUM
PSHT!

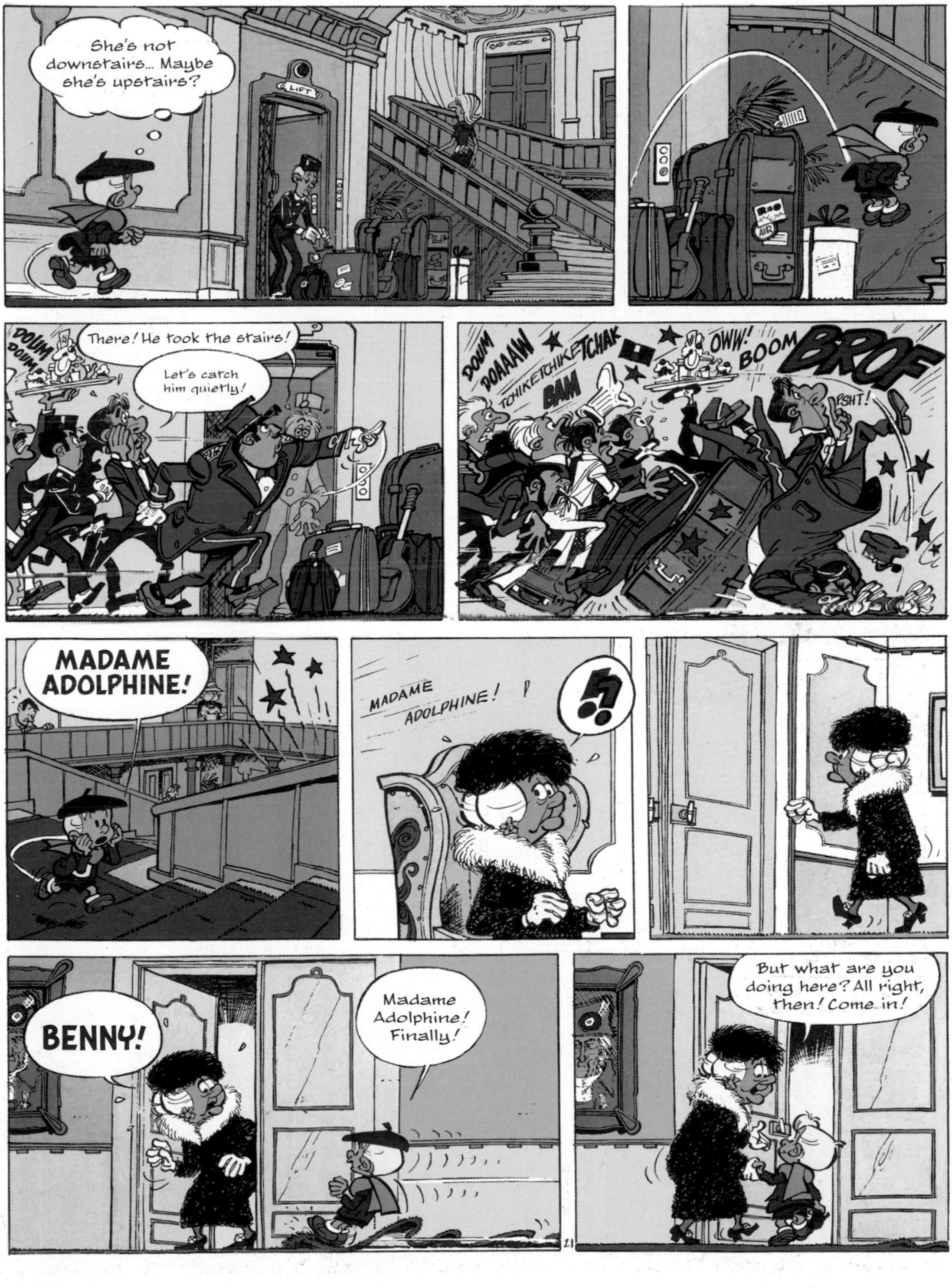
She's not downstairs... Maybe she's upstairs?
LIFT
DOUM DOUM
There! He took the stairs!
Let's catch him quietly!
DOUM DOAAAW TCHIKETCHIKETCHAK BAM OWW! BOOM BROF
PSHT!
MADAME ADOLPHINE!
MADAME ADOLPHINE!
BENNY!
Madame Adolphine! Finally!
But what are you doing here? All right, then! Come in!

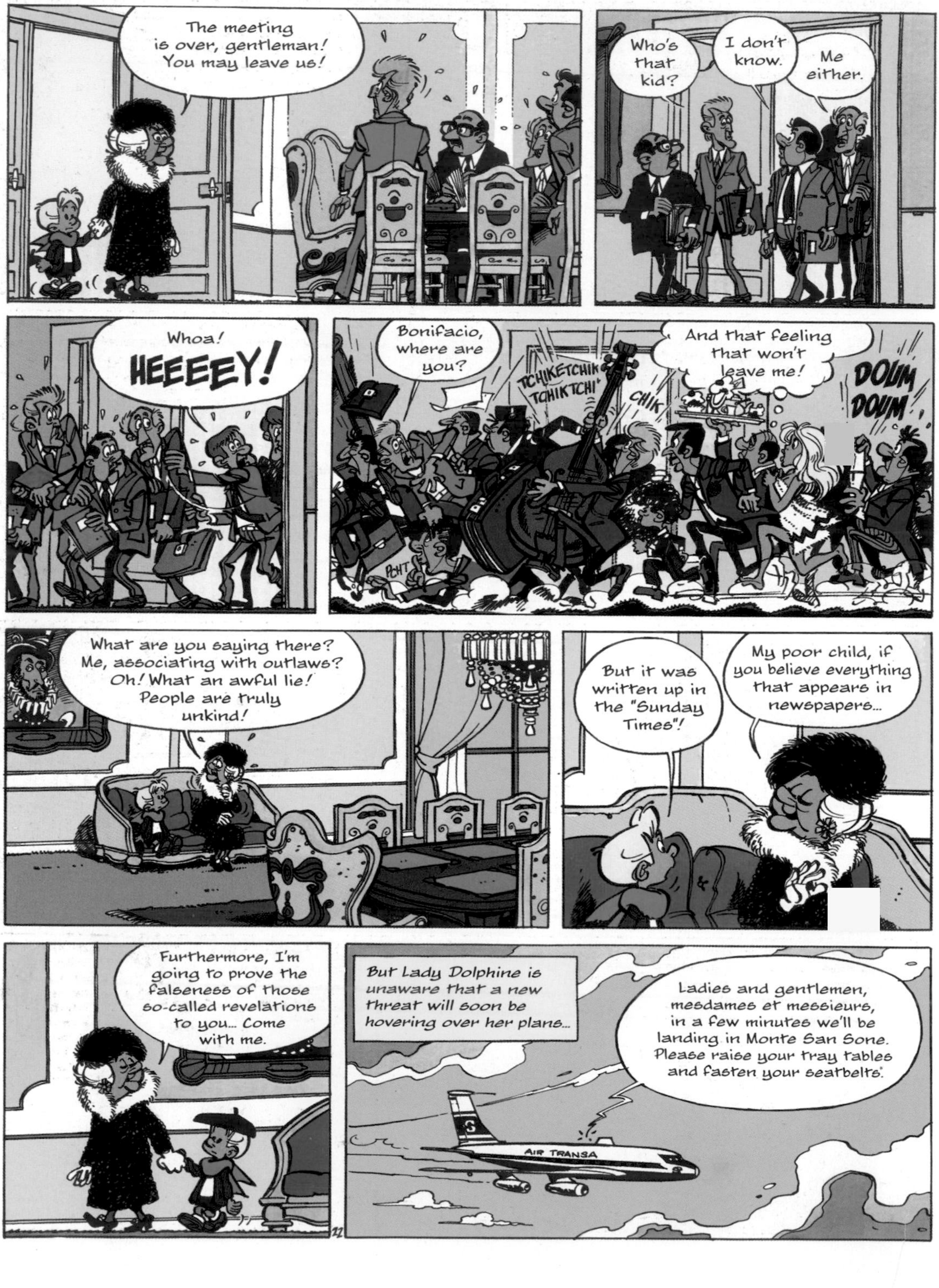

The meeting is over, gentleman! You may leave us!
Who's that kid?
I don't know.
Me either.
Whoa! HEEEEY!
Bonifacio, where are you?
TCHIKETCHIK TCHIKTCHI
CHIK
And that feeling that won't leave me!
DOUM DOUM
PCHT
What are you saying there? Me, associating with outlaws? Oh! What an awful lie! People are truly unkind!
But it was written up in the "Sunday Times"!
My poor child, if you believe everything that appears in newspapers...
Furthermore, I'm going to prove the falseness of those so-called revelations to you... Come with me.
But Lady Dolphine is unaware that a new threat will soon be hovering over her plans...
Ladies and gentlemen, mesdames et messieurs, in a few minutes we'll be landing in Monte San Sone. Please raise your tray tables and fasten your seatbelts.
AIR TRANSA

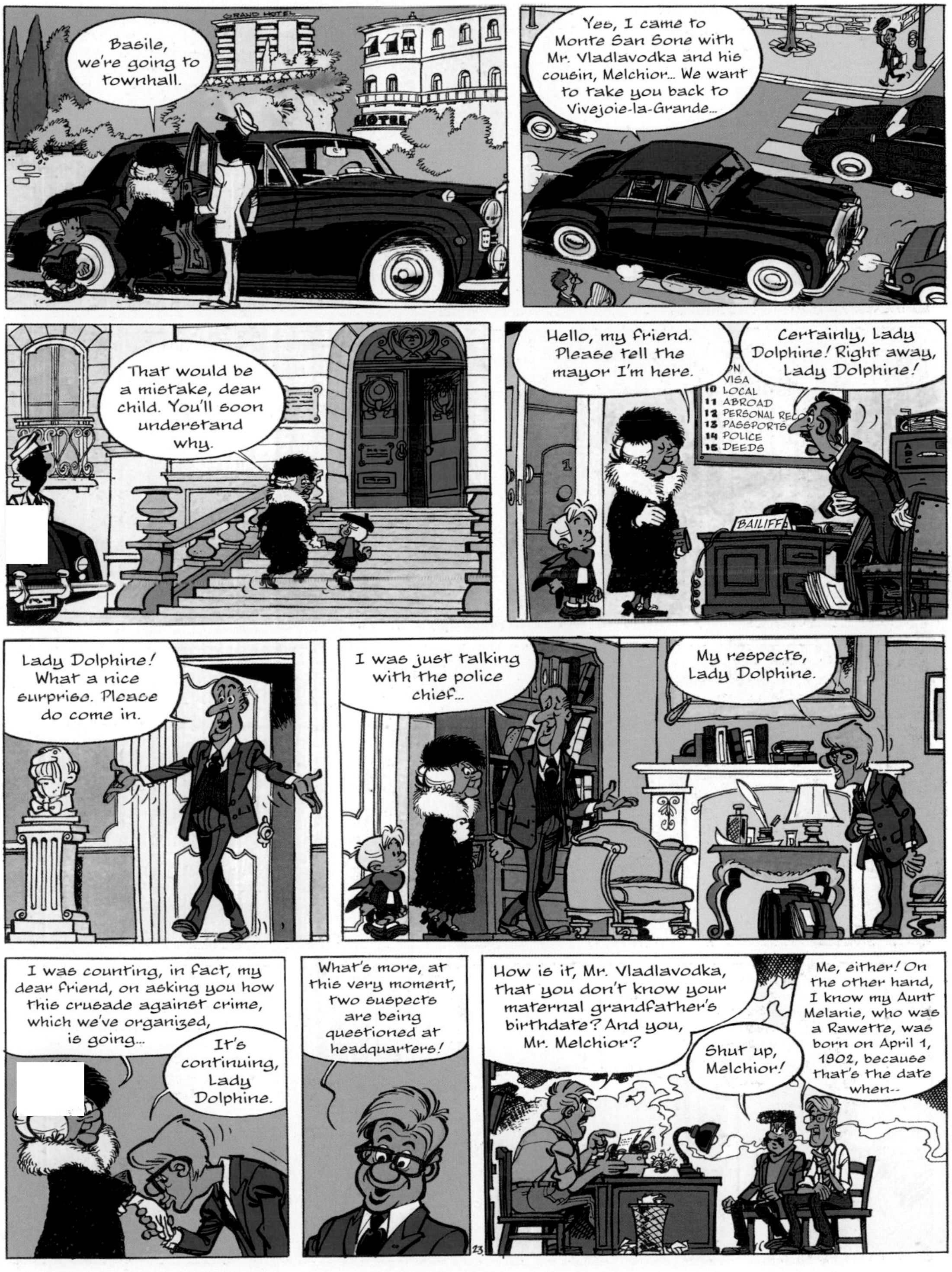
GRAND HOTEL
Basile, we're going to townhall.
HOTEL
Yes, I came to Monte San Sone with Mr. Vladlavodka and his cousin, Melchior... We want to take you back to Vivejoie-la-Grande...
That would be a mistake, dear child. You'll soon understand why.
Hello, my friend. Please tell the mayor I'm here.
Certainly, Lady Dolphine! Right away, Lady Dolphine!
VISA
10 LOCAL
11 ABROAD
12 PERSONAL
13 PASSPORTS
14 POLICE
15 DEEDS
BAILIFF
Lady Dolphine! What a nice surprise. Please do come in.
I was just talking with the police chief...
My respects, Lady Dolphine.
I was counting, in fact, my dear friend, on asking you how this crusade against crime, which we've organized, is going...
It's continuing, Lady Dolphine.
What's more, at this very moment, two suspects are being questioned at headquarters!
23
How is it, Mr. Vladlavodka, that you don't know your maternal grandfather's birthdate? And you, Mr. Melchior?
Shut up, Melchior!
Me, either! On the other hand, I know my Aunt Melanie, who was a Rawette, was born on April 1, 1902, because that's the date when--

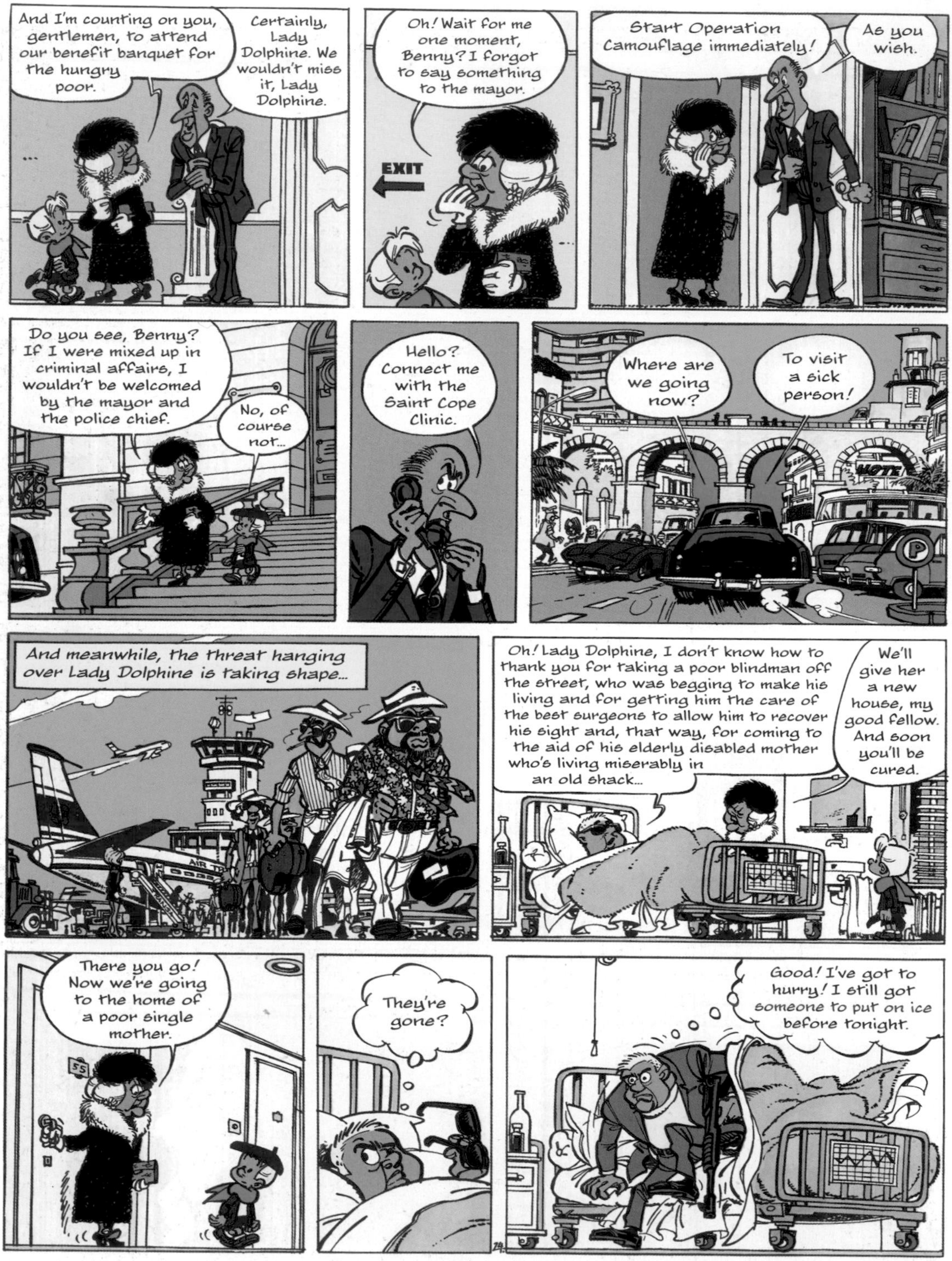

And I'm counting on you, gentlemen, to attend our benefit banquet for the hungry poor.
Certainly, Lady Dolphine. We wouldn't miss it, Lady Dolphine.
...
Oh! Wait for me one moment, Benny? I forgot to say something to the mayor.
EXIT
Start Operation Camouflage immediately!
As you wish.
Do you see, Benny? If I were mixed up in criminal affairs, I wouldn't be welcomed by the mayor and the police chief.
No, of course not...
Hello? Connect me with the Saint Cope Clinic.
Where are we going now?
To visit a sick person!
And meanwhile, the threat hanging over Lady Dolphine is taking shape...
Oh! Lady Dolphine, I don't know how to thank you for taking a poor blindman off the street, who was begging to make his living and for getting him the care of the best surgeons to allow him to recover his sight and, that way, for coming to the aid of his elderly disabled mother who's living miserably in an old shack...
We'll give her a new house, my good fellow. And soon you'll be cured.
There you go! Now we're going to the home of a poor single mother.
55
They're gone?
Good! I've got to hurry! I still got someone to put on ice before tonight.

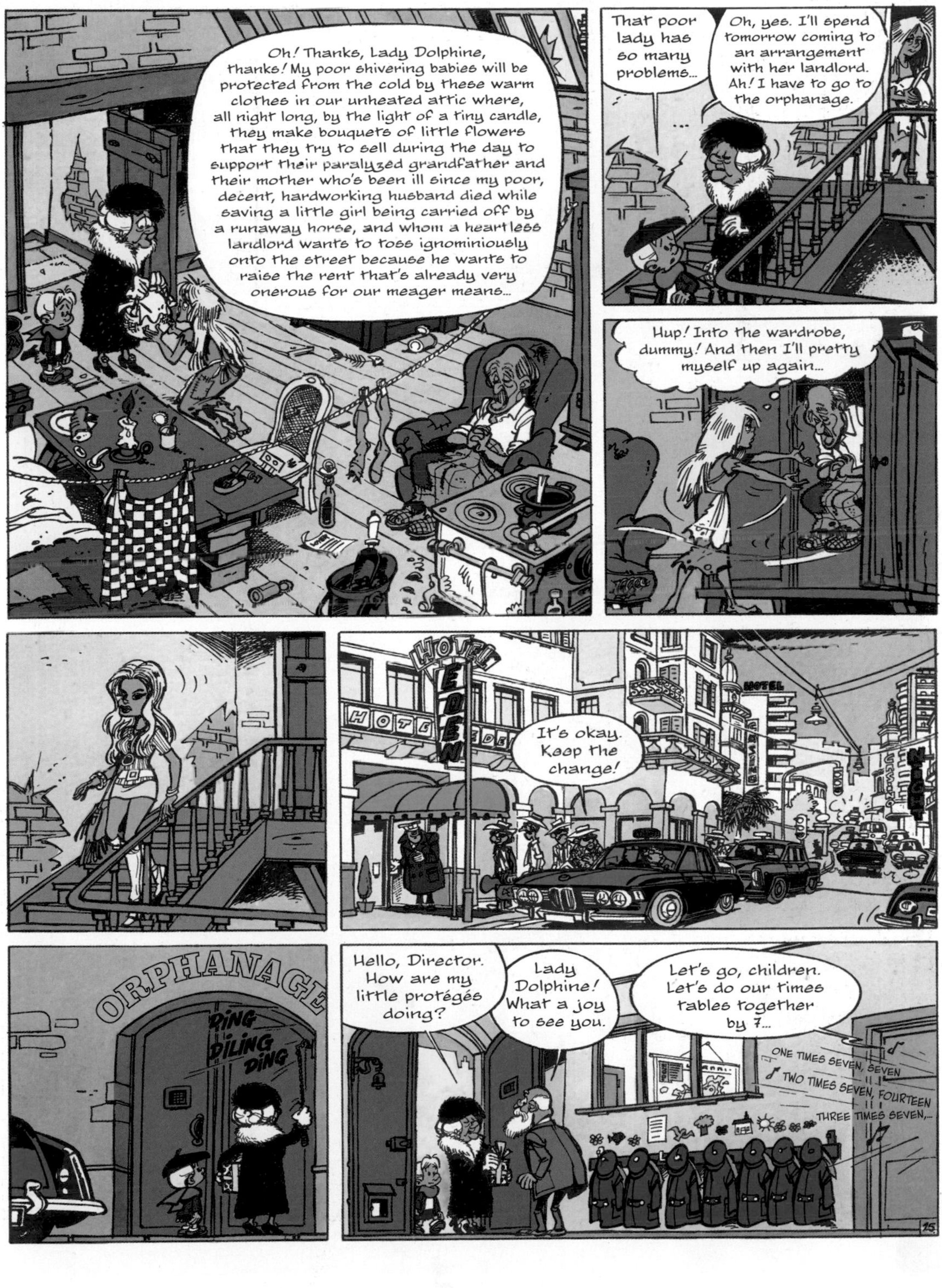

Oh! Thanks, Lady Dolphine, thanks! My poor shivering babies will be protected from the cold by these warm clothes in our unheated attic where, all night long, by the light of a tiny candle, they make bouquets of little flowers that they try to sell during the day to support their paralyzed grandfather and their mother who's been ill since my poor, decent, hardworking husband died while saving a little girl being carried off by a runaway horse, and whom a heartless landlord wants to toss ignominiously onto the street because he wants to raise the rent that's already very onerous for our meager means...
That poor lady has so many problems...
...
Oh, yes. I'll spend tomorrow coming to an arrangement with her landlord. Ah! I have to go to the orphanage.
Hup! Into the wardrobe, dummy! And then I'll pretty myself up again...
HOTEL
EDEN
HOTEL
It's okay. Keep the change!
ORPHANAGE
DING
DILING
DING
Hello, Director. How are my little protégés doing?
Lady Dolphine! What a joy to see you.
Let's go, children. Let's do our times tables together by 7...
ONE TIMES SEVEN, SEVEN
TWO TIMES SEVEN, FOURTEEN
THREE TIMES SEVEN,...

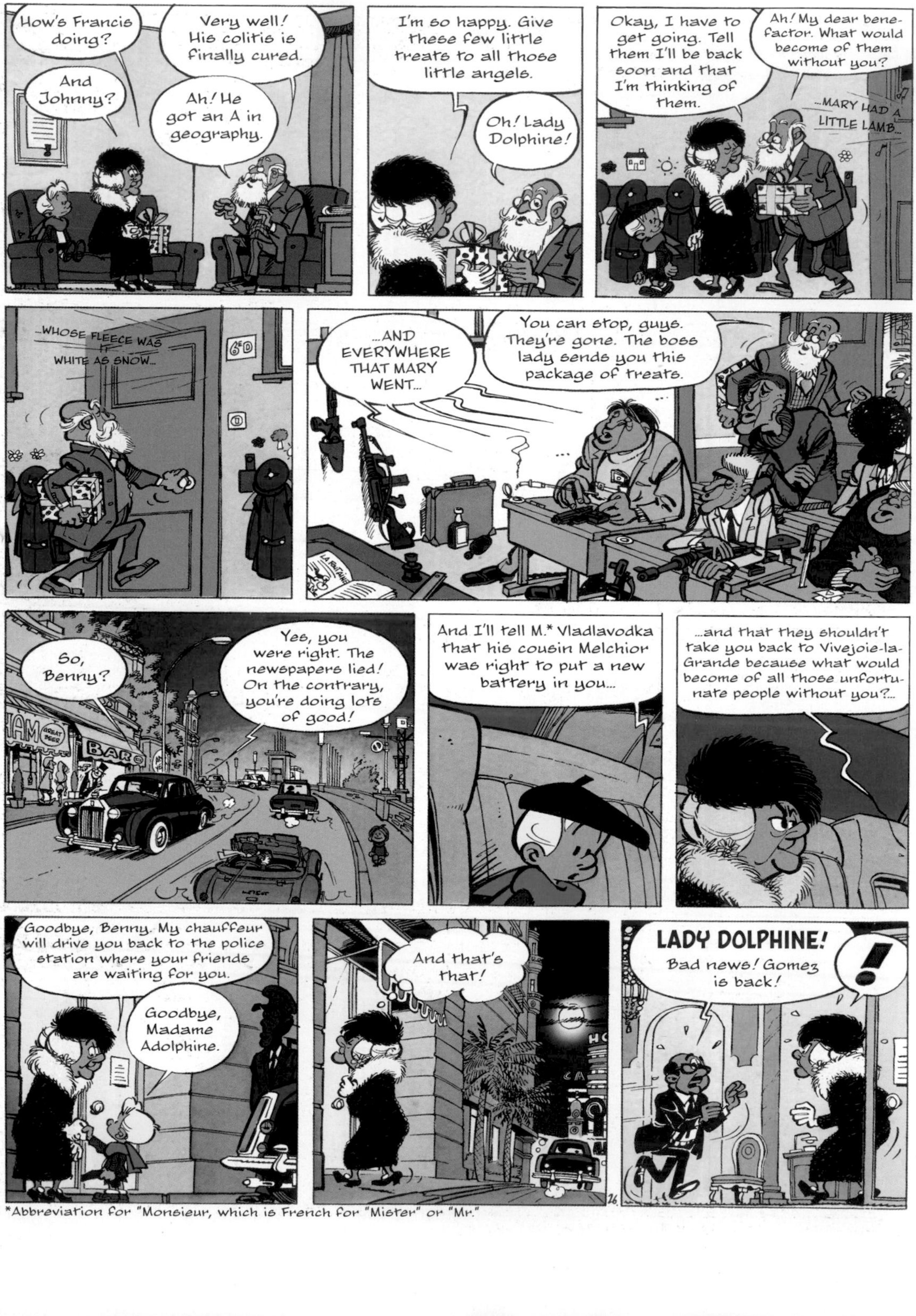
How's Francis doing?
Very well! His colitis is finally cured.
And Johnny?
Ah! He got an A in geography.
I'm so happy. Give these few little treats to all those little angels.
Oh! Lady Dolphine!
Okay, I have to get going. Tell them I'll be back soon and that I'm thinking of them.
Ah! My dear benefactor. What would become of them without you?
...MARY HAD A LITTLE LAMB...
...WHOSE FLEECE WAS WHITE AS SNOW...
...AND EVERYWHERE THAT MARY WENT...
You can stop, guys. They're gone. The boss lady sends you this package of treats.
So, Benny?
Yes, you were right. The newspapers lied! On the contrary, you're doing lots of good!
And I'll tell M.* Vladlavodka that his cousin Melchior was right to put a new battery in you...
...and that they shouldn't take you back to Vivejoie-la-Grande because what would become of all those unfortunate people without you?...
Goodbye, Benny. My chauffeur will drive you back to the police station where your friends are waiting for you.
Goodbye, Madame Adolphine.
And that's that!
LADY DOLPHINE!
Bad news! Gomez is back!
!

*Abbreviation for "Monsieur, which is French for "Mister" or "Mr."

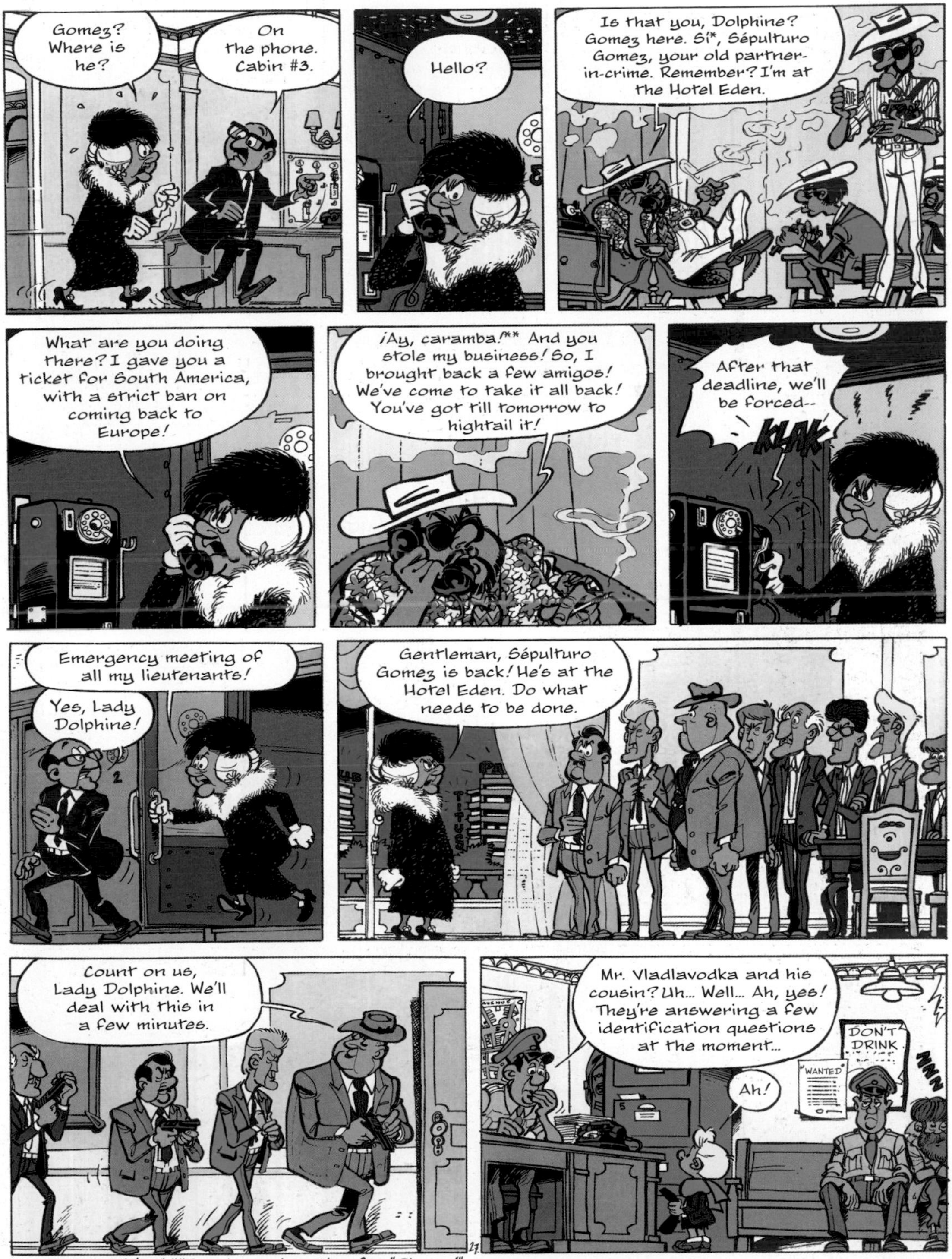
Gomez? Where is he?
On the phone. Cabin #3.
Hello?
Is that you, Dolphine? Gomez here. Sí*, Sépulturo Gomez, your old partner-in-crime. Remember? I'm at the Hotel Eden.
What are you doing there? I gave you a ticket for South America, with a strict ban on coming back to Europe!
¡Ay, caramba!** And you stole my business! So, I brought back a few amigos! We've come to take it all back! You've got till tomorrow to hightail it!
After that deadline, we'll be forced--
KLAK
Emergency meeting of all my lieutenants!
Yes, Lady Dolphine!
Gentleman, Sépulturo Gomez is back! He's at the Hotel Eden. Do what needs to be done.
Count on us, Lady Dolphine. We'll deal with this in a few minutes.
Mr. Vladlavodka and his cousin? Uh... Well... Ah, yes! They're answering a few identification questions at the moment...
DON'T DRINK
WANTED
Ah!
MMN

*Spanish for "Yes." **Spanish exclamation for "Oh, no!"

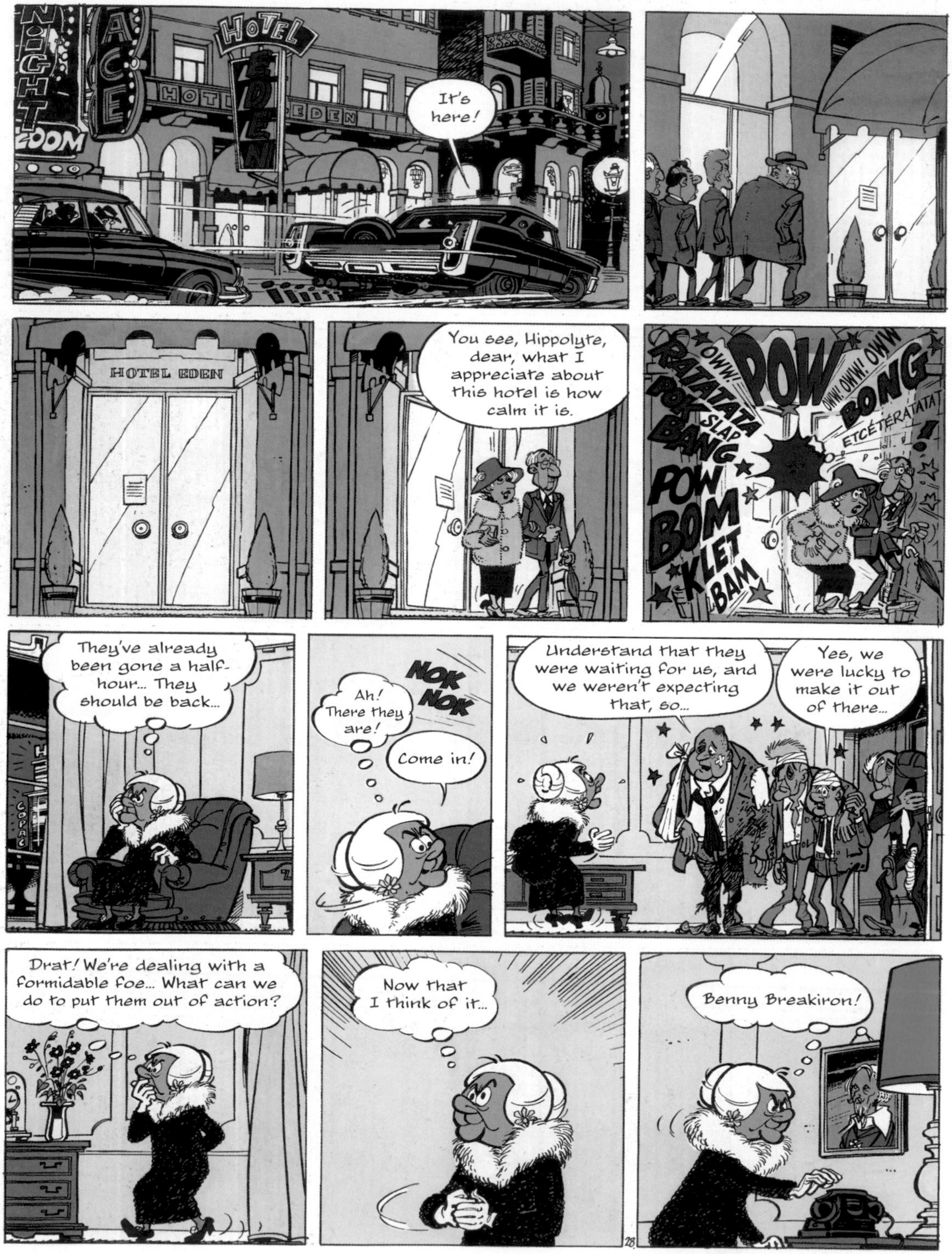

HOTEL EDEN
It's here!
HOTEL EDEN
You see, Hippolyte, dear, what I appreciate about this hotel is how calm it is.
RATATATATA
OWW!
POW
OWW! OWW! OWW
BONG
POK
SLAP
BANG
ETCÉTERATATAT
POW
BOM
KLET
BAM
They've already been gone a half-hour... They should be back...
NOK NOK
Ah! There they are!
Come in!
Understand that they were waiting for us, and we weren't expecting that, so...
Yes, we were lucky to make it out of there...
Drat! We're dealing with a formidable foe... What can we do to put them out of action?
Now that I think of it...
Benny Breakiron!

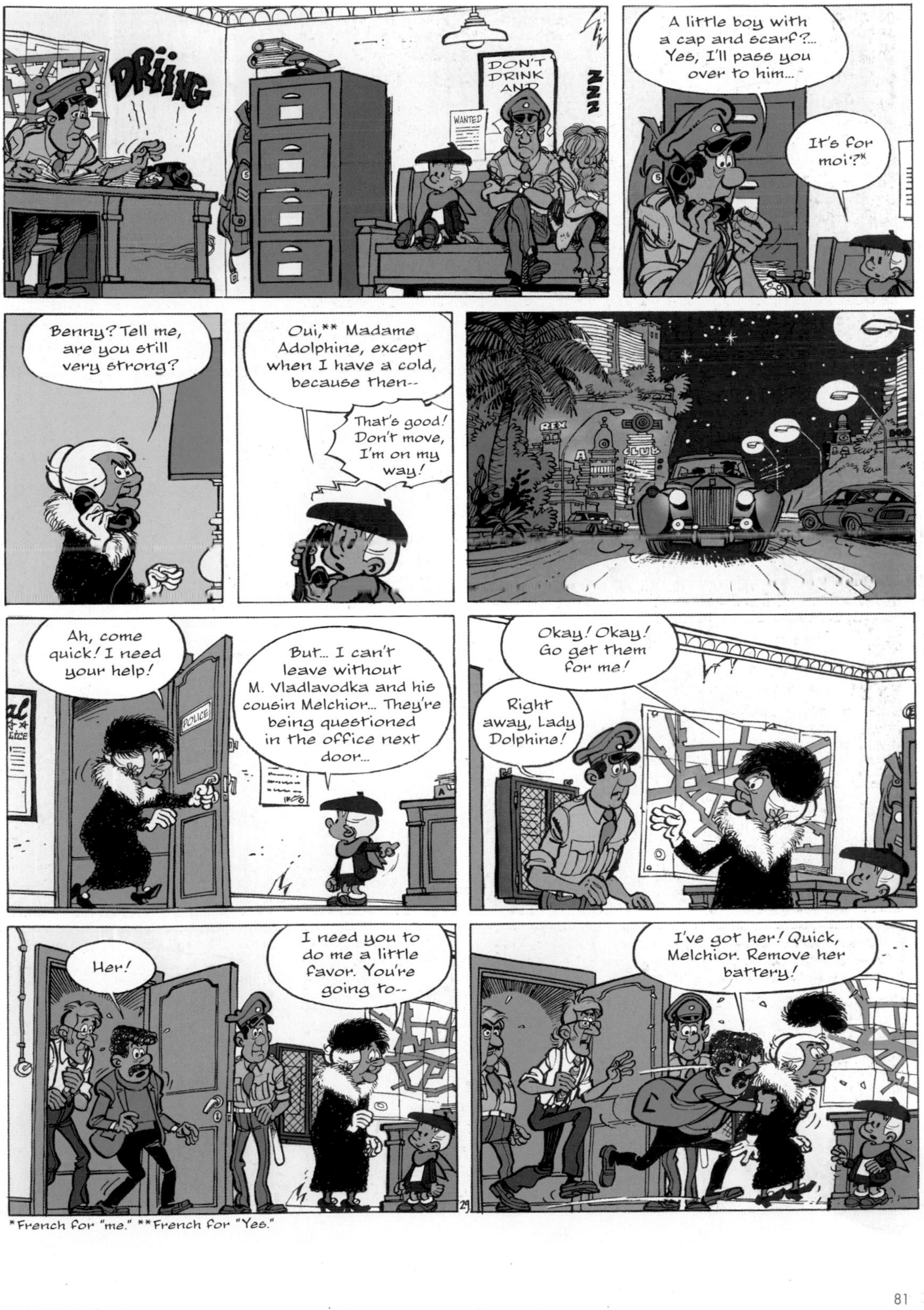
DRIIING
DON'T DRINK AND
WANTED
ZZZ
A little boy with a cap and scarf?... Yes, I'll pass you over to him...
It's for moi?*
Benny? Tell me, are you still very strong?
Oui,** Madame Adolphine, except when I have a cold, because then--
That's good! Don't move, I'm on my way!
REX
CLUB
Ah, come quick! I need your help!
POLICE
But... I can't leave without M. Vladlavodka and his cousin Melchior... They're being questioned in the office next door...
Okay! Okay! Go get them for me!
Right away, Lady Dolphine!
Her!
I need you to do me a little favor. You're going to--
I've got her! Quick, Melchior. Remove her battery!

*French for "me." **French for "Yes."

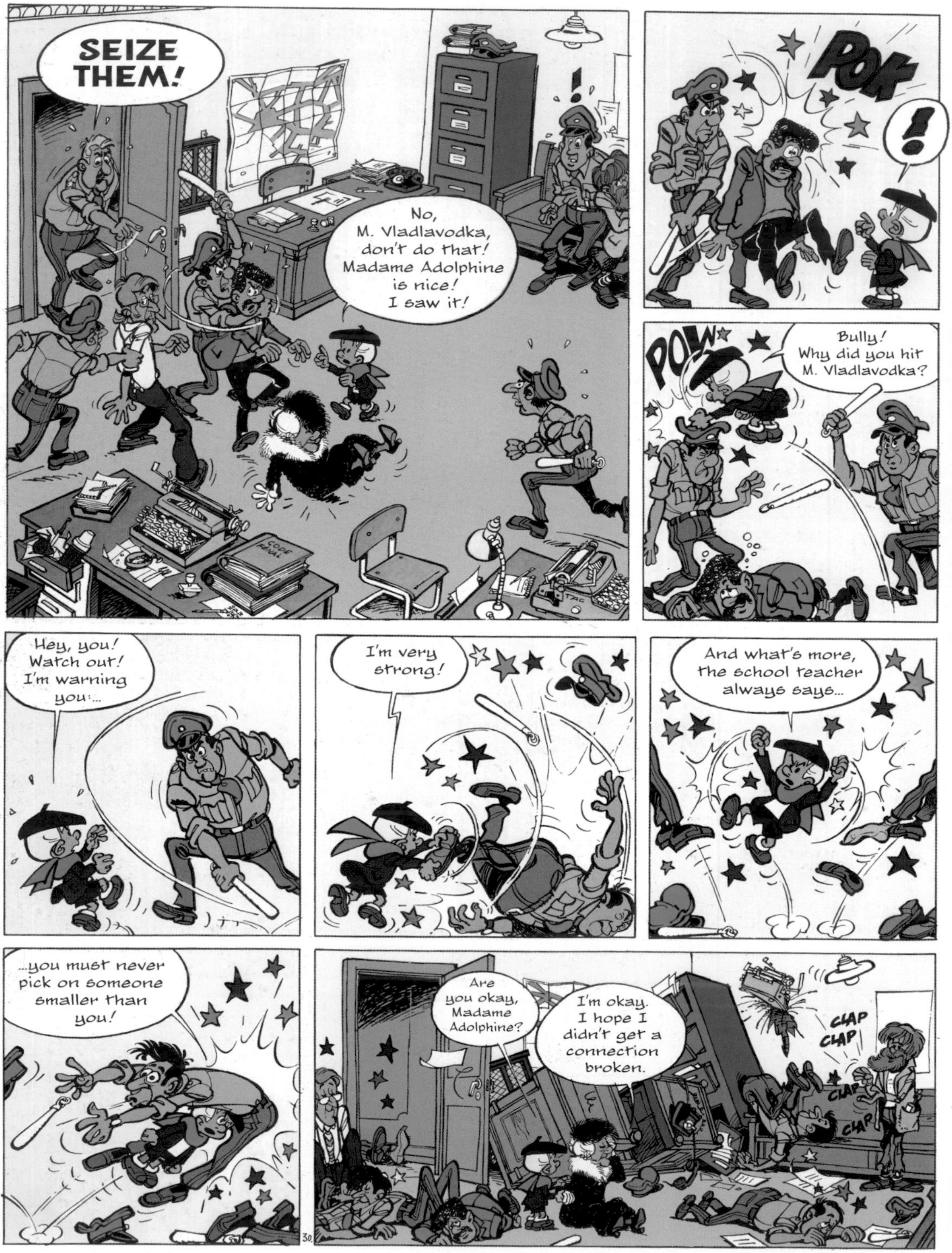
SEIZE THEM!
!
No, M. Vladlavodka, don't do that! Madame Adolphine is nice! I saw it!
POK
!
POW
Bully! Why did you hit M. Vladlavodka?
Hey, you! Watch out! I'm warning you:...
I'm very strong!
And what's more, the school teacher always says...
...you must never pick on someone smaller than you!
Are you okay, Madame Adolphine?
I'm okay. I hope I didn't get a connection broken.
CLAP
CLAP
CLAP
CLAP

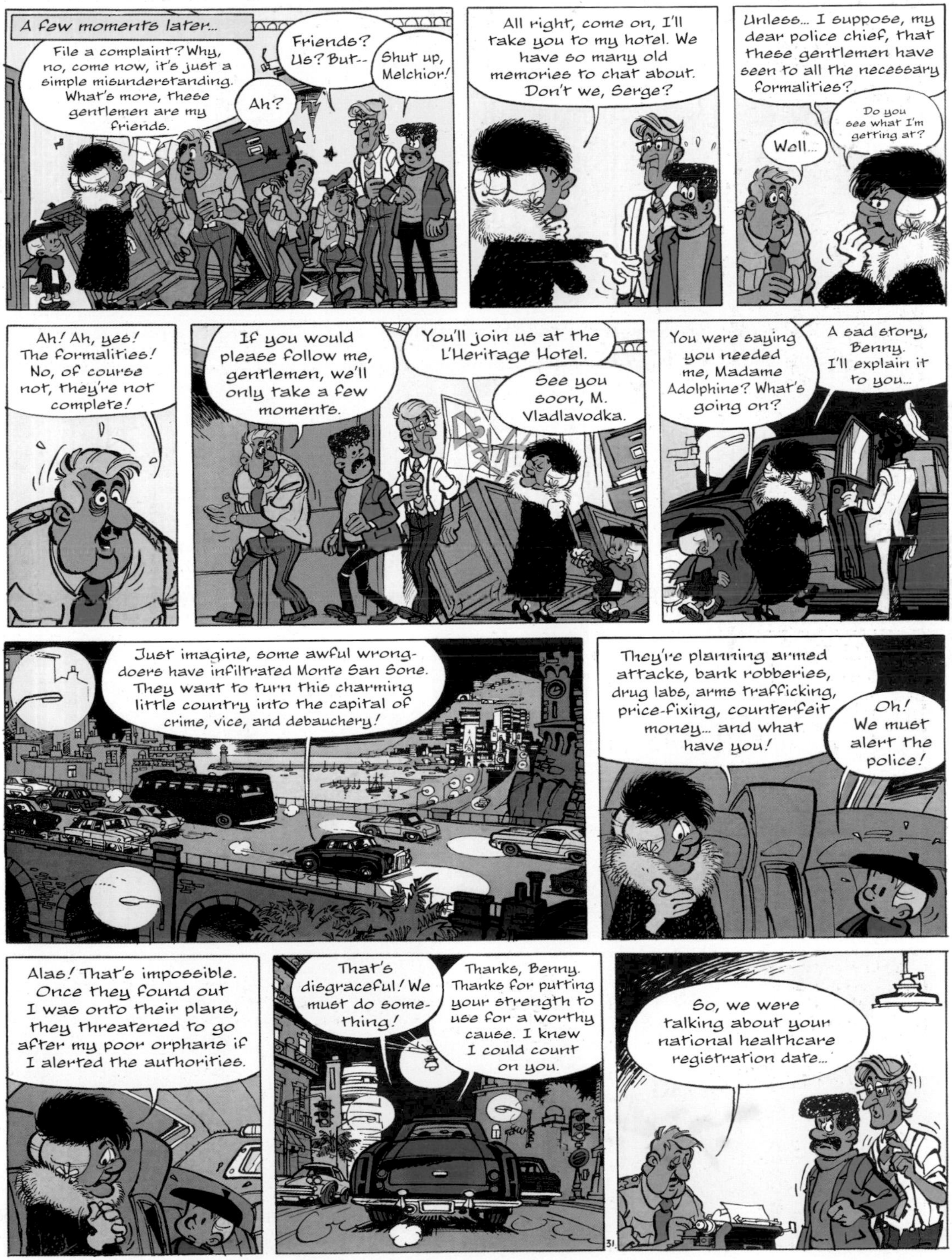
A few moments later...
File a complaint? Why, no, come now, it's just a simple misunderstanding. What's more, these gentlemen are my friends.
Ah?
Friends? Us? But--
Shut up, Melchior!
All right, come on, I'll take you to my hotel. We have so many old memories to chat about. Don't we, Serge?
Unless... I suppose, my dear police chief, that these gentlemen have seen to all the necessary formalities?
Well...
Do you see what I'm getting at?
Ah! Ah, yes! The formalities! No, of course not, they're not complete!
If you would please follow me, gentlemen, we'll only take a few moments.
You'll join us at the L'Heritage Hotel.
See you soon, M. Vladlavodka.
You were saying you needed me, Madame Adolphine? What's going on?
A sad story, Benny. I'll explain it to you...
Just imagine, some awful wrong-doers have infiltrated Monte San Sone. They want to turn this charming little country into the capital of crime, vice, and debauchery!
They're planning armed attacks, bank robberies, drug labs, arms trafficking, price-fixing, counterfeit money... and what have you!
Oh! We must alert the police!
Alas! That's impossible. Once they found out I was onto their plans, they threatened to go after my poor orphans if I alerted the authorities.
That's disgraceful! We must do something!
Thanks, Benny. Thanks for putting your strength to use for a worthy cause. I knew I could count on you.
31.
So, we were talking about your national healthcare registration date...

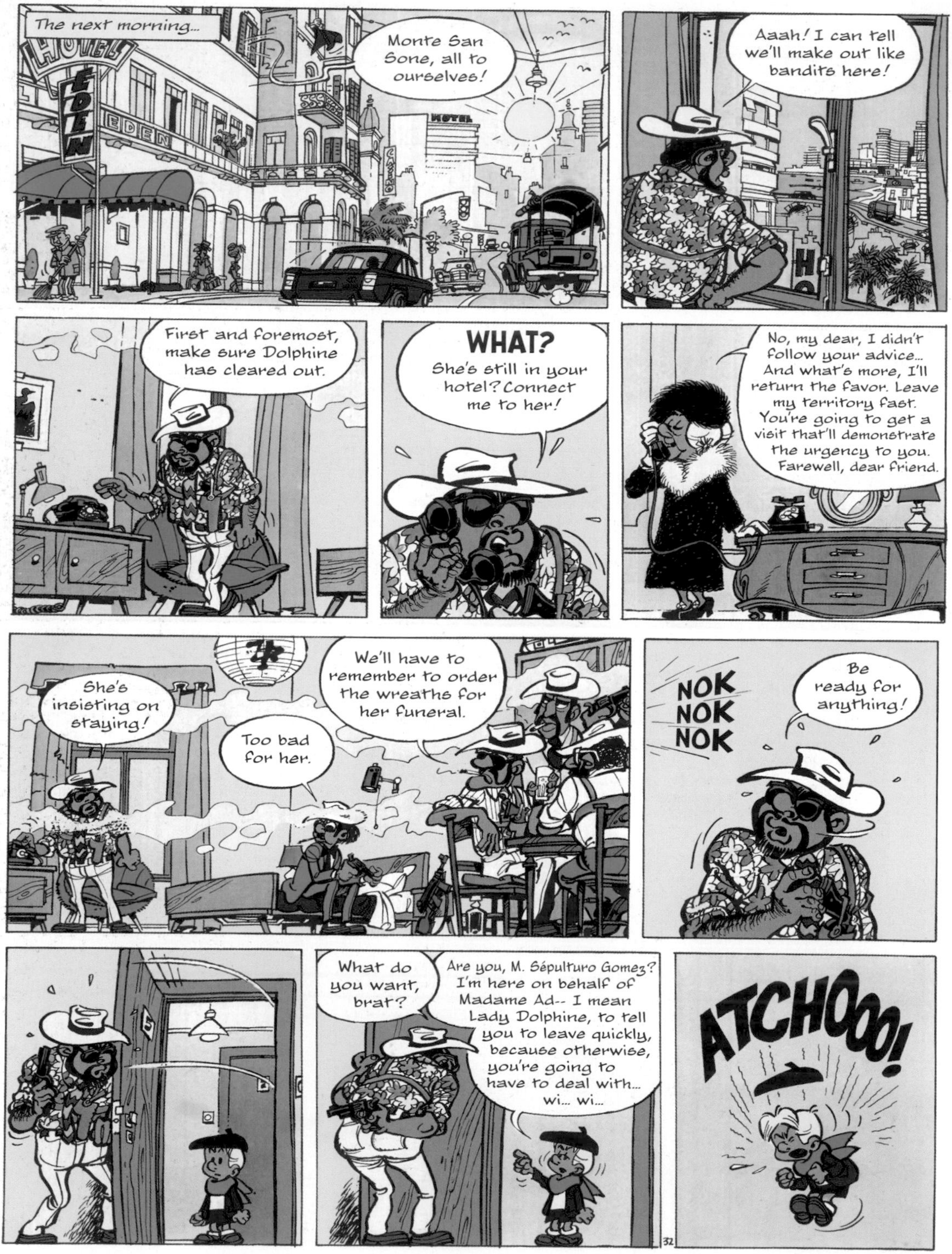
The next morning...
HOTEL
EDEN
Monte San Sone, all to ourselves!
Aaah! I can tell we'll make out like bandits here!
First and foremost, make sure Dolphine has cleared out.
WHAT? She's still in your hotel? Connect me to her!
No, my dear, I didn't follow your advice... And what's more, I'll return the favor. Leave my territory fast. You're going to get a visit that'll demonstrate the urgency to you. Farewell, dear friend.
She's insisting on staying!
Too bad for her.
We'll have to remember to order the wreaths for her funeral.
NOK NOK NOK
Be ready for anything!
What do you want, brat?
Are you, M. Sépulturo Gomez? I'm here on behalf of Madame Ad-- I mean Lady Dolphine, to tell you to leave quickly, because otherwise, you're going to have to deal with... wi... wi...
32
ATCHOOO!

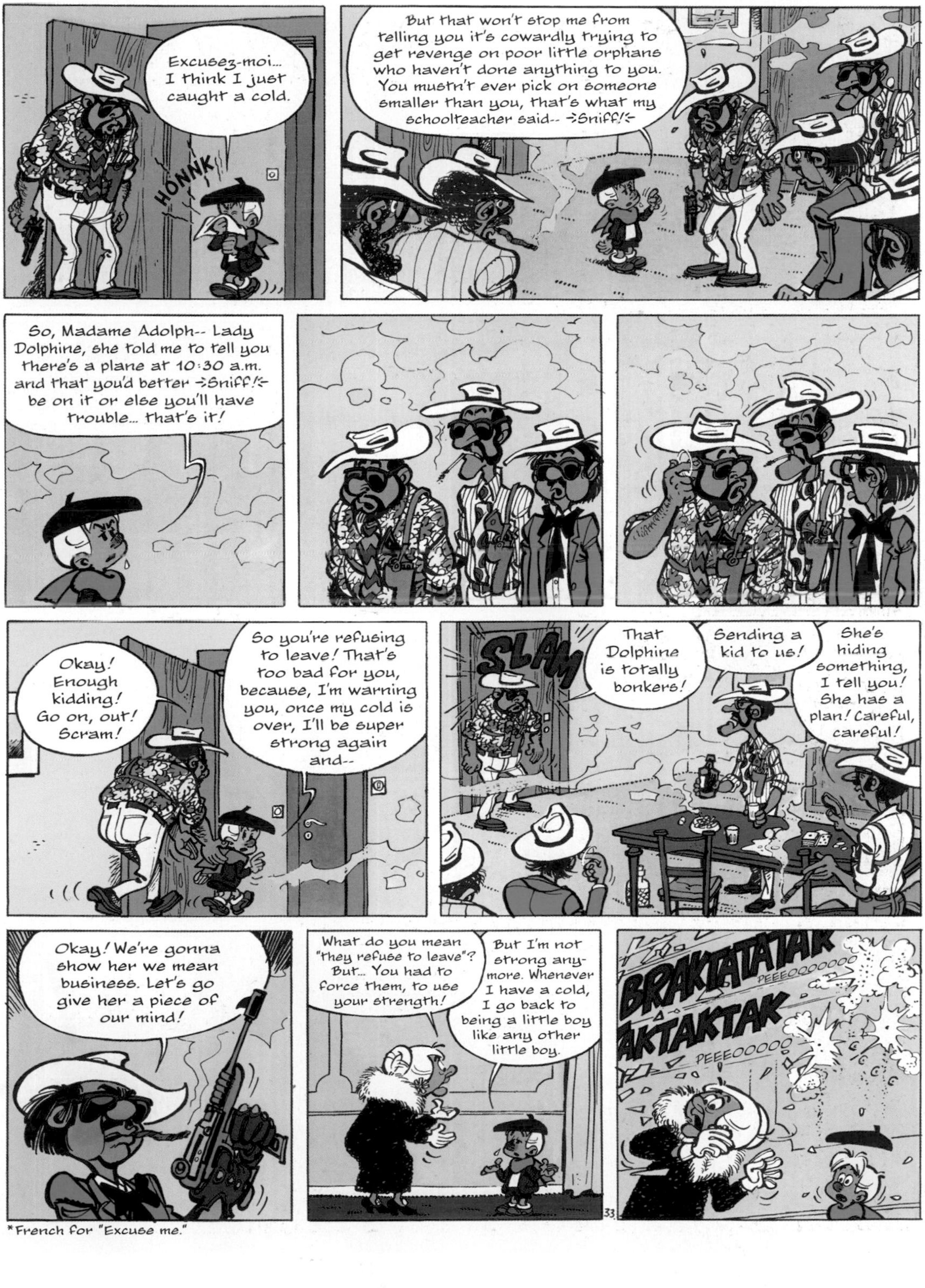

Excusez-moi... I think I just caught a cold.
HONNK
But that won't stop me from telling you it's cowardly trying to get revenge on poor little orphans who haven't done anything to you. You mustn't ever pick on someone smaller than you, that's what my schoolteacher said-- →Sniff!←
So, Madame Adolph-- Lady Dolphine, she told me to tell you there's a plane at 10:30 a.m. and that you'd better →Sniff!← be on it or else you'll have trouble... that's it!
Okay! Enough kidding! Go on, out! Scram!
So you're refusing to leave! That's too bad for you, because, I'm warning you, once my cold is over, I'll be super strong again and--
SLAM
That Dolphine is totally bonkers!
Sending a kid to us!
She's hiding something, I tell you! She has a plan! Careful, careful!
Okay! We're gonna show her we mean business. Let's go give her a piece of our mind!
What do you mean "they refuse to leave"? But... You had to force them, to use your strength!
But I'm not strong any-more. Whenever I have a cold, I go back to being a little boy like any other little boy.
BRAKTATATAK
AKTAKTAK
PEEEOOOOOOO
PEEEOOOOO

*French for "Excuse me."

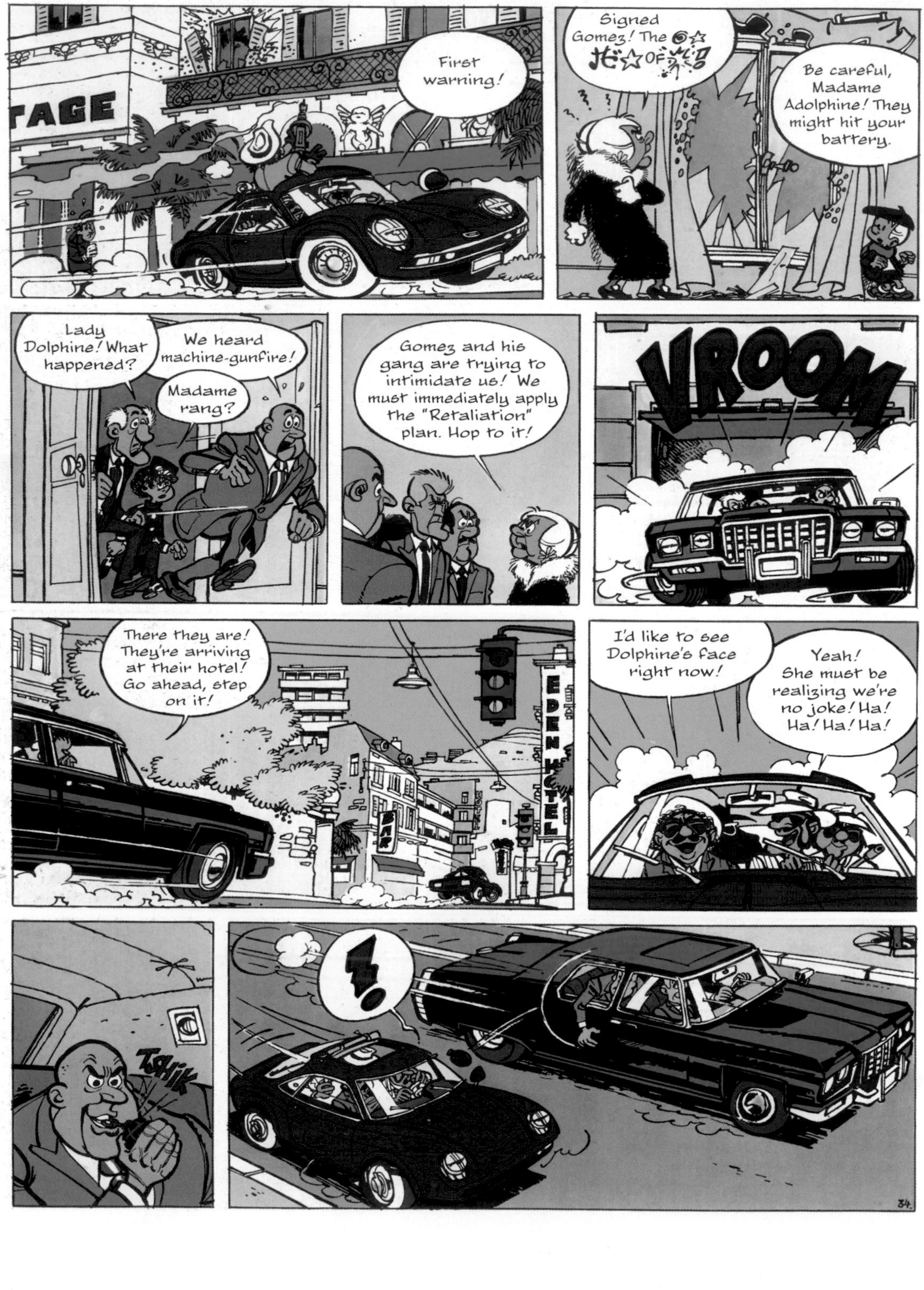

TAGE
First warning!
Signed Gomez! The
Be careful, Madame Adolphine! They might hit your battery.
Lady Dolphine! What happened?
We heard machine-gunfire!
Madame rang?
Gomez and his gang are trying to intimidate us! We must immediately apply the "Retaliation" plan. Hop to it!
VROOM
There they are! They're arriving at their hotel! Go ahead, step on it!
EDEN HOTEL
BAR
I'd like to see Dolphine's face right now!
Yeah! She must be realizing we're no joke! Ha! Ha! Ha! Ha!
TSHIK
34.

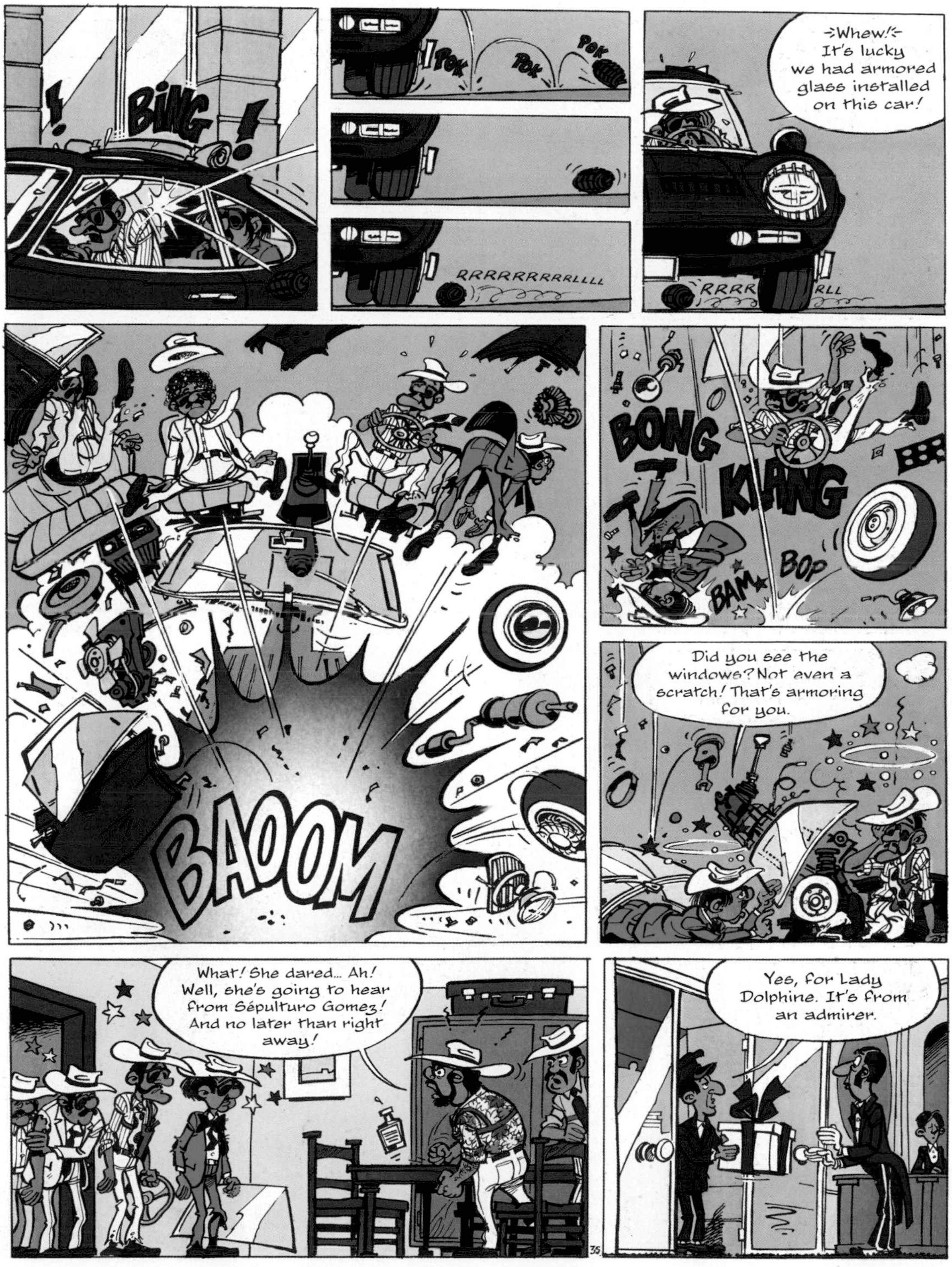
BING
POK
POK
POK
RRRRRRRRRLLLL
Whew! It's lucky we had armored glass installed on this car!
RRRR RLL
BAOOM
BONG
KLANG
BAM
BOP
Did you see the windows? Not even a scratch! That's armoring for you.
What! She dared... Ah! Well, she's going to hear from Sépulturo Gomez! And no later than right away!
Yes, for Lady Dolphine. It's from an admirer.

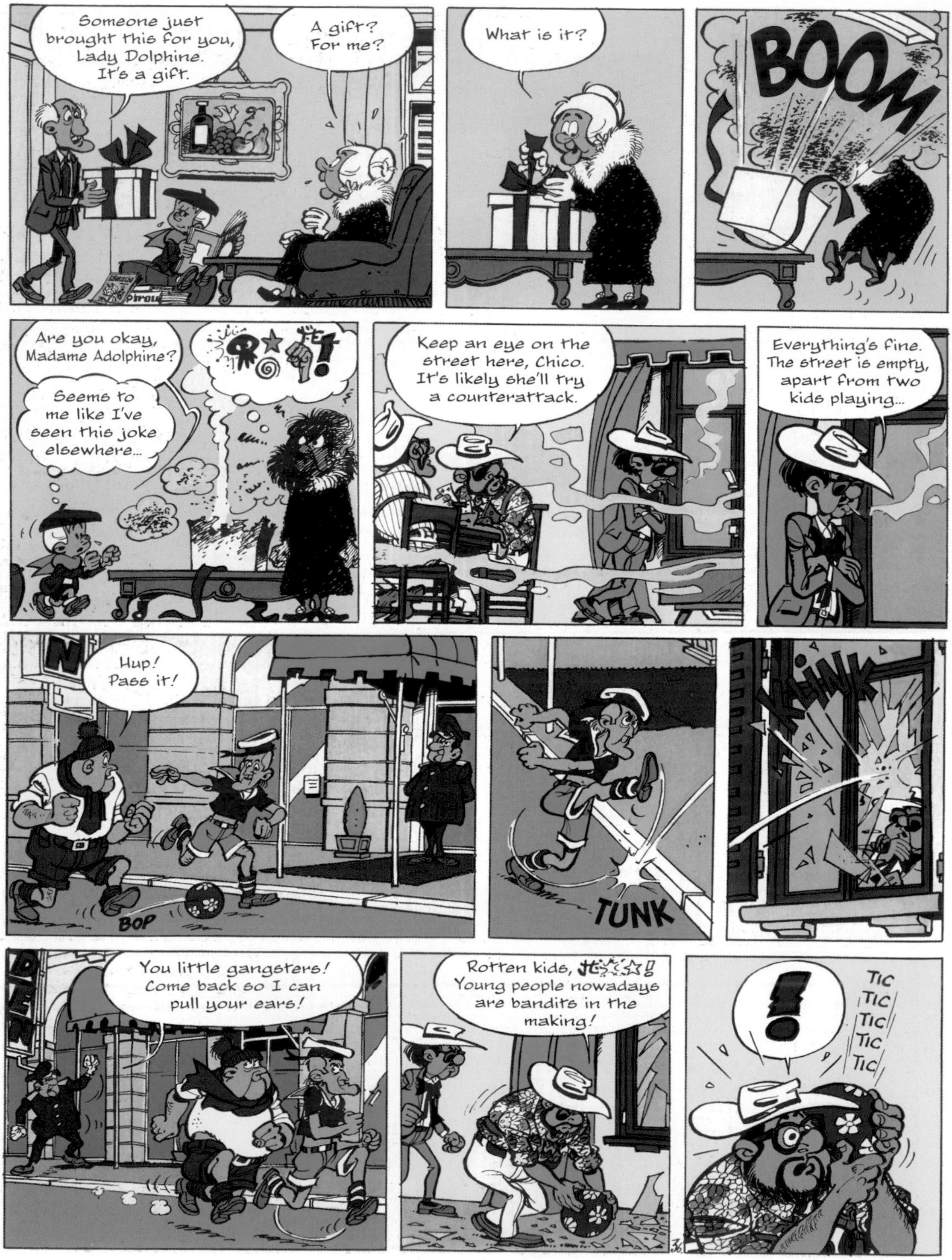

Someone just brought this for you, Lady Dolphine. It's a gift.
A gift? For me?
What is it?
BOOM
Are you okay, Madame Adolphine?
Seems to me like I've seen this joke elsewhere...
Keep an eye on the street here, Chico. It's likely she'll try a counterattack.
Everything's fine. The street is empty, apart from two kids playing...
Hup! Pass it!
BOP
TUNK
You little gangsters! Come back so I can pull your ears!
Rotten kids, Young people nowadays are bandits in the making!
!
TIC TIC TIC TIC TIC

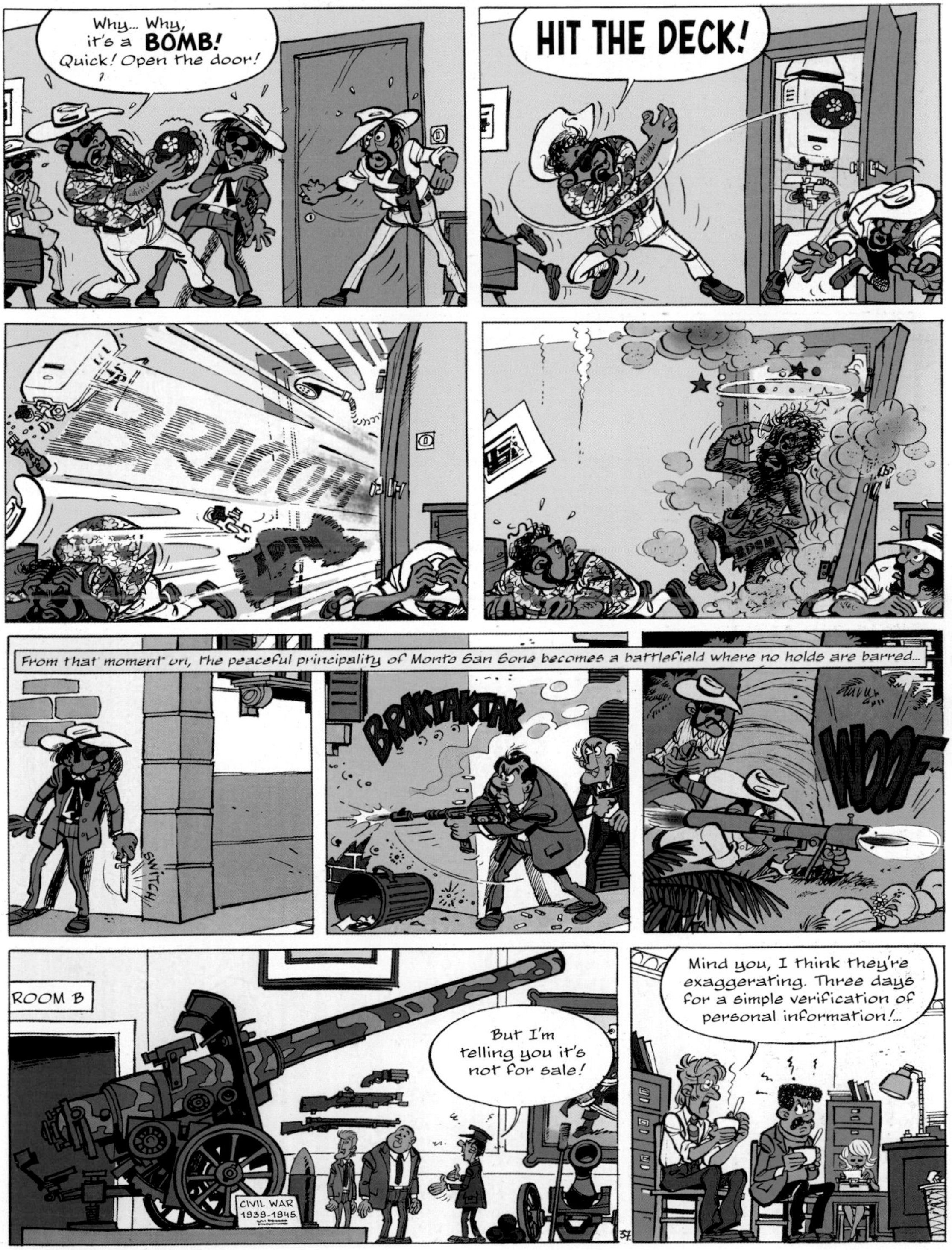
Why... Why, it's a BOMB! Quick! Open the door!
HIT THE DECK!
BRAOOM
From that moment on, the peaceful principality of Monte San Sone becomes a battlefield where no holds are barred...
SWITCH
BRAKTAKTAK
WOOF
ROOM B
CIVIL WAR 1939-1945
But I'm telling you it's not for sale!
Mind you, I think they're exaggerating. Three days for a simple verification of personal information!...

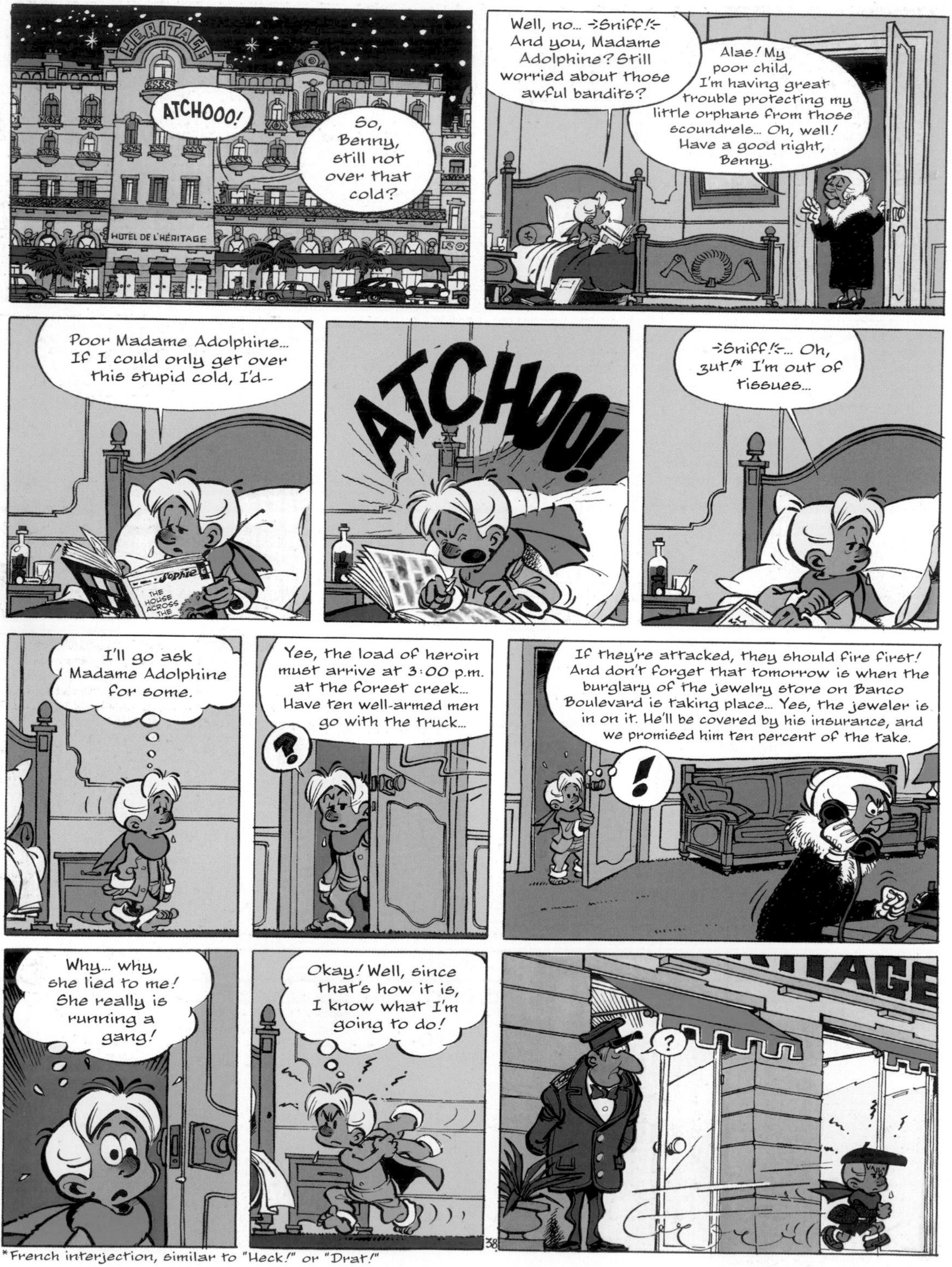
HERITAGE
HOTEL DE L'HÉRITAGE
ATCHOOO!
So, Benny, still not over that cold?
Well, no... ->Sniff!<- And you, Madame Adolphine? Still worried about those awful bandits?
Alas! My poor child, I'm having great trouble protecting my little orphans from those scoundrels... Oh, well! Have a good night, Benny.
Poor Madame Adolphine... If I could only get over this stupid cold, I'd--
Sophie
THE HOUSE ACROSS THE
ATCHOO!
->Sniff!<-... Oh, zut!* I'm out of tissues...
I'll go ask Madame Adolphine for some.
Yes, the load of heroin must arrive at 3:00 p.m. at the forest creek... Have ten well-armed men go with the truck...
?
If they're attacked, they should fire first! And don't forget that tomorrow is when the burglary of the jewelry store on Banco Boulevard is taking place... Yes, the jeweler is in on it. He'll be covered by his insurance, and we promised him ten percent of the take.
!
Why... why, she lied to me! She really is running a gang!
Okay! Well, since that's how it is, I know what I'm going to do!
ITAGE
?
38

*French interjection, similar to "Heck!" or "Drat!"

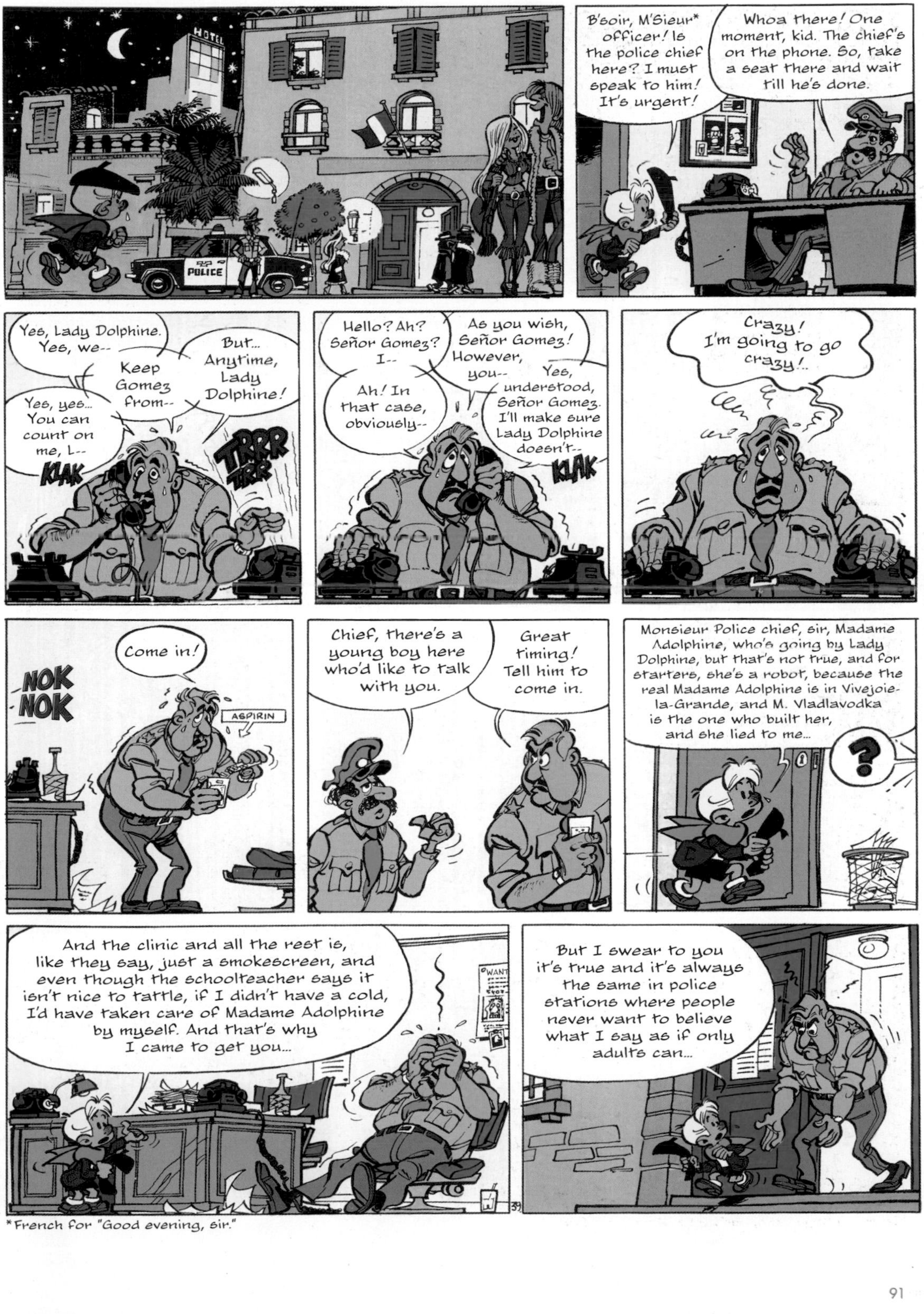
HOTEL
POLICE
B'soir, M'Sieur* officer! Is the police chief here? I must speak to him! It's urgent!
Whoa there! One moment, kid. The chief's on the phone. So, take a seat there and wait till he's done.
Yes, Lady Dolphine. Yes, we--
Keep Gomez from--
But... Anytime, Lady Dolphine!
Yes, yes... You can count on me, L--
KLAK
TRRR TRR
Hello? Ah? Señor Gomez? I--
As you wish, Señor Gomez! However, you--
Ah! In that case, obviously--
Yes, understood, Señor Gomez. I'll make sure Lady Dolphine doesn't--
KLAK
Crazy! I'm going to go crazy!..
NOK NOK
Come in!
ASPIRIN
Chief, there's a young boy here who'd like to talk with you.
Great timing! Tell him to come in.
Monsieur Police chief, sir, Madame Adolphine, who's going by Lady Dolphine, but that's not true, and for starters, she's a robot, because the real Madame Adolphine is in Vivejoie-la-Grande, and M. Vladlavodka is the one who built her, and she lied to me...
?
And the clinic and all the rest is, like they say, just a smokescreen, and even though the schoolteacher says it isn't nice to tattle, if I didn't have a cold, I'd have taken care of Madame Adolphine by myself. And that's why I came to get you...
But I swear to you it's true and it's always the same in police stations where people never want to believe what I say as if only adults can...

*French for "Good evening, sir."

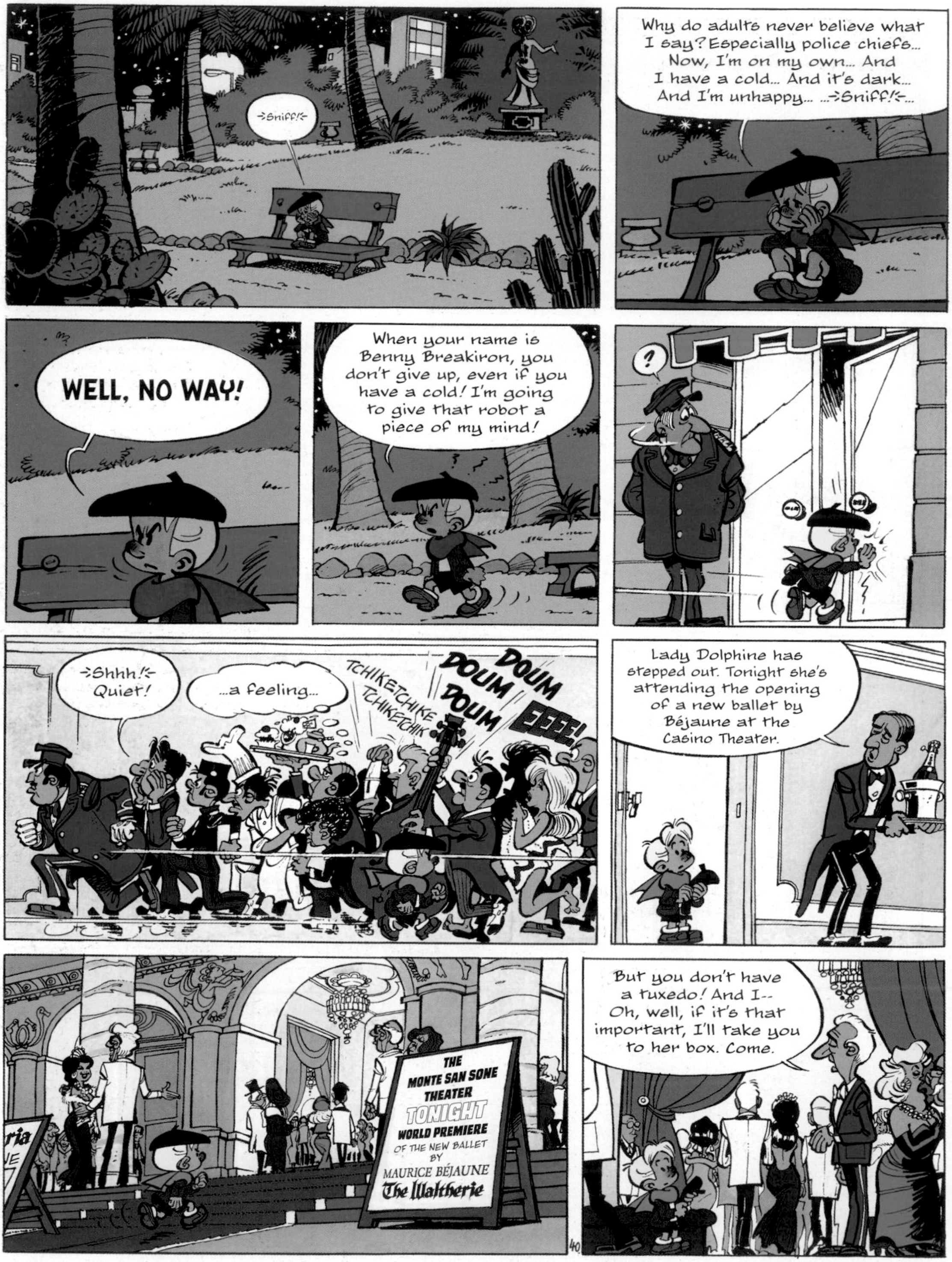

->Sniff!<-
Why do adults never believe what I say? Especially police chiefs... Now, I'm on my own... And I have a cold... And it's dark... And I'm unhappy... ...->Sniff!<-...
WELL, NO WAY!
When your name is Benny Breakiron, you don't give up, even if you have a cold! I'm going to give that robot a piece of my mind!
?
->Shhh!<- Quiet!
...a feeling...
TCHIKETCHIKE TCHIKETCHIKE TCHIKETCHIK
DOUM DOUM DOUM DOUM
EEEE!
Lady Dolphine has stepped out. Tonight she's attending the opening of a new ballet by Béjaune at the Casino Theater.
THE MONTE SAN SONE THEATER
TONIGHT
WORLD PREMIERE
OF THE NEW BALLET BY
MAURICE BÉJAUNE
The Waltherie
But you don't have a tuxedo! And I-- Oh, well, if it's that important, I'll take you to her box. Come.

Benny! What are you doing here? I thought you were sick!

Madame Adolphine, I know everything! You're in charge of awful trafficking, and I'm going to remove your batteries!

Come now, I see you haven't thought about it, my poor child...

If you take me offline, who will take advantage of that?... Gomez's gang, of course, who will wreak havoc in the whole city. Whereas if you wait a bit, I'll run them out of Monte San Sone...

...And then we'll plan our next move. What do you think of that?

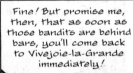

Well...

Fine! But promise me, then, that as soon as those bandits are behind bars, you'll come back to Vivejoie-la-Grande immediately!

Hush, the show is starting...

TATATZAAM

93

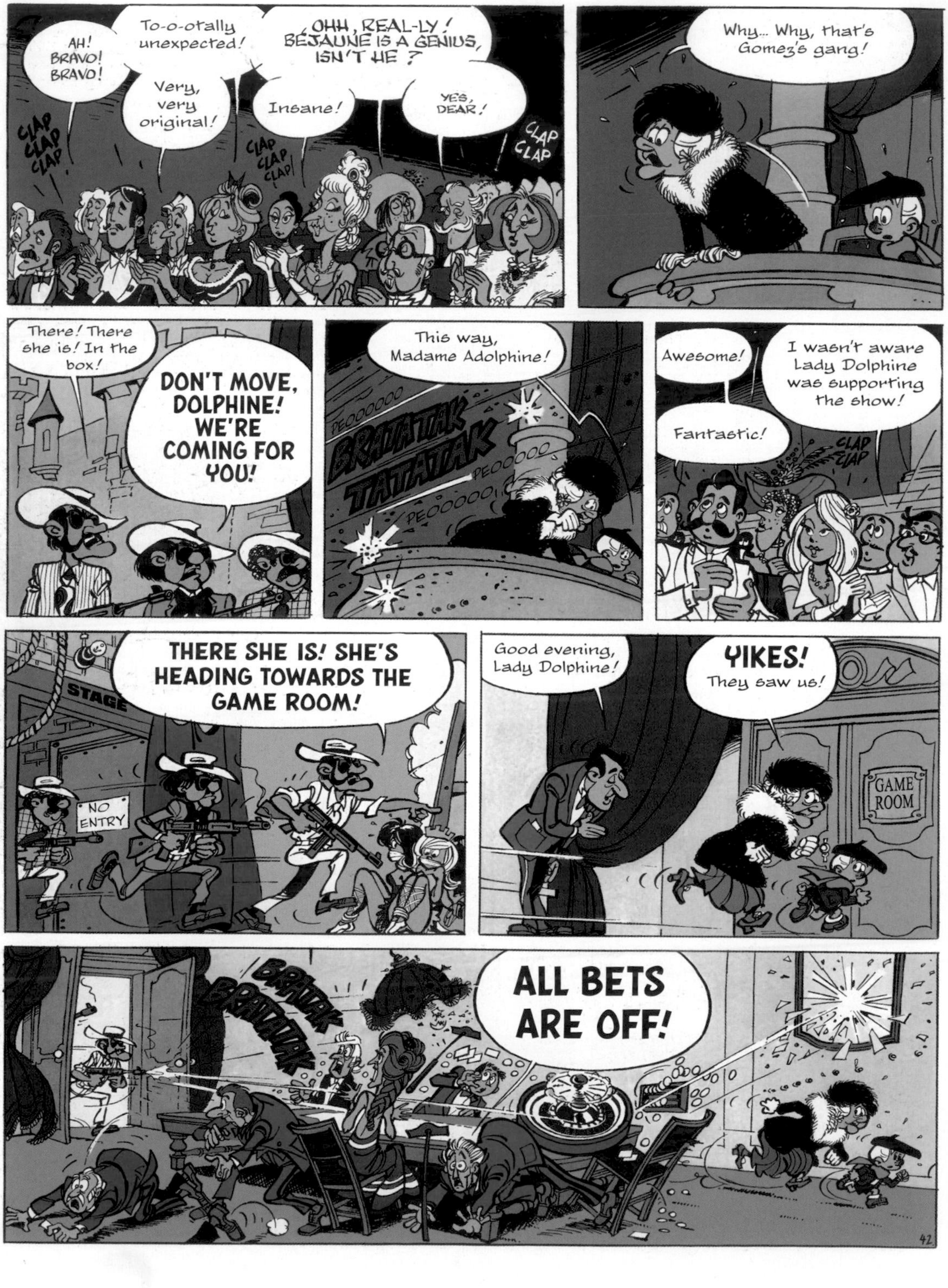
AH! BRAVO! BRAVO!
To-o-otally unexpected!
Very, very original!
OHH, REAL-LY! BÉJAUNE IS A GENIUS, ISN'T HE?
Insane!
YES, DEAR!
CLAP CLAP CLAP
CLAP CLAP CLAP
CLAP CLAP
Why... Why, that's Gomez's gang!
There! There she is! In the box!
DON'T MOVE, DOLPHINE! WE'RE COMING FOR YOU!
This way, Madame Adolphine!
BRATATAK TATATAK
PEOOOOOO
Awesome!
I wasn't aware Lady Dolphine was supporting the show!
Fantastic!
CLAP CLAP
THERE SHE IS! SHE'S HEADING TOWARDS THE GAME ROOM!
STAGE
NO ENTRY
Good evening, Lady Dolphine!
YIKES! They saw us!
GAME ROOM
BRATAK BRATATATAK
ALL BETS ARE OFF!
42

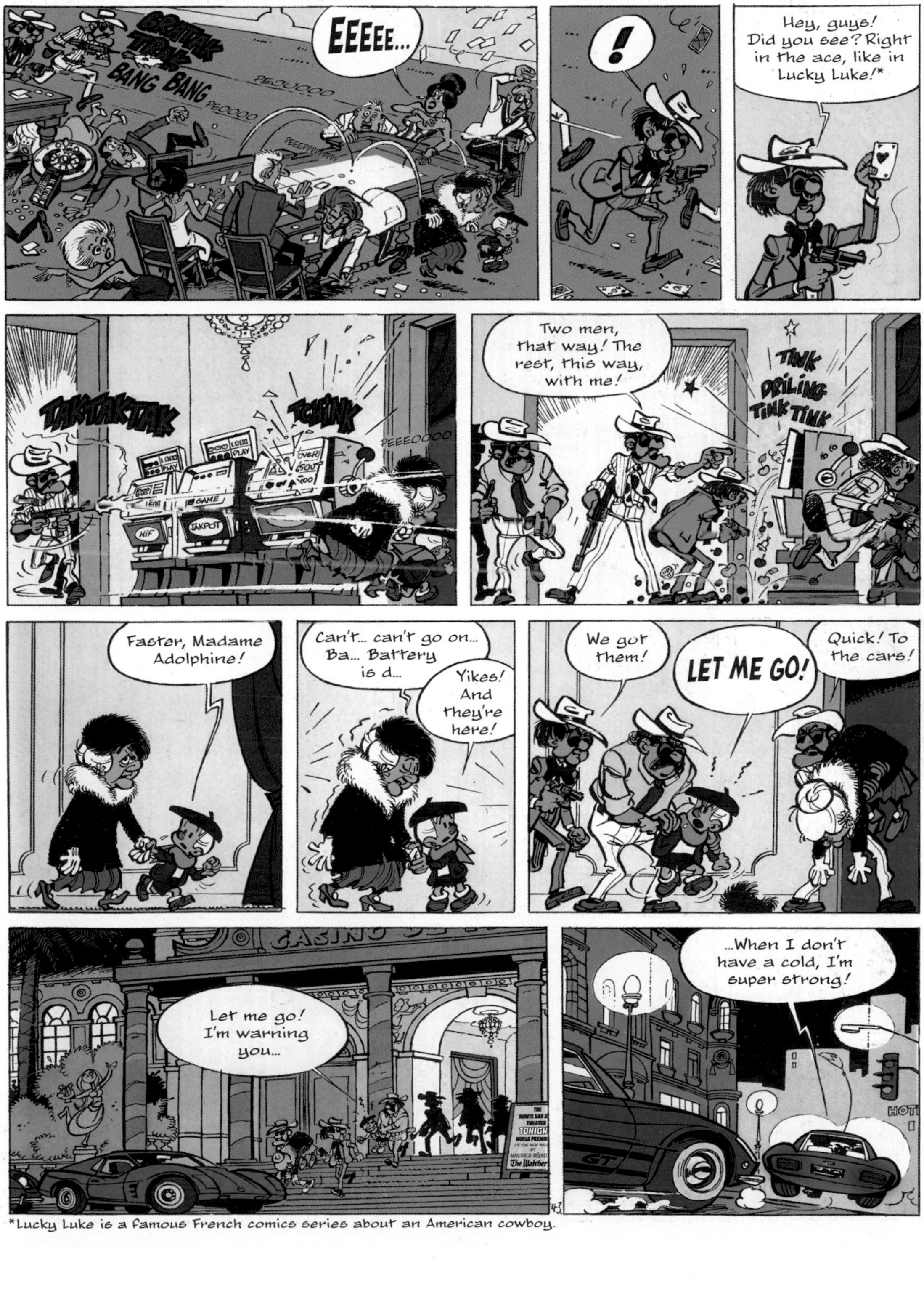

BRATATAK
TIBAK
BANG BANG
PEOOOO
PEOUOOO
EEEEE...
!
Hey, guys! Did you see? Right in the ace, like in Lucky Luke!*
TAKTAKTAK
TCHINK
PEEEOOOO
Two men, that way! The rest, this way, with me!
TINK
DRILING
TINK TINK
Faster, Madame Adolphine!
Can't... can't go on... Ba... Battery is d...
Yikes! And they're here!
We got them!
LET ME GO!
Quick! To the cars!
Let me go! I'm warning you...
...When I don't have a cold, I'm super strong!

*Lucky Luke is a famous French comics series about an American cowboy.

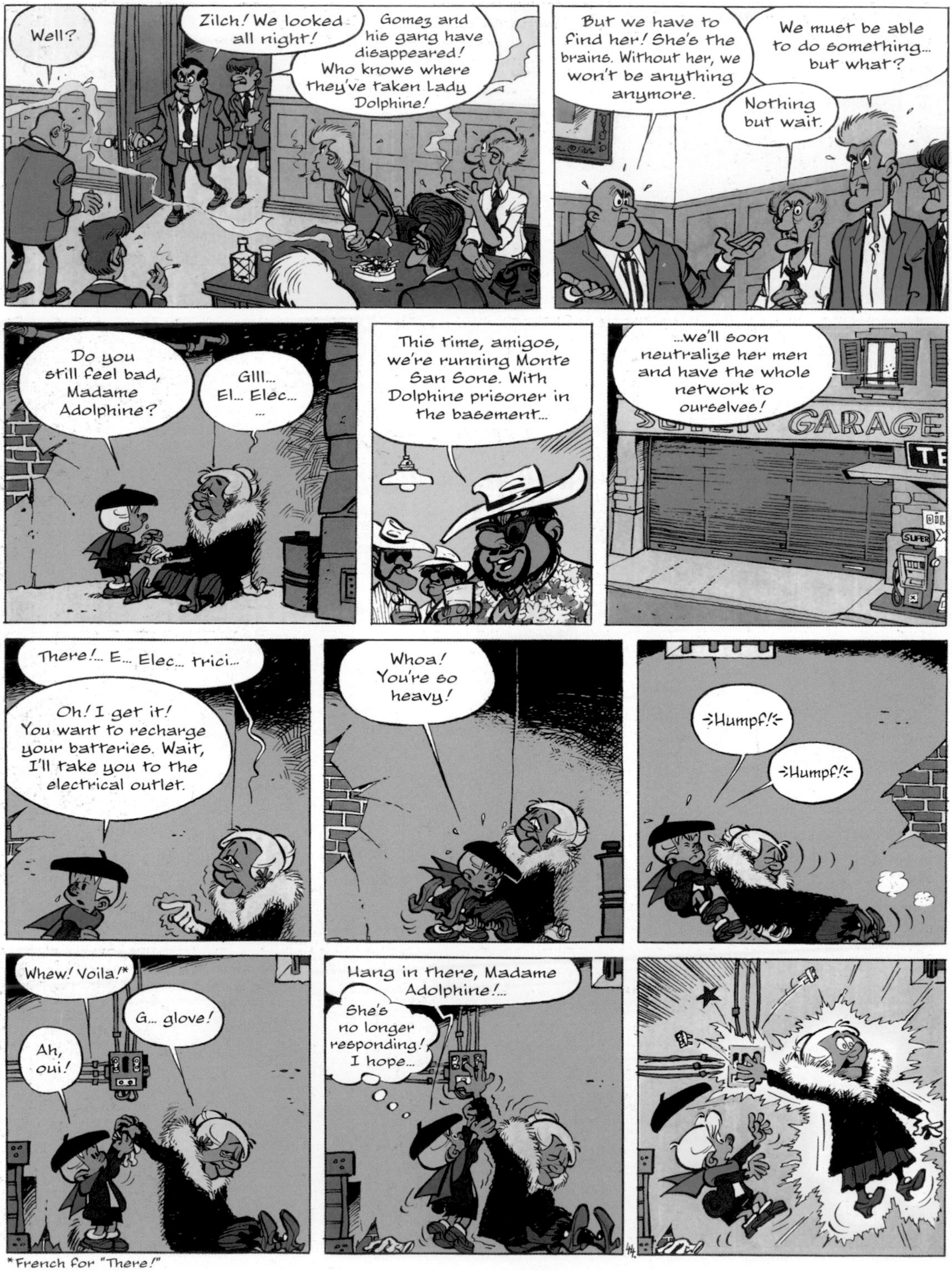
Well?
Zilch! We looked all night!
Gomez and his gang have disappeared! Who knows where they've taken Lady Dolphine!
But we have to find her! She's the brains. Without her, we won't be anything anymore.
We must be able to do something... but what?
Nothing but wait.
Do you still feel bad, Madame Adolphine?
Glll... El... Elec... ...
This time, amigos, we're running Monte San Sone. With Dolphine prisoner in the basement...
...we'll soon neutralize her men and have the whole network to ourselves!
GARAGE
SUPER
There!... E... Elec... trici...
Oh! I get it! You want to recharge your batteries. Wait, I'll take you to the electrical outlet.
Whoa! You're so heavy!
Humpf!
Humpf!
Whew! Voila!*
G... glove!
Ah, oui!
Hang in there, Madame Adolphine!...
She's no longer responding! I hope...

*French for "There!"

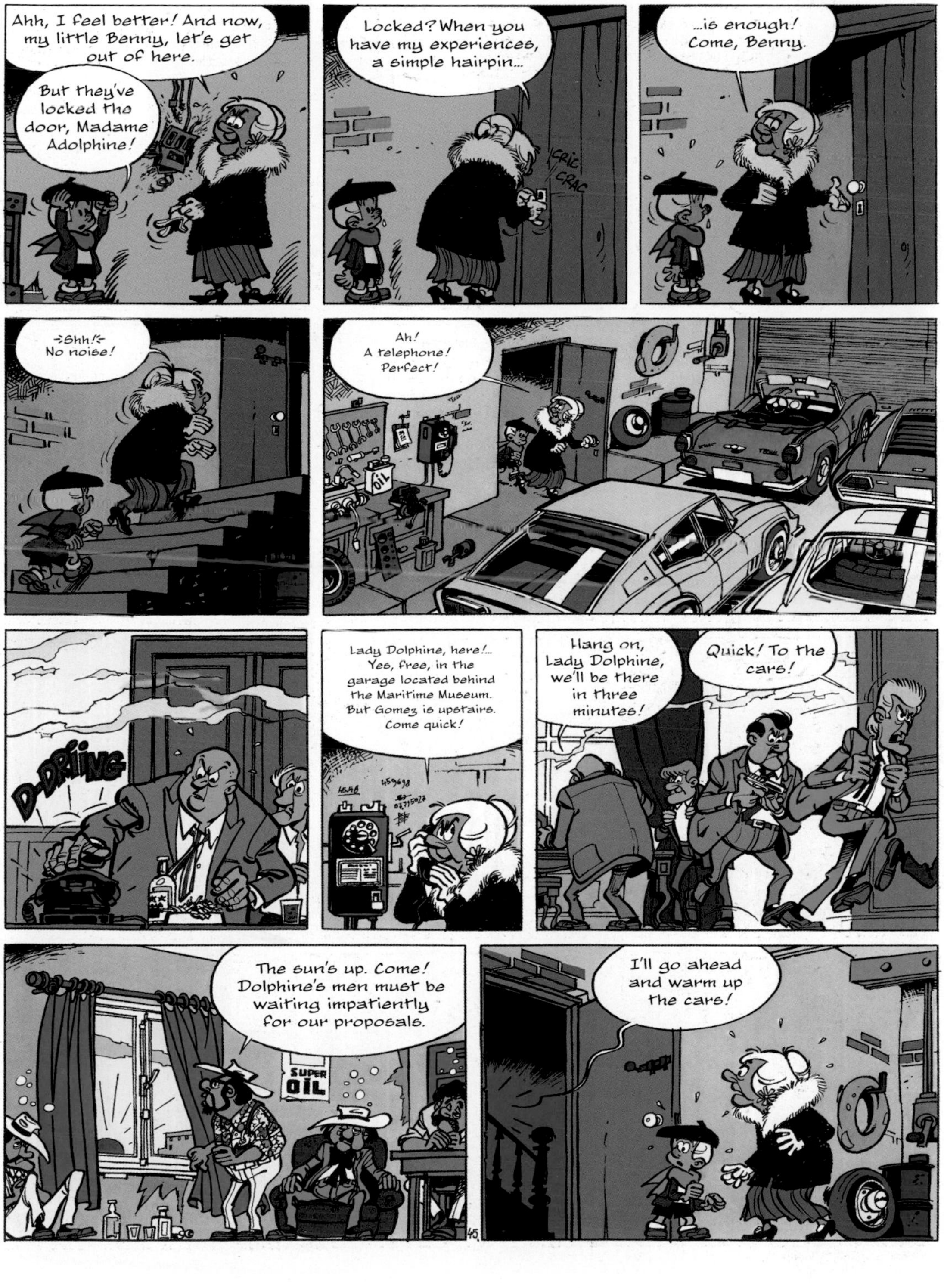

Ahh, I feel better! And now, my little Benny, let's get out of here.
But they've locked the door, Madame Adolphine!
Locked? When you have my experiences, a simple hairpin...
CRIC CRAC
...is enough! Come, Benny.
-Shh!- No noise!
Ah! A telephone! Perfect!
OIL
D-DRIING
Lady Dolphine, here!... Yes, free, in the garage located behind the Maritime Museum. But Gomez is upstairs. Come quick!
Hang on, Lady Dolphine, we'll be there in three minutes!
Quick! To the cars!
The sun's up. Come! Dolphine's men must be waiting impatiently for our proposals.
SUPER OIL
I'll go ahead and warm up the cars!

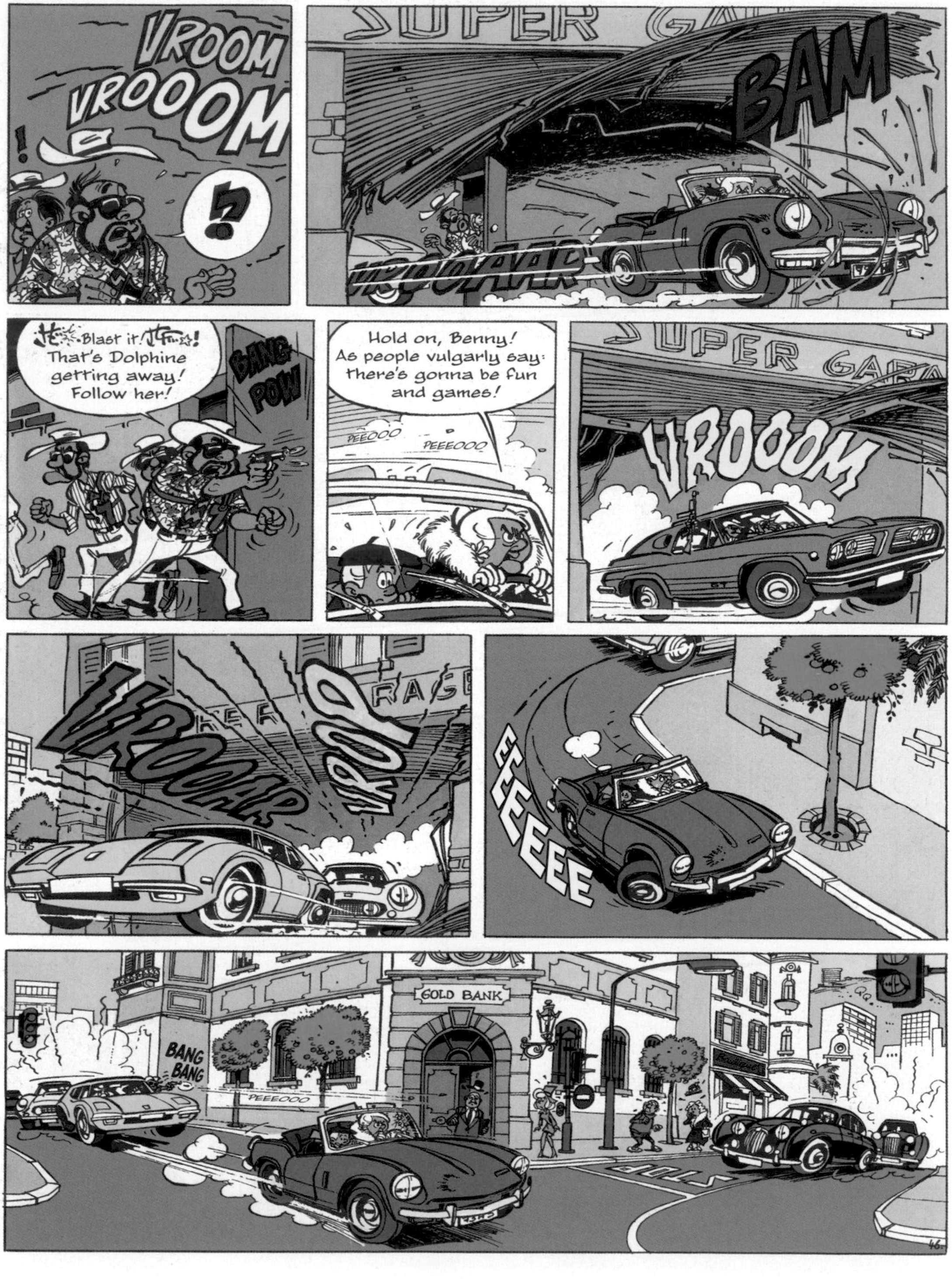
VROOM
VROOOM
BAM
Blast it! That's Dolphine getting away! Follow her!
BANG
POW
Hold on, Benny! As people vulgarly say: there's gonna be fun and games!
PEEOOO
PEEEOOO
SUPER GARA
VROOOM
EEEEEEE
GOLD BANK
BANG BANG
PEEEOOO

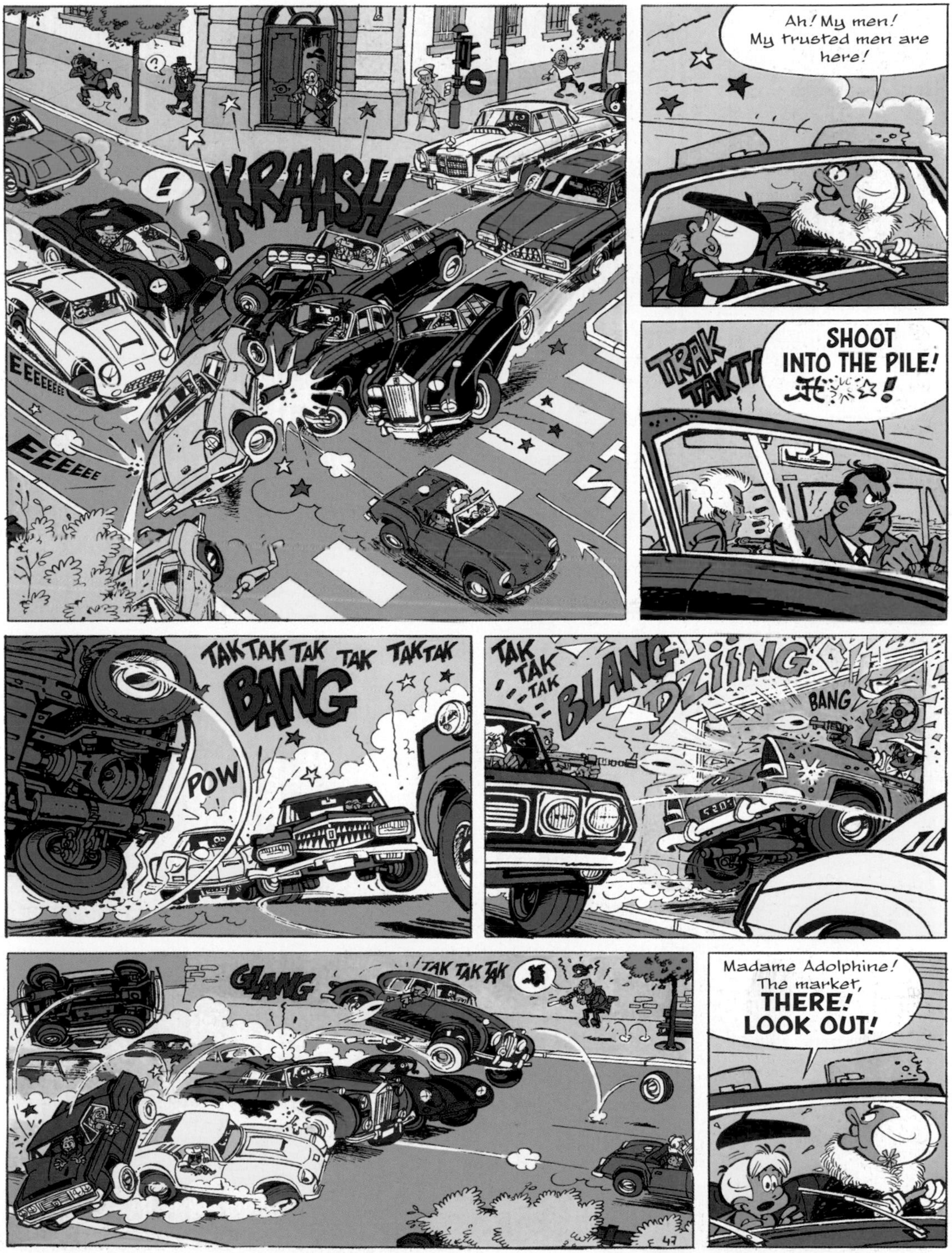
KRAASH
Ah! My men! My trusted men are here!
SHOOT INTO THE PILE!
TAK TAK TAK TAK TAK TAK
BANG
POW
TAK TAK TAK
BLANG
DZIIING
BANG
GLANG
TAK TAK TAK
Madame Adolphine! The market, THERE! LOOK OUT!

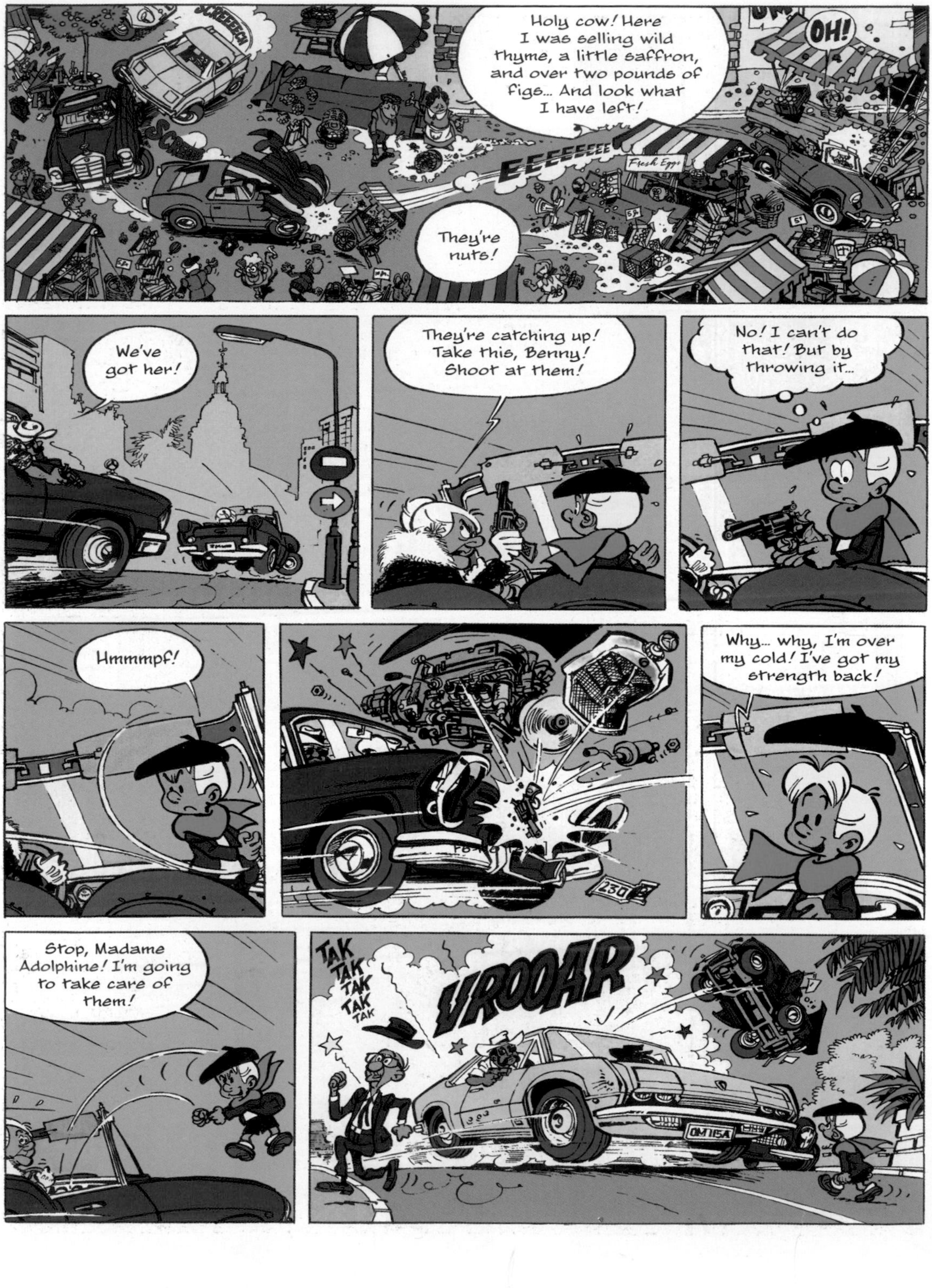
OH!
Holy cow! Here I was selling wild thyme, a little saffron, and over two pounds of figs... And look what I have left!
Fresh Eggs
They're nuts!
We've got her!
They're catching up! Take this, Benny! Shoot at them!
No! I can't do that! But by throwing it...
Hmmmpf!
Why... why, I'm over my cold! I've got my strength back!
Stop, Madame Adolphine! I'm going to take care of them!
TAK TAK TAK TAK TAK
VROOAR

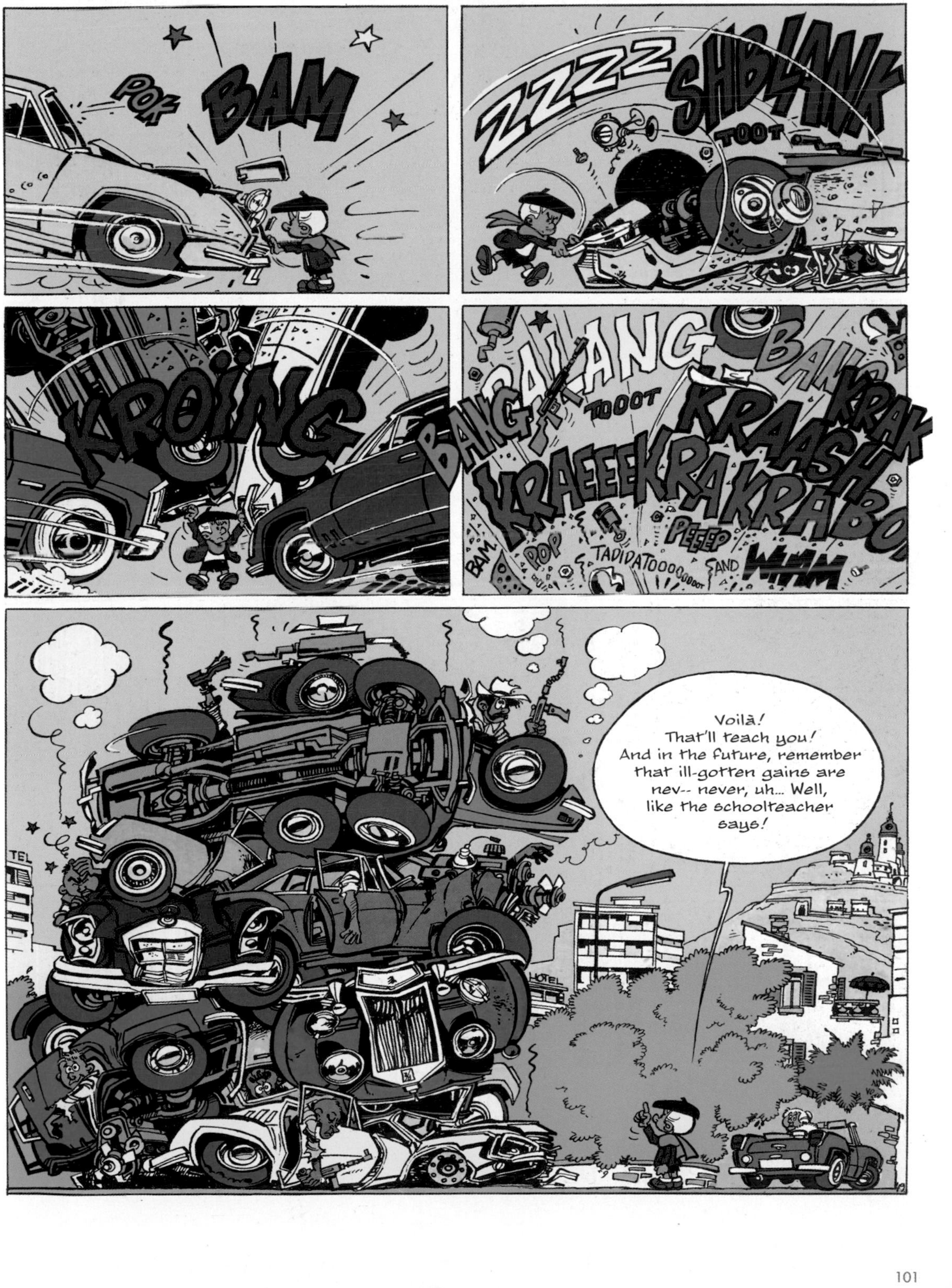
POK
BAM
ZZZZZ
SHBLANK
TOOT
KROING
BANG
TOOOT
KRAK
KRAASH
BAM
POP
PEEEP
AND
Voilà! That'll teach you! And in the future, remember that ill-gotten gains are nev-- never, uh... Well, like the schoolteacher says!

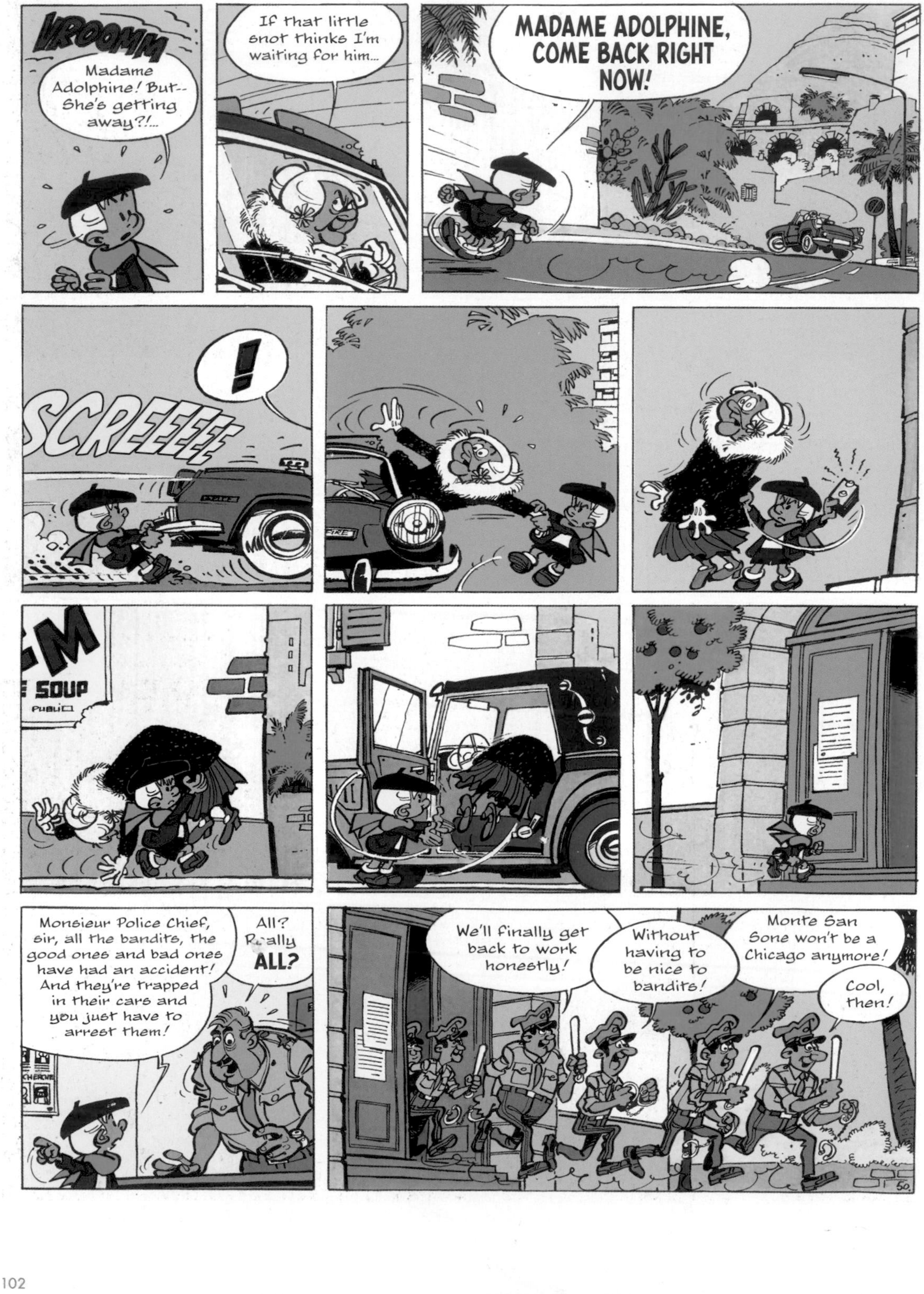

VROOMM
Madame Adolphine! But-- She's getting away?!...
If that little snot thinks I'm waiting for him...
MADAME ADOLPHINE, COME BACK RIGHT NOW!
!
SCREEEEEE
SOUP
PUBLICI
Monsieur Police Chief, sir, all the bandits, the good ones and bad ones have had an accident! And they're trapped in their cars and you just have to arrest them!
All? Really ALL?
We'll finally get back to work honestly!
Without having to be nice to bandits!
Monte San Sone won't be a Chicago anymore!
Cool, then!
50.

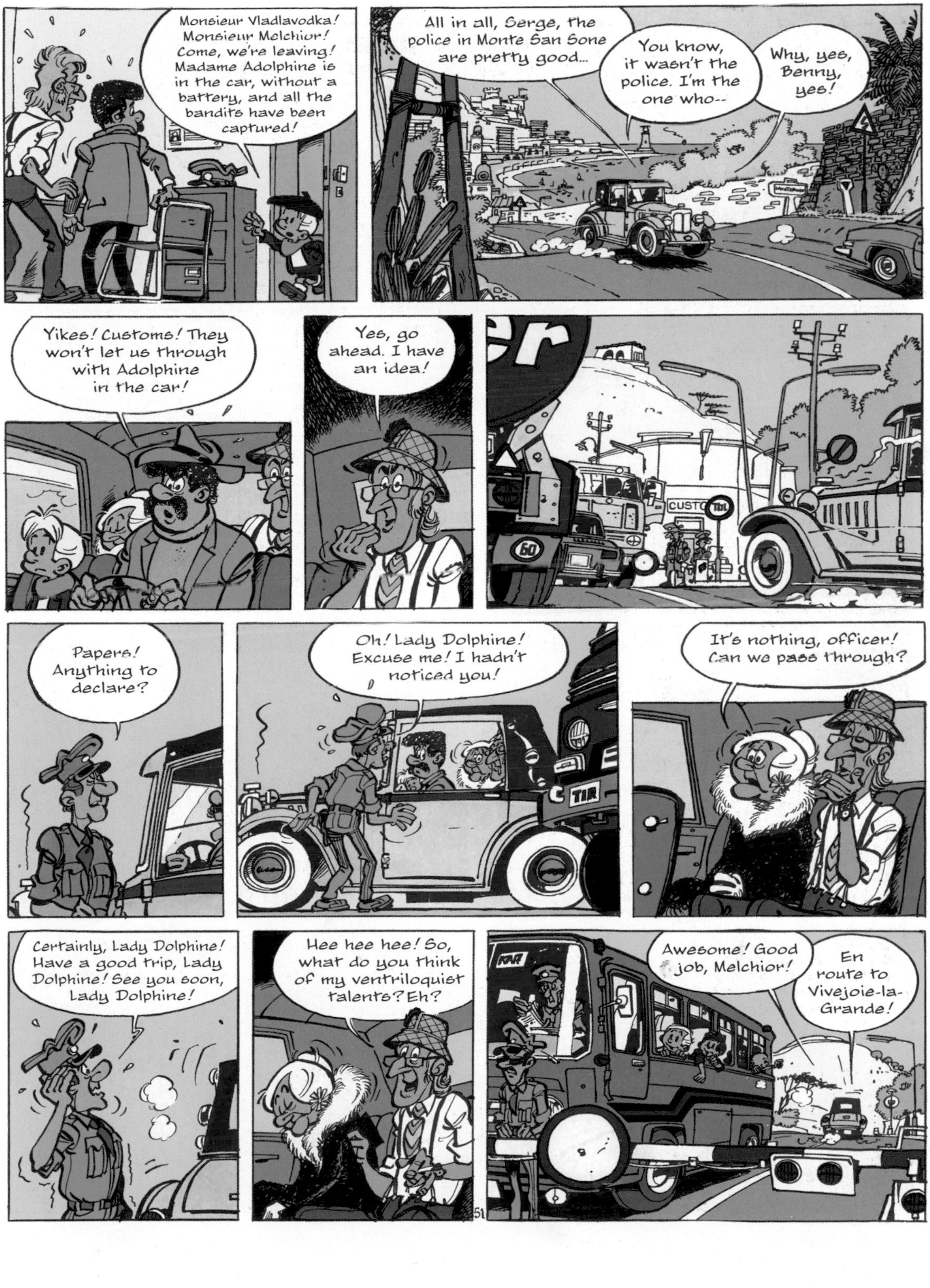
Monsieur Vladlavodka! Monsieur Melchior! Come, we're leaving! Madame Adolphine is in the car, without a battery, and all the bandits have been captured!
All in all, Serge, the police in Monte San Sone are pretty good...
You know, it wasn't the police. I'm the one who--
Why, yes, Benny, yes!
Yikes! Customs! They won't let us through with Adolphine in the car!
Yes, go ahead. I have an idea!
Papers! Anything to declare?
Oh! Lady Dolphine! Excuse me! I hadn't noticed you!
It's nothing, officer! Can we pass through?
Certainly, Lady Dolphine! Have a good trip, Lady Dolphine! See you soon, Lady Dolphine!
Hee hee hee! So, what do you think of my ventriloquist talents? Eh?
Awesome! Good job, Melchior!
En route to Vivejoie-la-Grande!

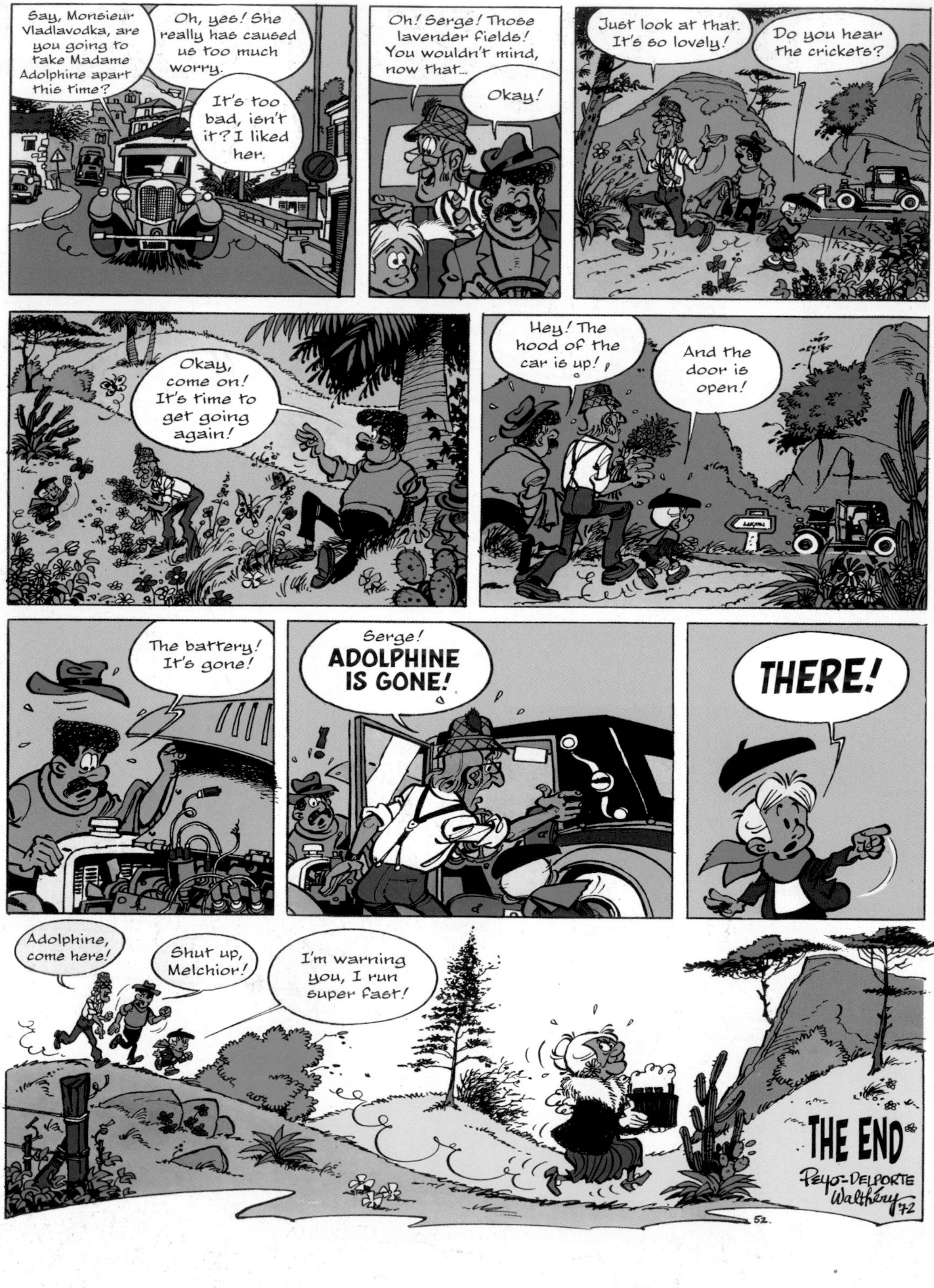

Say, Monsieur Vladlavodka, are you going to take Madame Adolphine apart this time?
Oh, yes! She really has caused us too much worry.
It's too bad, isn't it? I liked her.
Oh! Serge! Those lavender fields! You wouldn't mind, now that...
Okay!
Just look at that. It's so lovely!
Do you hear the crickets?
KZZZ
Okay, come on! It's time to get going again!
Hey! The hood of the car is up!
And the door is open!
The battery! It's gone!
Serge! ADOLPHINE IS GONE!
THERE!
Adolphine, come here!
Shut up, Melchior!
I'm warning you, I run super fast!
THE END
Peyo-Delporte
Walthéry 72
52.

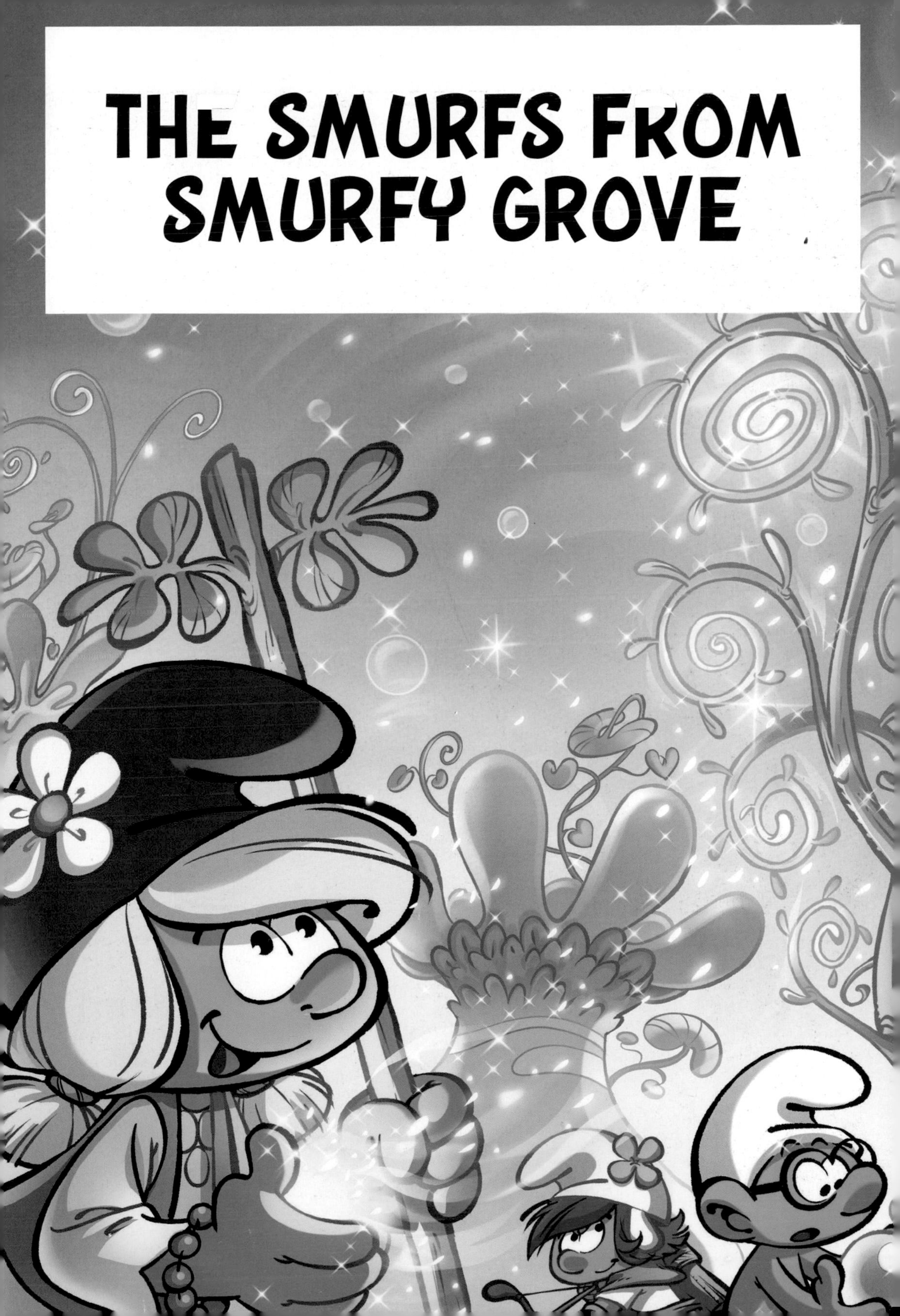
THE SMURFS FROM SMURFY GROVE

A New Beginning

A NEW BEGINNING

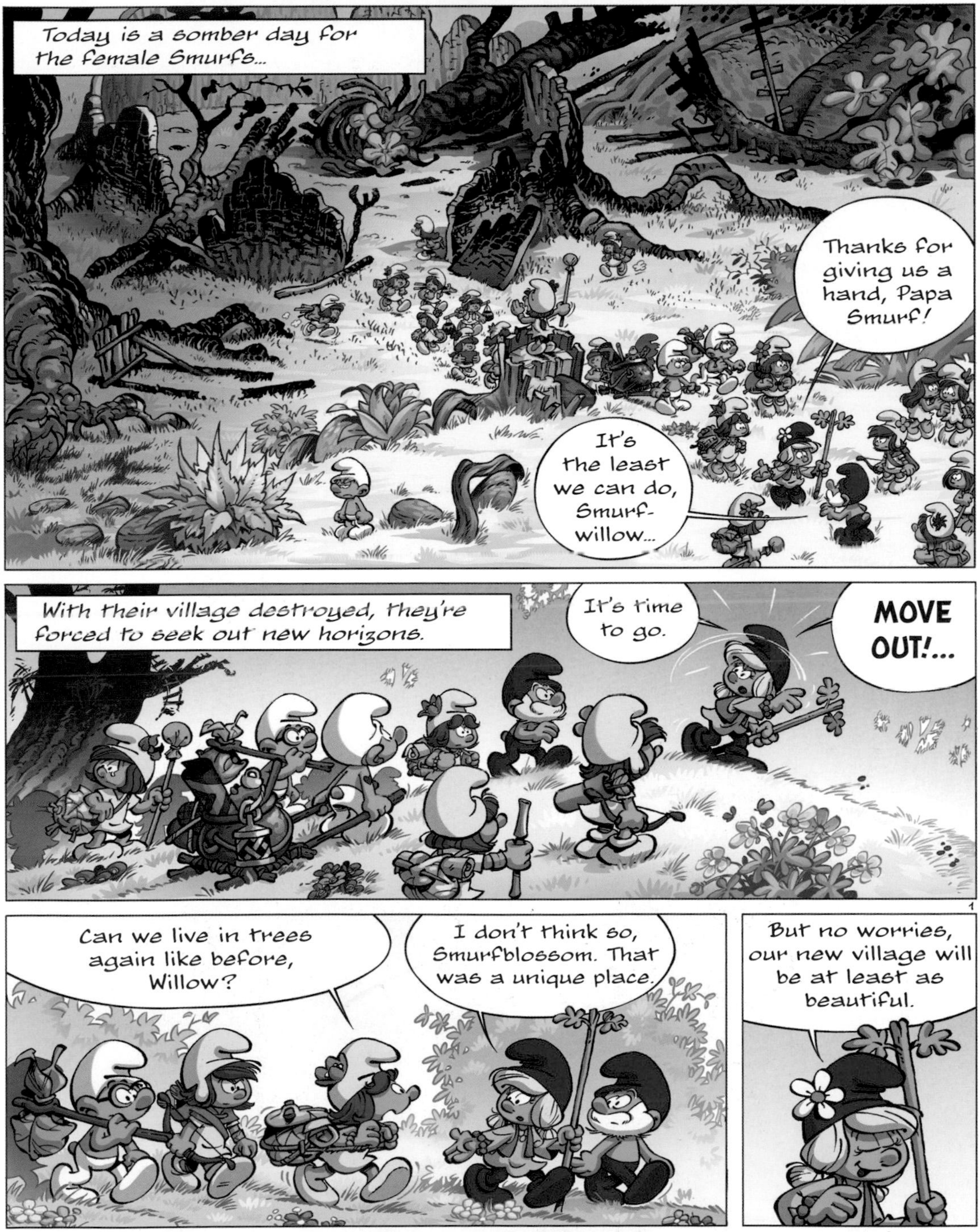
Today is a somber day for the female Smurfs...
Thanks for giving us a hand, Papa Smurf!
It's the least we can do, Smurf-willow...
With their village destroyed, they're forced to seek out new horizons.
It's time to go.
MOVE OUT!...
Can we live in trees again like before, Willow?
I don't think so, Smurfblossom. That was a unique place.
But no worries, our new village will be at least as beautiful.

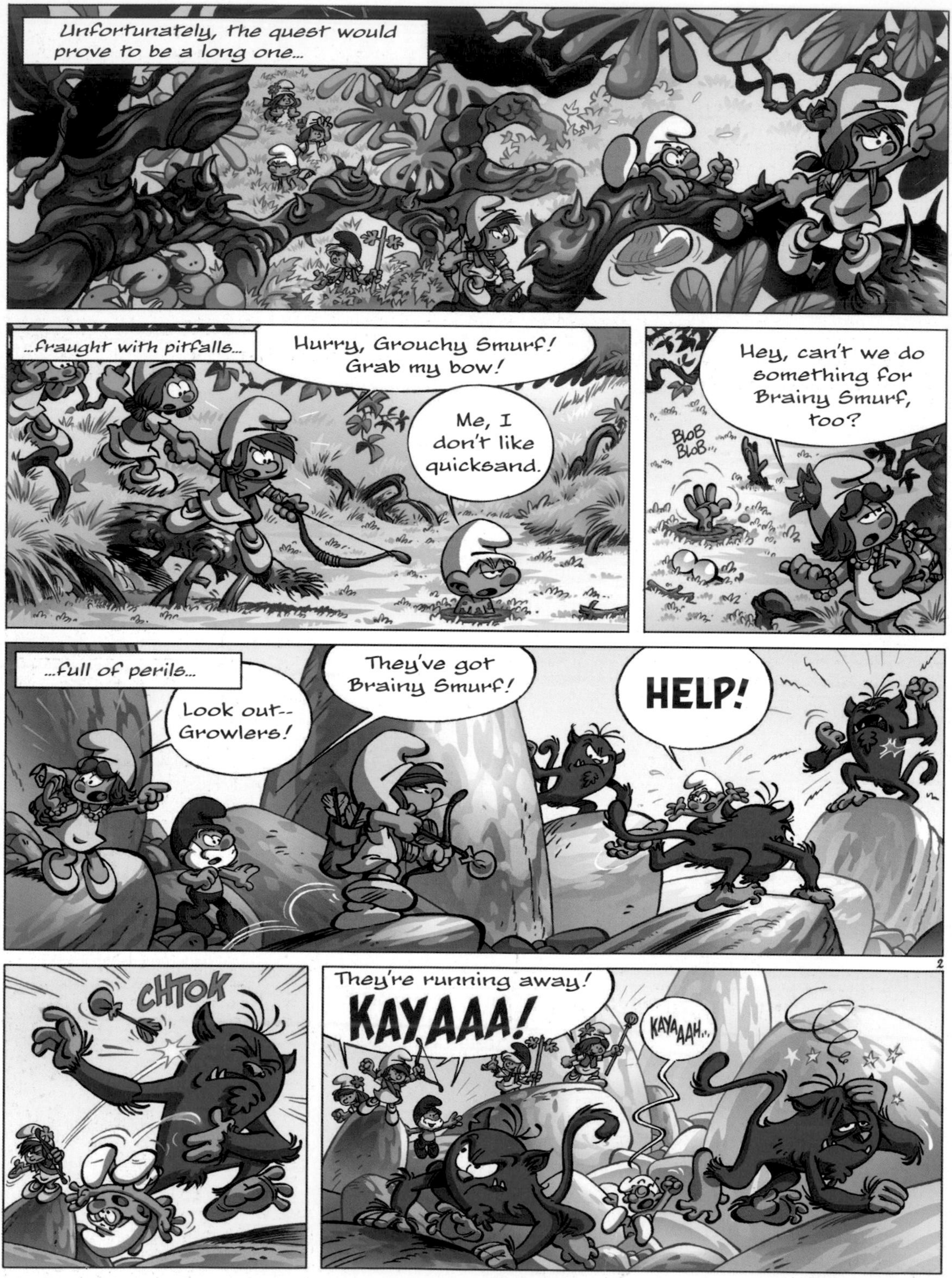
Unfortunately, the quest would prove to be a long one...
...fraught with pitfalls...
Hurry, Grouchy Smurf! Grab my bow!
Me, I don't like quicksand.
BLOB BLOB...
Hey, can't we do something for Brainy Smurf, too?
...full of perils...
Look out-- Growlers!
They've got Brainy Smurf!
HELP!
CHTOK
They're running away!
KAYAAA!
KAYAAAH...

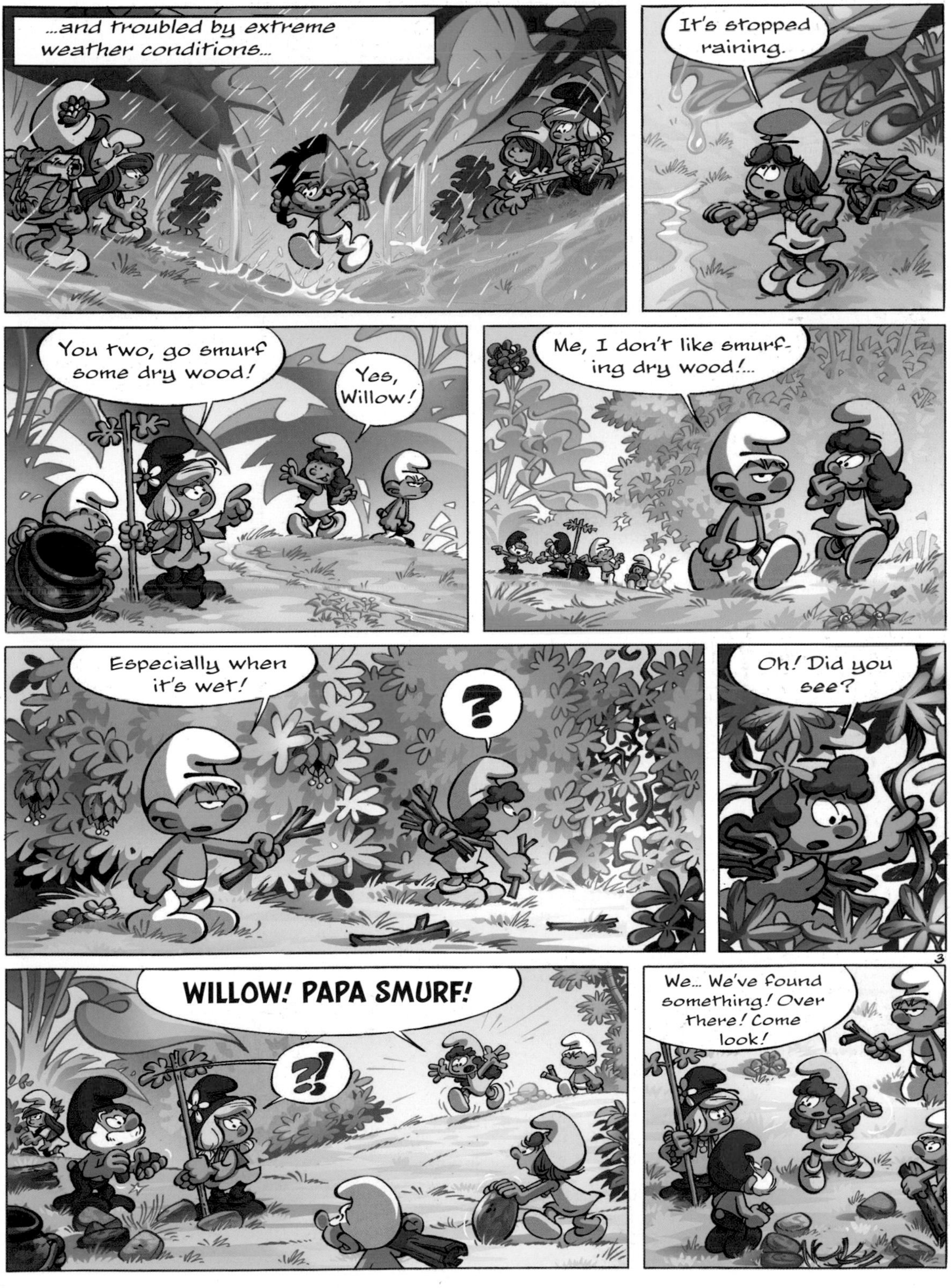
...and troubled by extreme weather conditions...
It's stopped raining.
You two, go smurf some dry wood!
Yes, Willow!
Me, I don't like smurf-ing dry wood!...
Especially when it's wet!
?
Oh! Did you see?
3
WILLOW! PAPA SMURF!
?!
We... We've found something! Over there! Come look!

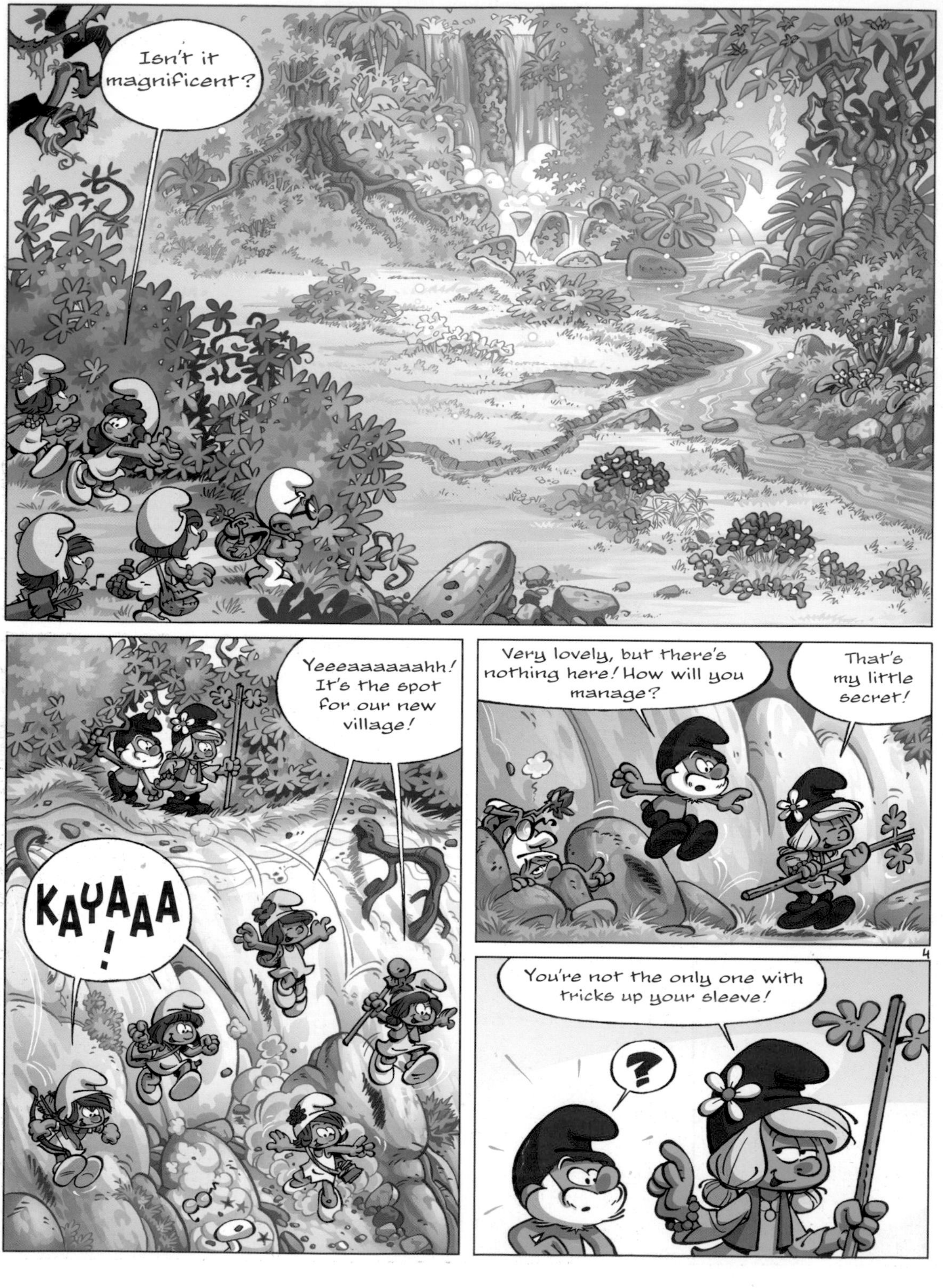
Isn't it magnificent?
Yeeeaaaaaaahh! It's the spot for our new village!
KAYAAA!
Very lovely, but there's nothing here! How will you manage?
That's my little secret!
4
You're not the only one with tricks up your sleeve!
?

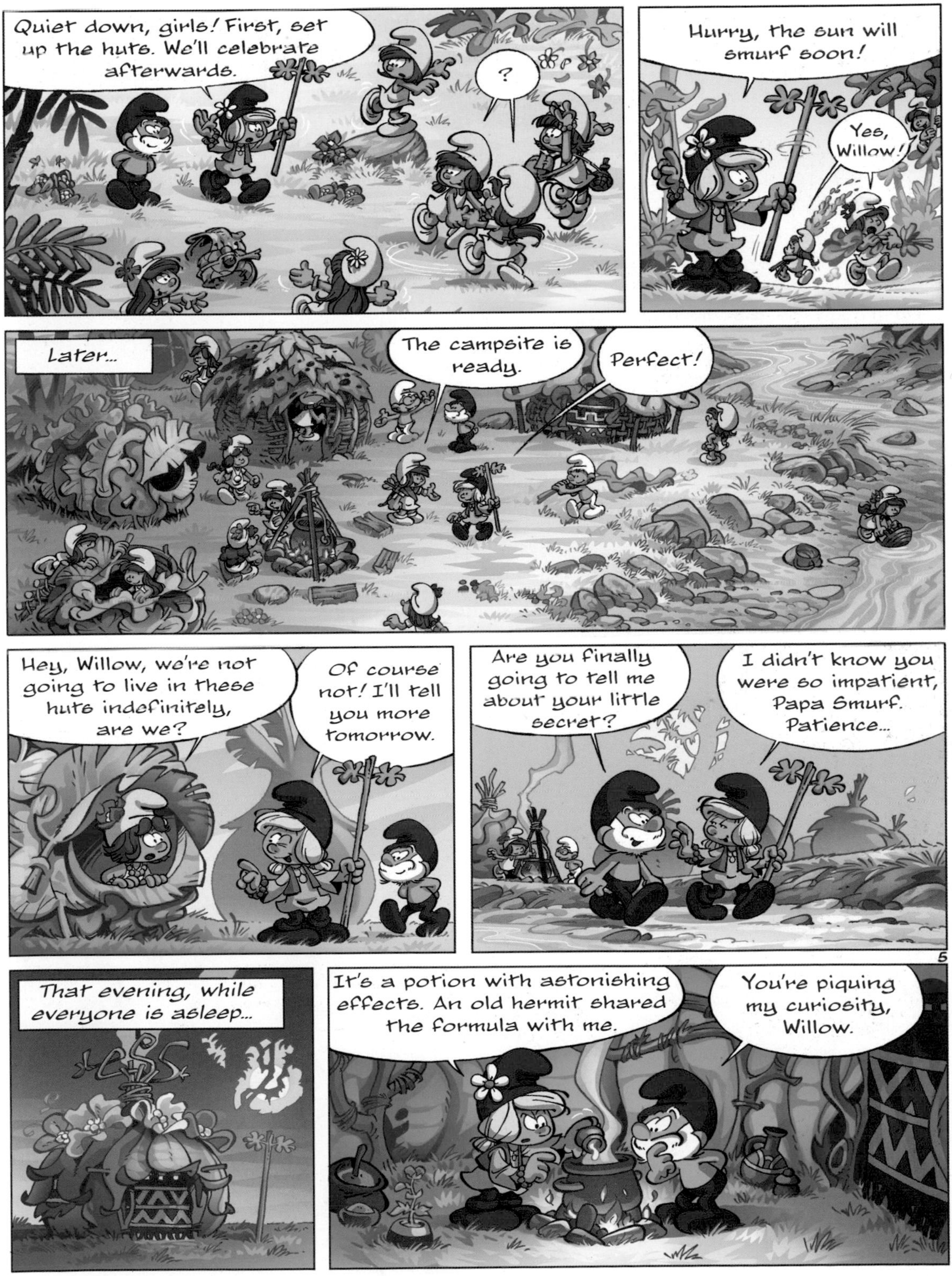
Quiet down, girls! First, set up the huts. We'll celebrate afterwards.
?
Hurry, the sun will smurf soon!
Yes, Willow!
Later...
The campsite is ready.
Perfect!
Hey, Willow, we're not going to live in these huts indefinitely, are we?
Of course not! I'll tell you more tomorrow.
Are you finally going to tell me about your little secret?
I didn't know you were so impatient, Papa Smurf. Patience...
5
That evening, while everyone is asleep...
It's a potion with astonishing effects. An old hermit shared the formula with me.
You're piquing my curiosity, Willow.

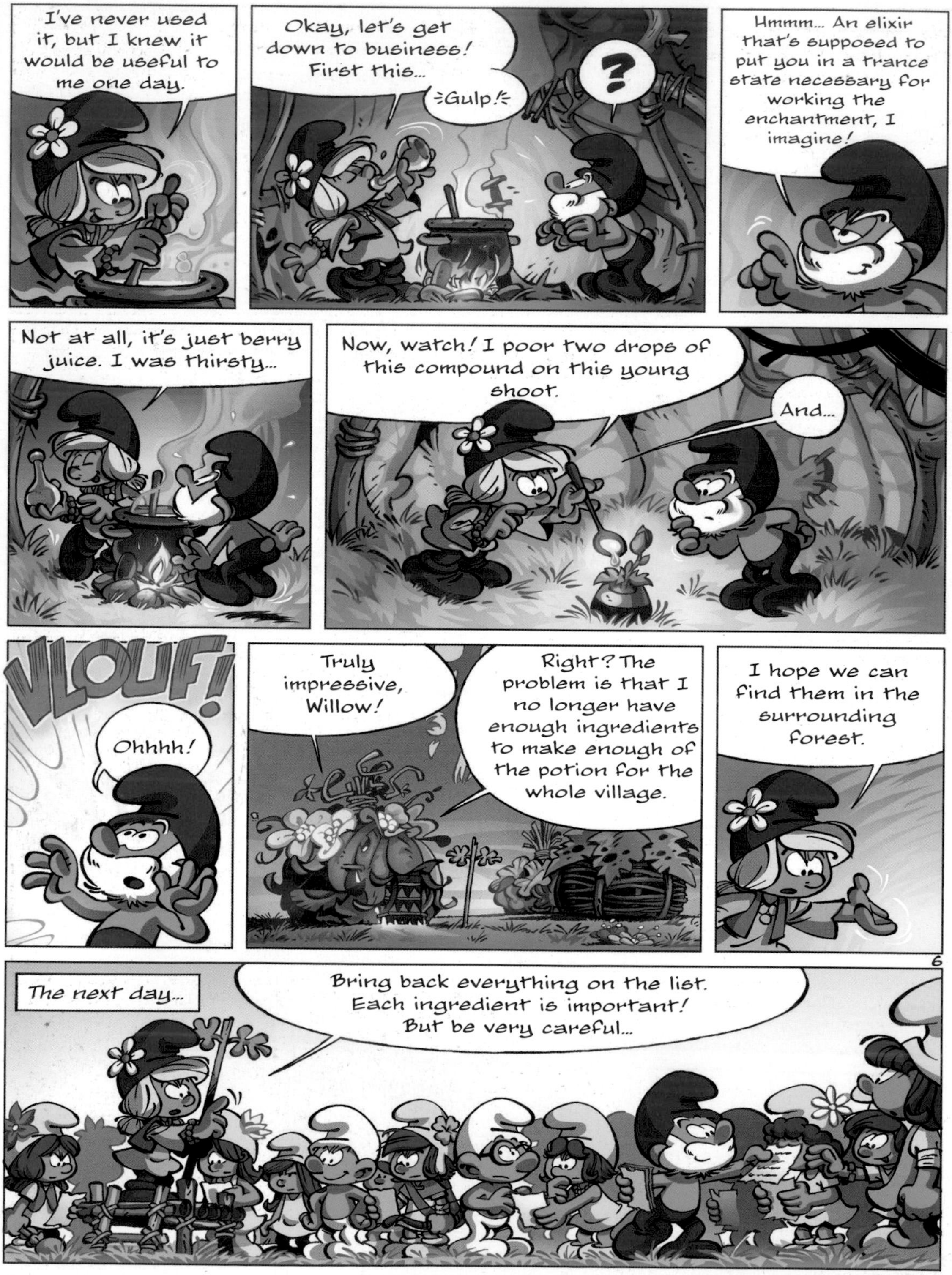
I've never used it, but I knew it would be useful to me one day.
Okay, let's get down to business! First this...
Gulp!
?
Hmmm... An elixir that's supposed to put you in a trance state necessary for working the enchantment, I imagine!
Not at all, it's just berry juice. I was thirsty...
Now, watch! I poor two drops of this compound on this young shoot.
And...
VLOUF!
Ohhhh!
Truly impressive, Willow!
Right? The problem is that I no longer have enough ingredients to make enough of the potion for the whole village.
I hope we can find them in the surrounding forest.
6
The next day...
Bring back everything on the list. Each ingredient is important! But be very careful...

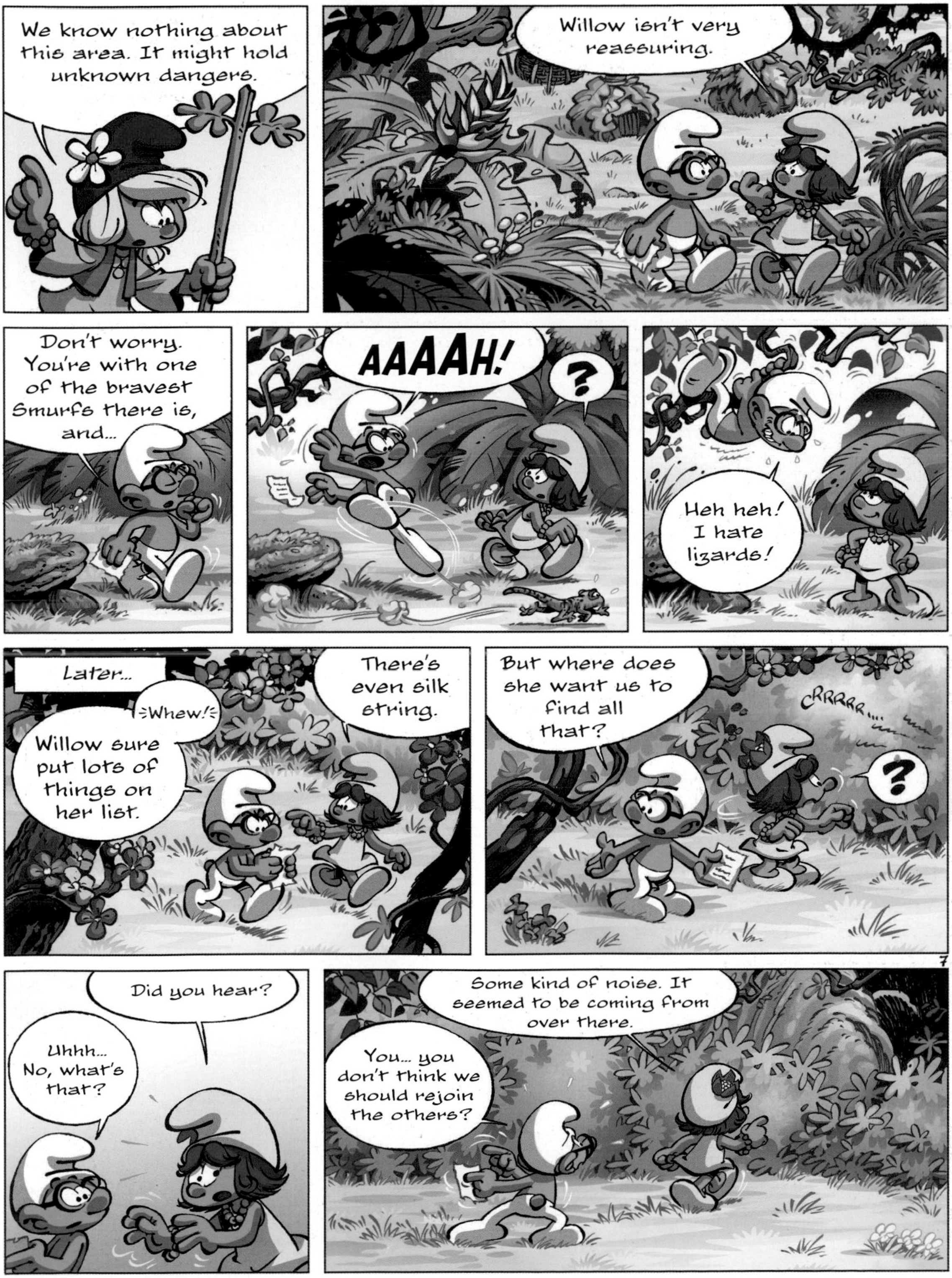

We know nothing about this area. It might hold unknown dangers.
Willow isn't very reassuring.
Don't worry. You're with one of the bravest Smurfs there is, and...
AAAAH!
?
Heh heh! I hate lizards!
Later...
Whew!
Willow sure put lots of things on her list.
There's even silk string.
But where does she want us to find all that?
CRRRRR....
?
7
Did you hear?
Uhhh... No, what's that?
Some kind of noise. It seemed to be coming from over there.
You... you don't think we should rejoin the others?

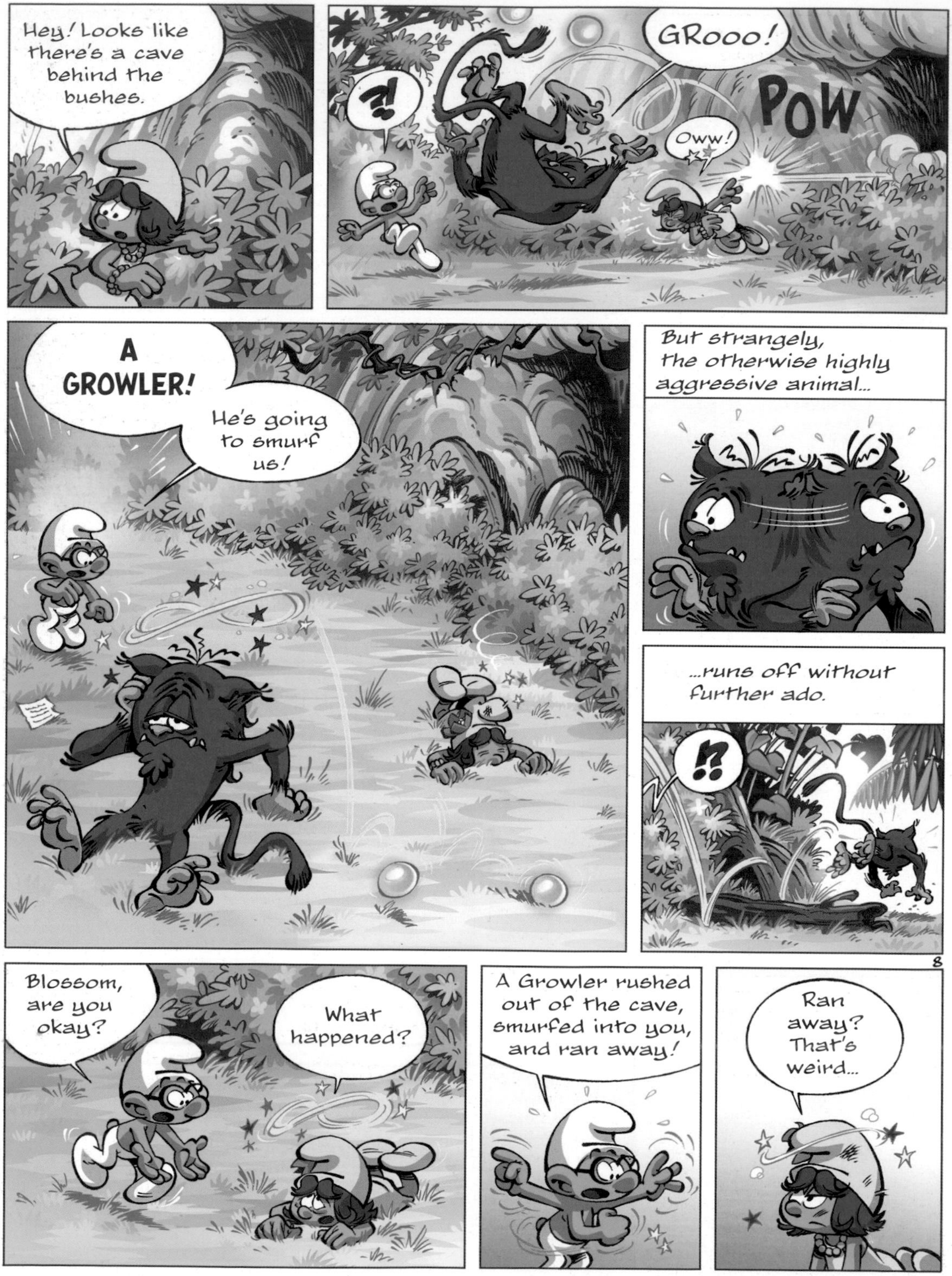
Hey! Looks like there's a cave behind the bushes.
?!
GRooo!
POW
Oww!
A GROWLER!
He's going to smurf us!
But strangely, the otherwise highly aggressive animal...
...runs off without further ado.
?!
Blossom, are you okay?
What happened?
A Growler rushed out of the cave, smurfed into you, and ran away!
Ran away? That's weird...

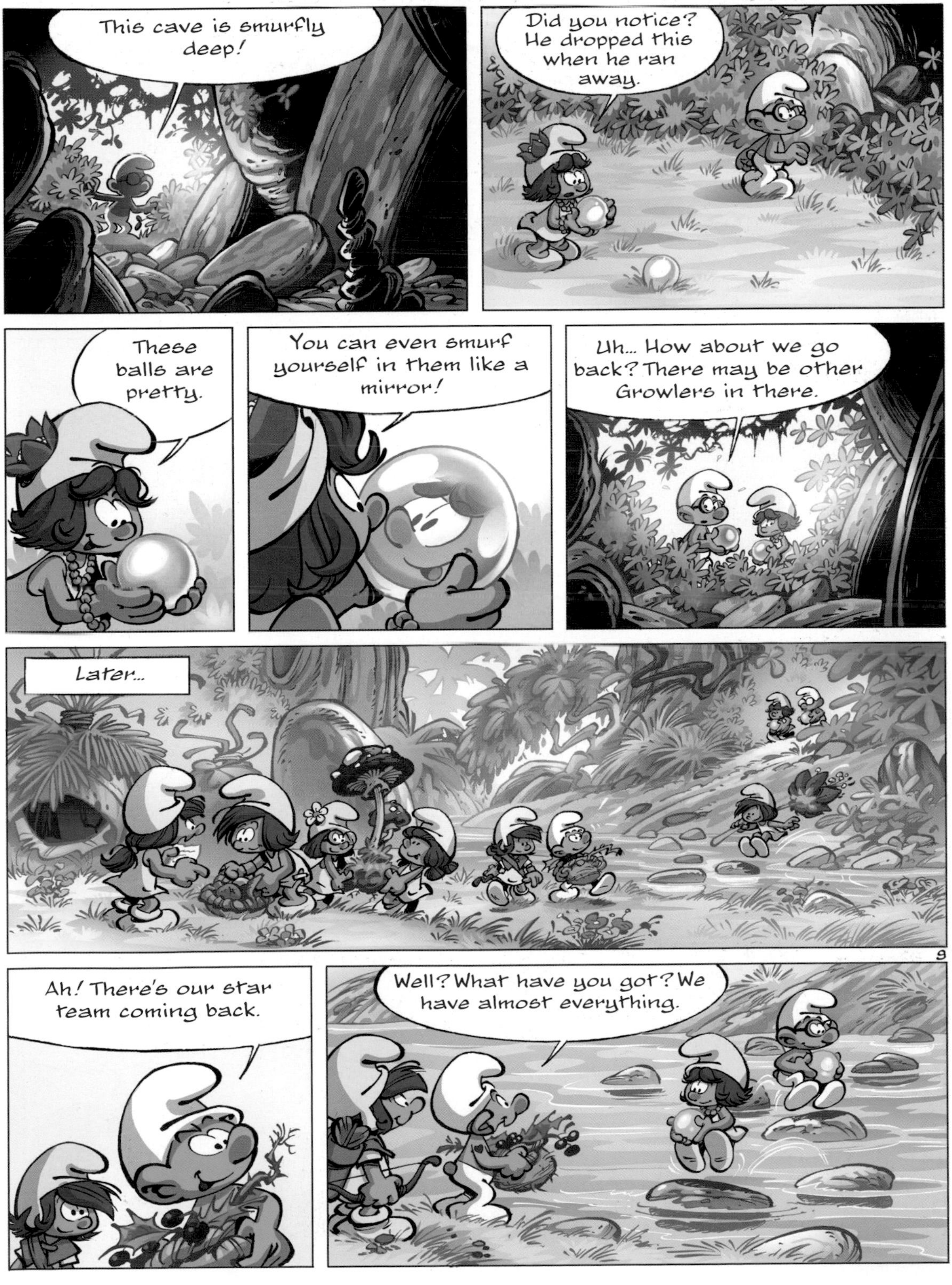
This cave is smurfly deep!
Did you notice? He dropped this when he ran away.
These balls are pretty.
You can even smurf yourself in them like a mirror!
Uh... How about we go back? There may be other Growlers in there.
Later...
9
Ah! There's our star team coming back.
Well? What have you got? We have almost everything.

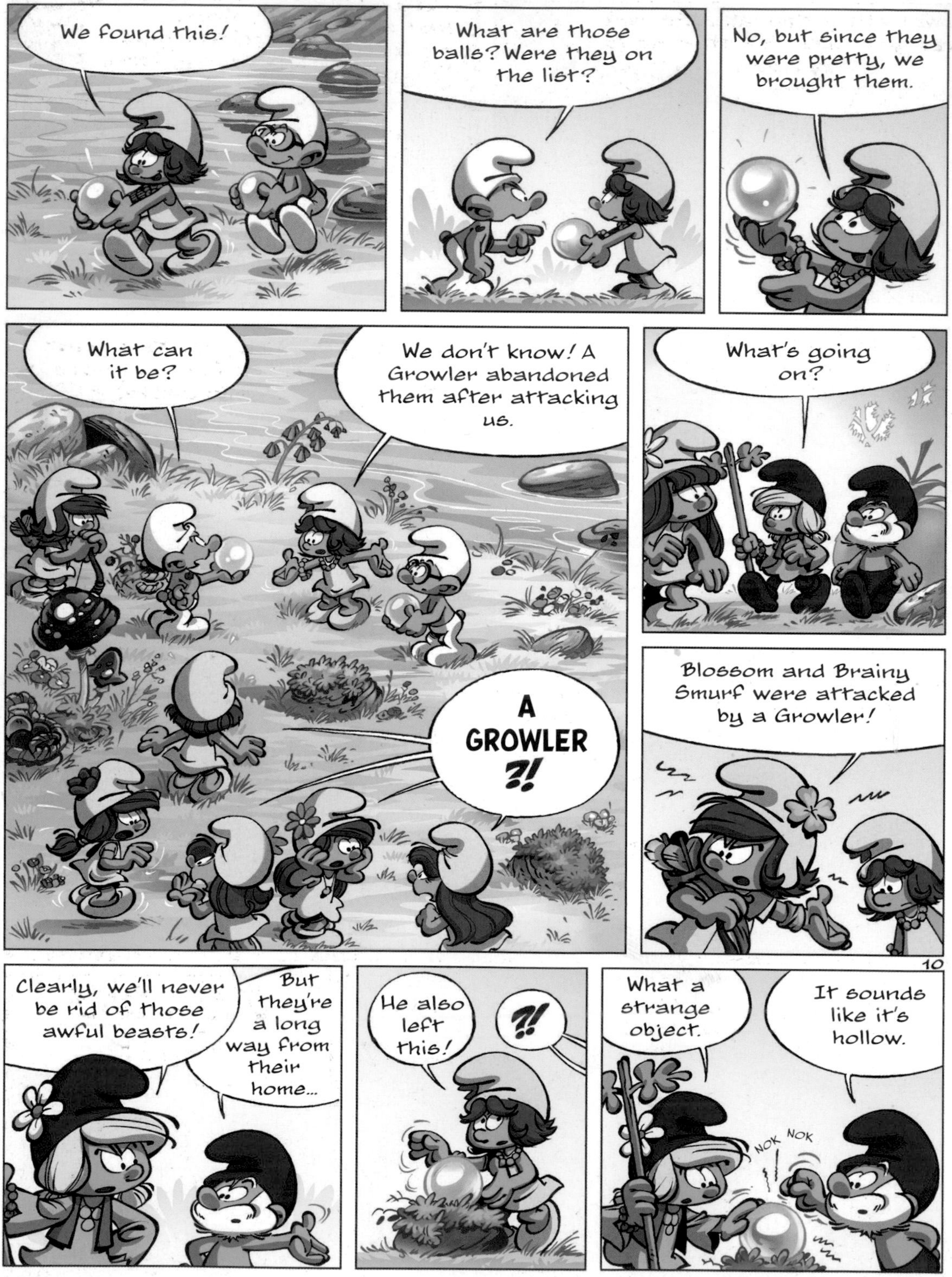

We found this!
What are those balls? Were they on the list?
No, but since they were pretty, we brought them.
What can it be?
We don't know! A Growler abandoned them after attacking us.
A GROWLER ?!
What's going on?
Blossom and Brainy Smurf were attacked by a Growler!
10
Clearly, we'll never be rid of those awful beasts!
But they're a long way from their home...
He also left this!
?!
What a strange object.
It sounds like it's hollow.
NOK NOK

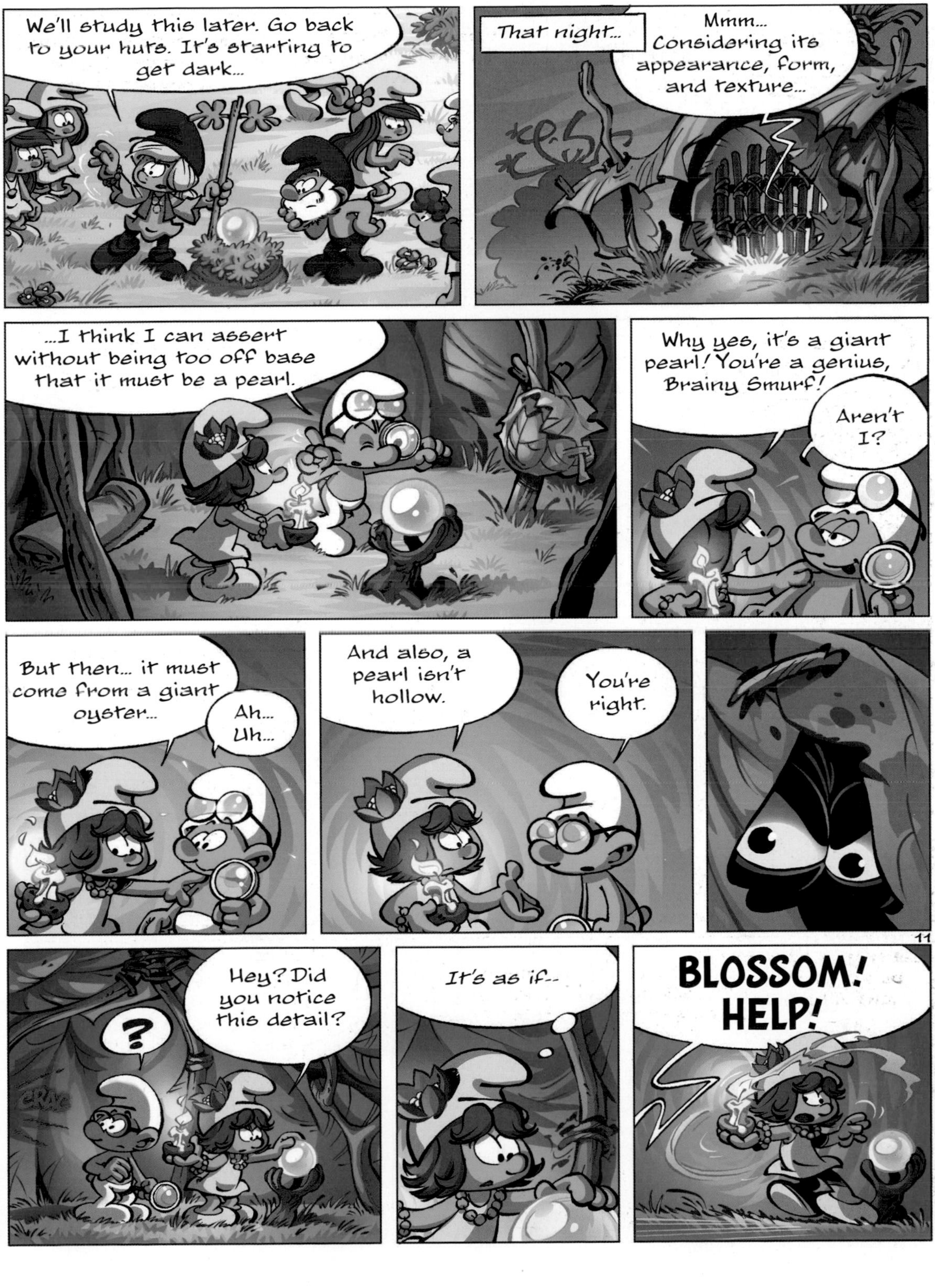
We'll study this later. Go back to your huts. It's starting to get dark...
That night...
Mmm... Considering its appearance, form, and texture...
...I think I can assert without being too off base that it must be a pearl.
Why yes, it's a giant pearl! You're a genius, Brainy Smurf!
Aren't I?
But then... it must come from a giant oyster...
Ah... Uh...
And also, a pearl isn't hollow.
You're right.
11
?
Hey? Did you notice this detail?
It's as if--
BLOSSOM! HELP!

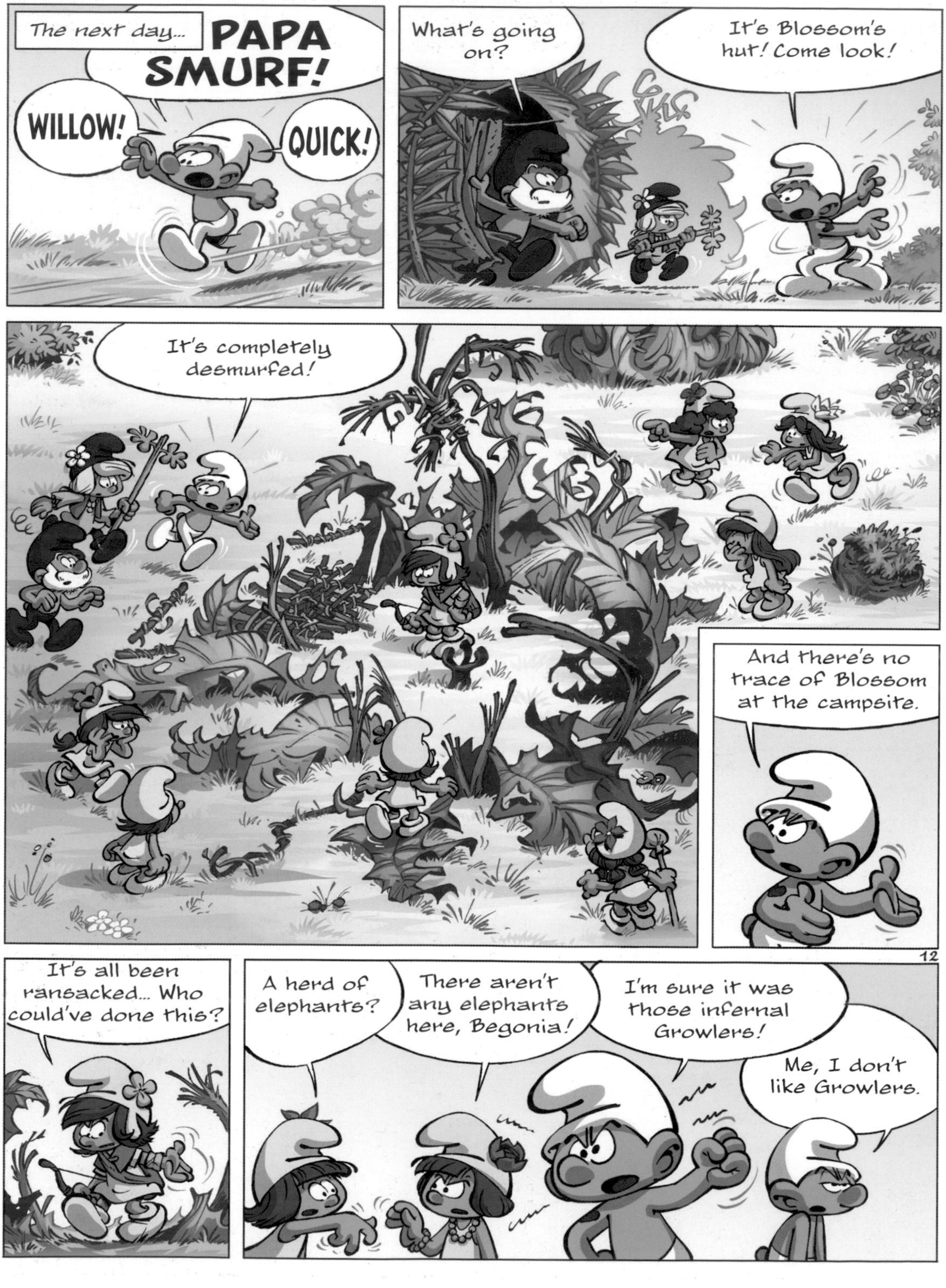

The next day...
PAPA SMURF!
WILLOW!
QUICK!
What's going on?
It's Blossom's hut! Come look!
It's completely desmurfed!
And there's no trace of Blossom at the campsite.
12
It's all been ransacked... Who could've done this?
A herd of elephants?
There aren't any elephants here, Begonia!
I'm sure it was those infernal Growlers!
Me, I don't like Growlers.

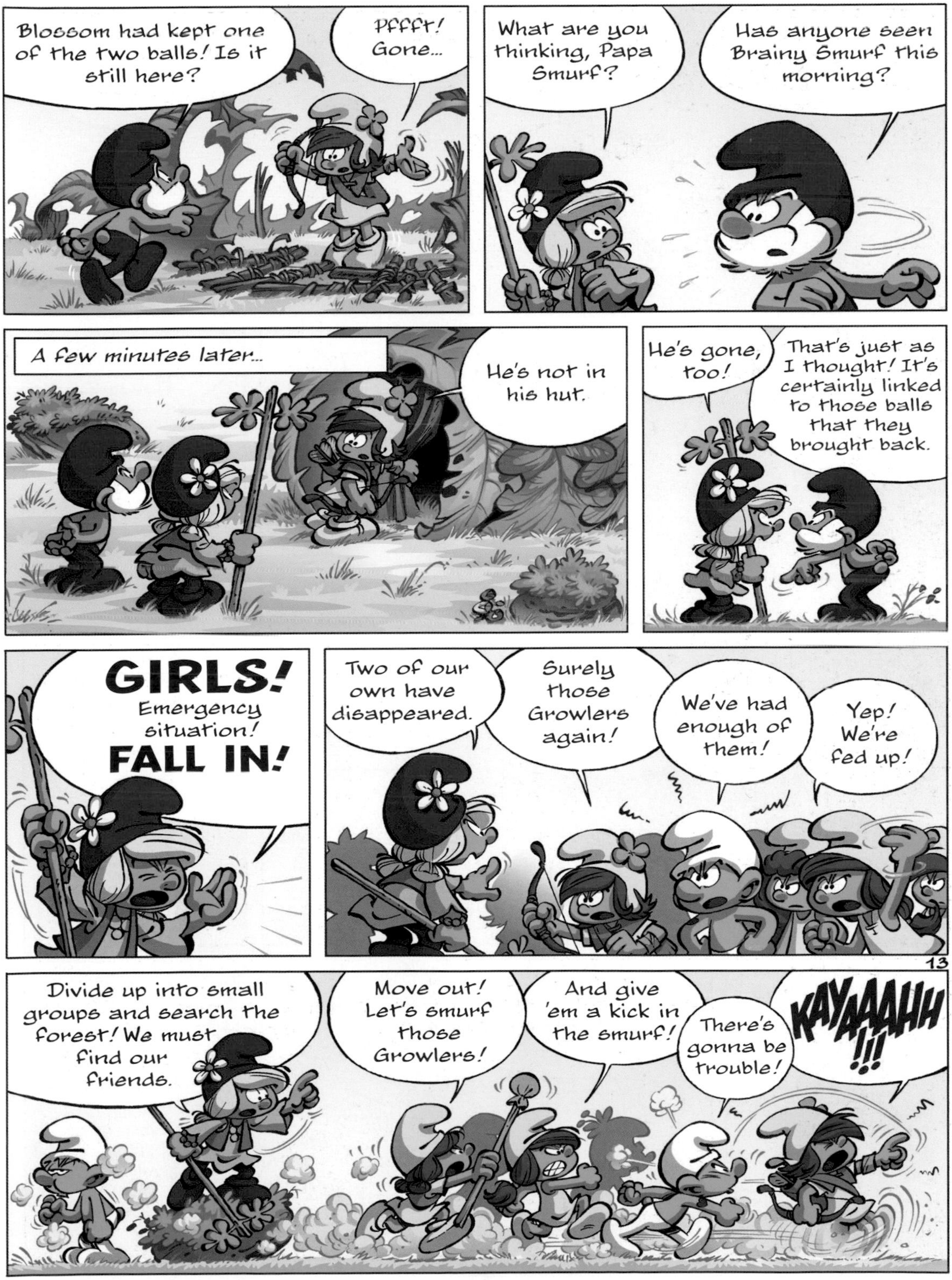
Blossom had kept one of the two balls! Is it still here?
Pffft! Gone...
What are you thinking, Papa Smurf?
Has anyone seen Brainy Smurf this morning?
A few minutes later...
He's not in his hut.
He's gone, too!
That's just as I thought! It's certainly linked to those balls that they brought back.
GIRLS! Emergency situation! FALL IN!
Two of our own have disappeared.
Surely those Growlers again!
We've had enough of them!
Yep! We're fed up!
13
Divide up into small groups and search the forest! We must find our friends.
Move out! Let's smurf those Growlers!
And give 'em a kick in the smurf!
There's gonna be trouble!
KAYAAAHH!!!

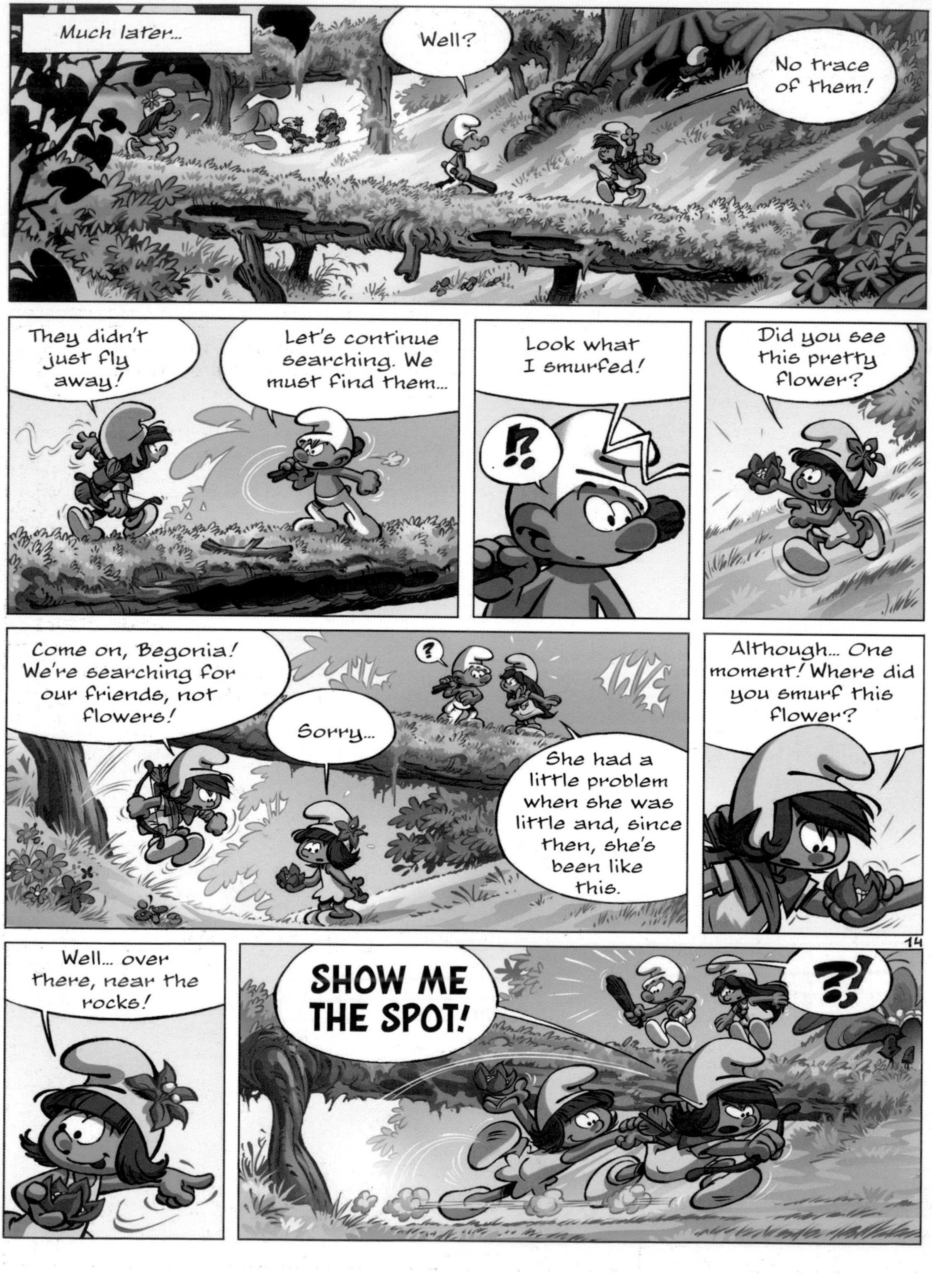

Much later...
Well?
No trace of them!
They didn't just fly away!
Let's continue searching. We must find them...
Look what I smurfed!
!?
Did you see this pretty flower?
Come on, Begonia! We're searching for our friends, not flowers!
?
Sorry...
She had a little problem when she was little and, since then, she's been like this.
Although... One moment! Where did you smurf this flower?
14
Well... over there, near the rocks!
SHOW ME THE SPOT!
?!

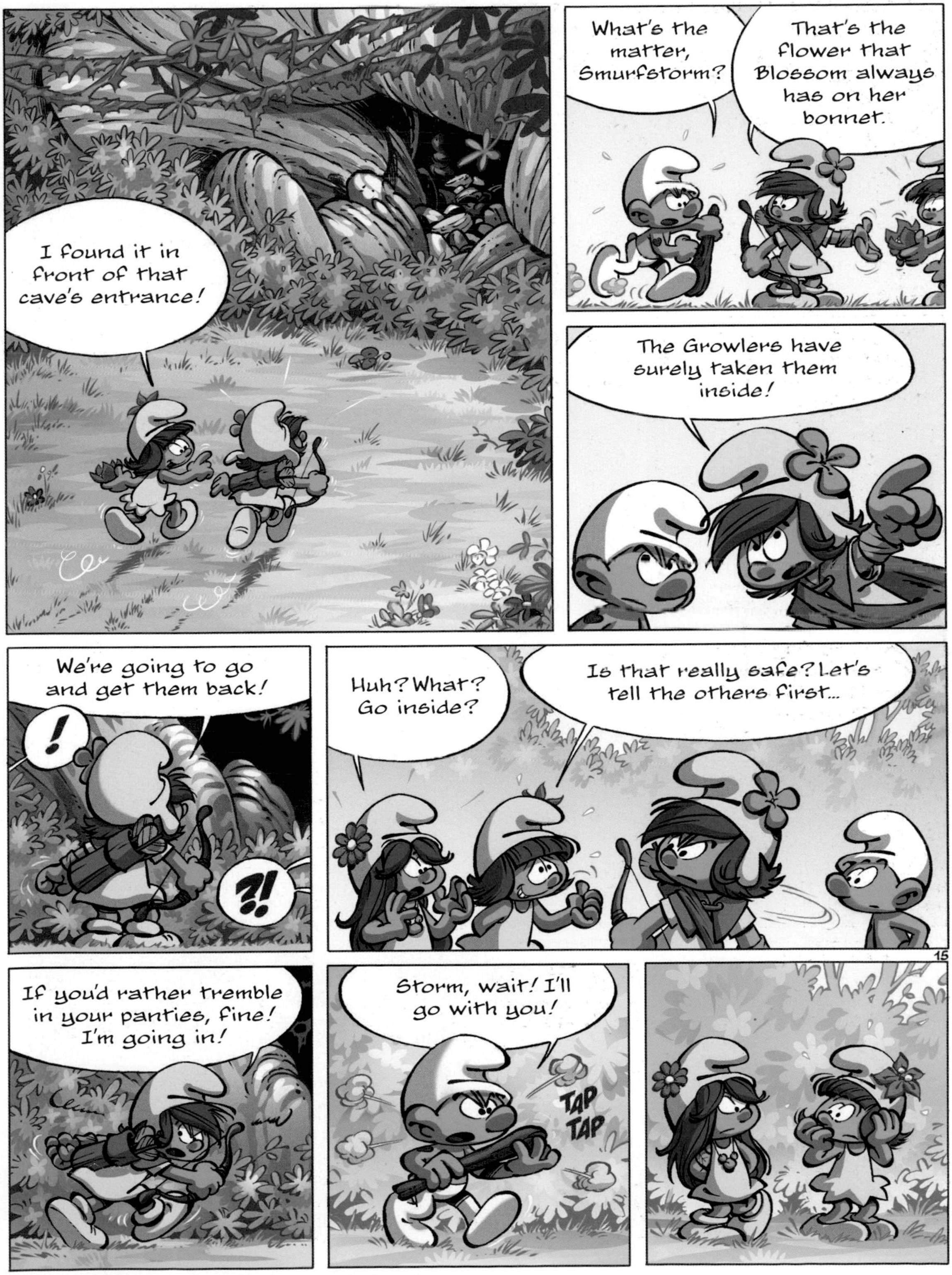

I found it in front of that cave's entrance!
What's the matter, Smurfstorm?
That's the flower that Blossom always has on her bonnet.
The Growlers have surely taken them inside!
We're going to go and get them back!
!
?!
Huh? What? Go inside?
Is that really safe? Let's tell the others first...
15
If you'd rather tremble in your panties, fine! I'm going in!
Storm, wait! I'll go with you!
TAP TAP

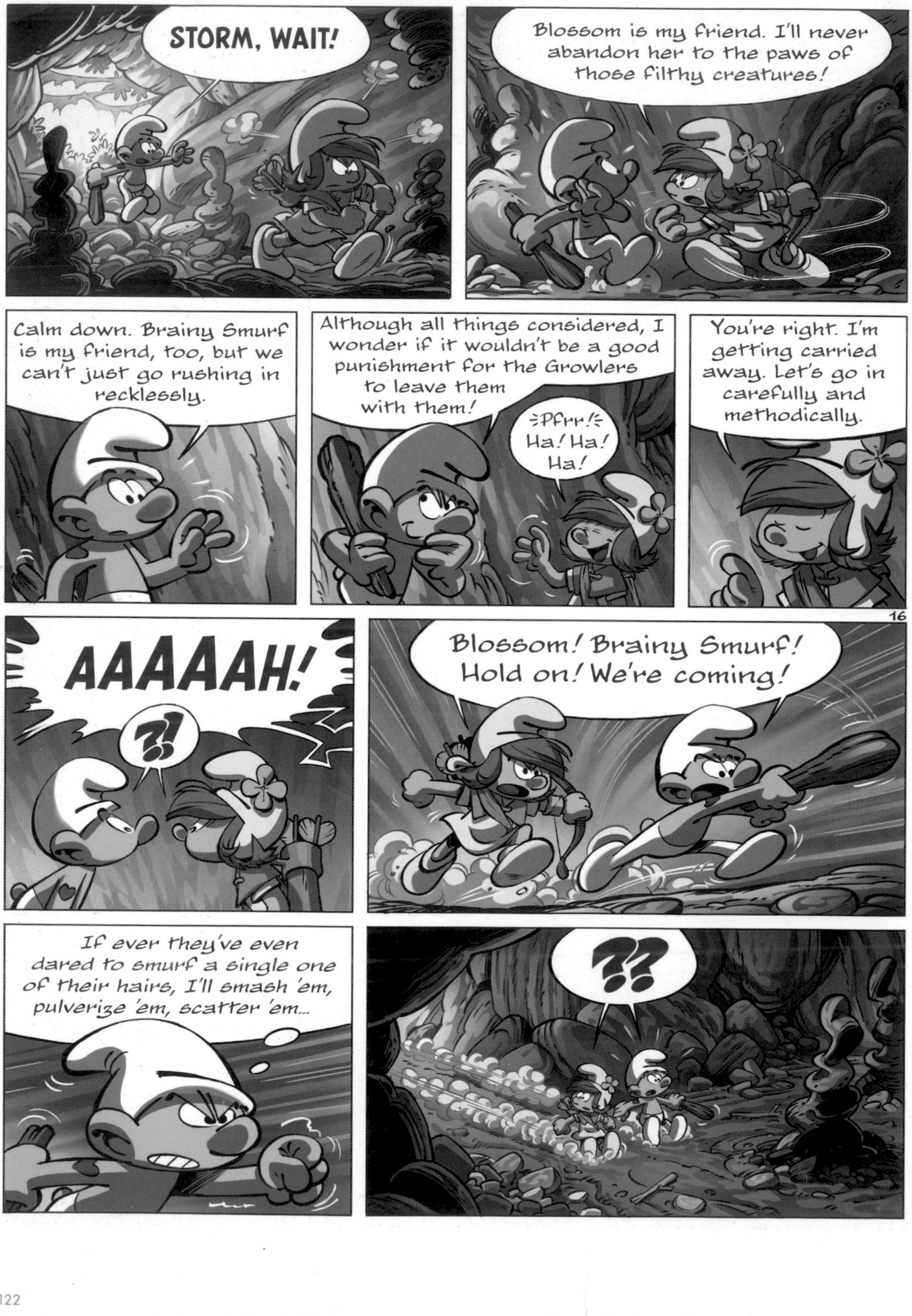
STORM, WAIT!
Blossom is my friend. I'll never abandon her to the paws of those filthy creatures!
Calm down. Brainy Smurf is my friend, too, but we can't just go rushing in recklessly.
Although all things considered, I wonder if it wouldn't be a good punishment for the Growlers to leave them with them!
Pfrr! Ha! Ha! Ha!
You're right. I'm getting carried away. Let's go in carefully and methodically.
16
AAAAAH!
?!
Blossom! Brainy Smurf! Hold on! We're coming!
If ever they've even dared to smurf a single one of their hairs, I'll smash 'em, pulverize 'em, scatter 'em...
??

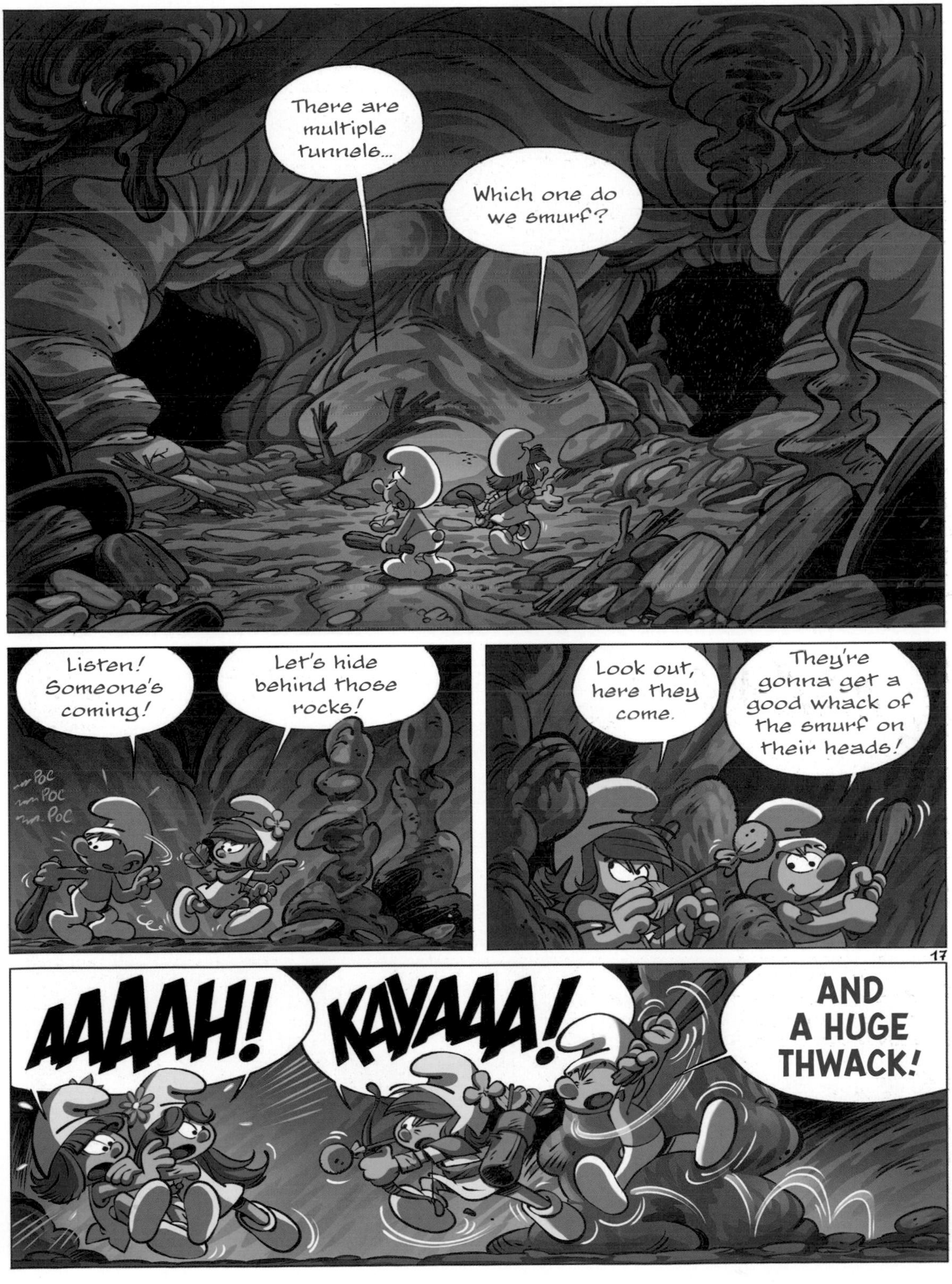
There are multiple tunnels...
Which one do we smurf?
POC POC POC
Listen! Someone's coming!
Let's hide behind those rocks!
Look out, here they come.
They're gonna get a good whack of the smurf on their heads!
17
AAAAH!
KAYAAA!
AND A HUGE THWACK!

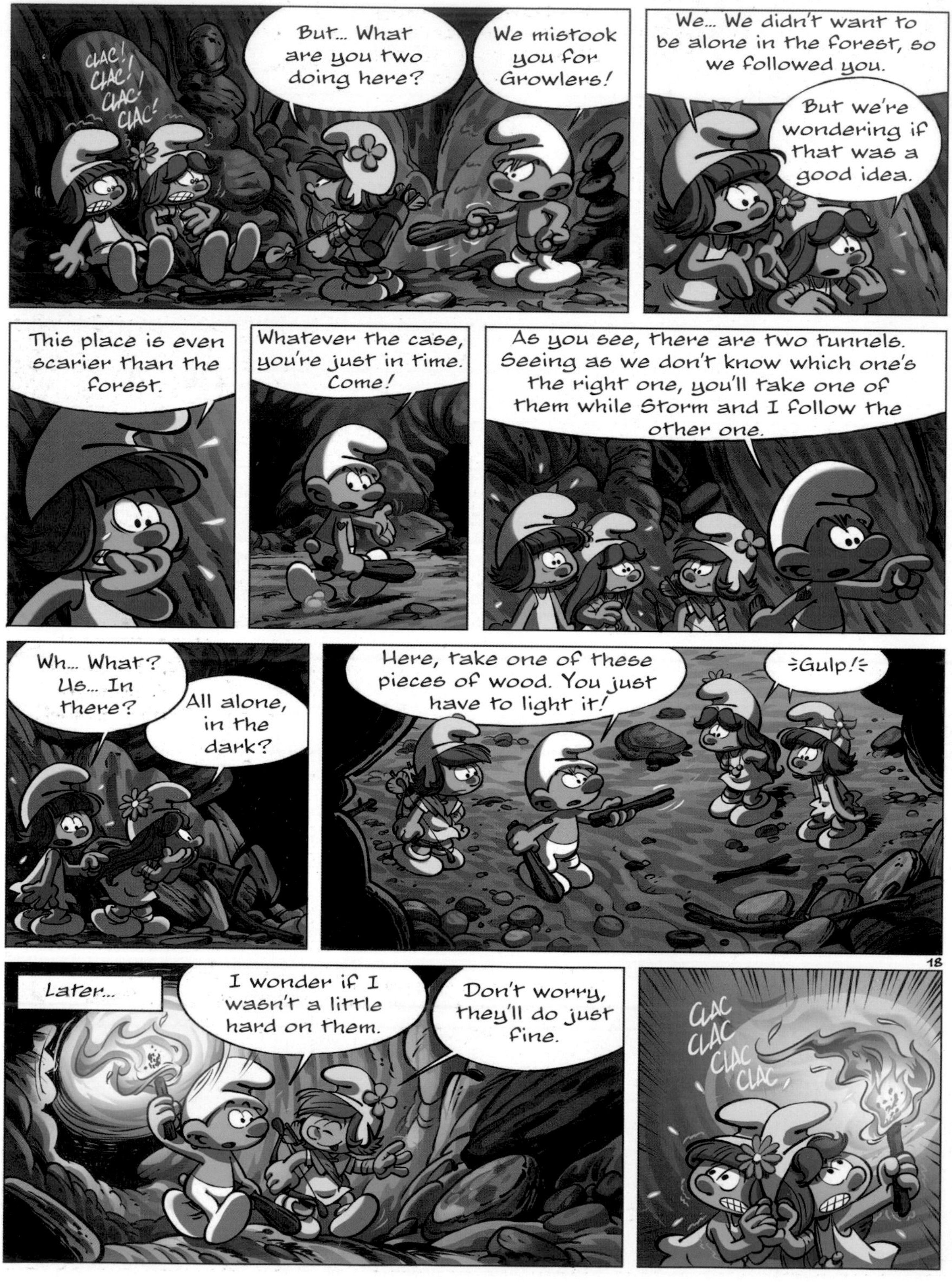

CLAC! CLAC! CLAC! CLAC!
But... What are you two doing here?
We mistook you for Growlers!
We... We didn't want to be alone in the forest, so we followed you.
But we're wondering if that was a good idea.
This place is even scarier than the forest.
Whatever the case, you're just in time. Come!
As you see, there are two tunnels. Seeing as we don't know which one's the right one, you'll take one of them while Storm and I follow the other one.
Wh... What? Us... In there?
All alone, in the dark?
Here, take one of these pieces of wood. You just have to light it!
Gulp!
18
Later...
I wonder if I wasn't a little hard on them.
Don't worry, they'll do just fine.
CLAC CLAC CLAC CLAC

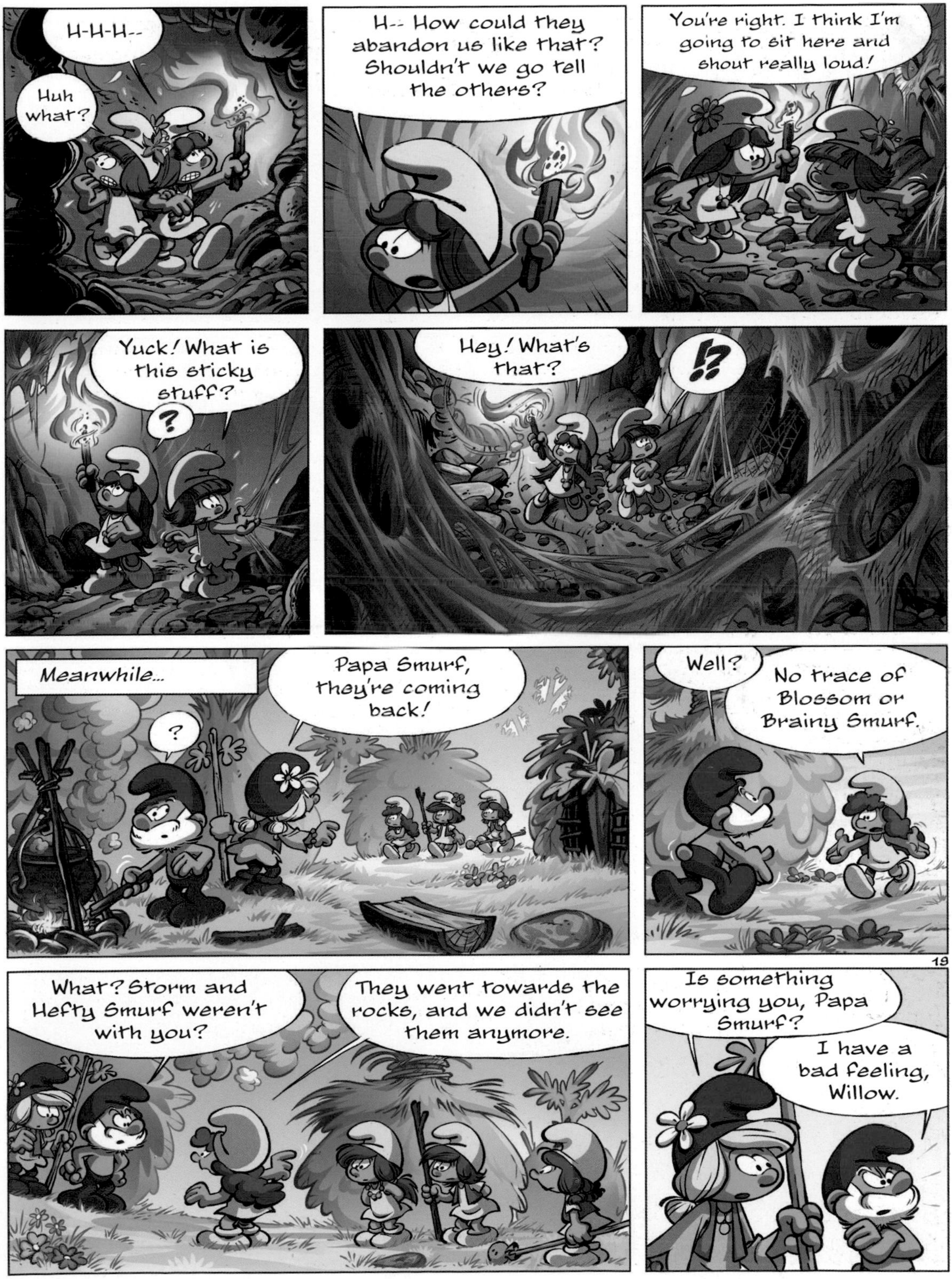

H-H-H--
Huh what?
H-- How could they abandon us like that? Shouldn't we go tell the others?
You're right. I think I'm going to sit here and shout really loud!
Yuck! What is this sticky stuff?
?
Hey! What's that?
!?
Meanwhile...
Papa Smurf, they're coming back!
?
Well?
No trace of Blossom or Brainy Smurf.
19
What? Storm and Hefty Smurf weren't with you?
They went towards the rocks, and we didn't see them anymore.
Is something worrying you, Papa Smurf?
I have a bad feeling, Willow.

We've been walking a long time and still haven't found anything.

Over there, a glow!

Have you see this funny stone?...

That's what's making the light.

And there are others!

No need for a torch then.

Over here!

Hey, look! These things are smurfly weird.

We'd better not touch it.

There's even some on the ground.

Watch where you smurf your feet. It's sticky.

Well, I never! By Papa Smurf's beard!

?

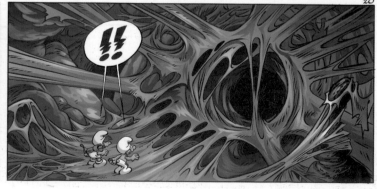

None of this tells me anything worthwhile.

Let's keep our guard up.

I don't understand. This doesn't look at all like a Growler nest.

∍Shh!∈ There's sound coming from ahead!

?

ᛚᚨᚾ ᛁᚹᛁ ᚢᚱᚨᛚᚠᛟ ·ᚷᛁᛚ smurf...

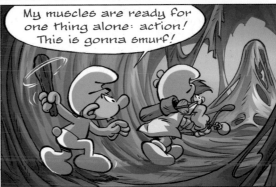

My muscles are ready for one thing alone: action! This is gonna smurf!

⁉

And as I was saying, the best way to smurf your hair obviously is to use soft soap.

That's not what Papa Smurf says! He uses an infusion of reed stalks for his beard!

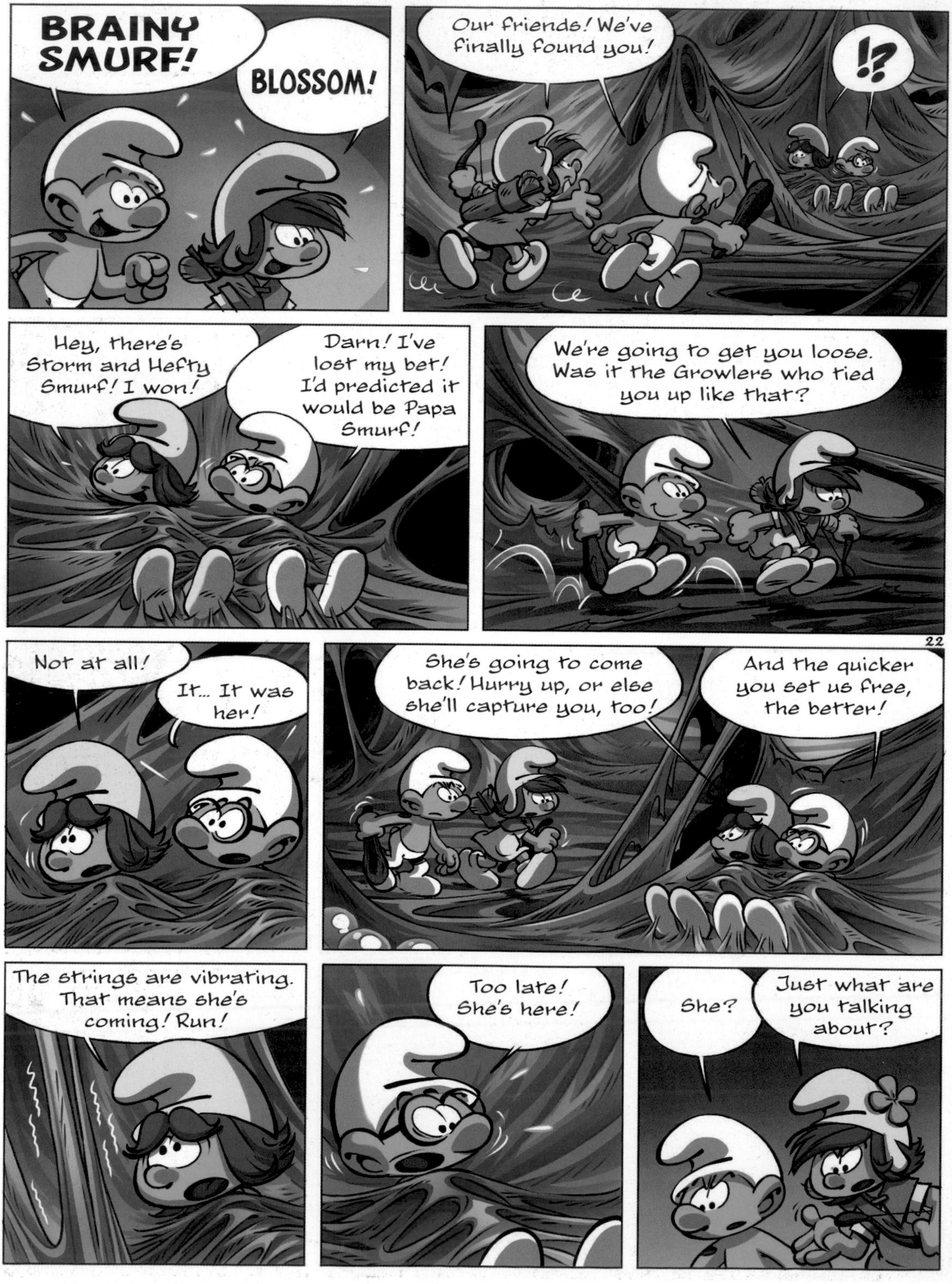
BRAINY SMURF!
BLOSSOM!
Our friends! We've finally found you!
!?
Hey, there's Storm and Hefty Smurf! I won!
Darn! I've lost my bet! I'd predicted it would be Papa Smurf!
We're going to get you loose. Was it the Growlers who tied you up like that?
22
Not at all!
It... It was her!
She's going to come back! Hurry up, or else she'll capture you, too!
And the quicker you set us free, the better!
The strings are vibrating. That means she's coming! Run!
Too late! She's here!
She?
Just what are you talking about?

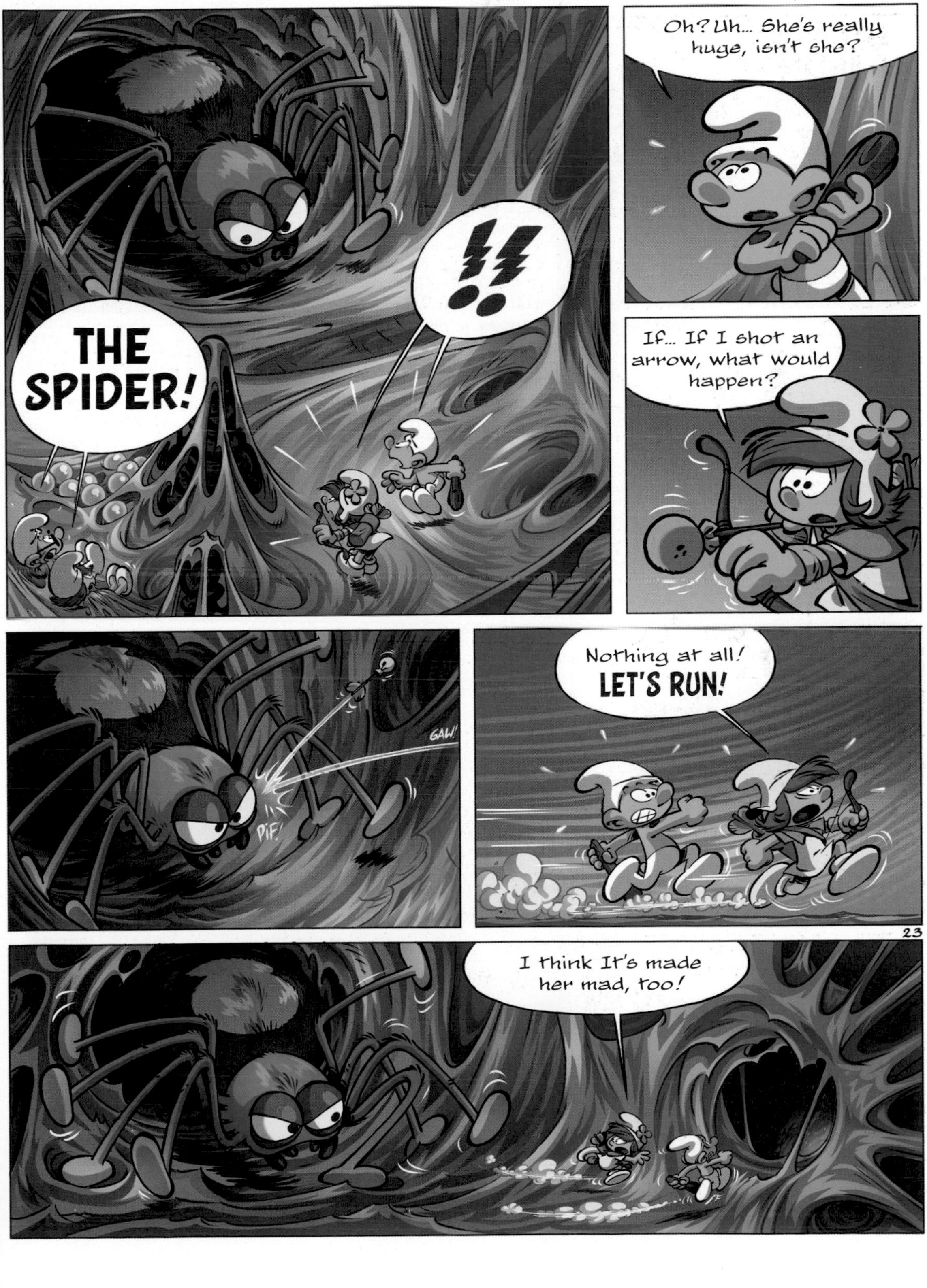
THE SPIDER!
!!
Oh? Uh... She's really huge, isn't she?
If... If I shot an arrow, what would happen?
PIF!
GAW!
Nothing at all! LET'S RUN!
23
I think It's made her mad, too!

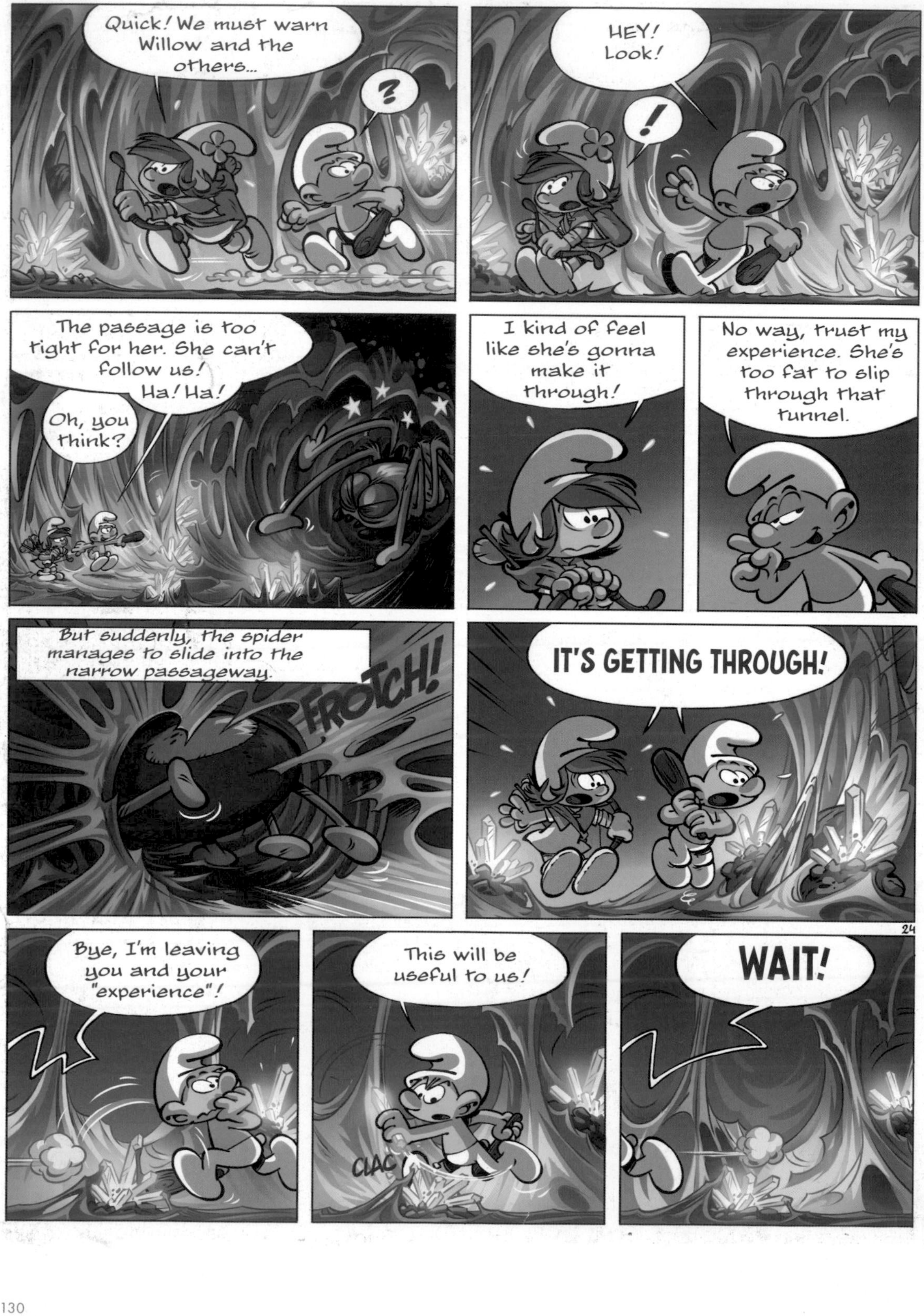
Quick! We must warn Willow and the others...
?
HEY! Look!
!
The passage is too tight for her. She can't follow us! Ha! Ha!
Oh, you think?
I kind of feel like she's gonna make it through!
No way, trust my experience. She's too fat to slip through that tunnel.
But suddenly, the spider manages to slide into the narrow passageway.
FROTCH!
IT'S GETTING THROUGH!
Bye, I'm leaving you and your "experience"!
This will be useful to us!
CLAC
WAIT!

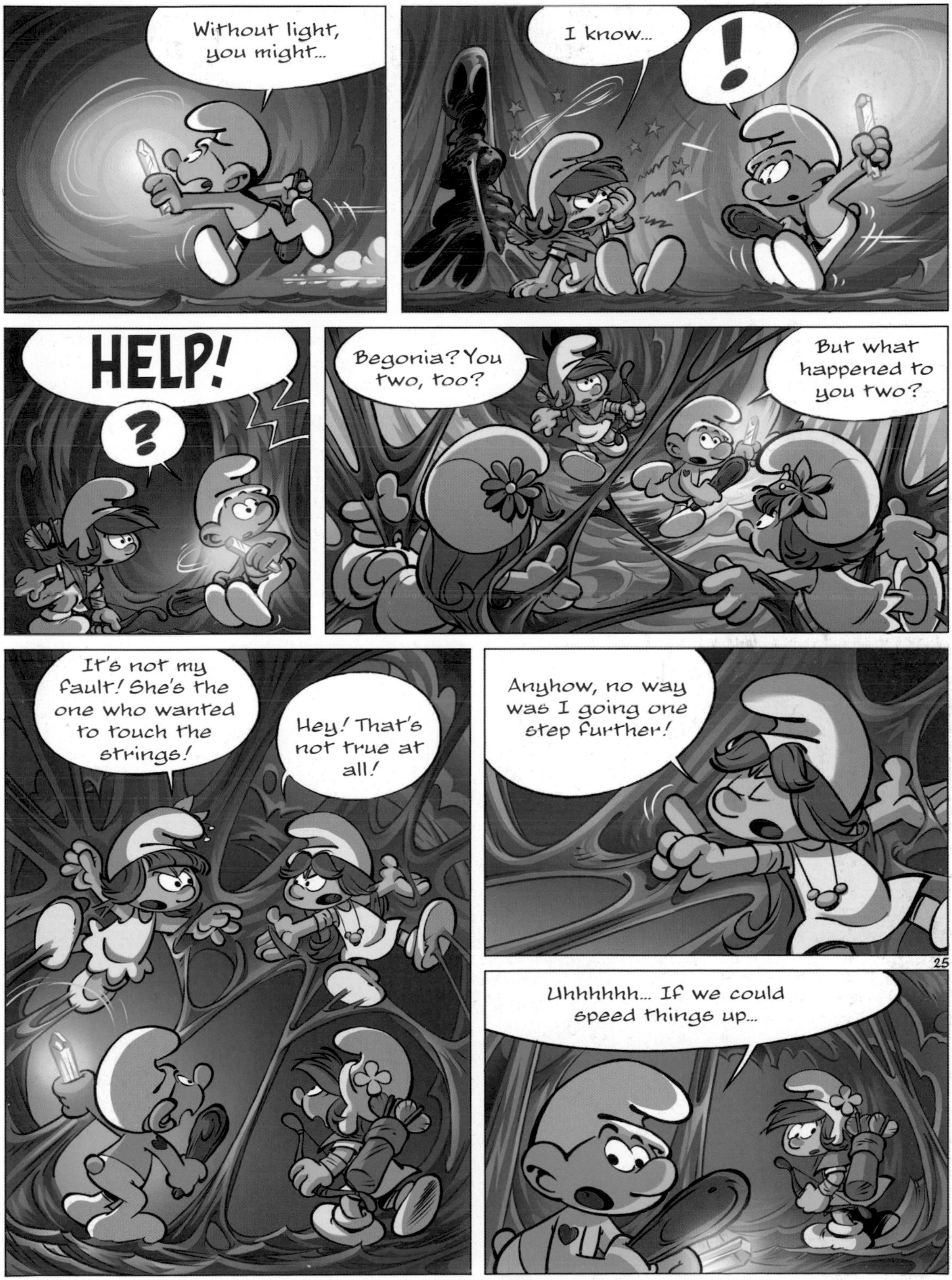

Without light, you might...
I know...
!
HELP!
?
Begonia? You two, too?
But what happened to you two?
It's not my fault! She's the one who wanted to touch the strings!
Hey! That's not true at all!
Anyhow, no way was I going one step further!
Uhhhhhh... If we could speed things up...

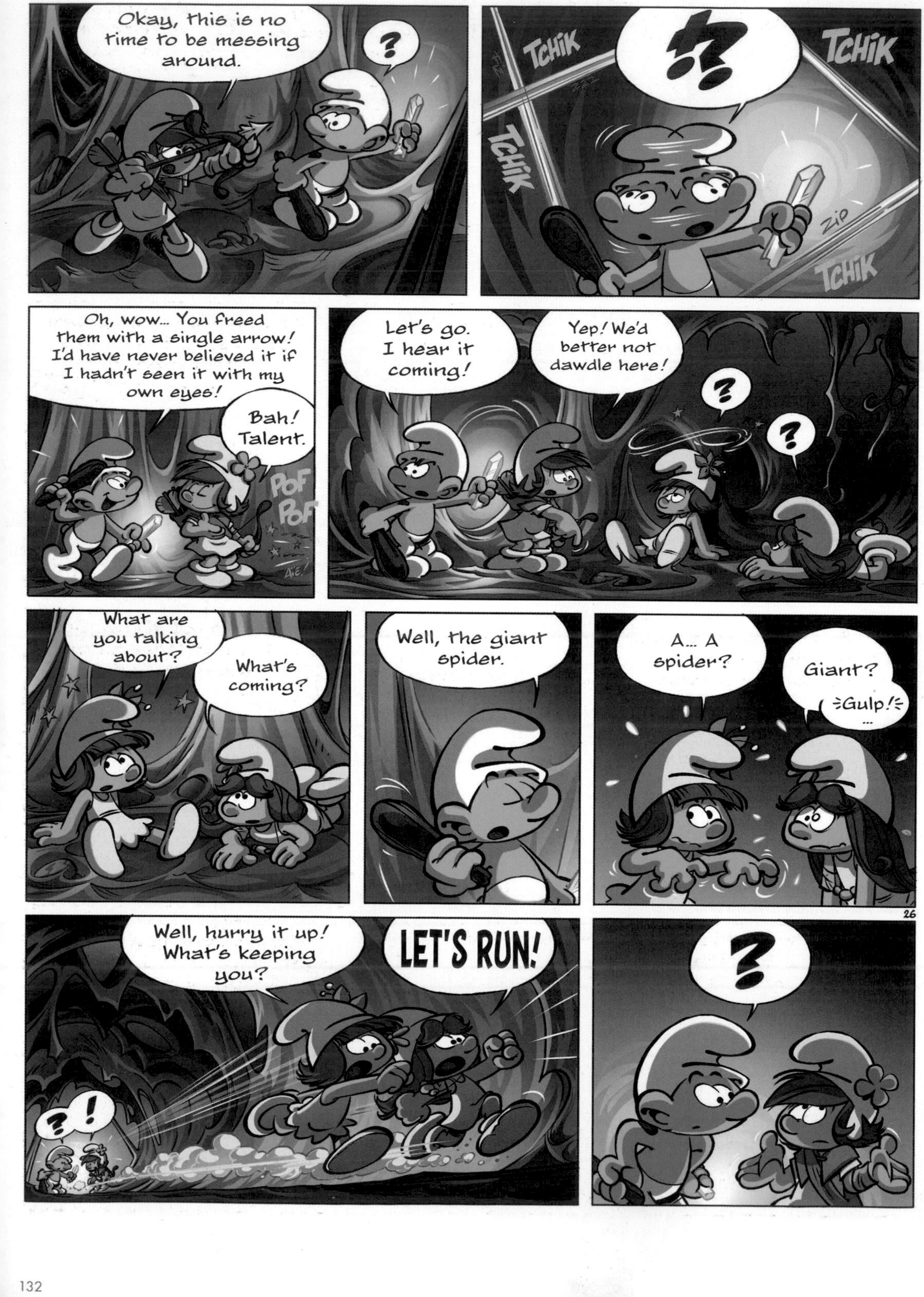
Okay, this is no time to be messing around.
?
TCHIK
TCHIK
TCHIK
ZIP
TCHIK
Oh, wow... You freed them with a single arrow! I'd have never believed it if I hadn't seen it with my own eyes!
Bah! Talent.
POF POF
AÏE!
Let's go. I hear it coming!
Yep! We'd better not dawdle here!
?
?
What are you talking about?
What's coming?
Well, the giant spider.
A... A spider?
Giant?
Gulp! ...
26
Well, hurry it up! What's keeping you?
LET'S RUN!
?!
?

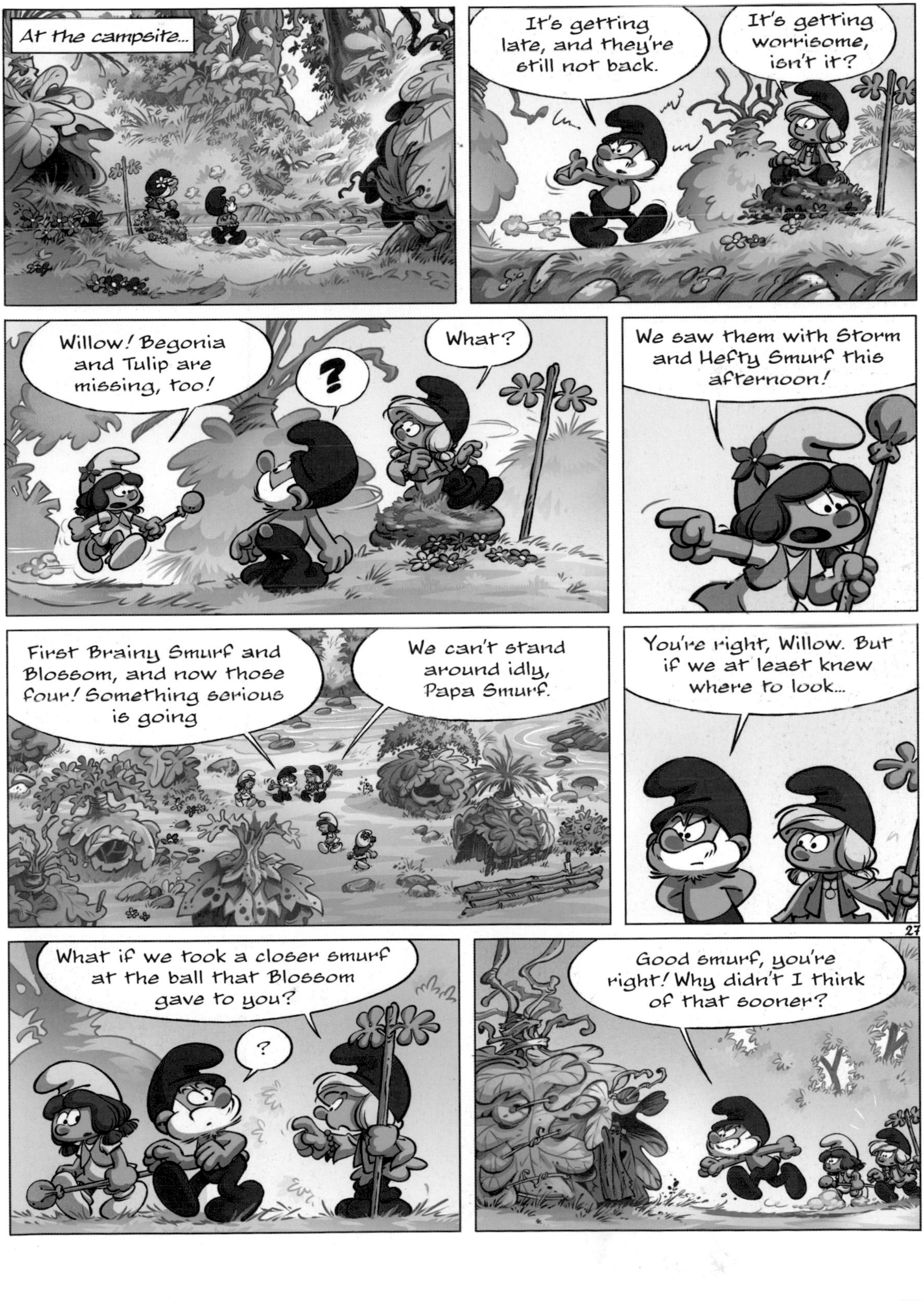
At the campsite...
It's getting late, and they're still not back.
It's getting worrisome, isn't it?
Willow! Begonia and Tulip are missing, too!
?
What?
We saw them with Storm and Hefty Smurf this afternoon!
First Brainy Smurf and Blossom, and now those four! Something serious is going
We can't stand around idly, Papa Smurf.
You're right, Willow. But if we at least knew where to look...
27
What if we took a closer smurf at the ball that Blossom gave to you?
?
Good smurf, you're right! Why didn't I think of that sooner?

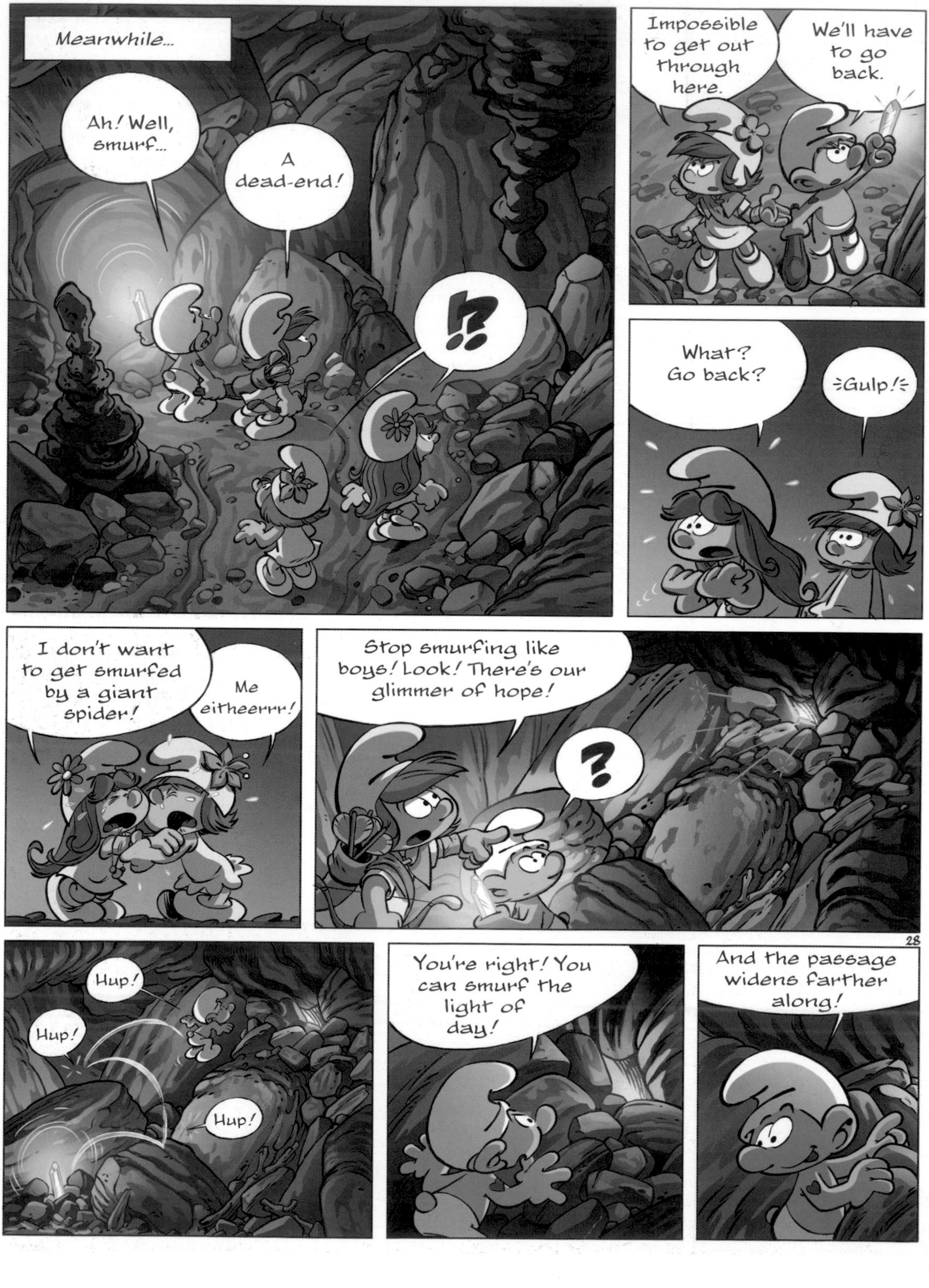

Meanwhile...
Ah! Well, smurf...
A dead-end!
!?
Impossible to get out through here.
We'll have to go back.
What? Go back?
Gulp!
I don't want to get smurfed by a giant spider!
Me eitheerrr!
Stop smurfing like boys! Look! There's our glimmer of hope!
?
Hup!
Hup!
Hup!
You're right! You can smurf the light of day!
And the passage widens farther along!
28

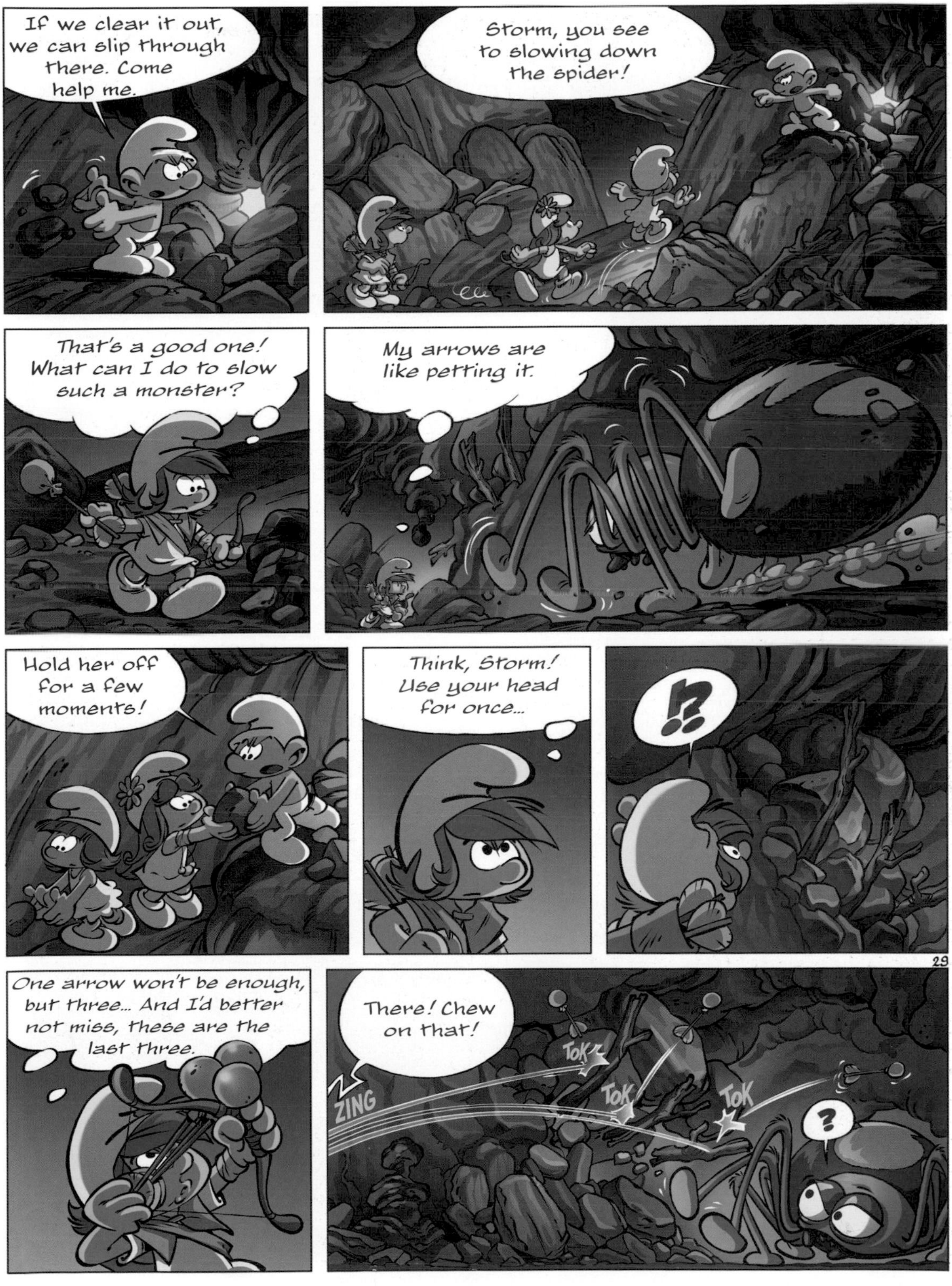

If we clear it out, we can slip through there. Come help me.
Storm, you see to slowing down the spider!
That's a good one! What can I do to slow such a monster?
My arrows are like petting it.
Hold her off for a few moments!
Think, Storm! Use your head for once...
!?
29
One arrow won't be enough, but three... And I'd better not miss, these are the last three.
There! Chew on that!
ZING
TOK
TOK
TOK
?

Storm's arrows loosen a pile of rocks.

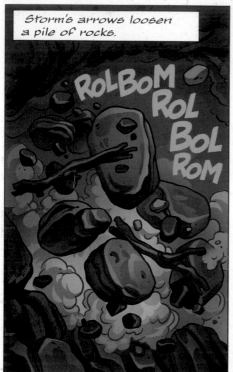

ROL BOM ROL BOL ROM

Which cut off the spider's path...

Okay, girls, it's now or never! I'm out of arrows and ideas!

It's wide enough. After you, ladies!

Let's go, then! Let's not hang around here!

30

Indeed, the spider has managed to break through the obstacle and is furious.

⇒Gulp!⇐ Move it, move it!

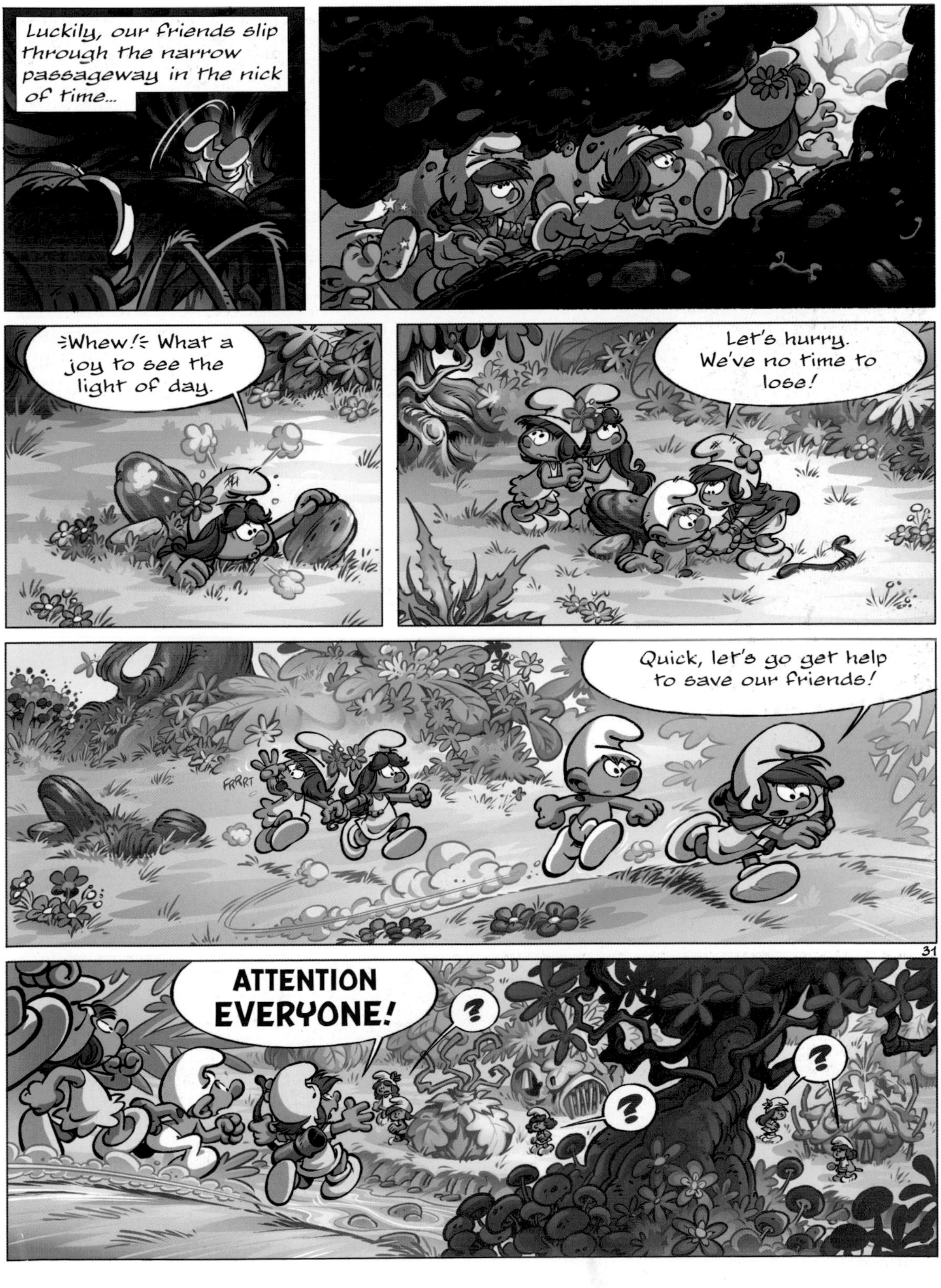

Luckily, our friends slip through the narrow passageway in the nick of time...
Whew! What a joy to see the light of day.
Let's hurry. We've no time to lose!
FRRRT
Quick, let's go get help to save our friends!
31
ATTENTION EVERYONE!
?
?
?

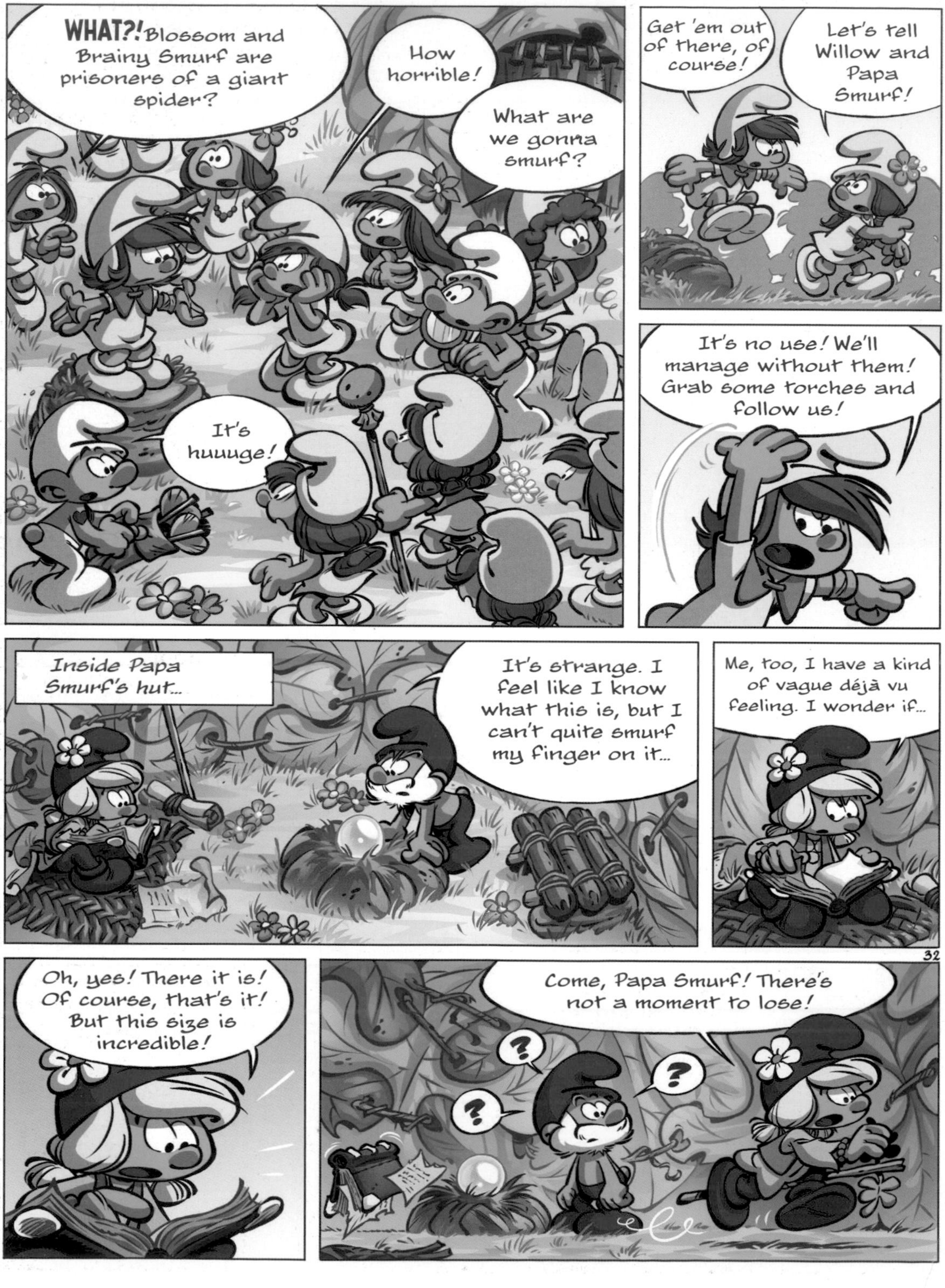

WHAT?! Blossom and Brainy Smurf are prisoners of a giant spider?
How horrible!
What are we gonna smurf?
It's huuuge!
Get 'em out of there, of course!
Let's tell Willow and Papa Smurf!
It's no use! We'll manage without them! Grab some torches and follow us!
Inside Papa Smurf's hut...
It's strange. I feel like I know what this is, but I can't quite smurf my finger on it...
Me, too, I have a kind of vague déjà vu feeling. I wonder if...
32
Oh, yes! There it is! Of course, that's it! But this size is incredible!
Come, Papa Smurf! There's not a moment to lose!
?
?
?

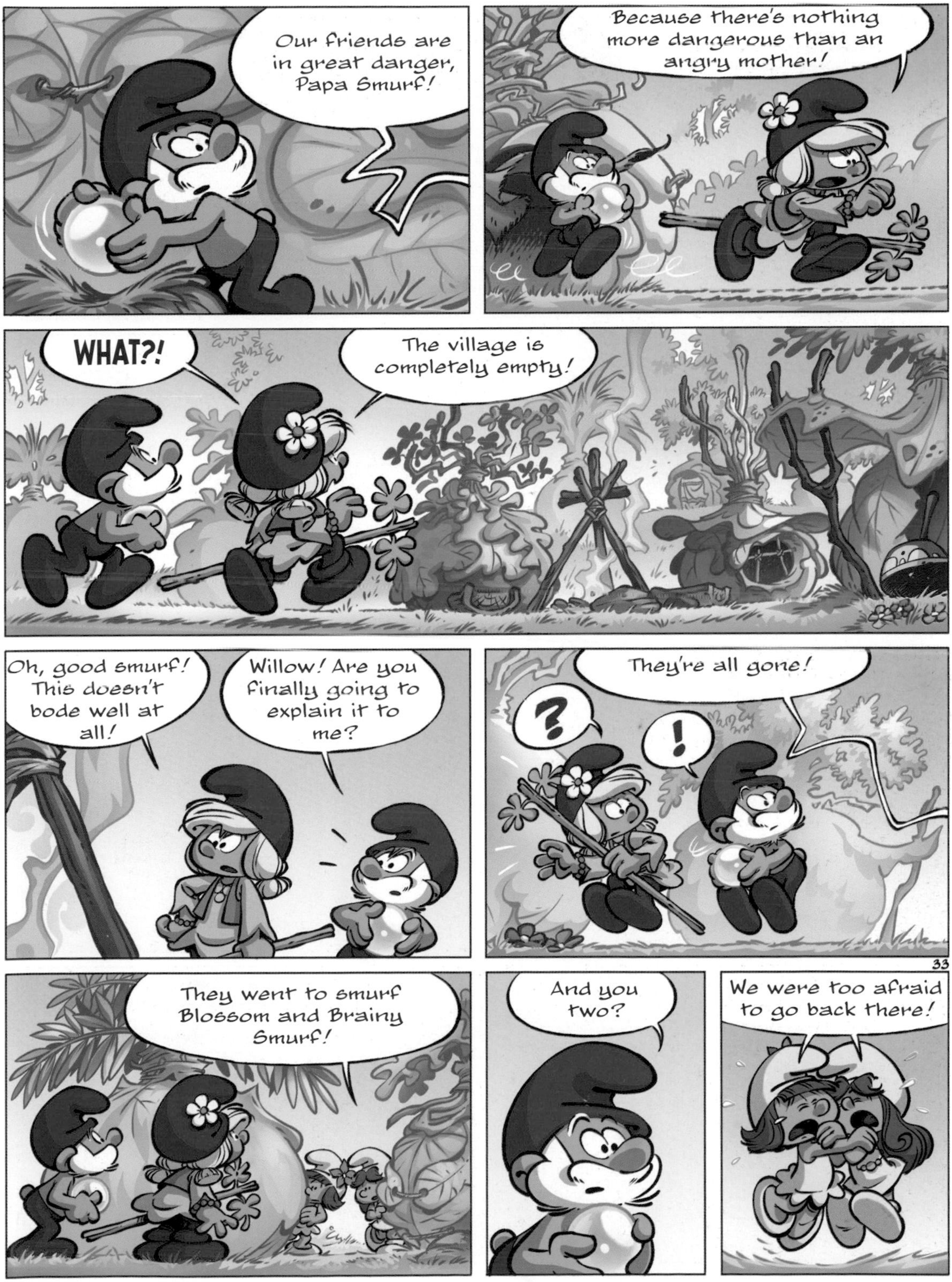
Our friends are in great danger, Papa Smurf!
Because there's nothing more dangerous than an angry mother!
WHAT?!
The village is completely empty!
Oh, good smurf! This doesn't bode well at all!
Willow! Are you finally going to explain it to me?
?
!
They're all gone!
33
They went to smurf Blossom and Brainy Smurf!
And you two?
We were too afraid to go back there!

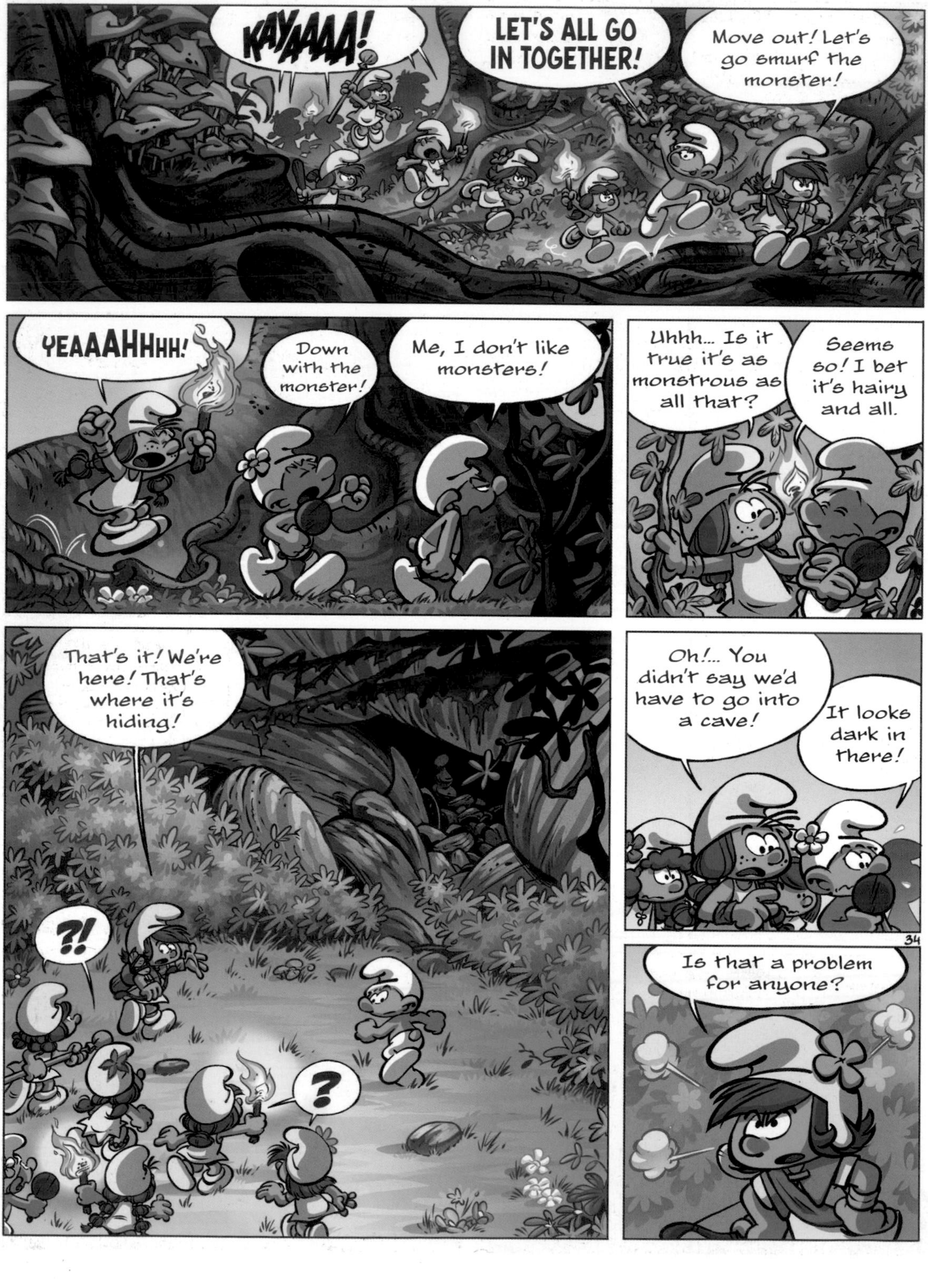
KAYAAAA!
LET'S ALL GO IN TOGETHER!
Move out! Let's go smurf the monster!
YEAAAHHHH!
Down with the monster!
Me, I don't like monsters!
Uhhh... Is it true it's as monstrous as all that?
Seems so! I bet it's hairy and all.
That's it! We're here! That's where it's hiding!
?!
?
Oh!... You didn't say we'd have to go into a cave!
It looks dark in there!
34
Is that a problem for anyone?

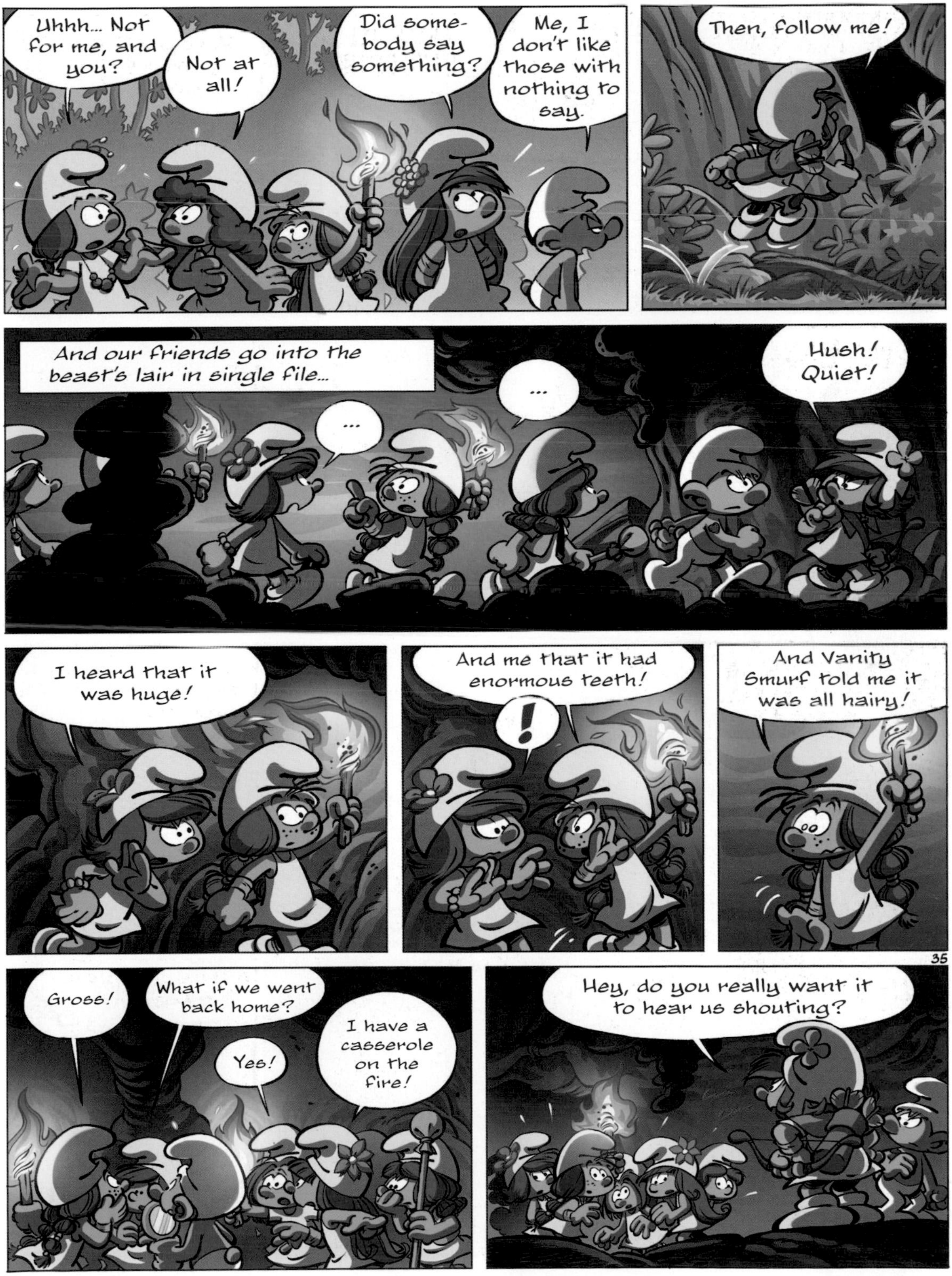
Uhhh... Not for me, and you?
Not at all!
Did somebody say something?
Me, I don't like those with nothing to say.
Then, follow me!
And our friends go into the beast's lair in single file...
...
...
Hush! Quiet!
I heard that it was huge!
And me that it had enormous teeth!
!
And Vanity Smurf told me it was all hairy!
35
Gross!
What if we went back home?
Yes!
I have a casserole on the fire!
Hey, do you really want it to hear us shouting?

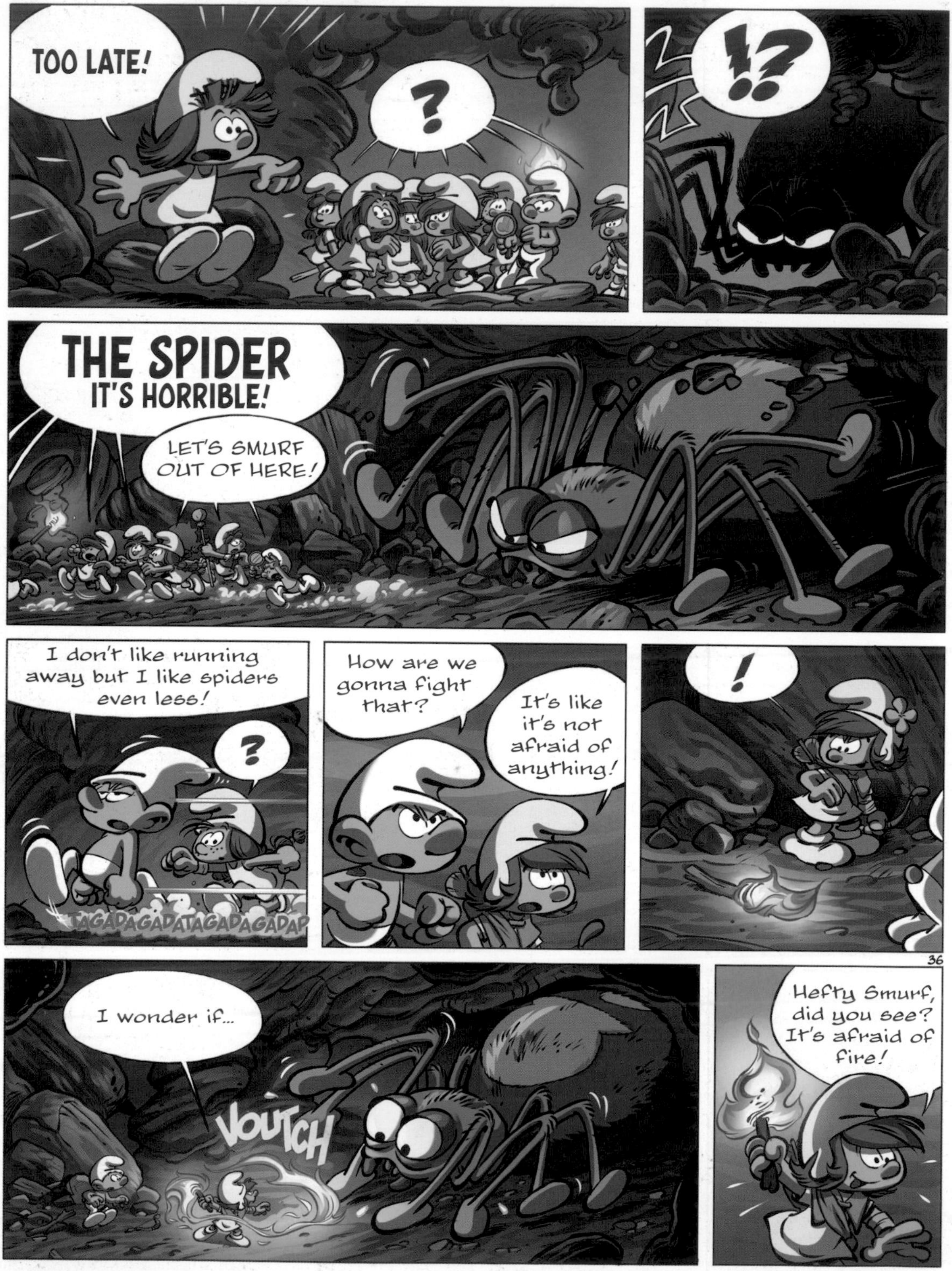
TOO LATE!
?
!?
THE SPIDER IT'S HORRIBLE!
LET'S SMURF OUT OF HERE!
I don't like running away but I like spiders even less!
?
TAGADAGADATAGADAGADAP
How are we gonna fight that?
It's like it's not afraid of anything!
!
36
I wonder if...
VOUTCH
Hefty Smurf, did you see? It's afraid of fire!

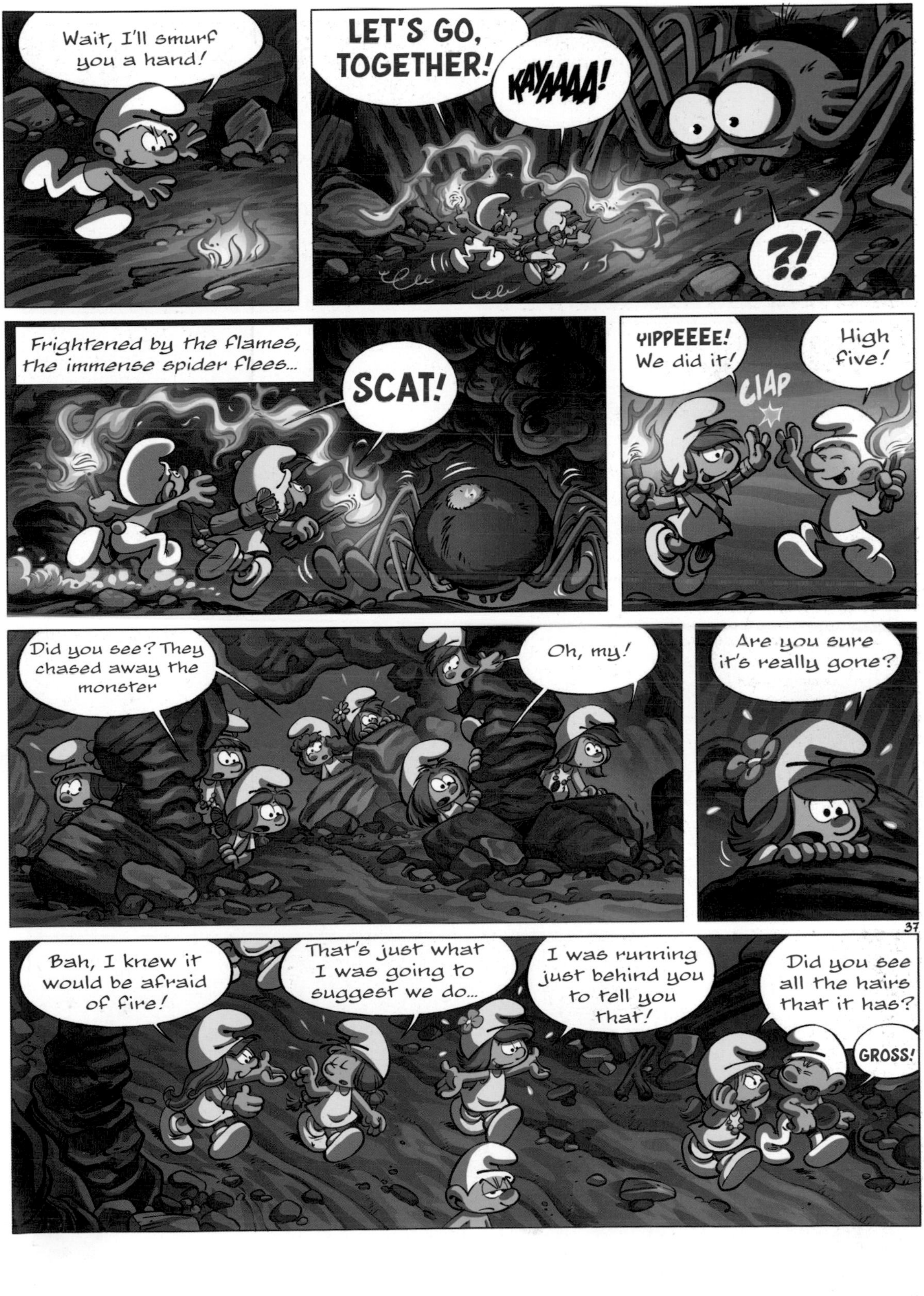
Wait, I'll smurf you a hand!
LET'S GO, TOGETHER!
KAYAAAA!
?!
Frightened by the flames, the immense spider flees...
SCAT!
YIPPEEEE! We did it!
High five!
CLAP
Did you see? They chased away the monster
Oh, my!
Are you sure it's really gone?
37
Bah, I knew it would be afraid of fire!
That's just what I was going to suggest we do...
I was running just behind you to tell you that!
Did you see all the hairs that it has?
GROSS!

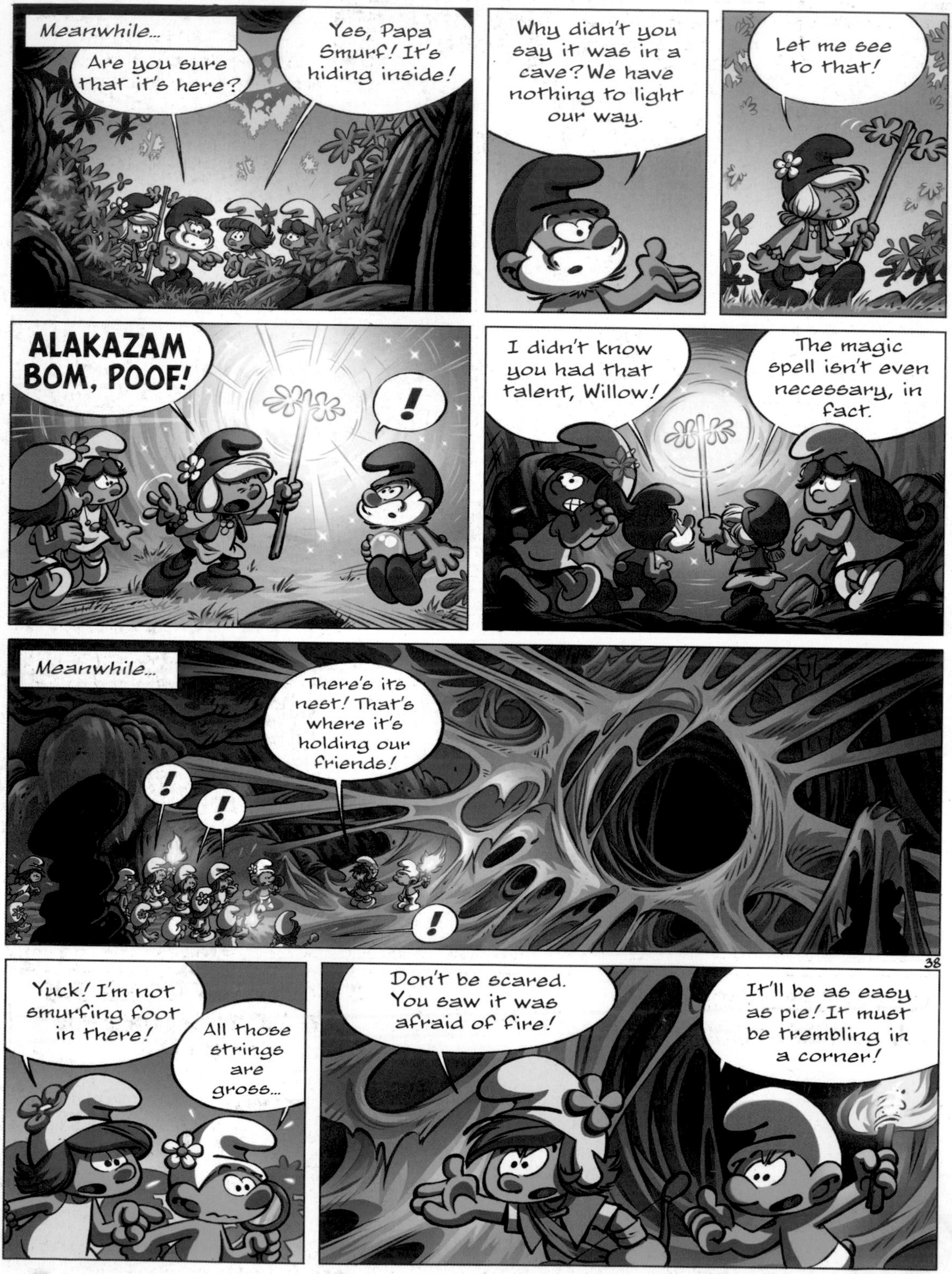
Meanwhile...
Are you sure that it's here?
Yes, Papa Smurf! It's hiding inside!
Why didn't you say it was in a cave? We have nothing to light our way.
Let me see to that!
ALAKAZAM BOM, POOF!
!
I didn't know you had that talent, Willow!
The magic spell isn't even necessary, in fact.
Meanwhile...
There's its nest! That's where it's holding our friends!
!
!
!
38
Yuck! I'm not smurfing foot in there!
All those strings are gross...
Don't be scared. You saw it was afraid of fire!
It'll be as easy as pie! It must be trembling in a corner!

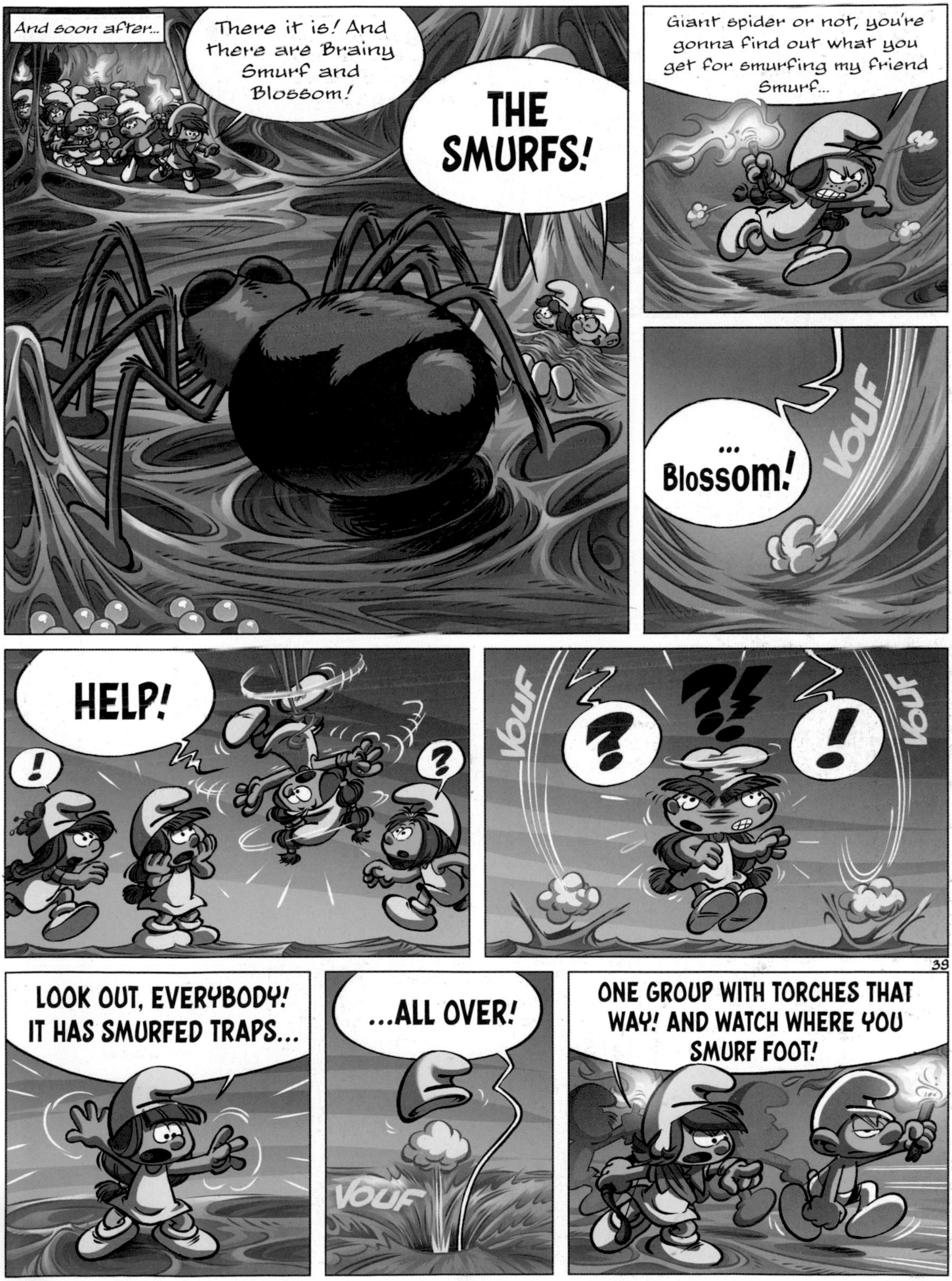
And soon after...
There it is! And there are Brainy Smurf and Blossom!
THE SMURFS!
Giant spider or not, you're gonna find out what you get for smurfing my friend Smurf...
... Blossom!
VOUF
HELP!
!
?
VOUF
?
?!
!
VOUF
39
LOOK OUT, EVERYBODY! IT HAS SMURFED TRAPS...
...ALL OVER!
VOUF
ONE GROUP WITH TORCHES THAT WAY! AND WATCH WHERE YOU SMURF FOOT!

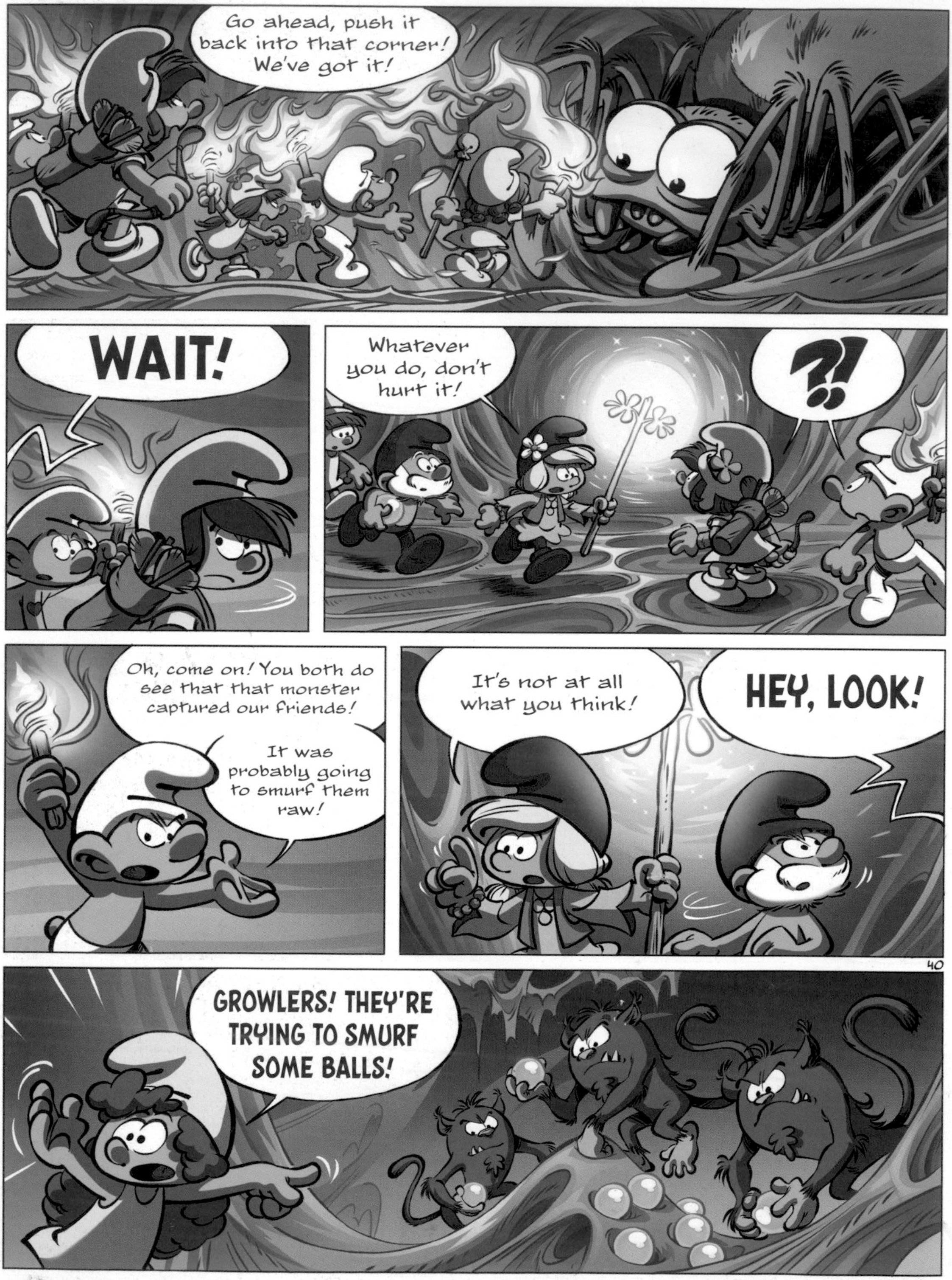

Go ahead, push it back into that corner! We've got it!
WAIT!
Whatever you do, don't hurt it!
?!
Oh, come on! You both do see that that monster captured our friends!
It was probably going to smurf them raw!
It's not at all what you think!
HEY, LOOK!
40
GROWLERS! THEY'RE TRYING TO SMURF SOME BALLS!

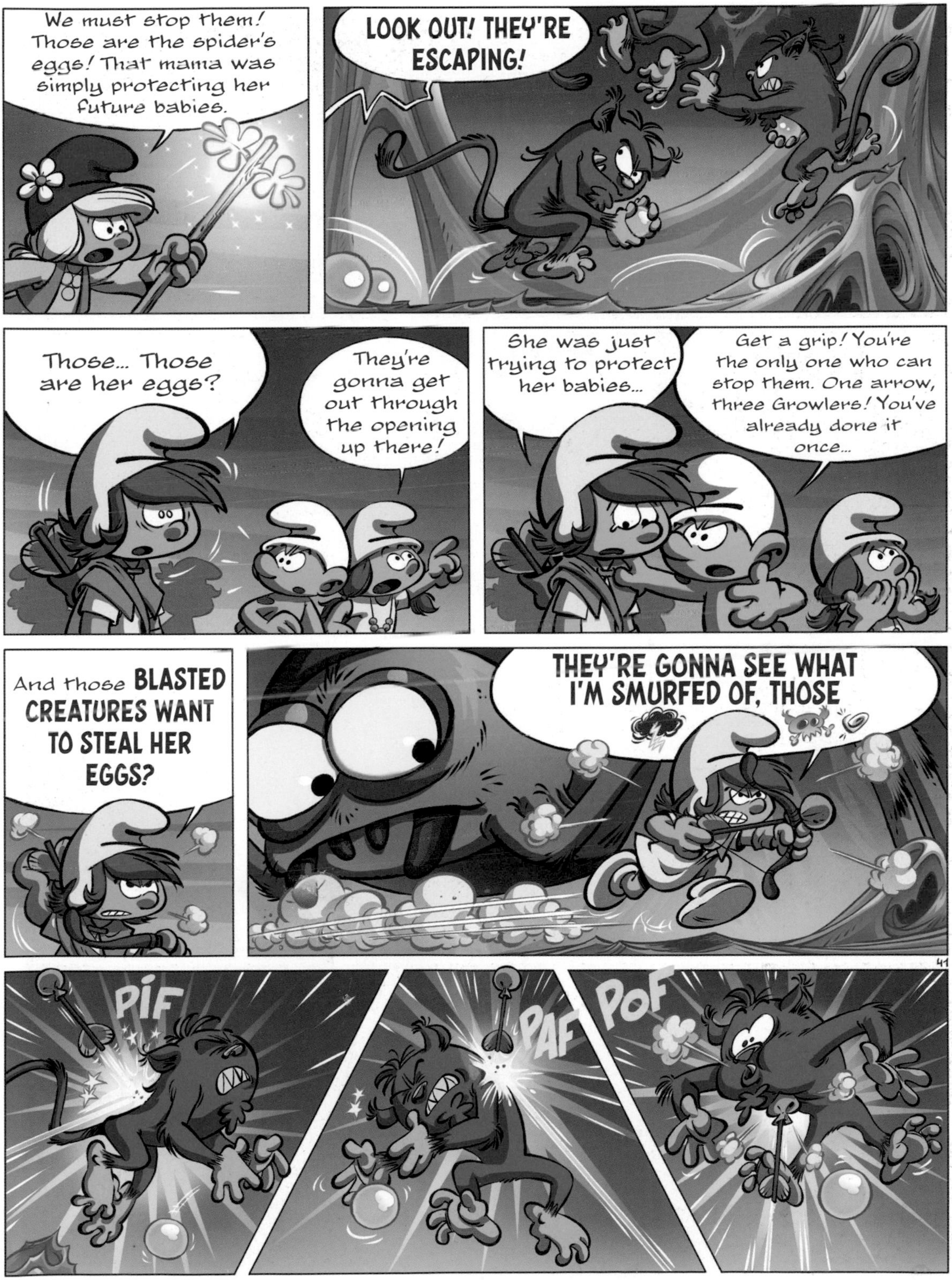

We must stop them! Those are the spider's eggs! That mama was simply protecting her future babies.
LOOK OUT! THEY'RE ESCAPING!
Those... Those are her eggs?
They're gonna get out through the opening up there!
She was just trying to protect her babies...
Get a grip! You're the only one who can stop them. One arrow, three Growlers! You've already done it once...
And those BLASTED CREATURES WANT TO STEAL HER EGGS?
THEY'RE GONNA SEE WHAT I'M SMURFED OF, THOSE
41
PIF
PAF
POF

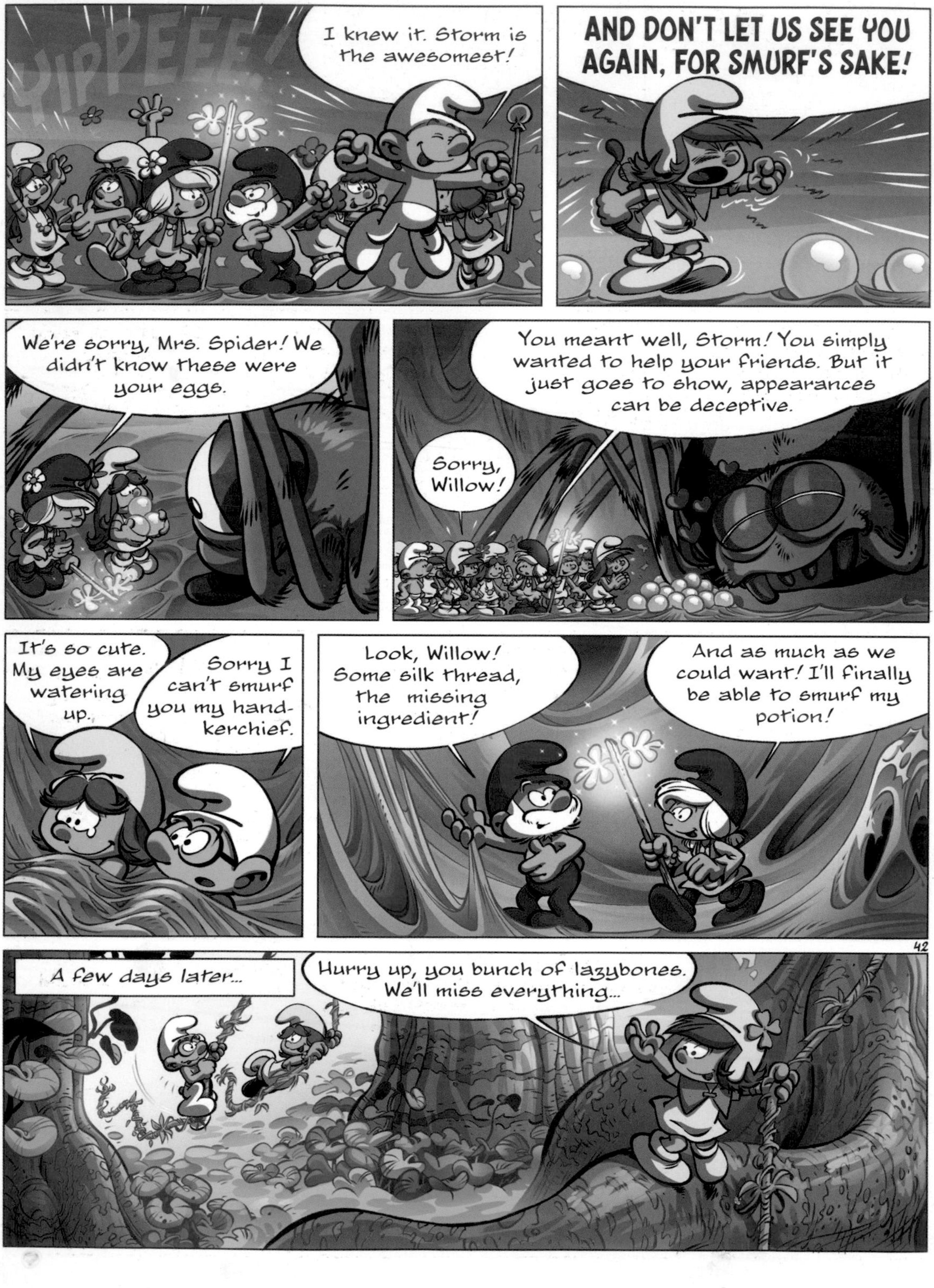
YIPPEEE!
I knew it. Storm is the awesomest!
AND DON'T LET US SEE YOU AGAIN, FOR SMURF'S SAKE!
We're sorry, Mrs. Spider! We didn't know these were your eggs.
You meant well, Storm! You simply wanted to help your friends. But it just goes to show, appearances can be deceptive.
Sorry, Willow!
It's so cute. My eyes are watering up.
Sorry I can't smurf you my hand-kerchief.
Look, Willow! Some silk thread, the missing ingredient!
And as much as we could want! I'll finally be able to smurf my potion!
42
A few days later...
Hurry up, you bunch of lazybones. We'll miss everything...

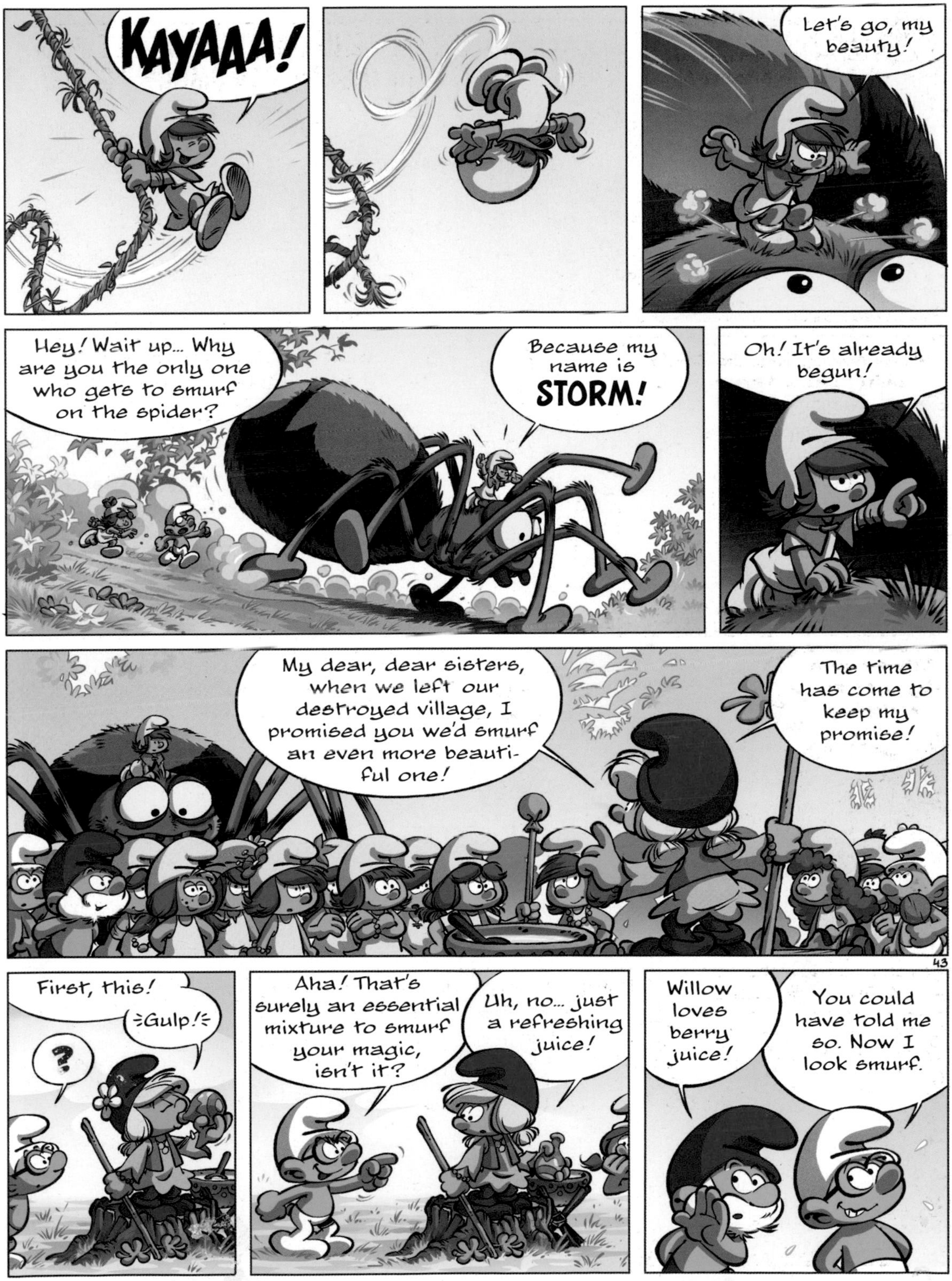
KAYAAA!
Let's go, my beauty!
Hey! Wait up... Why are you the only one who gets to smurf on the spider?
Because my name is STORM!
Oh! It's already begun!
My dear, dear sisters, when we left our destroyed village, I promised you we'd smurf an even more beautiful one!
The time has come to keep my promise!
43
First, this!
Gulp!
?
Aha! That's surely an essential mixture to smurf your magic, isn't it?
Uh, no... just a refreshing juice!
Willow loves berry juice!
You could have told me so. Now I look smurf.

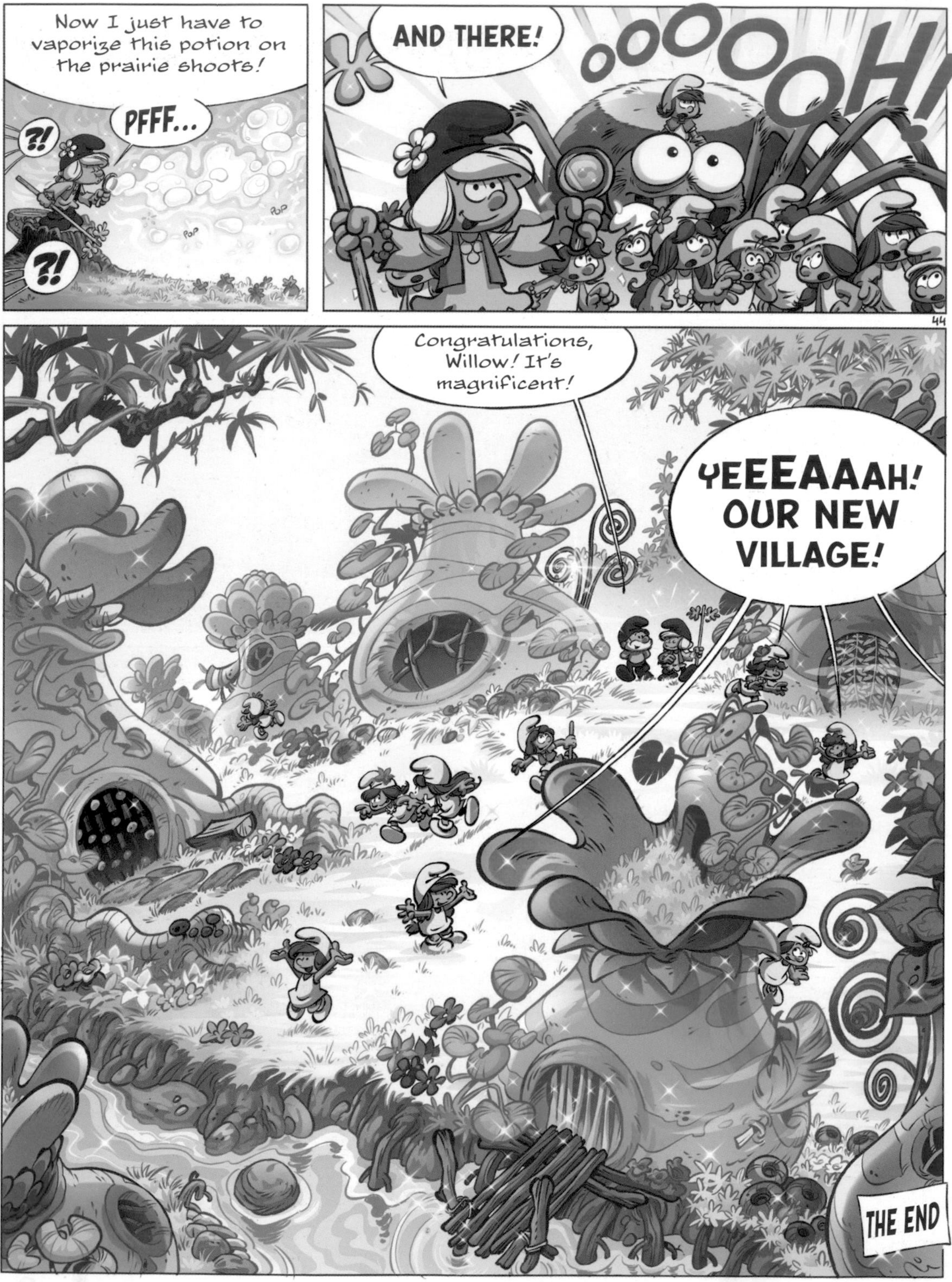

Now I just have to vaporize this potion on the prairie shoots!
PFFF...
?!
?!
POP
POP
AND THERE!
oOOOOOH!
44
Congratulations, Willow! It's magnificent!
YEEEAAAH! OUR NEW VILLAGE!
THE END

THE MINIATURE SMURFS

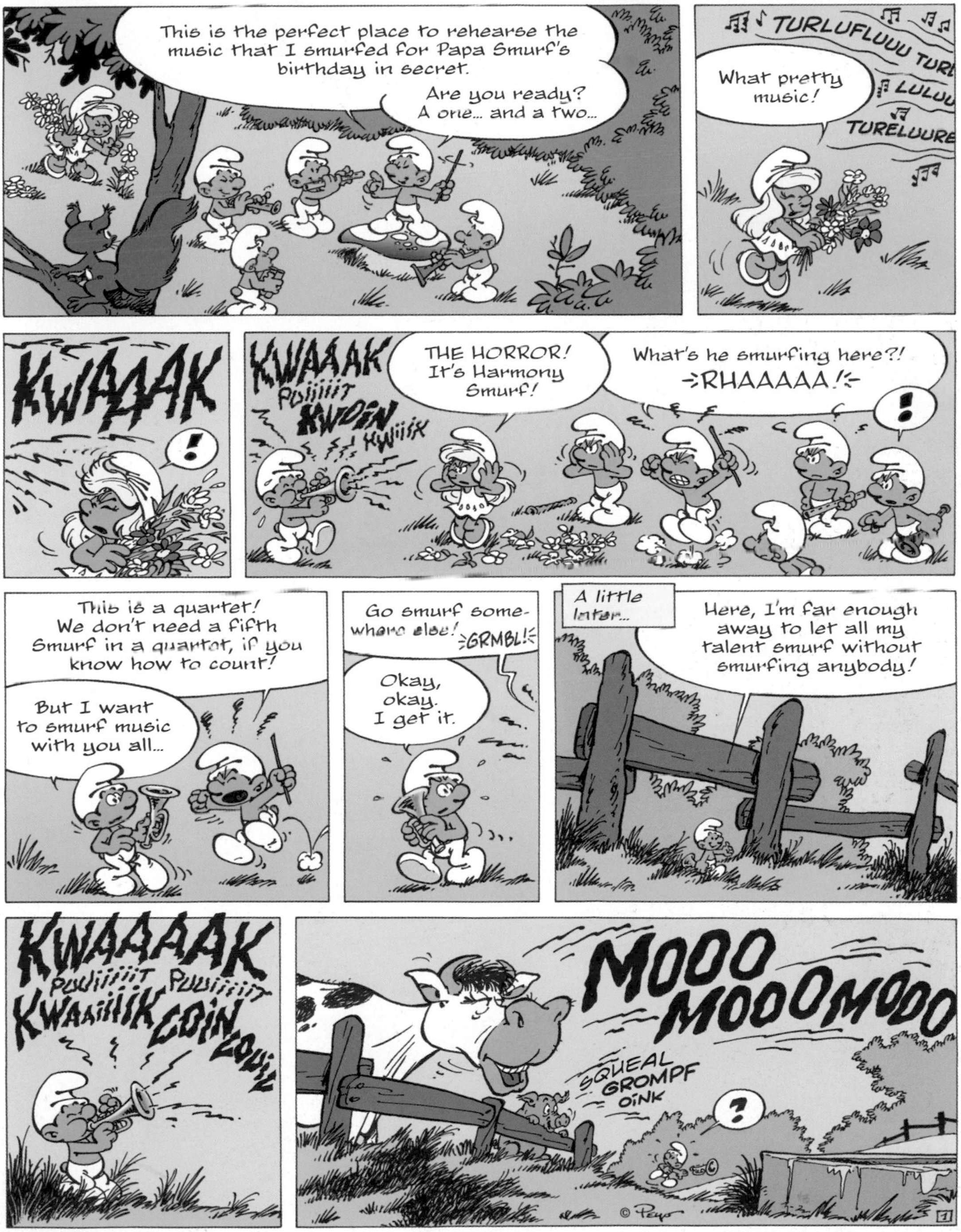

This is the perfect place to rehearse the music that I smurfed for Papa Smurf's birthday in secret.
Are you ready? A one... and a two...
TURLUFLUUU TURLULUU TURELUURE
What pretty music!
KWAAAK
!
KWAAAK PUiiiiiT KWOIN KWiiiiK
THE HORROR! It's Harmony Smurf!
What's he smurfing here?! RHAAAAA!
!
This is a quartet! We don't need a fifth Smurf in a quartet, if you know how to count!
But I want to smurf music with you all...
Go smurf somewhere else! GRMBL!
Okay, okay. I get it.
A little later...
Here, I'm far enough away to let all my talent smurf without smurfing anybody!
KWAAAAK PUiiiiiiT PUiiiiiiT KWAiiiiK COIN COUIC
MOOO MOOOMOOO
SQUEAL GROMPF OINK
?
© Peyo
1

MODO MODO

SQUEAL
OINK
GROINK

SPLASH

A cow! A pig! That's what I'm missing from my collection! Hee hee hee!

MOOO
MOOO-MOOO

OINK
GROINK

?!?!

ABRACA-DABRA!

Hup!

BOP MOOO

MINIMUM MINIMUS! Hee-hee, hee-hee!

GROMPF
BOP

MOOO?

POOF

OINK?!

POOF

Hee-hee-hee! It works! It always works. The cow and pig are miniature animals now.

?!

MOOO
OINK
NR OINK

My granddaughter will be happy to add this her collection! Hee-hee-hee!

MOOO
MOOO MOOO
OINK
SQUEAL

TURLUFLUUU
TURELURE FLUUUT
TURLUIIIT

?

GROINK
OINK
SQUEAL

MOOO
MOOO

Where's that melodious music coming from? Hee-hee-hee!

TURLUFLUUU
TURULUUU
TURLUU

MOOO
OINK

YIKES!

© Peyo

For smurf's sake! If that witch smurfs the quartert, she'll smurf them into miniature-Smurfs!

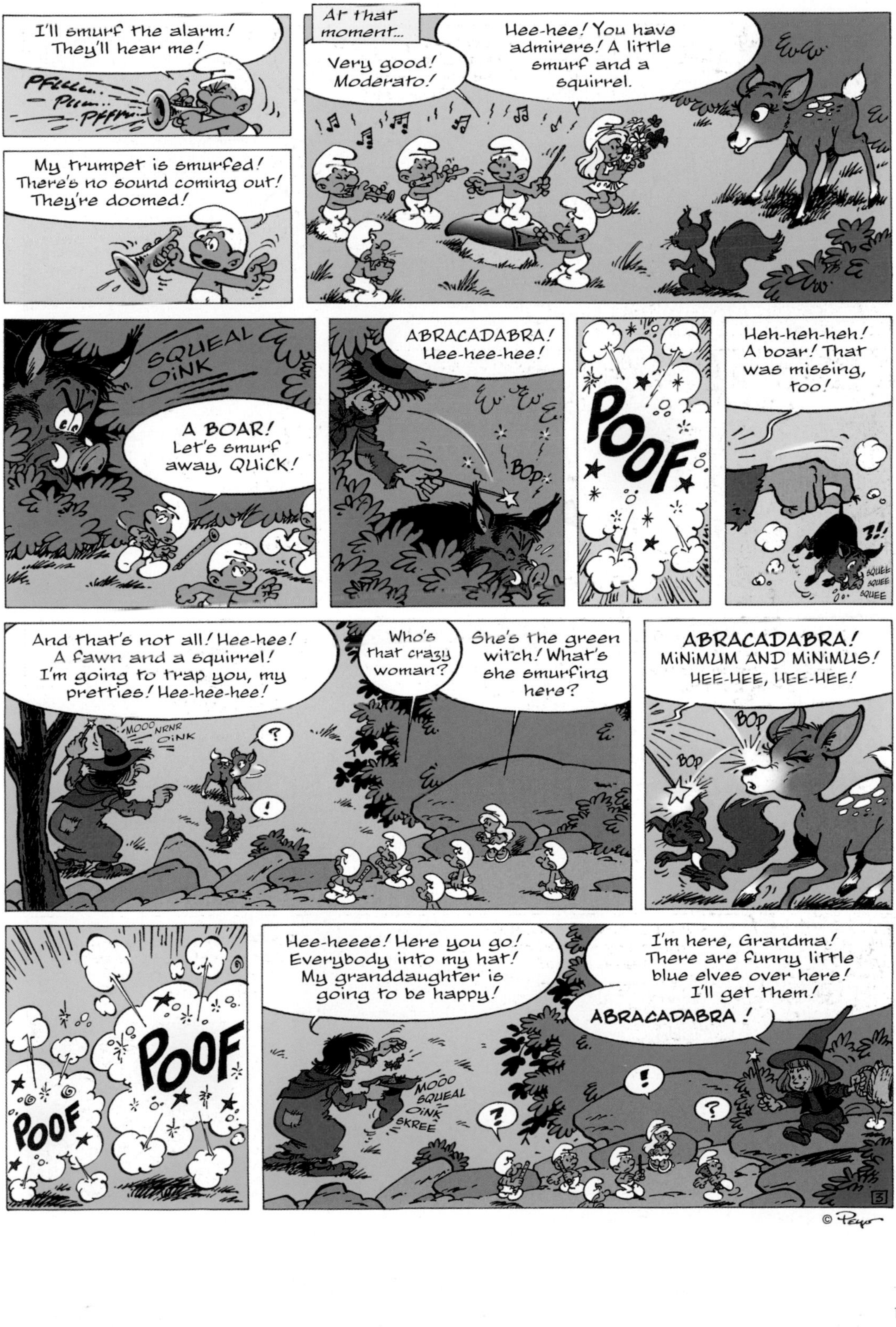

I'll smurf the alarm! They'll hear me!
PFiiiii... Piiii... Pfff
My trumpet is smurfed! There's no sound coming out! They're doomed!
At that moment...
Very good! Moderato!
Hee-hee! You have admirers! A little smurf and a squirrel.
SQUEAL OiNK
A BOAR! Let's smurf away, QUICK!
ABRACADABRA! Hee-hee-hee!
BOP
POOF
Heh-heh-heh! A boar! That was missing, too!
SQUEE SQUEE SQUEE
And that's not all! Hee-hee! A fawn and a squirrel! I'm going to trap you, my pretties! Hee-hee-hee!
MOOO NRNR OiNK
Who's that crazy woman?
She's the green witch! What's she smurfing here?
ABRACADABRA! MiNiMUM AND MiNiMUS! HEE-HEE, HEE-HEE!
BOP
BOP
POOF
POOF
Hee-heeee! Here you go! Everybody into my hat! My granddaughter is going to be happy!
MOOO SQUEAL OiNK SKREE
I'm here, Grandma! There are funny little blue elves over here! I'll get them!
ABRACADABRA!
3

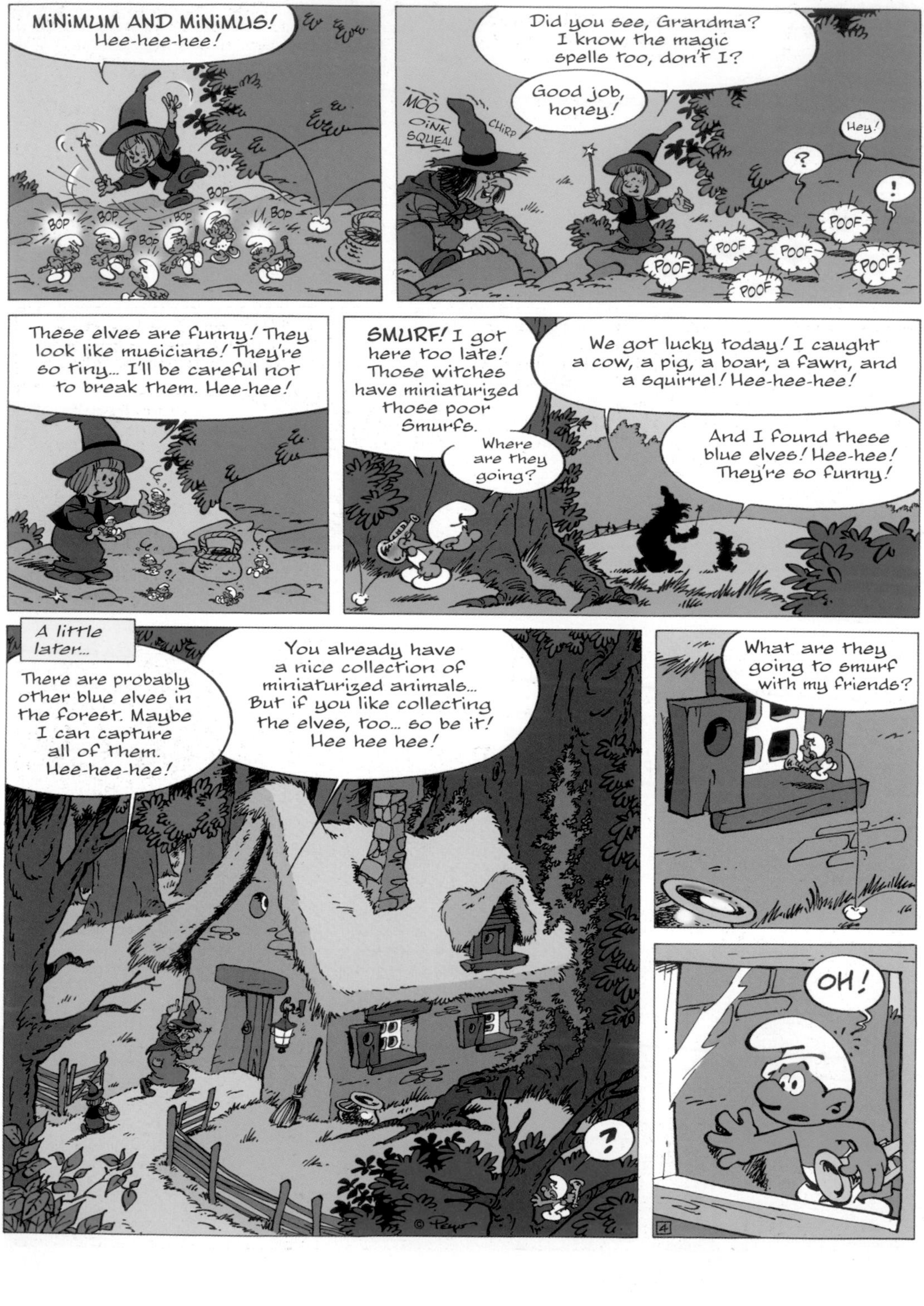
MINIMUM AND MINIMUS! Hee-hee-hee!
BOP
BOP
BOP
BOP
BOP
BOP
BOP
Did you see, Grandma? I know the magic spells too, don't I?
Good job, honey!
MOO
OINK
SQUEAL
CHIRP
Hey!
?
!
POOF
POOF
POOF
POOF
POOF
POOF
These elves are funny! They look like musicians! They're so tiny... I'll be careful not to break them. Hee-hee!
SMURF! I got here too late! Those witches have miniaturized those poor Smurfs.
Where are they going?
We got lucky today! I caught a cow, a pig, a boar, a fawn, and a squirrel! Hee-hee-hee!
And I found these blue elves! Hee-hee! They're so funny!
A little later...
There are probably other blue elves in the forest. Maybe I can capture all of them. Hee-hee-hee!
You already have a nice collection of miniaturized animals... But if you like collecting the elves, too... so be it! Hee hee hee!
?
© Peyo
What are they going to smurf with my friends?
OH!
4

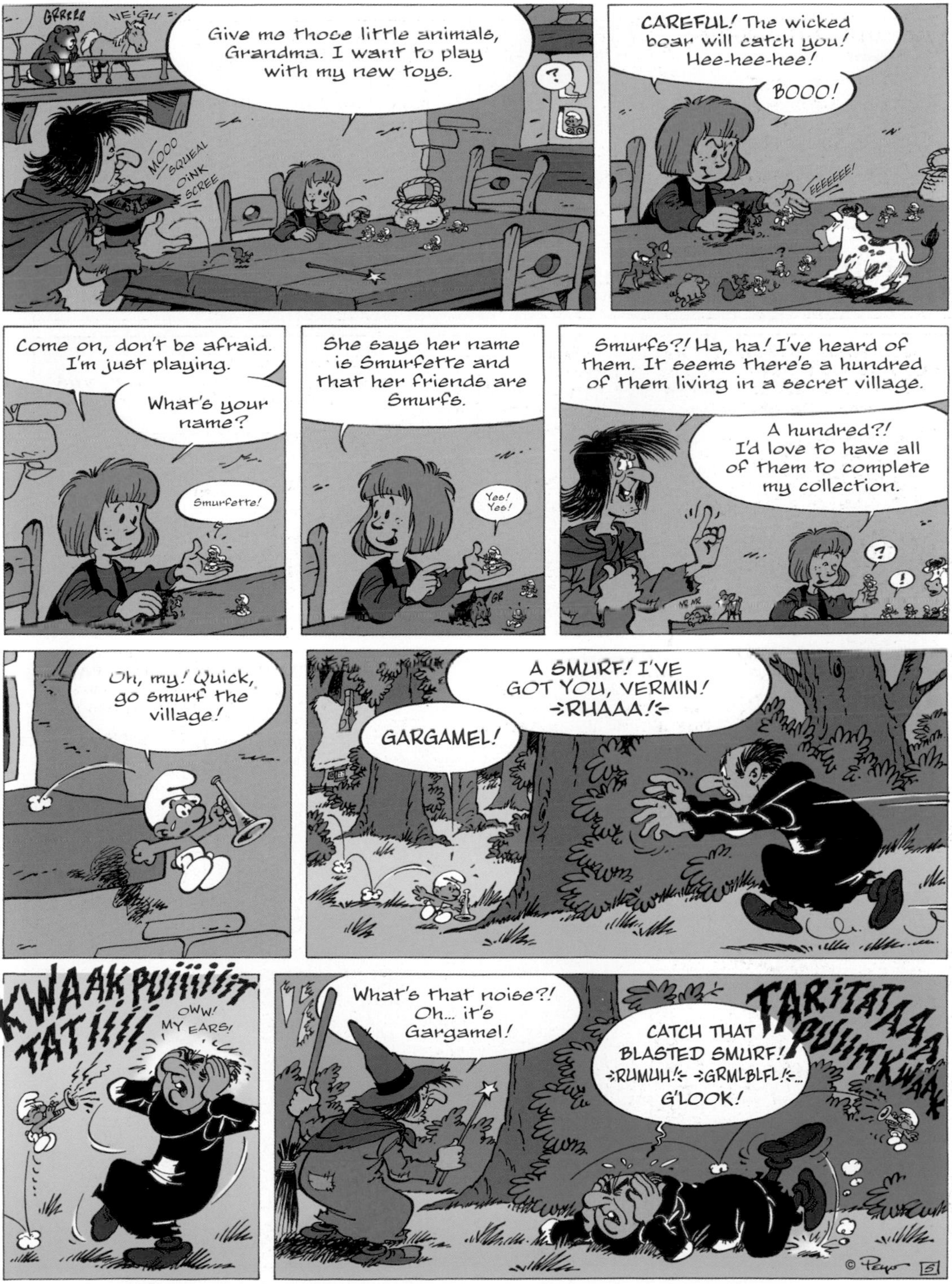

GRRRRR
NEIGH
Give me those little animals, Grandma. I want to play with my new toys.
?
MOOO
SQUEAL
OINK
SCREE
CAREFUL! The wicked boar will catch you! Hee-hee-hee!
BOOO!
EEEEEEE!
Come on, don't be afraid. I'm just playing.
What's your name?
Smurfette!
She says her name is Smurfette and that her friends are Smurfs.
Yes! Yes!
Smurfs?! Ha, ha! I've heard of them. It seems there's a hundred of them living in a secret village.
A hundred?! I'd love to have all of them to complete my collection.
?
!
Oh, my! Quick, go smurf the village!
A SMURF! I'VE GOT YOU, VERMIN! RHAAA!
GARGAMEL!
KWAAK PUIIIIIIT TATIIII
OWW! MY EARS!
What's that noise?! Oh... it's Gargamel!
CATCH THAT BLASTED SMURF! RUMUH! GRMLBLFL!... G'LOOK!
TARITATAAAA PUIIITKWAAK
© Peyo
5

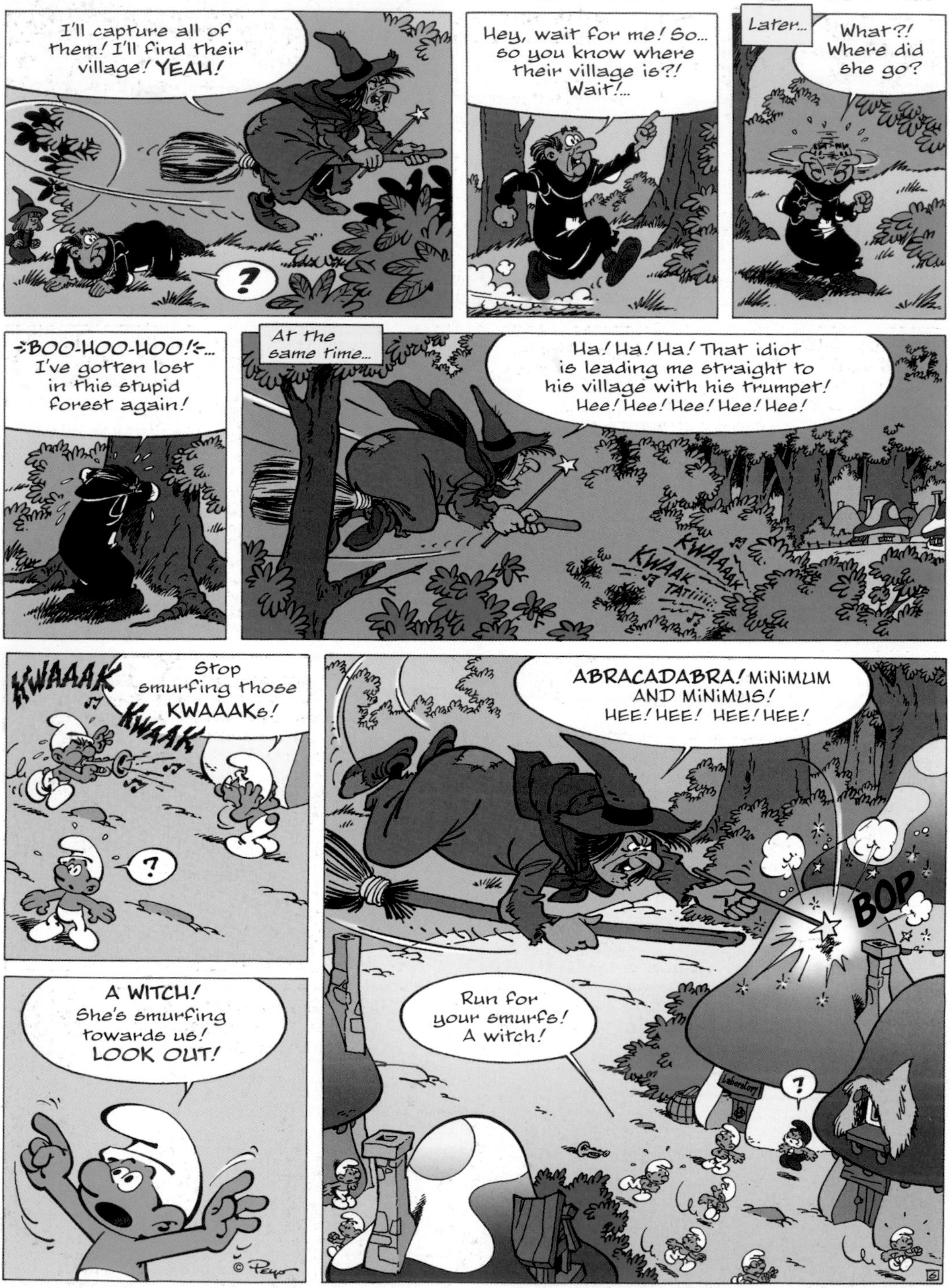
I'll capture all of them! I'll find their village! YEAH!
?
Hey, wait for me! So... so you know where their village is?! Wait!...
Later...
What?! Where did she go?
BOO-HOO-HOO!... I've gotten lost in this stupid forest again!
At the same time...
Ha! Ha! Ha! That idiot is leading me straight to his village with his trumpet! Hee! Hee! Hee! Hee! Hee!
KWAAAK
KWAAAK
TATiiiiii
KWAAAK
Stop smurfing those KWAAAKs!
KWAAK
?
ABRACADABRA! MiNiMUM AND MiNiMUS! HEE! HEE! HEE! HEE!
BOP
A WITCH! She's smurfing towards us! LOOK OUT!
Run for your smurfs! A witch!
?
© Peyo

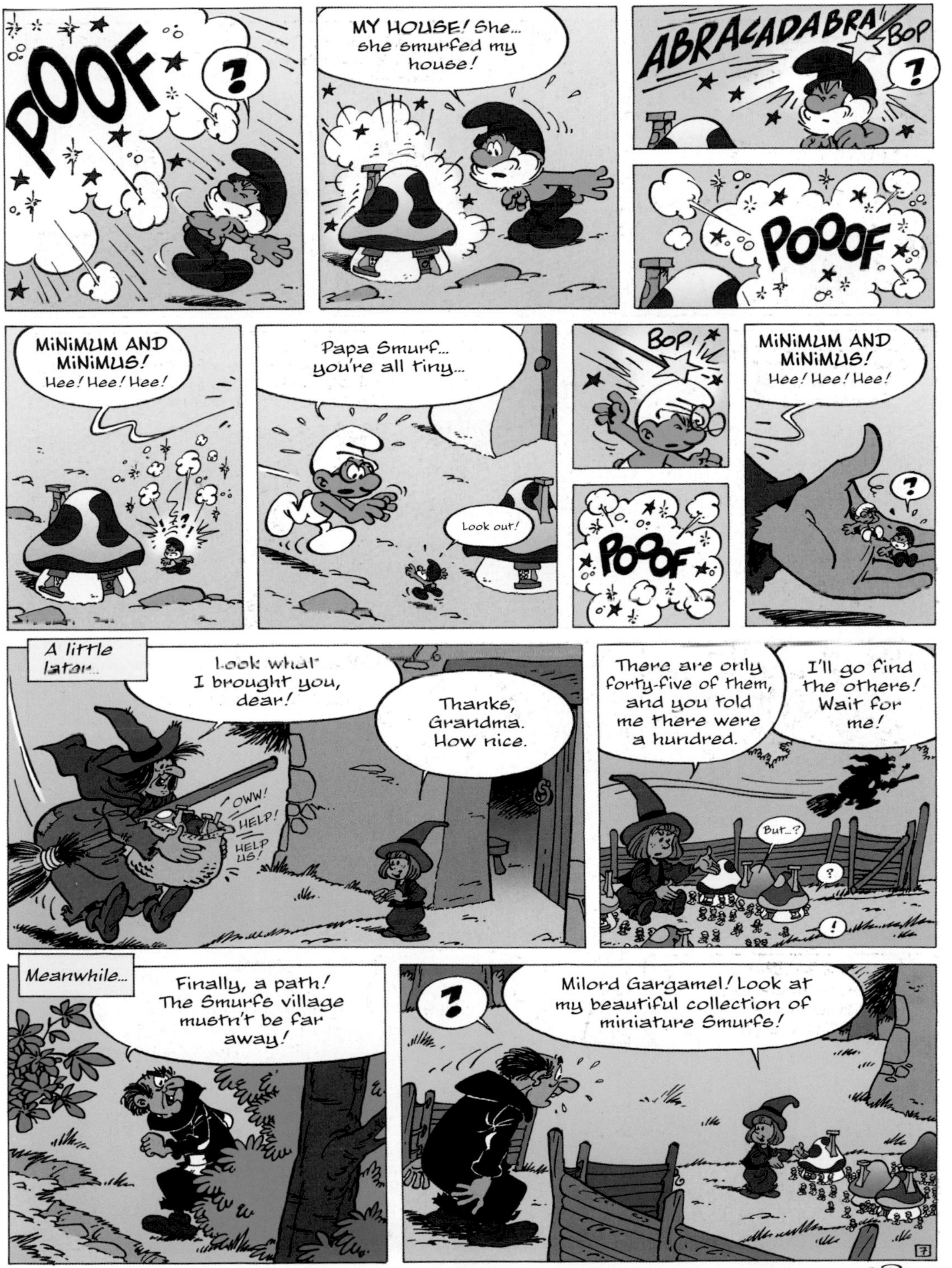

POOF
?
MY HOUSE! She... she smurfed my house!
ABRACADABRA
BOP
?
POOOF
MINIMUM AND MINIMUS! Hee! Hee! Hee!
Papa Smurf... you're all tiny...
Look out!
BOP
POOOF
MINIMUM AND MINIMUS! Hee! Hee! Hee!
?
A little later...
Look what I brought you, dear!
OWW!
HELP!
HELP US!
Thanks, Grandma. How nice.
There are only forty-five of them, and you told me there were a hundred.
I'll go find the others! Wait for me!
But...?
?
!
Meanwhile...
Finally, a path! The Smurfs village mustn't be far away!
?
Milord Gargamel! Look at my beautiful collection of miniature Smurfs!
7
© Peyo

Miniature Smurfs or not, I'm taking ALL of them! I'll give you a doll in exchange!

No! I don't want you to! They're mine!

PLAF

ABRACADABRA MINIMUM AND MINIMUS!

BOP

POOOF

That'll teach you, bad man! Now you'll stay tiny! ⇒NYAH!⇐

HOO! HOO! HOO!

HA! HA!

HEE HEE HEE!

Look out, Smurfette! The evil Gargamel is going to capture you! Heh-heh-heh!

Noooo! Mercy! I'm scared!

Oh, no, don't cry. I don't want you to be sad, little Smurfette. I'll set you free again.

And my friends?

I want you all to go back to your normal Smurf size!... ABRACADABRA! MAXIMUM AND MAXIMUS!

AND ME?

POOOF POOOF POOOF POOOF POOOF POOOF POOOF POOOF

⇒PFF⇐... I couldn't find their village again.

That's fine! I'd rather these nice Smurfs went back home. They aren't toys after all, they're Smurfs.

We'll return your magic wand once we've smurfed our houses in the village!

Keep Gargamel a little longer with you.

KWAAK! POUEEET!

Look, Gargamel, the little, bad wolf is going to eat you! Ooo Ooooo!

Soon, everything is put back to normal at Smurf Village...

MAXIMUM AND MAXIMUS! HA! HA! HA!

We have a surprise for you, Papa Smurf! HAPPY BIRTHDAY!

KWAAK! POUET! KWAIIK!

© Peyo

Far from there...

I'll turn myself into a GIANT and trample the whole forest! REVENGE!

GRMBL!

8 END

WATCH OUT FOR PAPERCUTZ ™

Welcome to the fifth, fully-packed volume of THE SMURFS TALES by Peyo—starring those little blue folks seen on the new hit Nickelodeon show, "The Smurfs." Brought to you by Papercutz, the somewhat taller folks dedicated to publishing great graphic novels for all ages. I'm Jim Salicrup, the Smurf-in-Chief and Golden Tree Polisher here to...

A) Not elaborate on the themes explored in "The Smurfs and the Golden Tree." The story speaks for itself.

B) Resist offering such platitudes as "There's no place like home" or "Home is where your heart is," regarding the events in "A New Beginning." I will, however, point out that this story picks up where the last story featuring the female Smurfs from Smurfy Grove left off in THE SMURFS TALES #3.

C) Not ask the eternal question "Does size matter?" in reference to "The Miniature Smurfs" short story, except to note that Peyo certainly enjoyed creating stories that featured classic "little guys." The Smurfs, Benny Breakiron, and Peewit (but not Johan), are all manifestations of that concept.

D) Avoid repeating all the wonderful things I usually say about Peyo, the brilliant cartoonist whose original name was Pierre Culliford, the man who created Johan and Peewit, The Smurfs, and Benny Breakiron. The mere fact that The Smurfs are still around over 60 years after he created them, and are more popular than ever, is tribute enough to the man's genius.

No, I'm here instead to talk about Benny Breakiron. Benny, the pint-sized powerhouse (when he's not suffering from a cold, that is!) is Peyo's loving parody of superheroes. Papercutz proudly published BENNY BREAKIRON graphic novels, but much to the chagrin of his many fans, the series ended after only five volumes. Papercutz wasn't about to abandon this young man, and we've since featured his adventures in the deluxe-sized series THE SMURFS & FRIENDS, and we're now alternating his adventures here in THE SMURFS TALES with those of Johan and Peewit.

While it's not necessary to have read any of Benny's previous adventures to enjoy this volume's "Lady Dolphine," we're betting that those of you that did enjoy Madame Adolphine's dramatic debut in BENNY BREAKIRON #2 are thrilled to witness her surprising return.

While The Smurfs and Johan and Peewit are set during an undefined period during Medieval times, which ironically makes their stories seem timeless, Benny's adventures are clearly set in France in the '60s and '70s. Let's face it, there's no way we can, or would even want to, "Americanize" these stories, which we do with such Papercutz series such as DANCE CLASS or THE SISTERS, to name a couple of examples. As a result, we've been letting Benny use select French words or phrases in his comics. In this volume, we're adding footnotes which will translate those word or phrases. It's something we started doing in another Papercutz graphic novel series, set in 50 BC, whenever Latin words or phrases are used.

And speaking of other classic European graphic novel series, there's a mention of Lucky Luke in the Benny Breakiron story. While Papercutz doesn't publish Lucky Luke, we decided to keep that reference intact as it's faithful to the original script, makes sense in context, and because we're also fans of that series, which is available in English editions in North America.

We do hope you enjoy Benny Breakiron as much as we do, and will be back again for more Smurftastic fun in THE SMURFS TALES #6, as well as THE SMURFS 3 IN 1 #7, all coming from your friends at Papercutz!

Smurf you later,

Jim

STAY IN TOUCH!

EMAIL: salicrup@papercutz.com
WEB: papercutz.com
TWITTER: @papercutzgn
INSTAGRAM: @papercutzgn
FACEBOOK: PAPERCUTZGRAPHICNOVELS
FANMAIL: Papercutz, 160 Broadway, Suite 700, East Wing, New York, NY 10038

Go to papercutz.com and sign up for the free Papercutz e-newsletter!

THE SMURFS GRAPHIC NOVELS AVAILABLE FROM PAPERCUTZ

the SMURFS
3 IN 1
THE PURPLE SMURFS
THE SMURFS AND THE MAGIC FLUTE
THE SMURF KING
PAPERCUTZ

THE SMURFS 3 IN 1 VOL. 1

the SMURFS
3 IN 1
THE SMURFETTE
THE SMURFS AND THE EGG
THE SMURFS AND THE HOWLIBIRD
PAPERCUTZ

THE SMURFS 3 IN 1 VOL. 2

THE SMURFS
3 IN 1
THE RETURN OF THE SMURFETTE
THE SMURF OLYMPICS
SMURF VS. SMURF
PAPERCUTZ

THE SMURFS 3 IN 1 VOL. 3

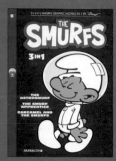

THE SMURFS
3 IN 1
THE ASTROSMURF
THE SMURF APPRENTICE
GARGAMEL AND THE SMURFS
PAPERCUTZ

THE SMURFS 3 IN 1 VOL. 4

SMURFS
3 IN 1
See THE SMURFS on Nickelodeon!
SMURF SOUP
THE BABY SMURF
THE SMURFLINGS
PAPERCUTZ

THE SMURFS 3 IN 1 VOL. 5

THE SMURFS
3 IN 1
THE AEROSMURF
THE STRANGE AWAKENING OF LAZY SMURF
THE FINANCE SMURF
PAPERCUTZ

THE SMURFS 3 IN 1 VOL. 6

THE SMURFS
TALES
The SMURFS & the BRATTY KID and other stories
PAPERCUTZ

THE SMURFS TALES #1

THE SMURFS
TALES
SMURFETTE IN CHARGE
and other tales
PAPERCUTZ

THE SMURFS TALES #2

THE SMURFS
TALES
THE CROW IN SMURFY GROVE
and other tales
PAPERCUTZ

THE SMURFS TALES #3

THE SMURFS
TALES
SMURF AND TURF
and other tales
PAPERCUTZ

THE SMURFS TALES #4

THE SMURFS
TALES

THE SMURFS TALES #5

THE SMURFS 3 IN 1 graphic novels are available in paperback only for $14.99 US each at booksellers everywhere. THE SMURFS TALES graphic novels are avaialble in paperback for $14.99 each and $22.99 each for hardcover at booksellers everywhere. Or order from us. Please add $5.00 for postage and handling for the first book, add $1.00 for each additional book. Please make check payable to NBM Publishing. Send to: PAPERCUTZ, 160 Broadway, Suite 700, East Wing, New York, NY 10038 (1-800-886-1223).

THE SMURFS graphic novels are also available digitally from **COMIXOLOGY**.com as well as at ebook sellers everywhere.

WWW.PAPERCUTZ.COM